Praise

"NIGHT STALKER suspense at the highest level of suspense! Dread evoked by a known enemy is frightening enough. But a sinister presence, close enough to touch your cheek, to stir the flowers in your garden, to know your innermost secrets—someone unknown and unsuspected, is the most dangerous of all."

—Ann Rule, author of *Without Pity*

In All the Wrong Places

"A chilling exercise in complete terror! Fascinating!"

—Ann Rule

Dead Silence

"Moves with the pace of a racing heart from beginning to end."

—Ann Rule

Another Life

"Suspense that will make your heart skip a beat."

—Ann Rule

The Flower Man

"Donna Anders brings the terror not only into your home, but directly into your heart. A terrific read."

—John Saul

"You will not put this book down before its outrageously suspenseful ending. . . . Donna Anders taps the darkest terrors of the human heart. . . . *The Flower Man* will scare your pants off."

—Edna Buchanan

Books by Donna Anders

THE FLOWER MAN
ANOTHER LIFE
DEAD SILENCE
IN ALL THE WRONG PLACES

Published by POCKET BOOKS

DONNA ANDERS
NIGHT STALKER

POCKET BOOKS
New York London Toronto Sydney

The sale of this book without its cover is unauthorized. If you purchased this book without a cover, you should be aware that it was reported to the publisher as "unsold and destroyed." Neither the author nor the publisher has received payment for the sale of this "stripped book."

This book is a work of fiction. Names, characters, places and incidents are products of the author's imagination or are used fictitiously. Any resemblance to actual events or locales or persons, living or dead, is entirely coincidental.

An *Original* Publication of POCKET BOOKS

 POCKET BOOKS, a division of Simon & Schuster, Inc.
1230 Avenue of the Americas, New York, NY 10020

Copyright © 2003 by Donna Anders

All rights reserved, including the right to reproduce
this book or portions thereof in any form whatsoever.
For information address Pocket Books, 1230 Avenue
of the Americas, New York, NY 10020

ISBN: 0-7434-2730-0

First Pocket Books printing December 2003

10 9 8 7 6 5 4 3 2

POCKET and colophon are registered trademarks of
Simon & Schuster, Inc.

Design and illustration by Jae Song

Manufactured in the United States of America

For information regarding special discounts for bulk purchases, please contact Simon & Schuster Special Sales at 1-800-456-6798 or business@simonandschuster.com.

ACKNOWLEDGMENTS

For their friendship, inspiration, advice, and support during the writing of this book I am eternally grateful to a few friends, relatives, and professionals. Many thanks to Diane and Erik Ronnegard, Glenn and Nancy Anderson, Ruth and Greg Aeschliman, Lisa and Bryan Pearce, Tina Abeel, Ann Rule, Leslie Rule, and of course Mike Rule for his thoughtful gift of flowers.

And again, special thanks to my agent, Sheree Bykofsky, and to Amy Pierpont, my talented editor at Pocket Books.

For the person who made this book possible

PROLOGUE

No, no! It wasn't possible. She was hallucinating. That was it.

That had to be it.

Topsy squeezed her eyes shut, but the image in her mind wouldn't go away. She had never faced such a horrifying moment, not in her wildest fantasy, not in all her imagined scenarios about the man in the clearing, so engrossed in his grotesque ceremony of death that he didn't know she was there.

That she'd followed him.

That she'd watched as he'd picked up the woman at the Happy Notes Singles Club in the seediest part of downtown Seattle. Her mind had tried to deny what her eyes had been seeing as she'd tracked them in her rented car, onto I-90 and out to this desolate place in the Cascade Mountain foothills.

But, now . . .

He'd been well into his ritual by the time she'd dared

creep closer, aware of stepping carefully. Somehow she'd known that he must not know she'd followed him.

That her life depended on it.

But she had to know for sure, had to know if her suspicions were true.

She crouched behind a cover of ferns and huckleberry bushes, her eyes opened again to the clearing. Her knees sagged, and she slumped against a tree trunk, sliding down the bark to the mossy floor of the forest. Gray mist swirled around her consciousness.

Don't faint.

"God, help me now," she whispered, gulping deep, silent breaths. She didn't allow herself to ask the "whys" or she'd lose her last thread of sanity. She only knew one thing.

She must be strong.

She forced herself to look back at the moon-dappled meadow where the woman strained against the rope that held her naked body spread-eagled on the ground. Although blackness shrouded the surrounding woods, the whites of the woman's eyes caught the moonlight as they darted wildly about. Her own bra gagged her and kept her screams trapped behind it.

And her pleas for mercy.

Topsy wanted to run forward, demand that he release the woman, but some primal instinct held her in place.

She, too, was expendable to this man.

This monster.

Paralyzed by the drama unfolding before her, Topsy watched in horrible fascination as the man played out his fantasy. Surely, he would let the woman go when it was over. Wouldn't he?

The man circled the woman slowly, as though he relished her helplessness. He didn't speak, but his breath came in ragged gulps. Occasionally he paused, taunting her with the hope that he might release her.

Please. *Let her go.* Topsy willed him to hear her silent plea.

And then it was too late.

His fingers, which had been so sensitive as they'd lightly skimmed his victim's skin, were suddenly pinching and kneading her flesh.

Then, with deliberate movements, the man stripped naked. When he turned back to his captive, a knife was clutched in his fist.

The woman cringed, trying to twist away as he bent over her, his erection grinding into her groin. The downward thrust of his hand was sudden.

Frozen in place, Topsy heard the muffled cry of agony as the blade flashed again . . . and again.

The scene tilted, out of focus. And Topsy slipped into oblivion.

CHAPTER ONE

ONE SECOND JULIA WAS JOGGING THE NARROW PATH, swerving to avoid overgrown evergreen branches, the next she was flung forward onto the hard-packed dirt. Skidding on her knees and the palms of her hands, she slid to an abrupt stop and collapsed onto her stomach. Too shaken to move, she gulped deep breaths, trying to regain her equilibrium.

"Damn shoelaces!" she muttered, knowing the replacements on her Nikes had been too long in the first place. But she had been in her typical hurry. Pressed for time because of her six part-time jobs, she'd skipped a stop at the store to buy the right length.

Julia Farley, Jill of all trades, she thought, mocking herself. It'd be a laugh if it wasn't so damn pathetic—and frightening.

Meeting work deadlines was why she was jogging during the evening rather than taking her usual early morning run. Today she'd had too many commitments, but being compulsive about exercising, she had squeezed in the time despite the late hour. Exercise helped her stay positive about the scary aspects of her life right now.

Her mind lingered on the thought: six part-time jobs. Oh God. Some things never changed. Years ago when she was in high school her mother used to caution her against taking on too many activities. But back then being too busy had meant being popular, having fun; these days it was an issue of survival. She needed all six little jobs to support her family now that she was the main source of income. She was not qualified for a high-paying position, as she lacked a college degree and an established career.

Despite throbbing knees and hands, Julia grinned. She had always believed a person could accomplish anything they set their mind to, come hell or high water. And she meant to work from home, make a living from the skills she did have, and stay close to her teenage daughters.

The fading sunlight filtered through the high pines and firs above her, splashing shadow patterns onto the final stretch of Highland Trail near her home in rural Issaquah, a bedroom community close to Seattle. The Cascade Mountain foothills to the east seemed to embrace the lowering temperature of approaching night, and the darkening blue sky, ringed by ominous clouds, threatened rain by morning. Typical fall weather in the Northwest, she thought, shivering. Despite having worked up a sweat, she now felt chilled to the bone, and in agony from her sudden fall.

Julia held up her hands. Pinpoints of blood dotted the heel of her palms. Her knees were in even worse shape, bleeding profusely. "Oh shit!—shit!—shit!" she chanted aloud as she managed to retie her laces. Gingerly, she got to her feet, testing her weight on them to make sure that no bones were broken.

She steadied herself, regaining her balance. She still had a way to go before she completed the run.

A snapping twig startled her, and she jerked her head to the left in the direction of the sound. Nothing moved within the dense underbrush, where the night was already settling its black presence. She was suddenly aware that she jogged alone on the remote wooded path. Other people had more sense than to be there at nightfall.

Because someone was killing prostitutes in the south Seattle area and dumping their bodies in just such a secluded place.

The hair on the back of her neck felt stiff. Was someone hidden in the woods—watching her?

She strained her ears, listening, hearing the faint rustle of dried leaves, the gentle slapping of branches caught by the strengthening currents of wind.

Did the sounds denote someone in the woods—someone creeping closer?

Don't be silly, she instructed herself. *You're a morning runner, unaware of the strange, indefinable noises of nocturnal creatures that come out at dusk.* Just because Peter was playing mind games, trying to scare her back to their marriage with his prowling around the house and dumb, if frightening, terror tactics, didn't mean that a serial killer was hiding in the bushes. Her former husband was emotionally disturbed, but she didn't believe he was a murderer. *I'm just on edge because of Peter,* she thought.

But her movements were quick as she jerked her headband from her head, allowing her long blond hair to fall free. She wrapped the elasticized strip of material around her right knee, which was the most injured, to stop the flow of blood. Then, without glancing around, she sprinted forward, gradually regaining her earlier speed, ignoring a sense of danger. Although she knew the rustling sounds that seemed to keep pace in the forest beside the path were normal, Julia's apprehension would not go away. Getting home—being safe—meant everything at that moment.

"The Paranoids are getting you, the Paranoids are getting you," Julia repeated over and over, punctuating each footfall with the words from a card her sixteen-year-old daughter, Alyssa, had given her as a joke.

Her headband slipped from her knee, and the blood ran down her leg into her athletic shoes. Julia stopped to adjust the makeshift bandage. The other skinned knee had stopped bleeding. About to start running again, Julia hesitated.

The woods had gone silent. There were no sounds from the underbrush, even though the wind still whispered through the high branches above her.

Because she was there, on the trail? Or because something—or someone—was in the underbrush, disturbing the rhythm of the forest?

A prickle of apprehension touched her spine. Something was wrong. It was as though the instincts of the night creatures had sensed danger, freezing them into place, waiting for what would happen next. Their fear was transferred to her, and for a moment she, too, was immobilized.

Shivering, Julia realized how vulnerable she was at that moment. *Stupid idiot*, she told herself. *Out here in the dark by yourself. Who cares if your body is in shape if you're dead? Your daughters won't. They'll only know that their mother is gone.* She glanced down the path. It was almost dark now; she could barely see the trail ahead of her.

Julia started forward, knowing she was almost to the end of her run. She gave a final burst of speed, anticipating a hot shower, antiseptic on her wounds, and a soothing glass of wine before she prepared supper for herself and her two daughters.

In all the years she'd been jogging the woodland trail near her home in Issaquah, she'd never been afraid. Her small community was nestled in the Cascade foothills and was far enough from the Seattle clamor of traffic and people to feel safe. But her apprehension now was not surprising, she reminded herself as she broke free of the woods into a lighted housing development near her house. Aside from a serial killer being on the loose in the Seattle area, she had never before been the target of someone dedicated to making her suffer—threatening her safety—so that she sometimes wondered if her life was in danger as well.

That someone was Peter, the man she had once loved.

The tension went out of her body as she jogged down the street to her house. She no longer felt an ominous presence near her. Now the woods behind her were only a backdrop to the big homes in the development. She had come back to civilization.

Once inside her Tudor-style house, the home her husband Peter had once built for them, Julia began to feel foolish. No one had been watching her. But as she closed the door between the garage and laundry room, went through the kitchen to the front hall and upstairs to her bathroom to tend her wounds, she also realized how a woman could get into trouble by ignoring good sense and jogging a remote trail alone at night. And as she showered, her thoughts lingered on the recent murders of women in the Northwest. Had they also flouted safety, disbelieving that anyone would be after them? *That they could be murdered?*

The thought was troubling.

Julia stood at the stove, stirring sautéed vegetables and low-fat marinara sauce into the cooked pasta. She sprinkled dill, a favorite herb from her own garden, onto the finished dish, checked the sourdough rolls in the oven, then walked to the doorway that opened into the front hall and called up the steps.

"Dinner's ready!" There was a silence. "Hey, you two, now!"

"Coming!" Alyssa answered.

"Be right there!" Samantha called. "As soon as I get off the phone."

Julia turned the food down to simmer, knowing that it would take at least five minutes for her teenage daughters to get downstairs. Resigned to their idea of promptness, she walked through the laundry room to the garage to check on the flowers that were drying in her work alcove. A boutique had ordered ten fall wreaths, and she was pleased to see that her hanging assortment of flowers and greens was ready to work into arrangements. She would do that first thing in the morning, after she had jogged and the girls had left for school. There would still be time before noon to prepare her talk on writing technical manuals for an annual writer's conference on Saturday. Her panel was in the late morning.

She sighed. There was scarcely time to accomplish all of her various projects: the three-tier cake she must bake and deliver for a Friday night wedding, her speech on

Saturday, the ten wreaths by Monday, two wallpapering jobs in the next seven days, and writing her bimonthly children's story for a small publishing house in California.

"Whew," she said aloud. She would not think about the computer program manual she had been commissioned to write by mid-November. Although she had already done one manual this year, the latest, a sophisticated upgrade by a local international software company, promised to be the most challenging yet. And she still needed to get up to speed on the latest advances to the program, a fact that she hadn't told her employer—because she knew she could do it.

She could not let them down; a close friend, another writer, had recommended her for the job, knowing she needed income after her divorce. Although she had been using a computer for years, as a writer and in her former husband's general contracting company, she was far from the brilliant computer nerd her employer believed her to be. While married, she had done all of the office and financial part of their business—billing, contracts, estimates and bookkeeping—on the computer. Creating a program manual required an expertise far beyond average computer knowledge, and each subject had taken weeks of research before she could write it up correctly. But she'd hung in there, working all night if necessary, because the pay was good. In fact, it was that income that tipped the balance and allowed her to be a stay-at-home mom.

She stirred her pasta dish and called the girls again, her thoughts on her own lack of a *real* profession. A glance out of the kitchen window reminded her that the weather was changing. There would be rain before she even went to bed tonight. She would have to cut her rosebushes tomorrow to save all the blooms for drying.

She turned back to the kitchen table, which was set for three, and added napkins. The only time she had ever regretted graduating from high school at seventeen, being married at barely eighteen, and a mother before she had turned nineteen, was after she had been divorced and needed a college degree to land a decent-paying job. Practical experience, common sense, and intelligence had not mattered to potential employers once they realized she was mid-thirties and lacked a B.A. They had not cared about her role in the family business, and her artistic accomplishments had been dismissed.

Their loss, she told herself. I'll make it without being conventional—despite academic prejudice.

"Hey Mom," Alyssa said, coming into the kitchen, her large blue eyes concerned. "Dad just drove up." A tall, slender girl of sixteen, Julia's firstborn was the more serious of her two. She wore her long blond hair straight and parted in the middle, an unintentional throwback to the late seventies, when Julia was a kid.

"Oh no," Samantha said behind her, her unruly red curls clipped into a ponytail. She gave a dramatic sigh and would have gone back upstairs but for Alyssa grabbing her sweatshirt. "I love Dad, but I can't stand another fight," she protested, trying to pull free of Alyssa's hold. "Dad is always mad at us," she said with the blunt wisdom of a fourteen-year-old.

"We could pretend we're not home," Alyssa suggested.

"Can't," Samantha said, her blue eyes darting to Julia. "Mom turned on the lights."

"I promise I won't get in a fight with your father." Julia swallowed hard. She hated the confrontations with Peter even more than the girls did. She could not dismiss the negative effect he had on them. The type of emotional abuse Peter had lowered on his family after they'd separated was horrific: rages and threats, sobbing and promises, and often all at once, his mood changing like a light switch. His mother had tried to help, explaining that Peter's first breakdown had happened in college, when the stress of grades and being away from the safety of his parents and home had caused him to flip out, family history Julia had not known about. With medication, counseling, and constant reassurances from his mother, Peter had gotten back on an even keel and stayed there—until years later, when business stress had overwhelmed him and a divorce had again threatened his sense of safety.

Dr. Hornsby, their family doctor, had referred him to a psychiatrist over two years ago, long before their separation, but neither the doctor nor medications had made an improvement in Peter's unpredictable personality and swinging moods. Living with him had been a frightening nightmare, and finally a matter of life and death. Julia had worried that he would snap and do something drastic, like killing her, as he had threatened each time he'd had a temper tantrum.

Dr. Hornsby had told him many times, "Peter, you're not listening." And when Peter would go into a tirade, "Peter, you're digging yourself another hole to fall into." It had been a scary time, and finally Julia had had no other option but to end the marriage, knowing she must avert a tragedy. Divorce had finally been her only option.

And then all hell had been unleashed on her and the girls. Peter wanted his family back. His abuse did not register with him; only his own needs did.

When reconciliation didn't happen, his fear tactics

began and then escalated into terrifying situations as he tried to manipulate her back to the marriage. And there was nothing she could do about it legally, since he had not broken the law—as far as anyone could prove. No one could pin him to the frightening incidents that kept happening to Julia; no one saw who flattened her car tires, stole her gas cap, cut her brake cable. No one witnessed the phantom in the night who threw rocks against the house, peeked in the windows, called her phone incessantly only to hang up, flooded her computer e-mail with spam, and hired people to chase her car and run her off the road. The police could do nothing without documented proof. As far as they were concerned, Peter had not broken the law. But after each incident Peter hinted to his daughters that he was behind everything, that it would all stop when they were a family again, that he would protect them. Alyssa and Samantha had recoiled, and they'd begged him to let go of their mom. He'd only smiled, said that wasn't possible, and repeated that they needed to be a family again.

Now, as Julia went to the door, she schooled herself to be calm. For the sake of the girls, she did not want a scene of histrionics and threats. Tomorrow she would call her lawyer, have him report Peter's infraction to the judge . . . again. She knew that the monthly child support check was due and that, court order or not, Peter had not been able to pass up the chance of coming to the door and delivering it in person.

"I'm going upstairs," Samantha said, bursting into tears. Then she rushed up the steps.

Julia turned, uncertain. It was another ruined evening—because everyone feared what Peter would do next. She started after Samantha, knowing how upset she was, afraid that a high-strung girl like Sam could break down one day, act out, and maybe run away from home as she had once threatened.

"Don't worry, Mom," Alyssa said. "I'll see to Sam, you take care of Dad." She hesitated before running after her sister, who'd just slammed her bedroom door. "Just tell Dad that Sam and I are gone."

Julia hesitated, hating the scenario that had become all too familiar of late: lie to save the peace—because no one could control Peter.

But she nodded. For the moment there was no other option. Alyssa went upstairs as Julia continued to the door, where the knocking had become urgent.

There was one other option, she reminded herself. She could sell the house and move, but both girls resisted the idea. Alyssa and Samantha had gone to school with their friends since kindergarten, and Julia realized a move would be the last emotional straw for them. Alyssa had said she wouldn't go, that her best friend's family would take her in. Samantha had simply threatened to run away. Somehow Julia needed to keep the status quo and hope that Peter would eventually come to his senses.

She grabbed the knob, hesitated, and then opened the door.

And wished she hadn't.

CHAPTER TWO

THE CLOYING FRAGRANCE OF ROSES HIT JULIA'S NOSTRILS the second she opened the door. Standing in rigid silence on the welcome mat, Peter offered her the bouquet.

Shit. Her heart sank. Another of his mood swings. She didn't want his damnable flowers, but she knew what would happen if she refused them. The powder keg would blow.

As though sensing her reservation, he shoved them against her. "Go on, take them."

"I wish you wouldn't do this, Peter."

"Can't a man give his wife flowers? Show her that he cares—that *he's a family man?*"

She searched for words.

Dr. Kornsweig said you weren't a family man, that you only thought you were a family man.

And I'm no longer your wife.

Julia clamped her lips over the words. What good would it do to quote Peter's psychiatrist? Or point out their marital status? Peter hadn't listened to an expert, so why would he hear her? He hadn't heeded anything she'd ever said in seventeen years of marriage.

"Thanks, Peter. I know Alyssa and Samantha will enjoy your gesture," she said instead of confronting him.

"And you don't?" The wild look was back in his eyes.

"Did you stop by with the support check?" she asked, trying to divert him from his anger. Although he was muscular without an ounce of fat, and his blue eyes were a startling contrast to his sun-weathered skin, his high-strung personality had become stamped onto his sharp features and took away from his attractiveness. What she'd once thought of as handsome, she now realized was suppressed anger that went far beyond their marital problems. "We could use it, that's for sure," she said, striving for normalcy. "Alyssa and Sam have lots of school expenses right now." She faked a laugh. "You know, the typical beginning-of-the-semester costs."

"Yeah, I've got the check."

She waited as he pulled it out of his wallet, then hesitated and made no attempt to hand it over. Instead, he went into his usual litany of complaints.

"Money wouldn't be a problem if we were still together, Julia." His tone was tight, his words clipped. "Your wanting to be single is standing in the way of us being a *real* family again."

His words froze the moment.

It was his blackmail tactic to do something nice, like the roses, then assume the position that his sensitive gesture had been thrown back into his face—so that he, not the family he was terrorizing with his bizarre and threatening behavior, became the victim.

"But we're not married anymore, Peter." She tried to sidestep his emotional trap, and reminded herself to instruct her lawyer to make sure Peter paid his child support to the court, not to her on her own doorstep in defiance of a court order.

What good was a law without teeth?

"No, we're not, because of your asshole writer friends."

His eyes flickered with anger, his hold on his emotions weakening. He blamed everyone but himself for their breakup, and he'd settled on the belief that she'd been led astray by the unrealistic thinking of "writer-types." She didn't dare take the bait. The situation was too volatile.

More emotional manipulation, she thought. Another of his ploys for control. Peter continued to get away with his every infraction, and no law enforcement agency or court seemed able to stop him, which was why she still opened the door to him, why she kept up her feeble attempt to keep him calm, to prevent public scenes for the sake of their daughters.

But Julia knew she was being manipulated by his inappropriate behavior. She knew why he acted out, stomped his feet and threatened violence: to get his family back at any cost. Although law enforcement officers were sympathetic, they were too overworked with murders, robberies and drugs to track down and enforce court rulings, relatively lesser offences—unless someone died. The process often took weeks.

"We'll always be connected, Peter," she said finally. "Our daughters belong to both of us."

"I'm talking about a marriage commitment here, Julia. Not divorce." His tone was threatening as he stepped closer, and she moved backward. "You're destroying our future, the future of our girls."

He believed that *she* was the destroyer, *not him*. Oh, God! She tried to push away her fear—that Peter could lose it completely—that he might really kill if his rage overcame rational thought.

Don't even think that, she told herself. Don't communicate negative thoughts.

She gave herself a mental shake. Maybe she was the one on the verge of losing it. She'd really begun to think that he could cue in on her thoughts, that he could pull them down from some universal thinking, that she couldn't hide anything from him, not even if it was to protect herself and their two daughters. His scrutiny of their lives had become a hell on earth.

He seemed to know everything they said and did.

Protect me from my own paranoia. Just because her fears had become manifest in his actions—banging on the door when she pretended not to be home, peeking in the windows, then trying master keys in the locks she'd had changed after he'd moved out—didn't mean Peter possessed the magical power of mind reading. Nor did it mean she was imagining his obsessive attention to their lives. It only meant he was always out there, watching.

"*You're the most normal young woman I've ever known*," a high-school counselor had once told her when she was in twelfth grade. But that was back in the years when she'd been class president, Girl's State candidate, girl's basketball star, and valedictorian. She'd even received the prestigious Activities Award at her high-school graduation.

So when had she started doubting herself?

Seventeen years ago, when she'd married Peter right out of high school, rather than going to college?

No, her fault had been in being too young, in disregarding her parents' disapproval. She'd naively believed love could change bad behavior. She still believed in love, but now she was smart enough to know about personality disorders and that they couldn't be changed—that Peter's problems weren't her fault. They had been in place years before she'd ever met him. That's how the shrink had described Peter, that his problem wasn't her fault.

And it wasn't her problem now, even though his two daughters lived with her.

But she wondered if she'd ever be free of him.

"So." His word was a sneer. "You want the roses or don't you?"

She didn't dare refuse, so she took the bouquet he offered, then again wondered about her own state of mind. Judy Gaston, her psychologist since the divorce, was directing her away from being so fearful about upsetting Peter, to just state her parameters and stay firm about her position. But then Judy didn't seem to completely understand the volatility of the situation.

"I need to get into the garage," he said.

"Why?"

"I think I left a level on the shelf above the workbench."

"It's not there, Peter. You took all of your tools months ago."

"Yes, it has to be. I must have overlooked it, and I need it for a particular job." His tone sounded hyper, almost out of control. "Remember, the judge said the tools were mine."

"I know that, Peter. But you took everything before."

"But I don't have it. I know it's there."

"Mom?" Alyssa's strained voice sounded behind her. "Just let Dad look, so he knows you aren't lying."

Still Julia hesitated, fearful of allowing Peter access to the garage. Finally she told him to go out to the driveway and wait for the garage doors to open. She realized that she could lock the door from the garage to the house, that she could call for help if he tried anything.

Minutes later Peter was in the garage searching for his level, and Julia and the girls were separated from him by the bolted door. Julia waited quietly in the laundry room for him to leave.

The sound of breaking glass startled her. She could hear Peter's profanity as the sound increased.

It sounded like her car windshield.

She resisted the urge to open the door. Peter was out of control . . . again.

She ran to call the police instead.

CHAPTER THREE

JULIA SAT IN HER OFFICE AND STARED AT THE LEDGER THAT was illuminated by the desk lamp. Beyond her the house was quiet, except for the faint ticking of the grandfather clock in the front hall. The girls had been asleep since around ten, and it was now two in the morning.

She chewed on the end of the pencil and wondered how she'd pay all the monthly bills and still be able to buy a pep club outfit for Alyssa and a basketball uniform for Samantha.

"Damn Peter," she muttered. How could a father deprive his own daughters? But she knew how. Peter's needs came first, rational or not. He believed their suffering would guarantee his return to the family unit.

Pushing back her chair, Julia stood up. She needed sleep, but she wasn't tired. The earlier episode with Peter in the garage had left her shaken. At first she'd believed he was breaking her car windshield, but when she'd run to see, she'd found him sobbing as he'd hammered the glass windows he'd left stored against the wall, remnants of his construction company inventory. Somehow she'd managed to get him out of there before the police came, and she'd closed the garage doors. He'd gotten into his pickup truck, then he'd sat there and cried while she and the girls had waited anxiously for him to go.

Julia sighed. Another staged episode to manipulate them. Something needed to be done. If she'd had him arrested, he'd just be free again in hours. And her daughters would have suffered another indignity. They worried about what the neighbors saw happening at their house.

Shit, it's hopeless, she thought. They'd never be free of him.

Unless they moved.

Go to bed, she instructed herself. *Things will look better when you're not exhausted.*

She switched out the light and went down the hall toward the kitchen, intending to get a drink of water before going upstairs. The sharp crack against the outside siding stopped her in her tracks.

Standing in the middle of the room, Julia strained her ears to listen. The night had gone silent.

Another rock against the house? she wondered. *Peter up to his usual terror tactics?*

She wasn't intimidated. And she wasn't about to be afraid.

But what if it isn't Peter? The question surfaced of its own volition, peppering her thoughts with doubt. *You don't really know that he's behind all the crazy little incidents.*

Nonsense, she thought, mentally arguing with herself. *Of course it's Peter.* It was predictable that he'd seen her light on and wanted to scare her, especially after the garage incident.

The next crack against the house was just outside the

kitchen, and she heard the stone bounce onto the concrete patio. Without hesitation, Julia flew to the sliding glass door, whipped back the drape, and looked out.

Two big rocks lay within feet of the house, out of place on the smooth surface. She flipped the floodlight switch, and the backyard was filled with instant illumination. Nothing moved. All was still.

Beyond the fence, the woods bordering her property were black and foreboding. Her skin prickled. Someone was out there. Someone who could see her framed in the window, a perfect target for anyone with a stronger weapon than a stone.

She jumped to the side, yanking on the drapery cord to close the window covering. Then she sagged against the kitchen counter, her legs shaking. Her breath came in short gulps, and she forced herself to slow it.

Admit it, she told herself. *You're scared.*

Peter—Peter! How can you do this to your family?

She checked the door locks, made sure the alarm system was still armed, and then went into the living room and sat down on the sofa. Minutes passed, and no other rocks hit the house. After a while she lay down and pulled her former mother-in-law's knitted afghan over her body.

She could never go upstairs to sleep now. Like a mother bear, she needed to protect her cubs against whoever was out there in the night, watching her house.

Surprisingly, Julia dozed off and slept until morning, awakening when she heard the girls getting up. She threw off the afghan, straightened the sofa pillows, and was already in the kitchen when Alyssa came downstairs.

"Up early, Mom?"

"Uh-huh." Julia filled the coffeemaker with water and switched it on. The sudden ring of the wall phone kept her from having to elaborate. She grabbed the receiver.

"Hello."

"It's Peter, Julia."

Her heart sank. Oh, God. Not again. Her first impulse was to hang up, but she resisted the urge. "Yes?" she answered.

"You have any problems during the night?" he asked.

She stiffened, turning away so Alyssa wouldn't see her expression. "What do you mean?"

"I was reading the morning newspaper. There's an article about a dead woman being found in the woods not a mile from our house." A pause. "I'm checking on my family, that's all."

She switched the phone to her left hand so she could pour coffee. "We're fine, Peter, but I have to go."

"Always in a rush, aren't you? Never time for the guy who cares enough about your safety to call, huh."

Her sigh was involuntary. His calling was another thing she needed to discuss with her lawyer. Like coming to the house, it was a court violation.

Alyssa stepped in front of her. "Dad?" she mouthed.

Julia nodded.

Alyssa put down her cereal bowl. "I'm not hungry." She turned and went back upstairs.

"I can't talk now, Peter." Anger washed over her. How dare he keep pestering them, not allowing any of them to get over the trauma of the divorce. He was obsessed . . . couldn't let go of what he wanted. "I'm hanging up now."

Carefully, she replaced the phone in its cradle. She began to shake, trembling so hard that her coffee splashed out of the cup.

It *had* been him out there last night. She glanced at the clock. It wasn't seven-thirty yet. She still had another couple of hours before her lawyer was in his office. Something had to be done about Peter.

He was getting worse, not better.

After the girls went to school, Julia scanned the newspaper article that Peter had mentioned. A woman who'd gone out for a short evening walk had been shot and killed, and Julia wondered if the murder had happened on a part of the trail she used. The article didn't pinpoint the exact location. Remembering her apprehension on the path the night before, she decided to skip her usual jog. Instead, she spent the morning working her dried flowers into door wreaths, waiting for her lawyer to return her call. Pleased when she'd finished her whole order of ten, Julia flexed her aching back muscles as she straightened up from the worktable in the garage.

"Whew." She felt stiff, but satisfied. One job down and several more to go. She headed for the kitchen. There was time to bake the three-tier wedding cake before the girls returned from school. She would freeze it to frost on Friday morning, just before delivering it.

At the moment she was ahead of schedule on all of her jobs. The Saturday speech still needed to be written, but she could do that tonight, after the girls were in bed. The sudden ring of the phone startled her.

"Julia?"

"Bill."

She recognized her lawyer's voice. "Thanks for calling back."

"What can I do for you?"

Briefly, she updated him about Peter's actions, that

he was still coming to the house with the support checks, and that he was calling incessantly on the phone.

"Okay, he's in violation again." A pause. "Did you tell me that you'd had the phone company block his calls?"

"Yeah, but he's on to that and rarely calls from his own phone numbers." She sighed. "And I have to pick up the calls that won't show up on my Caller ID. I have children and need to be available to them if they need me."

"Understood. I'll see what we can do about it, and I'll let you know."

"Today?"

"Probably not, but in the next few days, for sure." A pause. "As you know, legal procedures take time."

Julia hung up, vaguely disturbed. Why was it that the perpetrators always had their rights, while the victims had to wait—and hope that they survived. She washed her hands in the sink, and then took a mixing bowl from the cupboard. Julia was thoughtful as she pulled out the cake ingredients and recipe and placed them on the counter. The laws protected the person accused of breaking the law; it was up to the accuser to prove guilt.

Fucked-up system, she thought with a burst of anger, and then chided herself. Wasn't that the premise she'd always believed in, too? That a person was innocent until proven guilty? That no one should be institutionalized because another person said they should be?

The death of innocence, she told herself. Another thing Peter had taken from her. She was now in the unfortunate position of being stalked, hounded, and threatened by the man she'd once loved and been married to for seventeen years.

Shit. She needed to get strong. She could get past this and have a good future.

She had to.

The phone rang again as she was taking the first tier of cakes out of the oven. After slipping the tins onto a counter rack, she pulled off her oven mitt and grabbed the receiver.

"Hello?"

"Julia Farley?" a pleasant female voice asked.

"Speaking."

"This is Midge Fox, your panel moderator for the conference on Saturday."

"Hi, Midge." Julia was relieved the caller wasn't Peter. "What's up?"

"I'm just checking in." Her laugh was friendly. Although Julia hadn't met Midge, she knew the moderator wrote school textbooks. "Making sure that my panelists for the Truth in Nonfiction panel are all set," she went on. "Also, I wondered if you needed a map of the university campus."

"I'm familiar with the layout, Midge, but I appreciate your asking. And I believe I'm all set. You want me to speak for ten minutes on the subject at hand, and then when all the panelists have also spoken, to be prepared to answer questions."

"That's it." A pause. "And just one other update. Earl Paulsen has been added to the panel."

"Earl Paulsen, the criminal lawyer who coauthored that book on a high-profile murder case he successfully defended two years ago?"

"That's him." Midge's lilting words came over the lines. "We're so lucky he's appearing on our panel. His book has been an instant best-seller."

There was a silence.

"I hadn't realized this panel included true-crime writing." Julia switched the phone to her other ear so that she could check her second oven, where the bigger cake layers were about ready to be removed. "My nonfiction writing is about software manuals, the other panelists write articles, and you write textbooks." She hesitated. "A best-selling crime book doesn't seem to fit the format."

Midge laughed. "No, it doesn't. But it was the only nonfiction spot on the program we had left. His publicist said it didn't matter, so long as he had a platform somewhere at the conference."

Midge went on to explain that a headliner like Earl Paulsen enhanced the coverage by the local media and gave the conference much-needed publicity. "So it's beneficial to everyone." Midge drew in a long breath. "Do you have a problem with Earl being on the panel, Julia?"

"Of course not. I only wondered why he'd agree to appear with authors who are amateurs compared to him."

"Hey, he's just richer than the rest of us. Don't forget, he was a rank amateur just last year, before he hit the lists." Midge gave another laugh. "To his credit, I heard he's a nice guy."

They said their good-byes, and as Julia hung up, she felt a new urgency about her unwritten speech. Jeez, she was in a whole new ballgame now that Earl Paulsen was on the panel. She needed to make her talk meaningful, even if the subject matter was technical and boring.

Earl Paulsen would attract a big, intelligent audience, not the few dozen people she'd expected.

She could not come across like a beginner. She must

seem knowledgeable about the current market. Damn it! Her talk would take more work than she'd intended. She needed to get busy on it right after supper.

She just hoped Peter wouldn't make another dramatic appearance. And if he did . . . she'd just have to report him. Again.

CHAPTER FOUR

Topsy stared out of the front window, watching as the ferry moved away from Bainbridge Island to cross Puget Sound and head toward Elliott Bay. The Seattle skyline loomed in the distance, directly across the water from her beachfront house, an enchanting view once the lights came on at night. Moving into her home had been a dream come true: loving the sweeping vista of the city across the sound, living with the island community of family-oriented people, and enjoying the peaceful ambiance while living so close to a major West Coast port, yet being so separate.

Topsy turned away from the window. If everything was so perfect, then why did she feel such a sinking sensation in the pit of her stomach—such a sense of impending danger? Why was she so fearful in her own house that she couldn't sleep at night?

And why did she have to take antianxiety and antidepression drugs? Judy, her psychologist, was trying to help her recognize that she might be suppressing something so traumatic that she couldn't face its ramifications.

Why she only felt safe enough to talk about her distant past or her children.

She'd tried so hard to remember, but nothing ever surfaced, the locked door in her mind never opened. Topsy drew in a shaky breath. Maybe Judy was wrong and nothing had happened. Maybe she'd just gone crazy and there was no event to blame for her mental state. All she knew for sure was what triggered the panic attacks: hearing about killing sprees on the television news, reading newspaper articles about murder victims, being alone in a dark place, and sex with her husband.

During her waking hours she was like someone trapped in a horror movie—someone who'd been blinded and didn't know where the terror would strike next but was always expecting the fatal blow at any second.

While asleep she couldn't run from her recurring nightmare, in which she was unable to move even though a faceless black shape was closing in and death was moments away. She always woke up with her heart in fibrillation, her terror so great that she couldn't even scream.

What had happened to her? Topsy asked herself for the umpteenth time. And why now? Was her problem the result of something from her childhood, of being the daughter of a sixteen-year-old mother and seventeen-year-old father? Had being born to irresponsible children, whose own parents had demanded they marry, given her such insecurity that she'd had a mental breakdown when faced with a life-altering event?

A life-altering event.

What?

It was what Judy had implied might be the cause, something so horrific that her mind had shut down, and whatever happened had buried itself in her subconscious.

Topsy wasn't sure about anything anymore. Maybe her debilitating migraine headaches of recent years had developed into the anxiety and depression problems. Maybe her therapist was wrong about her suppressing something so hideous that she wasn't allowing it a voice.

She hated herself for being so pathetic, for being such a burden to her family. Why couldn't she accept her own weaknesses, and go on like everyone else? Why couldn't she just live up to her husband's expectations of a wife and mother?

Her husband. He was so successful, so perfect.

Then why did he repel her? Why did she have to control herself so that she didn't flinch at his touch?

It was another shameful issue she needed to discuss with Judy. Why had her feelings for him changed so drastically, coinciding with the onset of her first anxiety attack.

Oh, God! Topsy prayed that she was salvageable. That she still had a future with her husband, the man she'd once loved so desperately. And with her children, who meant more to her than anything else.

If not, she had nothing.

CHAPTER FIVE

JULIA BACKED OUT OF THE DRIVEWAY ON SATURDAY morning, preoccupied with getting to the university campus for her panel. She was pressed for time, having had to cope with the latest of Peter's tirades. He'd called earlier with new pleas for reconciliation. Unfortunately, Alyssa had answered the phone and gotten the full force of her dad's volatile mood swings. Julia had grabbed the receiver, angrily confronted Peter about his narcissism at the expense of their daughter's well-being, and then hung up on him. But she'd had to spend the next hour trying to undo the emotional damage. Consequently, she was running late.

I may have to sell the house after all, she thought. If there was no legal way to control Peter, then she'd have no other choice. It would be less of a disruption for Alyssa and Samantha to move than to be subject to Peter's mental illness.

Julia drove into the campus parking lot, placed her

Reserved card from the conference committee on her dashboard, then got out of her car and headed for the building she'd been told would hold her panel.

She was the last person to arrive at the speaker's platform, only several minutes before the session was scheduled to begin. "Sorry I'm late," she told Midge, who'd just introduced herself. "Family emergency."

"You made it and that's what matters," Midge replied, looking relieved to see her. "Take a seat and we'll get started once you've caught your breath."

Nodding, Julia glanced along the table at the other three writers. She recognized Mary Allison, who wrote travel articles, and Jill Graham, who penned a local gardening column and was working on a cookbook, but not the bearded man at the end. She realized he must be Earl Paulsen, although he looked bigger and more attractive in person than he did in his photos in the Seattle newspapers.

He caught her gaze, and she smiled before looking away. The sudden intensity in his dark eyes momentarily disconcerted her. She hadn't felt such a rush of attraction since she'd first met Peter years ago.

Julia sat down in the empty chair at the opposite end of the table from Earl as Midge welcomed the several hundred people to the panel. The next two hours passed quickly, and her talk seemed well received by the audience. By the time the question-and-answer period completed the segment, Julia felt uplifted, confident that she'd done a good job answering questions and explaining software manuals.

Earl Paulsen was surrounded by fans when she picked up her notes, said her good-byes to the other panelists, and headed for the door. The hand on her arm that stopped her was, therefore, unexpected.

"Hey." Earl Paulsen's deep baritone voice sounded behind her. "Anyone ever tell you how talented and intelligent you are?"

She turned and faced him, her eyes immediately caught by his admiring gaze. "Not recently." She wanted to add that most people didn't give outrageous praise to strangers, but decided against it.

"Well, they're remiss then." A flash of humor softened the set lines of his features. "I was so impressed by your talk that I'm considering trading in my law license to write computer manuals."

The amusement in his eyes belied his words, although she recognized the sincerity in his compliment.

"Thanks, Mr. Paulsen." She smiled and tried to not seem flattered, or in awe of him like his adoring fans, who waited behind them. "But I was only talking nuts and bolts about a very boring subject."

"But you made it interesting."

She laughed outright. "I know how to write a software manual because I have to. Interesting? I hardly think so."

He stood in momentary silence, a tall, attractive man in a gaunt, ruggedly handsome way. It was his quick wit and engaging personality that made him so appealing, she decided. Passionate about his subject when he spoke, his animated words brought his face to life, his brown eyes lighting with fervor, his mouth suddenly smiling because of his inherent humor and his ability for instant repartee.

A hard man to forget, Julia realized. Earl was one of those men that women found irresistible. She'd never met anyone quite like him. His talk had been informative, explaining his role in defending the rights of a high-profile killer, police procedure, why he'd decided to write about the case, and the movie option on his book. He'd held her and the audience enthralled from the beginning to the end of his talk. And most of the ensuing questions had been directed to him.

He has charisma, she thought as he momentarily explained his thoughts about their panel. As he talked, Julia found herself wondering how it would feel to be the woman in his life.

Silly . . . silly, she reprimanded herself, glancing away so he wouldn't divine her wayward thoughts from her expression. He was simply an outgoing man who couldn't help his attractiveness—just as she couldn't help responding to a fellow writer with a brilliant mind. She forced back thoughts of Peter, a total opposite of Earl in both manner and emotional stability. Earl was calm and precise; Peter was easily upset and scattered.

She thanked him again for his compliment, and when he was suddenly surrounded by fans, Julia made her getaway. She was done for the day as far as the conference was concerned. Tonight she planned to attend the awards banquet, but for now she was headed home.

There was no point in entertaining a lingering thought about Earl Paulsen. He had enough fans without her being at his feet, too.

"Gosh, Mom," Samantha said, coming into Julia's bedroom. "You really look pretty."

The awe in her youngest daughter's voice brought a smile to Julia's lips. Their eyes met in the mirror. "That might be because I haven't dressed up since last year's conference banquet," she said, grinning wider. "Do you approve, sweetie?"

"Yeah." Samantha slumped onto the bed behind the

vanity, where Julia sat, applying mascara to her eyelashes. "And I love the red dress. Didn't you buy that two Christmases ago to wear at the party you and Dad had for his employees?"

Julia's hand hesitated momentarily. She nodded, her eyes averted to her task. That had been the only time she'd worn the long-sleeved, scooped neck velvet sheath, the night she'd walked in on Peter embracing his young bookkeeper in their home office. He'd explained later that he was only expressing holiday cheer, had just given the girl a one-hundred-dollar bonus check away from the other employees, and she'd reacted by hugging him.

Julia had known instantly that he was lying, that he was covering his ass, but she'd let it go—until after the party. And later her demand for an explanation had produced shouts, accusations of jealousy, and, finally, him sobbing. For the first time she'd recognized that he was emotionally disturbed, a realization she'd been avoiding for several years. Since that night, almost two years ago, his emotional state had gone downhill, and their family doctor had admitted to her that Peter wasn't coping. That's when Dr. Hornsby had referred him to Dr. Kornsweig, a psychiatrist.

Then, as Peter had gotten worse, threatening her with scenarios of how she should die, preferably in front of their daughters, she'd pleaded with his psychiatrist for help in how to handle the situation. To her horror, the doctor wouldn't violate his confidentiality with Peter, would not reassure her that her life was not in jeopardy.

That had been her own breaking point. What the doctor wouldn't say had said volumes. Peter had been a powder keg about to blow up, and when he did, she could die at his hands, even if he regretted it a moment after the fact.

She'd had to leave the marriage or possibly die.

Their separation had marked the beginning of her reign of terror.

"Yeah, you look so young you could be our sister," Alyssa said, stepping from the doorway and bringing Julia's thoughts back to the present. She'd obviously overheard Samantha's praise. "You look beautiful, Mom."

Suddenly overwhelmed, Julia put down the mascara wand and turned on her stool to embrace her girls. They were so special; she was so lucky to have them.

A few minutes later she hesitated at the laundry room door to the garage and turned back to Alyssa and Samantha.

"I won't be late, probably home before nine." She hesitated. "My cell phone will be on, no matter where I am. Call if anything comes up and I'll come right home."

"It's okay, Mom," Alyssa said. "We aren't scared." She gave a nervous laugh. "We'll call Aunt Diana and Uncle Ted if we get spooked. Her house on Lake Sammamish is only ten minutes away."

Her words gave Julia pause. "You're to call 911 first if there's ever a problem," she said with contrived calmness. *Maybe I should just stay home*, she thought. Maybe Judy, her psychologist, was wrong, maybe they couldn't "just go on with their lives" at this point.

Oh God, she thought, getting into her ten-year-old Jeep Cherokee. She even felt guilty about attending a dumb writer's banquet. Peter's presence was always out there in the periphery of her life, trying to sabotage her. She couldn't let him do that. With resolve, she pressed the garage door opener, waved to the girls, and backed out onto the driveway. But all the way down the hills to the freeway she felt unsettled, as though she'd compromised the safety of her daughters by going.

"You need to get past those feelings," her psychologist had told her many times. "Or you'll never get past Peter's control."

With Judy's words in her mind, Julia drove over the Lake Washington floating bridge and into Seattle. A few minutes later she found a parking place on campus and headed for the huge cafeteria, where the banquet was being held. She'd tried to put a lilt in her step and a relaxed expression on her face. It was a break from her terror, and she needed it . . . desperately.

Peter would never harm his daughters, she reassured herself. His anger was against her, not them. Julia was depending on that or she would never have left them alone, even though she'd alerted Diana and Ted about being gone for the evening.

"About time you're getting out," her sister had commented when Julia had called to make sure they'd be home. "I understand your concerns, Julia, but sometimes your precautions tip into overkill. You need a little relaxation, too."

Overkill, she thought. But that's how it was these days. She and her girls had to be protected against the mental illness of their own father.

"Hey, I think I just won the lotto!"

Julia's gaze flew to the man who'd jumped up from a nearby table as she moved through the dining room looking for her name card in the area reserved for program presenters. She was surprised—and pleased—to find she'd been seated next to Earl Paulsen. He pointed to the empty chair as she walked toward him, his admiring glance taking in the red dress that emphasized her slender figure.

"Thanks." She grinned. "I couldn't seem to find my place without help."

Glancing around the table of eight, she saw that her moderator and the two other panelists, all three with husbands, completed their group. Greeting them all, she realized that she and Earl were the only ones without partners.

As she sat down next to him, he took her matching red jacket and draped it behind her on the chair, and the conversation at the table turned to talk of their earlier panel. While dinner was being served, and the attention of the group turned to the food, Earl directed his next comment to her alone.

"Tell me about you, Julia." His eyes reflected the interest she heard in his tone of voice.

She shrugged and glanced away. "Not that much to tell, Earl."

"Hmmm. I can't believe that."

"What?" Her laugh was spontaneous. "We don't all have exciting lives like yours."

"Exciting? That doesn't describe mine."

Julia lifted her gaze, and it was instantly captured by his. "Really? It's hard to believe that a successful, high-profile lawyer, not to mention a national best-selling author who is everywhere in the media, doesn't have an exciting life."

His black brows slid up his forehead. "But true." It was his turn to look away. "To misquote an old cliché, fame and fortune don't always guarantee personal happiness."

She could only nod.

"I struck a chord?"

"Not really, Earl. I'm neither rich nor famous." A pause. "But I know that real happiness is much more elusive than achieving either of them."

A brief silence went by.

"Of course, I agree." Another pause. "Sounds like you've suffered."

The server refilled Julia's coffee cup, and she was saved from answering. When the conversation resumed, it was more general. Then, unexpectedly, Earl reverted to a direct question.

"You aren't married, Julia?"

She shook her head. "Divorced."

"Any kids?"

"Two daughters, fourteen and sixteen. You?"

"Married, also two kids, Jenny is eighteen and Mitch is twelve."

He sounded stilted, and she wondered about the state of his marriage, if his life wasn't what it seemed on the surface. She faced him and managed a smile.

"You know there's an old statistic that claims the perfect family is a mother, father, son, and daughter." A pause. "Maybe that was what was wrong with mine. I had two daughters instead of a son and daughter."

"Are you joking? Or being cynical?" His serious tone belied the return of humor in his eyes.

She snorted a laugh. "Both, I guess."

"I'm sorry," he said. "But believe me, I understand what you're saying."

She didn't question him further. The conversation was becoming too personal. Instead, she changed the subject to writing again, answering his questions about her published fiction. She explained that all her sales had been children's stories, but she hoped to eventually write novels when she could afford the time.

"Writing is an expensive addiction for those of us who don't make much money at our craft and must work at other jobs to support ourselves." She smiled. "I can't even begin to make a living from what I write."

"You will," he said seriously.

"Thanks, Earl. That was a nice tribute, especially since you've never seen any of my published work."

He grinned suddenly. "Hey, I'm a criminal lawyer, remember? I read people, and I can tell you'd be good," he said, then turned away to answer another question from one of the husbands.

Julia was glad that his attention had been diverted from her. His close proximity was almost overpowering, and she'd found herself breathless at times. It was easy to see why he was so successful in his profession. She wondered if his adversaries ever had a chance in the courtroom, or in his private life, for that matter.

She smiled to herself, listening to the ebb and flow of the conversation until the dinner dishes were cleared away and the program began. When it was over she said her good-byes and managed to slip away while Earl was once again surrounded by adoring fans.

Julia sighed as she drove home. She would probably never see Earl again. Just as well, she told herself. He was a married man, and she was a beleaguered and terrorized divorcée.

Not a good combination.

CHAPTER SIX

EVERY LIGHT IN THE HOUSE WAS ON AS JULIA DROVE UP TO her house and into the garage. She wasn't even out of the Cherokee before the door to the laundry room burst open and both Alyssa and Samantha stood waiting for her on the threshold.

Something was wrong. Julia could tell by their darting eyes, as though they feared someone would enter behind her before the garage door finally swooshed shut.

"We tried to call you, Mom," Alyssa said, motioning for her mother to hurry.

"But your cell phone was turned off," Samantha added before Julia could get a word out of her mouth.

"What's happened?"

"We'll tell you in a minute." Alyssa yanked the door closed behind Julia, then locked it. As they moved into the kitchen, Julia pulled the phone from her purse. It *was* off—oh, God. The power switch must have accidentally bumped against something in her handbag.

Once safely inside the house, the girls started talking at once.

"Wait," Julia instructed. "One at a time."

"Someone was looking in the kitchen window when Samantha was washing a pan," Alyssa blurted. She put an arm around her younger sister. "Sam was really wigged out, screamed so loud I figured the neighbors would have heard her—if they'd been home."

A knot of panic tightened in Julia's stomach, but she strove to appear calm. A glance told her that all the blinds were tightly closed, and she knew the doors were locked. "When did this happen?"

"Just a few minutes ago."

"Did you call the police?"

Alyssa shook her head.

"Why in hell didn't you?" Of its own volition, Julia's fear was unleashed in a burst of anger. "I've told you girls time and again to call for help if there's anything wrong. *Anything at all.*"

Julia ran to the windows and peeked from behind the blinds. The whole backyard was illuminated as bright as day. No one could still be out there. There was nowhere to hide once the exterior lights had been switched on.

Unless someone was beyond their yard watching from the woods.

"But, Mom, we couldn't." Samantha's voice wobbled. "What if it was Dad out there, you know, snooping like he does sometimes."

Julia turned from the window, forcing back the retort that sprang to her lips. Lashing out at the girls wouldn't do any good. She realized that she was misdirecting her anger, that it was a reaction to her own fear and frustration.

Would it ever end? Would they ever lead normal lives again?

"I called Aunt Diana instead—like you told us to do." Alyssa sounded hesitant, as though she feared upsetting her mother even more. "She's on her way over right now."

"With Uncle Ted?"

Alyssa shook her head. "Uncle Ted went to a Mariners game with some of his men friends."

Julia was momentarily stunned. What was Diana thinking of, to come alone when there was a prowler, to not call the police herself?

"Aunt Diana told us to shut all of the blinds, then turn on all the lights, inside and out," Samantha said.

"And to make sure the doors were locked and the alarm system turned on," Alyssa told Julia, nervously tucking her long blond hair behind her ears. "I unarmed it when I saw you turn into the driveway."

"Mom?" Sam asked. "You aren't mad at us, are you?"

"Of course not." She went to them, pulling both girls into her arms for a hug. "But now that whoever was out there is gone, tell me exactly what happened." Julia stepped back, relieved that she sounded calmer, even though her mind still raced, and all of her nerve endings tingled.

Should she call the police? she wondered, her glance flickering to the window over the sink where Samantha had seen someone. The blinds were never closed on that window—until now—because it was so high a person would need a short ladder to look into the house. Her mind boggled. Unless you'd been the one who'd built the house and knew there was a narrow ledge over the outside facet, that it was strong enough to support the weight of an adult.

No, Julia instructed herself. She wouldn't jump to the obvious conclusion: Peter. She'd wait until she knew what had happened. She sat both of them down at the kitchen table, explaining that everything looked okay now, that they were safe. After a little prodding, Samantha was calmer and began to explain.

"I was only washing my spaghetti pan and—" She broke off, twisting her hands into a knot. "I wanted to make sure the kitchen was cleaned up before you got home, Mom."

"Go on, sweetie." Julia's prompt was gentle. "I know you got scared, but you're okay now."

Samantha nodded, and after a gulp of air, related what she'd seen. "At first I thought it was a reflection of me—it happened so fast that all I know is that it was a face, and then it was gone before I could even make out the features, if it was even a man or a woman." More tears rolled down her face. "But I had the impression that it was a man." She hesitated. "I thought it was Dad, Mom. But I can't believe it was. My dad wouldn't scare me like that."

Damn that Peter, Julia thought behind her calm façade. That son of a bitch *was* scaring his own daughters, and all he cared about were his own motives, his own perceived comfort zone. He needed to know what was going on, who was home. *If she was home.*

This was the final straw—his last act of manipulation. He'd finally gone too far. He had to be stopped before he damaged everyone beyond repair.

"That's when I screamed," Samantha went on. "Alyssa came running from the family room, we tried to call you and then called Aunt Diana."

The sudden sound of the front doorbell startled all of them.

"It's Aunt Diana," Alyssa announced, jumping up to start through the room toward the hall.

"Wait!" Julia cried.

Alyssa stopped short in the doorway, allowing her mom to go ahead of her. A glance though the peephole verified that it was Diana. Julia flung open the door to her sister—and a police officer.

She hesitated.

"I called the police," Diana announced, stepping into the foyer. "There was no way that I couldn't—under the circumstances."

"I understand," Julia said, after a moment of silence. "It's what I expected you'd do." Another pause. "Thanks."

Her sister, taller but equally blond and blue-eyed, was far more assertive than Julia. Diana, seven years younger, had gone to college and gotten her degree, their parents being in a better financial position to help than when Julia had graduated high school. Later, after Diana and Ted married, she'd received an architecture degree at the University of Washington and now had a successful career at a prestigious firm in downtown Seattle. Diana was a blunt, no-nonsense person, but also loyal and loving. She adored her two nieces and hated them being emotionally abused by their own father.

The uniformed officer stepped into the hall behind Diana. Beyond him, Julia could see his patrol car parked in the driveway.

"Officer Dolby," he said. "I've met you before." A hesitation. "What's the problem tonight?"

Julia blushed, remembering. The tall, lanky officer had responded to a neighbor's call when Peter had been in the driveway shouting obscenities and threatening to break down the front door. She and the girls had been humiliated. In the end Peter had calmed down and she hadn't pressed charges, because both girls had begged her not to.

"Hey, this isn't your fault, Sis." Sensing her embarrassment, Diana dropped an arm around Julia. "I had to call the police, you know that." A long sigh escaped her lips. "Even though this is such ongoing ugliness, each infraction needs to be reported, so that everything is on file in case—"

Julia sucked in a long breath, knowing what her sister had avoided saying. *In case something bad happened.*

What? Someone dying? Her?

Her and Diana's parents were dead, their father of a stroke six years ago, their mother two years later in an automobile accident. She knew that Diana was very attached to her only living family: herself, Alyssa and Samantha.

So, was Diana overreacting now?

No. Julia answered her unasked question. Her sister was far more rational about the situation than she was at times. When Julia had been embarrassed to call the police in the past because the incidents had become so frequent, Diana had been emphatic that she must. When Julia hesitated out of concern for her girls, Diana told her in no uncertain terms that it was for everyone's sake that she not sweep Peter's mental illness under the carpet, because if she did, she and her daughters might never recover from the trauma of the divorce and all the terror since. "It's what is," Diana was fond of saying. "Whether we like it or not."

"I know," Julia had agreed many times.

"So what happened?" the officer asked, interrupting Julia's mental dialogue. "It seems that whatever it was is no longer a threat. Is that right?"

Julia nodded.

"Humph," he said. "My partner is checking out the grounds, making sure that no one is out there, okay?"

His attitude was detached, as though handling a domestic violence/stalking situation was old hat. Julia felt the familiar frustration, the sense of not being heard by the authorities, the very people she'd once believed protected society from wrongdoers. But she'd come to realize that they were as frustrated as she was; they needed proof to arrest, even if they believed that Peter, a solid citizen in every other area of his life, was threatening his family. The system didn't recognize her accusations that he was obsessive, narcissistic, and dangerous. So she and the girls had slipped through the cracks to find real help.

"Tell me what happened?" the officer asked again. "The dispatcher said that two young teenage girls were home alone and someone was prowling the house."

"That's correct," Julia said. "I was at a banquet."

The officer's whole demeanor was one of disapproval. "Let me get this straight, Mrs. Farley. You accuse your husband of being volatile, yet you left your daughters alone?"

"Hey!" Diana interrupted. "My sister is not the perpetrator here, and she didn't abuse her daughters— aged sixteen and fourteen—by leaving them alone while she attended a business banquet." In sweats and her long hair in a ponytail, Diana stepped forward, her expression angry. "Let's stick to the facts, Officer!"

He blinked. "That's what I'm trying to do."

Within the next few minutes he took down Samantha's and Alyssa's statements, gave the usual litany of keeping the doors locked, and went out to join his partner, who'd said the property was secure. Julia was glad to see them go. They'd never been much help, even though she understood that their hands were tied, too.

A fucked-up legal system, Julia thought again. There wasn't a problem until someone died. Peter must be caught in the act in order to be prosecuted.

Diana insisted on staying the night. "Don't try to talk me out of it," she told Julia. "I'm staying," she said when Julia protested. "You and the girls are my life, my background. Ted understands, and agrees. He just wishes he didn't have early morning appointments that preclude him from staying, too."

Julia could only smile. How lucky it was for her younger sister to have found Ted, who always said that very same thing about finding Diana.

For tonight, Julia was glad to have her little sister stay overnight. Somehow she felt safer.

Everything was quiet over the next week. There were no further incidents, and gradually Julia and the girls began to feel that the situation with their father might be improving.

Julia thought about Earl often, wondering about his personal life as she read about his autographing events in the newspaper. He was hugely successful, a realization brought home to her when she turned on a midafternoon TV talk show to see Earl and his coauthor discussing their true-crime book. Julia was frosting a wedding cake, but she stopped to watch the program.

Aside from the case itself, the focus of the show was on obsessive/compulsive behavior, and a psychologist rounded out the format. The doctor spoke about men who, like the predator in Earl's book, wouldn't let go, who would go to any length, even murder, to hold on to their security, which usually meant their wife or girlfriend. Earl agreed that such women were in jeopardy, and it pleased Julia that he understood their plight. She could identify.

The psychologist's words popped into her head several times over the next few days as she worked on her various projects. She hoped that Peter was not typical of the disorder, that he'd get over his obsession with being a "family man" and move forward, maybe meet another woman.

It was almost noon when the phone rang. She'd just completed her children's story for the California publisher, the tale of a child who'd learned the gift of honesty after lying. She was pleased with it, having drawn from a real incident that had occurred when Alyssa was seven.

"Hello," she said, grabbing the receiver on her desk next to the computer.

"Do I hear a smile in your voice?" a man said in her ear.

She hesitated, her mind registering the person on the other end of the line. For long seconds, surprise froze her response. He was the last person she'd expected to call. It was as though she'd conjured his image from her own thoughts.

"Is this Earl?"

"Yeah, it is." A hesitation. "Do I still hear a smile?"

"You do, Earl," she said finally, satisfied that her tone sounded normal. "I just finished my monthly kid's story for a publisher in California."

"And you're pleased with it, I can tell."

"Yeah, I guess I am. It encompasses a value that I've preached to my daughters for years." Julia switched the receiver to her other ear. "I'd just e-mailed it to my editor seconds before your call—thank goodness."

"Thank goodness?"

"Uh-huh. Today was my deadline."

"Jeez. You e-mailed the story? The wonders of modern technology." His sigh came over the wires. "But then I forgot, you're computer hip—you're a person who writes computer manuals."

Julia laughed. "Not because I want to."

"Then why, for God's sake? I can't imagine anything more boring for a creative person."

"Income."

A silence went by.

"Sorry, Julia. My comment was out of line."

She smiled into the receiver. "Hey, it's okay. I'm not the only divorced mother who has to make a living."

"Uh, that's true." His tone was softer. "I don't know what my wife would do if she had to make a living." He expelled a long breath. "She doesn't have your talents."

"Oh," Julia said, inanely. "I thought I'd read somewhere that your wife was a model, had been on the covers of most American magazines."

"That's true, but it happened over twenty years ago." A pause. "Nowadays we're lucky if she leaves the house for five minutes."

"Oh, I'm sorry, Earl. I had no idea."

"It's okay. Kaye's under medical care for her problems and sees a therapist for the agoraphobia." She sensed the upset in his voice. "We, Mitch and Jenny and I, feel she's making progress." He gave a laugh. "At least we tell ourselves that."

"I'm sure you're right." There was a pause while she tried to think of an appropriate response to his obvious heartache.

"So, how about you, Julia? What's your situation, if you don't mind me asking." A pause. "I know you're divorced and you have two teenage daughters, not that you seem old enough to have teenagers."

"Yeah, I am." She smiled into the phone, sensing his smile. "My scenario is much different from yours." She hesitated, wondering how much she should share. "My former husband won't let go." She forced a laugh. "It seems like he's one of those guys you and the other guests talked about on television the other day."

"So, you saw the program?"

"Uh-huh. It was fascinating."

"Aberrant behavior is always fascinating to normal people," he said. "Despite all the criminal cases I've handled, I still don't know why some people do what they do, or what happened to make them so different from the rest of us." He drew in a breath. "Why they never developed a conscience—why they lack empathy for their fellow human beings." He cleared his voice. "You aren't serious about your husband having a personality disorder, are you?"

Julia hesitated. "I'm not sure what to call it, Earl. I wish I could say Peter's behavior was just an emotional phase, but it's lasted too long—" She broke off, uncertain. "I'm awfully scared that it's far more serious than that."

"Shit, I hope you're wrong, Julia. But it sounds like you've given the subject a lot of thought."

"Yeah, I guess I have," she replied. "All seventeen years of my marriage."

His whistle came over the wire. "I've spent a lot of time with psychopaths," he began, and then gave a wry laugh, "but I confess to not understanding what happened to these guys to make them that way. Even the experts don't really know."

"Darn, I was hoping you had some sage advice." Her own laugh was half serious. "I could sure use some help in my own situation."

His sigh came over the line.

"I'm really sorry, Julia. A woman like you doesn't deserve that kind of treatment." He'd taken her words seriously. "If there's anything I can do to help you, please let me know. I'm glad to offer my services."

She hesitated, considering her response.

"Hey, I appreciate your words, kind sir," she said, attempting to lighten their conversation. Somehow they'd become too serious, and they hardly knew each other. She realized that she didn't know why he'd called, and so she asked him, changing the subject.

"I need your help—and a favor," he replied in answer to her query.

"From me?" Surprise registered in her voice.

"Uh-huh."

"I can't imagine what?"

"Your expertise as a fiction writer."

"Are you kidding? I've only sold children's stories."

"I know. But you plot those stories, don't you?"

"Well, yes."

"Julia, I'm serious. I know I've just had a nonfiction book published, but I don't know anything about writing fiction, and I hope to write mystery novels based on some of my old cases." There was a pause as she digested his words. "So I need to learn technique—and I don't know any fiction writers aside from you."

"I'd be happy to help you, Earl, but I write children's stories, not adult mysteries."

"I know. But doesn't plotting technique apply to both?"

"It does, but—"

"Then I'd like to hire you to help me," he said, interrupting.

"For goodness' sake, I wouldn't charge you anything for discussing writing. Writers do that all the time."

"Like I said, I don't know any fiction writers." A pause. "Would you help me get started? Say over lunch one day next week?"

She laughed. "Your power of persuasion is pretty compelling, Earl. I'll say one thing for sure. If I ever need a criminal lawyer, I'll come to you."

"But would you help me write fiction?"

They both laughed, and then she agreed. They set the time and place to meet during the following week. After they'd hung up, she found herself humming as she worked.

A good sign, she thought. She couldn't remember the last time she'd felt the anticipation of being with a man. That he was a married man didn't matter. She wasn't looking for romance, only a friend.

CHAPTER SEVEN

It was amazing to Julia how much she'd looked forward to lunch with Earl. Even Alyssa, who'd stayed home from school with menstrual cramps, had commented about how nice she looked. "If I didn't know better, I'd think you had a hot date, Mom," she said when Julia left the house.

As Julia drove the Cherokee away from her development in the hills above Issaquah and headed for the I-90 freeway, she smiled, remembering her daughter's comment. Good thing she didn't see me blush, she thought.

Damn, go easy, girl, she told herself. *Remember, this is only a lunch to help a fellow writer.*

But she knew better. Hadn't she juggled her busy schedule to go? Taken longer than usual to figure out what to wear? And hadn't her whole state of mind improved after she knew she'd be seeing Earl again?

I'm attracted to him, she thought, and then immediately qualified her feelings. She admired him, loved the brilliance of his mind—his quick retorts, his humor, and his instant grasp of any situation. It was no wonder that a cover-girl model, desired by many men, had chosen Earl to marry.

Another positive aspect of meeting Earl was that she'd realized there could be a life for her with someone else after Peter. Maybe not until her girls were past the trauma of the divorce, but her hope for a decent future was all she needed now.

As she drove past the Bellevue exit and continued across Mercer Island in Lake Washington and then on to the final bridge into Seattle, Julia felt uplifted. Peter hadn't bothered them since the night of the banquet. She wondered if a police officer had talked to him, warned him that such actions could land him in jail.

Don't think of that now, she instructed herself, heading for Ivar's, the famous waterfront seafood restaurant next to the Bainbridge Island ferry terminal. She parked under the Alaskan Way Viaduct, crossed the street that paralleled Elliott Bay, and went inside, knowing she was a few minutes early.

"That's what I like," Earl said, unfolding his tall frame from an overstuffed chair where he'd been waiting. "A woman who's on time, and a beautiful blonde at that." He grinned. "I should have guessed, knowing you."

She smiled back. "But you don't know me, Earl. This could be a first for me."

His dark brows shot up as he thoughtfully stroked his beard. "Doubt it, sweetheart. You're a woman who respects her fellow humans. You're not a taker."

"Taker?"

He sobered, taking her arm. "Just a figure of speech." They started walking. "I have a window table on the water side," he said, changing the subject.

They sat down facing each other. The waiter was immediately at their table, handing them menus.

"We'll need a few minutes to order," Earl told him.

"Anything to drink?" the waiter asked.

Earl's gaze shifted to Julia. "How about a Chardonnay?" His grin was questioning, slightly reckless, as though the event called for setting routine aside. "Or is it too early in the day for you?"

She hesitated, realizing he remembered that she'd drunk Chardonnay at the banquet.

"We'll each have a glass of Chardonnay," he told the waiter, then glanced back at her with raised brows. "We don't have to drink it, but it'll be good for a proper toast to our new friendship as struggling writers."

She laughed. "I'm struggling; you're a huge success, Earl."

"With one nonfiction book." His dark eyes were suddenly serious. "I was talking about fiction."

"Which you haven't tried to do yet."

He nodded.

"I suspect that you'll do great in that genre, too." She cleared her throat and tried to look serious. "I really think that at this point in our, uh, writing careers, that you're light-years ahead of me."

His glance flickered to her mouth as she spoke, then back to meet her eyes. "But I don't know how to plot," he said, deadpanning, avoiding a direct reply.

"And you think I can help you do that?"

"That's what one of our fellow panelists said when she traded seats with me at the banquet."

"You traded chairs to sit next to me?"

He leaned back, his eyes suddenly alight with humor and—what? Admiration? Attraction?

"No, I traded seats to learn more about . . . plotting."

The waiter brought their wine, and she was saved from responding. She was at a loss; what did Earl really want from her? Her limited writing expertise? Or just the company of another writer? Surely he, a married man, wasn't interested in anything else.

Grow up, she told herself. Married men had affairs, and maybe he did, too. His wife, a woman disabled by emotional problems and a fear of leaving her house, may no longer be sexually appealing to him. And Earl was definitely a virile man who'd want sex with his wife.

Julia lowered her eyes, not wanting him to read her thoughts. Had she made a mistake by coming? Was she in over her head? Damn! She was not experienced enough to know for sure, having married her first steady date—Peter. All she had were her instincts to go on. And they'd raised a huge caution sign in her mind.

"Hey," he said. "To new friends."

She raised her eyes.

"A person I value." He'd raised his glass for a toast. "And to writing success for us both."

She smiled and sipped. Maybe her instincts had been wrong. Maybe she was reading into his play on words, his own sense of humor. Maybe. She'd have to see.

A moment later the waiter returned to take their orders. Earl ordered a seafood grill, and she chose the crab salad. After the waiter was gone, Earl changed the subject completely, asking about Peter. Briefly, she replied that he was an eastside builder of high-end homes, that his company was still in operation, but that he'd been distracted since their divorce.

"You mean he's fixated on you?"

Julia watched a ferry as it eased into the slip down the waterfront from their window and began to unload vehicles. "I guess you could say that," she said finally. "He can't seem to adjust to living alone."

"How long have you been divorced?"

"We've lived apart for eighteen months, divorced for the last six."

"And he isn't getting past it, huh?"

Julia took another sip of wine, her eyes locking with Earl's as she glanced up. "It doesn't seem so."

"I'm sorry, Julia." A pause. "Does that mean your social life has stopped because of him?"

She nodded. "Pretty much, for the time being." She looked away from his obvious questions and his concerned expression. "He keeps pretty close tabs on us, that is, me and our two daughters."

"And he'd be upset if you, uh, say, started dating?"

"I think that's putting it mildly."

There was a brief silence.

"So how about you, Earl?" She wanted to change the subject. "I know your wife has some medical problems, but aside from that I assume you have a good life."

Now it was his turn to seem preoccupied with the ferry beyond their window. Finally he turned back to her. "You ever heard the cliché 'It takes one to know one?'" His grin was brief. "I'm married all right, but things aren't perfect for me, either." He took a large swallow and then placed the glass on the table. "Although my situation isn't anything like yours, it isn't good. Mine is a life of quiet desperation." He laughed. "Another cliché." Immediately sober, he went on, "I have to consider my kids. Jenny is overly emotional about her mother's illness, while Mitch seems oblivious to it." He took another swallow of wine. "Mine is a wait-and-see game."

The tyranny of weak people, she thought, as the waiter placed their food on the table. Earl hadn't said so, but again she felt his unhappiness, that he was even more trapped in his situation than she was in hers, that he would like to end his marriage. But how could anyone leave a sick spouse? At least she could leave hers.

"So, shall we talk about plotting?" Earl asked.

He'd shifted topics again, and this time she was relieved. She wasn't comfortable talking about either of their marriages, at least not in the early stage of knowing each other. When they became real friends there would be time enough to learn about personal matters.

Over the next hour she explained how she plotted her children's stories, and how a story would have to be developed to become a whole book.

"In other words, there has to be enough of a story, the basic plot, and all the subplots to warrant a book-length treatment of the theme," she said.

He asked good questions, took a few notes, and jotted down titles of books on fiction writing. She could see that he was completely serious about becoming a mystery author.

Julia was sorry when it was time to go, and Earl also looked regretful. It wasn't often that she had such a stimulating conversation on a topic she avoided with most of her friends, largely because it bored them.

He walked her out to the street and hesitated.

Then he bent and brushed a kiss on her forehead. "Let's do this again, okay?"

A bit disconcerted, she nodded.

"Today's lesson on plotting only told me that I have a lot more to learn."

And then he was gone, striding down the sidewalk

toward the ferry terminal. She stood there until he was gone, then she walked across the street when the light turned green. A glance at her watch told her that she'd better hurry to miss the rush-hour traffic over the bridges.

But she was preoccupied . . . with Earl. She'd never met anyone like him in her entire life.

The midafternoon traffic was already heavy as Julia drove back across Lake Washington to the East Side. It didn't help that it had started to rain, that the wheels of hundreds of cars were throwing up a mist of road spray, making it difficult to see. Although it was slow going, Julia's thoughts lingered on her lunch with Earl, not on the vehicles behind her. She hadn't noticed the pale blue Honda Civic on her bumper until she had to slam on the brakes to avoid another car that had cut in front of her. The Honda's screeching brakes told her that she'd almost been rear-ended.

"Stop daydreaming. Pay attention to traffic," she muttered aloud. She needed to stay focused.

Once she'd noticed the blue Honda, it seemed to stay right behind her in the line of slow traffic. When she suddenly saw a chance to change lanes she did, and it followed. She watched it in the rearview mirror, unable to determine if the driver was a man or woman. Her impression was that it was a woman—or a man with longer hair than the usual male haircut.

Was she being followed?

Silly, stupid question, she told herself. The driver was only doing what she was trying to do—get home.

But as the car continued to trail her lane changes, Julia felt vague apprehension. Common sense told her that her imagination was out of control, that drivers took similar chances in traffic, but still her uneasiness wouldn't go away. She reminded herself that the scary incidents that had happened around her house at night had sharpened her sensitivity to anything out of the ordinary—like a blue Honda that made the same moves in traffic.

One thing she didn't want to do was to become paranoid.

Their window peeper, the rock thrower, the phantom in the night were all part of the same reign of terror that was being perpetrated by one person.

Peter.

Julia veered off I-90 at the Issaquah exit. Another glance behind her sent a shiver down her back. The blue Civic was only a car length back, slowing for the light at the end of the ramp, just as she was. She gulped a deep breath.

It had to be a coincidence. No one was after her.

She made her right turn to head for the foothills above Issaquah. The blue car suddenly went left, onto the street that led under the freeway.

The air escaped her lungs in a deep sigh. Oh God, she was becoming a basket case—because of Peter.

She *was* imagining a threat where it didn't exist. She needed to regain her equilibrium—or lose it big time.

CHAPTER EIGHT

JULIA OPENED THE DOOR THE NEXT MORNING TO HER SISter, who rushed into the house looking upset. The girls had already left for school, and Julia still had the frosting spreader in her hand when she answered the ring of the front doorbell.

"Thank goodness!" Diana cried.

"For what?" Julia asked, trying to hide her smile.

It was her younger sister's personality to always have a cause—from little kid disputes in the past, to adult dilemmas in the present. It sometimes amazed Julia that Diana was such a successful architect, that she drew elaborate designs for building construction in the Northwest, and that she made a good income. Diana, so like their father, who'd owned a small construction company until he'd died ten years ago, was high-strung and a little histrionic. Those traits, combined with Diana's blunt, no-nonsense approach to life, gave her the needed edge in business but made her so unlike

Julia, who was more inclined to turn the other cheek and give second chances—her fatal flaw when it had come to Peter. Their mother had been the opposite of their father and had kept the family on an even keel, doing the bookkeeping for her husband and calming every situation with optimism and love. Julia had realized long ago that she'd patterned after her mother.

Julia inclined her head as she listened to her sister talk about another woman who'd been shot at earlier that morning several miles away, in the same woods where Julia jogged.

"Where did you say?" Julia asked, sobering.

"At the other end of the trail where you jog, Julia." Diana's words shot out of her mouth like machine gun bullets. "That's what I've been telling you." She gulped air. "You can't jog alone anymore. At least not until that serial shooter is caught." She paused, gulping air. "Haven't you been following the morning news on TV?"

"No, I haven't." Julia led the way back to the kitchen, where she'd been frosting a fortieth wedding anniversary cake. "There was no time. My cake needs to be delivered this afternoon."

"Good thing you have me," Diana retorted. "And good thing I had the morning off so I could stop by—keep you from heading up that trail." She poured herself a cup of coffee and then faced Julia. "I know you're obsessive about exercise, but you'll have to do something else, like ride your exercise bike." She took a gulp of coffee. "That trail is dangerous. This is the second shooting incident. The first victim is dead."

"But that path is many miles long," Julia said, putting down the spreader and refilling her own coffee cup. Her mellow mood from the day before suddenly vanished. "This end of it has never had problems with people being accosted, probably because we aren't close to the freeway." She hesitated. "When did you say the shooting happened?"

Diana sighed, as though Julia was too dumb to understand what she'd said. "Right after daylight. Can you believe that a female jogger can be so obsessed that she would take such a chance?"

"She wasn't hurt?"

Diana nodded. "That's what the newscaster said."

Julia lowered her eyes. *She'd been frightened by a sense of someone watching her in the woods that night when the first woman was killed.* Had she been in the shooter's sights?

"Why would someone do such a thing?"

"Why does a lunatic do anything?" Diana replied. "No one knows what sets them off. We just have to stay out of the way if we know there's a danger, like being on your jogging route." Her eyes were direct. "And that means staying off that trail until they get the wacko."

They sat down at the table, facing each other as Julia explained her own experience the night when the first woman died. "I didn't see anyone—just heard snapping twigs and felt like I wasn't alone." She paused. "It was a creepy feeling, especially since it was getting dark."

"It was a bad decision, Julia."

"What?"

"Jogging that late on a remote trail." Diana sighed. "You're the older sister. You're supposed to be the one with the most sense. I hope you use it next time."

"I promise." Julia grinned. "I think I've been properly chastised."

"Good." Diana finished her coffee, then took the cup to the sink. "I gotta run," she said. "I have a busy afternoon at work." She hesitated at the door to the hall. "I just needed to know the unidentified woman who'd been shot at wasn't you."

Julia hugged her sister, suddenly realizing how scared she must have been about the latest shooting. "I'm sorry, Diana. I promise I'll be careful."

Diana stepped back, her question direct. "Nothing else going on, is there? Uh, Peter behaving himself for a change?"

"Nothing's happened since Saturday night."

"So that's why you're looking so pleased."

"Pleased?"

"Uh-huh. Like something good is happening in your life."

Unexpectedly, Julia blushed.

Diana's eyes widened. "I can tell—something is. What?"

"Nothing much, except that I had lunch with a new friend yesterday."

"And this friend is responsible for that glow I haven't seen on your face for years?" Diana grinned. "It's a man, right?"

Julia nodded. "A fellow writer who just wanted to talk about plotting."

"I see. And?"

"And, nothing. I just had a good time, that's all." Julia hesitated, formulating words. "I met him on my conference panel." She quickly explained Earl, who he was, and that he was married. "As I said, he's only a friend."

"Damn that he has to be married! I was hoping you'd met a nice guy you could date." Diana headed down the hall toward the front door. "But you're right. A man with a wife can never be more than a friend."

As Diana stepped onto the porch, she paused. "You know, I thought I'd seen another dead woman as I turned into your street earlier."

"What do you mean?"

"It wasn't, of course." Diana tucked her blond hair behind her ears. "This blue car was parked with a woman behind the wheel. She was resting her head back on the seat at an odd angle, and for a second I thought she was another corpse, until she straightened up. Then I realized she was only relaxing, probably waiting for someone."

"A blue car? What kind?"

Diana stepped off the porch. "Honda, I think. She really took off in a hurry when she saw me, like I'd scared the shit out of her or something."

A moment later Diana climbed behind the wheel of her BMW, waved, and was off down the street. Julia was thoughtful as she went back into the house.

Hmmm. *Just coincidence*, she told herself. A big percent of all cars on the road were Hondas, and blue was a popular color.

But she made sure the door was locked before she went back to the kitchen.

The phone rang as Julia was about to take the finished cake out to her Cherokee. She grabbed the receiver, praying it wasn't Peter.

"It's Mother," Peter's mother said in her ear.

The high, whiny voice raised goose bumps on Julia's arms. Frances was the last person she wanted to talk to. Julia could mentally picture the round, smooth face that never stopped smiling, even when she was upset. A superficial phony, she thought, holding the phone away from her ear as though the condition were contagious.

"Hello, Frances." Julia had never been able to call her Mother. "I'm surprised to hear your voice in the middle of the day. As you know, the girls are in school."

"I wanted to talk to you this time, Julia." Her laugh sounded even more false than usual. "I know the long-distance rates are high right now, me being in Chicago and all, but we won't chat long."

Another thing Julia disliked about her former mother-in-law: she always had to be in control, even for a phone call. The woman was diabolical, sickly sweet while she manipulated for her own way.

"That's good, as I have an appointment and was just leaving." Julia couldn't resist exercising her own control. "But I have a couple of minutes to spare."

"That's good, my dear. I'll get right to the point."

Julia adjusted the receiver under her hair and waited.

"I'm planning a trip to Seattle, haven't settled on a date yet, but I wanted to make sure that I can see the girls while I'm with Peter."

There was a pause.

"Of course you can, Frances. I'm surprised you felt a need to ask."

"Well, uh, Peter said that you might object."

"Why in the world would he say that?" Surprise registered in Julia's voice. "I've never kept the girls from Peter or you. Samantha and Alyssa are both old enough to make those decisions themselves."

"Well, yes, of course they are. It's just that Peter sort of implied that things were not all that congenial between you and"—another forced laugh—"and I decided to make sure that your problem with Peter didn't include me."

"My problem?"

"You know, I'd hate to come over and be arrested, or something."

Instant anger flashed through Julia. How dare the woman twist the truth and make her the bad guy. At the last moment she managed to stifle her retort. Instead, she spoke with stilted calm.

"I assure you that you've nothing to worry about, Frances, unless you intend to peek in the windows or throw rocks at the house." She gave a laugh. "I'm sure the girls will love to hear about your upcoming visit." She glanced at the wall clock. "I'm afraid I have to hang up or I'll be late for my appointment."

"No, you mustn't be late. Will you tell the girls I'll call to chat with them this weekend?"

"Of course."

"Good-bye for now, then." The smile was back in her voice, but Julia knew the woman was livid.

As she replaced the phone in its cradle, Julia felt a pang of pity for Peter. How had he ever had a chance to grow into a normal man when his own mother had given him mixed signals from the day he was born? Julia wondered if Peter really disliked the woman. She knew that he'd moved from Chicago after college to get away from her.

If only I'd realized how dysfunctional his family was, she thought as she backed out of the garage, the cake secure in the back of the Cherokee. *If only I'd been older, smarter, more aware that every kid didn't grow up in a secure family just because I did. If only, if only.* What was done was done, and it was time to move forward. She just hoped Peter would let her.

She headed down I-90 to the Bellevue exit, wove down side streets until she found the address, and then delivered the cake. She'd decorated it with special care, as it was intended for the parents of a woman she knew from her aerobics class. Word of mouth, that's how she got most of her business. Once she'd handed over her bill and been paid, she retraced her route back to Issaquah.

There was no blue Honda parked anywhere in sight when she turned into her street. She drove into the garage, knowing she still had a little time to work on the computer manual before the girls got home.

Ugh, she thought, stepping into the kitchen. She was behind on it and needed to catch up if she was to meet her deadline. One day I'll make enough money so I don't have to write boring manuals, she promised herself, and noticed that the message light on her answering machine was blinking.

She pressed the button, and Earl's voice filled the kitchen.

"I need help," he said. "My plot has bogged down." His deep laugh brought a smile to her lips. "I sure hope a certain writer will take pity on a struggling novelist and let me buy dinner in return for a few nuggets of wisdom." Another laugh. "I'll call back tomorrow."

Julia felt a surge of energy as she went to her computer to work. The day had started out on an upbeat note, but then Diana's news, the blue Honda, and Frances's call had managed to lower her mood.

The day had come full circle, she told herself. She was definitely on a high now. Earl's invitation had canceled the negative thoughts. She looked forward to his call.

CHAPTER NINE

JULIA WORE A BASIC BLACK WOOL DRESS WHEN SHE MET Earl on Wednesday night at a little Italian restaurant in Pioneer Square, walking distance to the Bainbridge ferry terminal for Earl.

"I'm a foot passenger," he'd explained when he'd called her the day after his message. "I leave my car on the island, walk on the ferry and off in the city." He'd laughed. "I can hike up the hills to my office and take a taxi if I need to go anywhere else beyond walking distance."

"Sounds like the perfect plan," she'd replied.

"It is—although I have to keep my business appointments in town." He'd hesitated. "I hope you won't mind driving in—that is, if you're free to share supper?"

They'd settled on the place and time, and after Julia had hung up, she'd found herself humming off and on for the remainder of the day.

Now, as she parked on First Avenue, Julia hoped she

wasn't overdressed. Because the weather was overcast and unpredictable, she'd worn a long hooded raincoat and leather boots. Good thing, she thought as it started to rain. She made a dash for the restaurant a block away.

Earl was waiting by the entrance, looking tall and fit in his black business suit, and he stepped forward when he saw her. "Hey! You're dripping."

She flipped back her hood, grinning. "My raincoat is dripping."

His return smile altered the rugged angles and lines of his face, accentuating his good looks. Julia let him take her coat to check with the hostess, who then seated them by the fireplace at the back of the small restaurant.

Once they were alone, his dark gaze was suddenly direct, probing her face. She glanced away, pretending interest in the fire behind him. For a moment she wondered what she was doing, why she'd agreed to meet him—a married man. His next words put her concern to rest. He didn't have ulterior motives.

"I'm really bogged down, Julia. This damn writing thing is not easy." His expression was sincere when she met his eyes again. "I've come to the conclusion that I need to outline the story, fit the fictitious characters into the real background, making sure that I don't put myself in a position of being sued by the real people involved in the case."

"Good thinking, Earl. You're writing what is called fiction based on fact and—" About to say more, Julia raised her brows, indicating her comments could wait until after the approaching waitress had handed them menus and taken their order for drinks.

"Merlot for me, your best Chardonnay for my guest, and we'll order later," he told the young woman.

"You remembered my wine choice again," Julia said when they were alone. She was unable to hide her admiration. "I'm impressed."

"Remembering detail is the secret of my success. I've had a photographic memory since childhood." He shrugged. "So I've been told, anyway."

"Now I'm really impressed."

His expression softened, although he suppressed an outright grin. "Anyone ever told you how beautiful you are, Julia?" His question was unexpected, disconcerting.

"Thank you, Earl," she said. "That was a nice compliment."

"You're welcome." A pause. "But you didn't answer my question."

"Maybe I didn't want to."

His brows shot up. "Because you're uncomfortable with the truth about your looks?"

She shook her head. "Nope, nothing so complicated."

"I'm intrigued." His gaze intensified. "May I ask what, then?"

She spread her hands. "Just a residue from my marriage. My former husband was superficial when it came to how people looked." She laughed wryly. "He would never be interested in a woman if she wasn't attractive, even if she was dumber than a stump."

"I'm surprised he let you go."

"Well, he hasn't exactly done that, as I've mentioned before."

He tilted his head, even more interested. "Things haven't improved?"

She shook her head.

"In a certain way I understand him not wanting to

let go." Earl leaned closer. "If you belonged to me, I wouldn't want to lose you, either." He was abruptly serious. "Is he withholding child support?"

She shook her head. "He's only using it for ongoing contact, like coming to the door with his check—against a court order."

He raised his brows, looking concerned. "I'm not prying, Julia. Just thought you might need some free legal advice. After all, you're giving me free writing advice."

She managed a smile. "Thanks anyway. I have a lawyer."

There was a brief silence.

"You aren't in danger, are you?" He reached out to momentarily place his hand over hers on the table. She hadn't realized that she'd tightened hers into a white-knuckled fist.

"To be honest, I sometimes wonder." She withdrew her hand to her lap under the table. "Peter, uh, that's my husband, seems pretty unstable at times." Julia cleared her throat, disliking the turn of conversation, but she didn't want to throw Earl's genuine concern back into his face without clarifying herself. "He seems unable to go on with his life since our divorce."

"Is he stalking you?"

She hesitated, and then was saved from answering when the couple at the next table got up to leave. Once they were gone, Earl raised his glass.

"To future happiness—for both of us."

"Cheers."

They both sipped, and Julia put down her glass. "Just to finish the conversation, yes, Peter does watch what goes on at my house pretty closely. It's . . . uh . . . unnerving at times."

"I can imagine." He still held his glass, and the firelight seemed to be reflected in the red wine. "My wife hasn't been stable at times, either." His expression tightened. "Unfortunately, with her maladies she couldn't cope if she were on her own."

Julia wondered what he implied. That he'd like to end his own marriage when possible? That he was as unhappy as she'd been for several years before her divorce?

"I'm sorry, Earl. That has to be hard on you, and her, too," Julia added, thinking they'd had a variation of this conversation before and that it had not been productive.

"Let's have another toast," he said, lifting his goblet again. "To a pleasant evening talking about our mutual love of writing."

"Hear, hear." Julia smiled over her glass, glad he'd broken the somber mood, wondering if he'd tuned in to her hesitancy to discuss their marriages.

True to his word, they discussed his plot problems and then went on to share thoughts on current bestsellers. The meal, which ended with coffee and liqueur, passed too quickly for Julia, and when Earl glanced at his watch and announced that he had to catch a ferry in thirty minutes, she couldn't believe it was so late.

"I need to get on the road, too. My daughters will think I had an accident or something."

"Or something?" He grinned as he placed his credit card on the tray with the bill.

"Uh-huh. Like being abducted by some crazy writer."

"They knew you were meeting me?" he asked casually, but she caught the note of caution in his tone.

"They knew I was having dinner with a writer to discuss writing." She busied herself with her purse. "I didn't mention your name."

He didn't reply for a moment.

"Thanks, Julia. I've enjoyed our getting together immensely, but—" He broke off, and she suddenly understood what he was having difficulty saying. He was a married man.

"I understand, Earl. My daughters—and your wife—might not understand us having dinner together, even though we're nothing more than friends." She gave a laugh. "New friends at that."

An emotion flickered momentarily on his face. Disappointment? Relief that she understood? Whatever. She had no plans to be anything more than a friend to him. In a way, his reaction was a sober ending to a wonderful evening.

But when he took her arm to escort her out to the street, chatting again about mutual interests, she forgot her moment of annoyance. He was quite right to be careful with a wife who sounded so fragile. She knew all about dealing with a mentally ill person.

He walked her the block to her Cherokee, stating emphatically that it was unsafe for her to be alone in Pioneer Square at that time of night. "Besides, it's on my way to the ferry."

"Hey, I like your vehicle. I would have guessed you drove a Mercedes."

"Nope." She grinned. "I need an SUV for my various jobs."

"I'd like to hear about the things you do, Julia," he said seriously. "Maybe next time?"

"Maybe." She was deliberately noncommittal. She needed to think about a next time. *If there should be a next time.*

She slipped into the driver's seat and lowered the window to say good-bye, when he suddenly bent and brushed a kiss onto her forehead.

"Drive carefully, Julia." Something glinted in his eyes as he straightened. "I'll call you."

And then he was striding away, headed for the ferry terminal a couple of blocks away. For long seconds, she stared after him, then started the engine and headed for the freeway.

She didn't know what to think about the man. She only knew that her feelings for Earl were different from anything she'd ever felt before.

She let herself into the house, careful to be quiet, knowing her daughters would be in bed. She took off her shoes and, holding them in her hand, tiptoed up the stairs, peeking in on the girls before she went on to her own bedroom. She was beat, and tomorrow was a big workday. She needed her sleep.

Julia had just climbed into bed and was about to turn out the bedside lamp when the door opened and Alyssa stepped into the room.

"Hey, I thought you were asleep," she said, sitting up as her daughter hesitated at the foot of the bed. A second glance told her that something was wrong, that Alyssa was upset about something.

"I was just waiting for you to get home, Mom." A smile flickered on her face and was gone. "Thought I'd let you get into your nightgown before I bothered you."

"Bothered me?"

Alyssa's long blond hair swung forward as she nodded. "Grandma Frances called tonight, and I thought you should know what she said."

Julia sat up straighter, and her duvet-covered comforter slipped into her lap. *Oh, God*, she thought. *What's happened now?*

"What?"

"She's upset, Mom—about Dad. She thinks that he's close to a breakdown, that if something isn't done, he'll do something drastic."

"She called to tell you this . . . and didn't call me first?"

"She didn't think you'd be receptive to Dad's mental state."

There was a sinking sensation in the pit of Julia's stomach. What next? Not only was Peter trying to emotionally manipulate his daughters but his mother was, too.

How dare she do that! Julia thought, suddenly furious. Although Peter was her son, Alyssa and Samantha were her granddaughters and should be considered first, above their adult parent who was emotionally ill.

"I'm sorry that she upset you, sweetie," Julia said. She managed to keep her tone normal. "She's obviously worried about your father, and I can understand that, but to call long-distance and put a guilt trip on her granddaughter is not in my frame of forgiveness."

"She wasn't trying to do that, Mom," Alyssa said. "She's just so worried about Dad. In the week she's been here she hasn't been able to make much progress with his anguish over the divorce."

Julia swung her legs over the edge of the bed but restrained herself from jumping to her feet. It was another need-for-sleeping pill night. She wished she had one.

Frances was in Seattle? How long had she been here?

Worse, she'd lied to Julia, saying she was planning a trip in the near future. No wonder Peter hadn't stalked them in the past week; his mother had been visiting, holding him on a tight rein. But why would she have lied, pretended to be calling long-distance?

Julia hid her anger, speaking softly to her daughter. After all, Peter was her father and Frances was her grandmother. She needed to remember that for the emotional well-being of her daughter.

Mostly she needed Judy, her shrink, to advise her on the right course of action right now. Left to only herself, Julia would have verbally shredded Frances. How dare she put her worry—her trip—onto her granddaughters!

Instead, Julia listened patiently as Alyssa expressed her grandmother's view that Julia wasn't trying hard enough to keep the family together, that Peter wanted nothing more than a second chance. Abruptly, too angry to suppress her feelings, Julia jumped out of bed. *The old witch!* she thought. Frances just wanted someone else to be responsible for Peter other than herself, the someone—her—who had kept him stable for all the years of their marriage.

The bitch!

"I'm sorry, sweetheart, I don't understand your grandmother." She turned her face, not wanting Alyssa to see her expression, which she couldn't hide. "I didn't know she was in Seattle, but she had no business laying her concerns on you." Julia gulped a breath. "This isn't your problem—or your fault. Parents sometimes have issues and get divorced." A pause. "The kids have nothing to do with it and shouldn't be burdened by the old baggage of grandparents."

"What do you mean, Mom?" Alyssa sat down on the bed.

"Only that we parents don't always make the right decisions, for right or wrong reasons, and that isn't the fault of the next generation."

Julia met her daughter's eyes. "I don't want you losing sleep over a problem that isn't yours. Your grandmother should have spoken to me directly, and I thought she had. Instead she lied to me, didn't tell me she was in town, only that she was coming out from Chicago soon." Julia's voice wobbled with anger. "I'll have a talk with her in the morning. She's out of line here, grandmother or not."

"She's leaving in the morning, Mom. Early, like seven."

"Then I'll catch her at home later, Alyssa." Julia drew in a sharp breath. "I won't have this, and she needs to hear that straight from the horse's mouth—me."

"But—"

"But nothing. Your dad may be her son, but you and Alyssa are my daughters."

"What do you mean?"

Julia suddenly felt exhausted, but she tried to explain, knowing it was important. "The difference is that Peter is almost forty, and you girls are young teens. He should know better than to influence his mother to implicate you girls in his sick manipulations."

How dare Frances unload on Alyssa! she thought. *She isn't getting away with it!*

They talked a little longer, until Alyssa was relieved of the guilt her grandmother had placed on her. Intentional or not, Julia would not allow that to happen again. She'd have to lay down the rules again.

Later, after Alyssa had gone back to her own room, Julia was thoughtful. Earl was a married man, Peter was a troubled man, and neither was right for her. But as she dozed she wondered if she could change both situations. Peter could get on with his life without her, and Earl could get on with his . . . with her?

Her thoughts faltered. And she knew no more.

CHAPTER TEN

JULIA AWAKENED IN THE MORNING WITH THE SAME HOPE she'd gone to sleep with: Peter would move on with his life without her, and Earl with her.

Faulty judgment, as her psychologist would say about people who based their conclusions on wishful thinking. "Pollyanna situations only exist in fiction, not real life."

So silly to fantasize about impossible hopes, Julia thought as she showered and got ready for the day. It was what she might have done in the second grade, buying into the fantasy of fairy tales and dreams coming true.

My own flaw, Julia reminded herself. Because she'd married right out of high school, because she'd never known her parents to have a serious marital conflict, and because she'd had no harsh life experience before being married to Peter, she'd had a tendency to romanticize, believe that bad situations could be fixed. And some things could never be fixed no matter how hard she tried. She'd learned that the hard way.

The girls were still asleep when she went downstairs and started coffee, then strode toward the front porch to get her morning newspaper. She opened the door, grabbed the paper, and turned to step back inside.

Then she froze, her eyes glued to the empty hook on the heavy paneling. Her door wreath was gone.

She whirled around to look at the front yard. Heavy dew lay over the grass and beaded the elaborately spun spiderwebs that connected the boxwood shrubs lining both sides of the walkway. It was just past daylight, and all of the houses in her development were still shuttered and draped against the night.

Then Julia spotted the wreath at the edge of the grass near the street. Without thinking, she darted forward to retrieve it. About to pick it up, she paused, her hand in midair, staring at the dried flowers and greens that had once been her own creation. Now it was a crushed piece of thin sticks and twigs. Her artistry in blues, pinks, and greens was gone, the crushed petals scattered over the grass.

Someone had deliberately destroyed it.

She glanced along the street. Everything was quiet; most of her neighbors were still asleep. But her skin prickled, as though she was being watched.

Her gaze skimmed over the manicured yards that lined the sidewalk, then beyond to the woods that bordered the development. Night still lingered under the evergreen boughs and dense underbrush.

Someone could be watching from the dark places.

Julia left the wreath to dump into the garbage can later, then ran back to the door, slamming it harder than she'd intended as she reached the safety of her house.

Even the closed barrier between herself and the outside did not dispel the feeling of watching eyes—that someone was out there.

Peter?

Oh God, she hoped not, even though the alternative might be even scarier. Her daughters needed to have a father they could be proud of, not one they feared and were ashamed of knowing.

It was still an hour before they had to get up for school. Thankfully they hadn't heard the door slam. She went to pour herself a cup of coffee. They didn't need to know that someone had destroyed the door wreath. But she wondered, why?—and who could have done such a vindictive thing?

Surely it hadn't been Peter—or his mother, who'd been showing her upset to her granddaughters lately. No, it wouldn't be Frances. Just because she was Peter's mother, and had lied about her being in Seattle, didn't mean she was nuts, too.

By the time the girls were ready to head out to meet the school bus, Julia had cleaned up the mess from the door wreath, and neither girl noticed that it was gone.

Julia hurried to clean up the breakfast dishes and straighten the house before she gathered her wallpapering equipment together. She was exchanging the job for a two-hundred-twenty-five-dollar balance on her therapy. Judy, her therapist, was letting her compensate what she owed with labor; Judy had bought the wallpaper and other minor materials needed for the job.

"Hey," Judy had said. "I know the arrangement isn't typical, not to mention it not being professional, but it works for us. You need your bill paid, and I need my bathroom wallpapered."

Julia had only grinned, her gratitude too great to express in words. If—when—she was ever past the nightmare in her life and no longer needed a therapist, Judy would still be her friend. Their current arrangement for payment may not be professional, as Judy had said, but it enabled Julia to have counseling, which was lifeblood for someone who was coping with a mentally ill husband who might, in fact, be dangerous.

She loaded the Cherokee in the garage and then backed it into the driveway before remembering that she hadn't watered the fall mums in the backyard. They were planted in the flowerbed next to the house under the roof overhang and thus didn't get the benefit of rain, which had been sparse in the last few days.

After a glance at her watch, Julia realized she had time to grab the water bucket and give them a drink. She used the outside backdoor from the garage, quickly filling the container. Then half running with the dripping bucket, Julia headed for the burgundy and white mums. Reaching the flowerbed, she stopped so fast that the water from the spout splashed onto the legs of her jeans.

The plants lay uprooted on their sides, already wilted and dying.

"Oh my God!" The words rushed out of her mouth on one breath. She flung the watering bucket aside. Someone had pulled all eight plants out by the roots.

Suddenly aware that she was alone, that all of her close neighbors were gone, Julia whirled around and ran back to the garage. After locking the paneled door behind her, she rushed through the two-car parking area that was still open to the driveway, jumped into the Cherokee, and drove it back inside, its wheels bumping along for those few feet. Before the barrier had closed behind it she was already running for the door to the laundry room. She needed to call the police, report both cases of vandalism, her door wreath and the mum plants.

No, three incidents, she thought, stopping in the doorway to the house, her eyes focused on why the Cherokee had seemed different. Within the few minutes she'd been in the backyard, her two back tires had gone flat.

Someone had vandalized her Jeep in broad daylight. Who?

She continued on to the kitchen. It was only after she'd dialed 911 that she realized the perpetrator could have gone into the house ahead of her, while she'd still been in the backyard. That person could be hiding somewhere, waiting for her to step into the next room.

The hairs on the back of her neck felt like they were scraping the collar of her sweatshirt. She backed away from the counter, the portable phone still in her hand.

The dispatcher's voice sounded in her ear.

Julia quickly explained what had happened, her voice shaking, her back to the way she'd come into the house, her eyes on the shadows beyond the doorways to the kitchen.

"Stay on the line," the woman instructed. "A patrol car is on its way."

By the time the police car pulled up outside and two officers hurried up the walkway to the door, Julia was shaking so hard that she couldn't stand.

"You better sit down, lady," one of the uniformed cops told her. "Officer Lloyd will check out the property while I take your statement, okay?"

She could only nod. What in hell was happening? Had Peter really flipped out this time?

She'd soon find out.

"Jeez! You've got to be kidding!"

Judy, a buxom woman around fifty, was about to leave for the office when Julia finally arrived an hour late for her wallpaper job. Judy's usually composed expression registered shock as Julia explained what had happened, that the police had had to take down her statement, bizarre as it all seemed. Even the two officers had shaken their heads, but they'd finally come to the conclusion that the vandal was probably a teenager, maybe someone who was upset with either Samantha or Alyssa.

"You mean they aren't checking out Peter?" Judy asked, trying to hide her worry.

Julia knew what her therapist was thinking but couldn't express aloud because of professional integrity: if Peter was behind such craziness, then he'd lost it completely, maybe needed hospitalization.

Julia lowered her eyes, suddenly hit by a barrage of emotions: fear, humiliation, and anger. If Peter was the skulking presence capable of such threatening acts of vandalism, he did need to be stopped—even if Samantha and Alyssa were shamed in front of their peers, even if they had to adjust to the last resort of having to move completely away from Issaquah.

"Yes, they are talking to Peter," Julia said. "They'd already known about the domestic disturbances at our house over the past months, and they took it from there."

Judy nodded. "It's all in the police computers, and the officers get the information almost immediately when they're called out like this."

"Yeah, so I've learned."

Judy dropped an arm around her. "I'm so sorry, Julia. Somehow we've got to make this stop." She hesitated. "I have appointments and have to leave in a few minutes." She tried to interject an upbeat note into her voice. "Why don't we put off your job here for today, reschedule when you're feeling better?"

Julia shook her head and managed a smile. "I need to keep to my schedule, Judy, if I'm to meet my financial obligations." Her lips still curved, but she felt like crying.

Judy started to speak and then closed her mouth. "Okay, then. You're safe here while you work." She hesitated. "But please, please, Julia. By all that's holy, be careful."

Julia nodded, and then switched the topic to her few wallpapering questions for Judy before she left. A short time later, she was alone.

Her mind worked overtime as she cut and pasted the paper to the wall, and when she was finally done several hours later, she stepped back, pleased. The job looked perfect. Every seam was flawless, the pattern fitting so well that no one could ever detect an imperfection.

She cleaned up her mess, gathered her tools, and loaded them back into the Cherokee. But all the way home one question circled her mind. How could she stop the reign of terror?

She had no answers. But she knew she had to come up with one—and soon.

CHAPTER ELEVEN

"OH, GOD, NO!"

Shock took her breath, and Topsy slumped over the steering wheel to rest her face in her arms. *I won't cry*, she told herself. *It'll be okay.*

It can't be a bad thing. It just can't be.

Of all the scenarios she'd imagined, Topsy had never considered the possibility that was undeniable now. She'd watched the woman who owned the house leave her street, and she'd been about to go herself when another car had swung out of an overgrown lane that led to the jogging trail. She'd recognized the driver, who'd been concentrating on following the woman and hadn't seen Topsy parked in a side road.

"Thank you, God," she'd murmured shakily, staring at the tree-lined street where the cars had disappeared. It had taken several minutes before her breathing had returned to normal. Gradually, she'd come to realize that what she'd seen might be fortunate in the long run.

Maybe this time she could change things before anyone else had to die.

And maybe she'd been mistaken about recognizing the driver of the second car, she thought hopefully. There were lots of blue cars on the road, even her own. She could have been wrong about who the person was behind the wheel.

But now, a few hours later, only minutes after she'd come back to her hiding place to watch as the woman returned to her house, she was devastated all over again. Mindful of not being spotted, Topsy had backed her car behind a cluster of trees just in case the woman was still being followed. Seconds later she would have congratulated herself for being so farsighted if she hadn't been so devastated. The second car was back as well, and its driver was the person Topsy had thought it was in the first place.

Topsy swallowed against the tightening in her throat, working the muscles that threatened to close off her air. She wouldn't have returned for a second time today if she hadn't spotted the blue car following the woman. She'd hoped to prove to herself that her imagination was working overtime. Her body was suddenly wracked by tremors. *God help me,* Topsy pleaded silently. She'd been right.

Don't think about it now, she told herself. *Remember, you can fix it.* She didn't allow herself to consider what would happen if she couldn't—if her time was running out.

She needed to get home, shut out the world, blank out the images in her mind that were clamoring to surface. But she didn't dare leave her hiding place. What if the blue car left its cover at the same time? She'd be seen—and recognized.

Then all hope would be gone—*for everyone*.

Trying to be patient, Topsy wondered how long her shattered nervous system would allow her to sit still. Her mind was close to flat-lining; she could feel the nothingness surging inward from its edges. She was a hair away from losing it altogether.

She had to risk it, even if it meant exposing herself. There was no other choice. If she lost it, they'd find her anyway.

Starting the engine, she steered onto the road, her eyes on the lane that led to the jogging trail. Once she had passed it without incident, she pressed down on the gas pedal, rolled down all the windows so that the fresh air could wash over her, and turned on the radio to blaring rock music. Anything she could do to distract the ugly images flashing on the mental screen of her mind. By the time she was headed downhill toward the freeway, the grayness was ebbing again.

She was safe—this time.

CHAPTER TWELVE

"Is this Mrs. Phinnortner, entrepreneur and world-famous children's writer?"

"Mrs.—who?"

"Phinnortner?" The male voice in Julia's phone receiver sounded assured, slightly amused, and vaguely familiar. "I thought I'd called the right number." He repeated it.

"Yes, that's my number," she began slowly, "but there's no one here by that name. I'm afraid you have the wrong—"

"Julia?" he laughed, interrupting. "Don't hang up."

She suddenly connected the voice with a name, now that he'd dropped the intonation he'd used to tease her.

"Earl?"

"Yeah, the struggling novelist who needs more writing advice, who is hoping a successful writer of children's stories will have mercy on him." He cleared his throat, as though controlling his amusement with her. "Sorry about putting you on—I couldn't resist."

"Because you think I'm gullible? Or because you just like to tease new friends?" Julia didn't know exactly what he meant, not yet having a real fix on the man behind his professional persona. She'd noticed his quick wit and quirky humor before and found it attractive. She'd seen how his talent for turning a phrase had captivated an audience, part of his being a successful attorney, she supposed.

"Let's just say you're very bright, yet trusting, not a trait I see very often in women these days." A pause. "I perceived that your first instinct is to believe what another person tells you, and I just proved myself right."

"Is that good or bad?" She didn't know if she approved of his perception. She saw herself as a capable, intelligent woman who tried to cope with life honestly.

"Definitely good. Innocence is an attractive and feminine quality." His tone had lowered, and she suspected that he was smiling at the other end of their connection.

"That's a relief," she retorted, hoping she didn't sound defensive. Her first reaction had been annoyance.

A silence went by.

Julia wondered if his definition of innocence was different from her own. She'd always been trusting—to a fault, according to her sister. But she hadn't considered herself innocent for several decades, especially during the last few years, after Peter had become so irrational that she'd had to pick up the family slack so she and her girls could maintain a semblance of their earlier lifestyle.

"You're unique, Julia," he went on, jumping into her

silence. "I suspect that you've been told that many times by men."

She managed to laugh. "No, I haven't. But if that's a compliment, thanks," she said, finally.

"You're welcome." His inhaled breath came over the line. "So, Julia, when are you gonna be up to give me another writing lesson?" The note of humor was back in his voice.

There was a silence as she considered his offer.

"I'll throw in a great dinner, good wine, and stimulating conversation. What do you think?" he added. "I can clear my schedule most any night this week." A hesitation. "But not the weekend."

She glanced out through her kitchen window to the woods beyond her backyard, wondering how to answer. He was married, hence not free on the weekend, although she'd definitely gotten the impression that his was not a happy marriage. Then what was the status of his marital commitment, she wondered. One of obligation—of being too responsible for a wife with emotional problems? She turned away from the window. Maybe she'd misread the signals and he was happily married and really was only interested in someone who could give him writing tips, just as he'd said. In either case, she hesitated to become more deeply involved with Earl because she was so attracted to him, in a way she'd never felt before.

"Hey, you still there, Julia?"

"Un-huh." She licked her lips, considering. "Sorry, I was thinking about my week's schedule, if I was free to get away for an evening."

"So, how about a little pity on a guy who can't plot?"

Her desire to see him won over her good sense. "Okay, if it can be Thursday night."

"Done." His pleasure reverberated in the word. "Is Ivar's okay for a second time?"

She said it was, and they settled on the time. A minute later, they hung up, and Julia went back to frosting a cake, aware that she was behind schedule if she was to deliver it on time.

What are you doing? Julia asked herself as she worked. Even if Earl's intentions were genuine, it might be a mistake to continue seeing him, because she was beginning to care about him as more than a writing friend.

By the time she finished and went upstairs to change her clothes, she'd decided that dinner with Earl was harmless. She could control her feelings because she wasn't ready for a romantic relationship with anyone, especially a married man.

She had enough problems without that, too.

Thursday night with Earl at Ivar's Fish House on the Seattle waterfront was wonderful. Julia had never had such a nice evening with any man before. They talked about their mutual passion for writing, and then went on to other subjects, from political views to the 9-11 terrorist attack, to religion, and, finally, their personal hopes for the future. Their views were so in sync that Julia was reminded of a recent article she'd read in a national magazine about "soul mates," one she'd dismissed as unrealistic. Now she wasn't so sure.

Over the next fourteen days Julia saw Earl several times a week, grateful that Peter seemed to be finally accepting their divorce and leaving her and the girls alone. She looked forward to each date, planned what she'd wear, and took extra care with her hair and makeup.

Silly goose, she told herself. You can't fall for a married man, even if he is in an unhappy marriage. But she forced caution aside and continued to see him, knowing her feelings were deepening each time they were together for a platonic dinner of talk, sharing, and laughter. Earl was a good man in a desperate relationship. Who knew what could happen in the future? Maybe he'd be free, and in the meantime she could be his friend. Julia would not allow herself to admit how deeply she felt about him, and wondered if he felt similar feelings for her.

After yet another dinner on the waterfront, where she and Earl sipped wine as they talked writing again, laughed about the flaws of other writers, and shared more of their personal histories, Julia felt as though he were an old and trusted friend. He was so understanding—and concerned—about her situation with Peter, even as she was sympathetic about his marriage to an emotionally damaged woman he felt obligated to protect until she'd recovered enough to stand on her own.

As he walked her to the Cherokee after their stimulating evening together, Earl suddenly took hold of her shoulders and turned her to him.

"I'm really fond of you, Julia," he said gently, the intensity in his dark eyes saying much more than his words. "I've come to need our times together."

"Need?"

He nodded. "I know that I'm not a free man, and I have nothing to offer you for continuing to see me—" He broke off, releasing her to spread his hands, as though in supplication. "I hope you'll want to maintain our friendship and won't want to end it because I'm married." He seemed to search for words. "You're an attractive woman who'll want to date soon."

She tilted her head, waiting for him to finish.

"I'm hoping you'll save some time for me for—"

She stared into his eyes for long seconds. "I'm not sure I understand, Earl. What are you suggesting?"

His gaze dropped momentarily to her lips, and for an instant she thought he would kiss her. But when his eyes met hers again, they were inscrutable.

"A connection between good friends, friends who care about each other." He hesitated, and his eyelids lowered slightly. "Friends who, because of circumstances, can't have a closer commitment."

Julia glanced away, breaking the hold of his gaze. What did he mean by friends? Commitment? Didn't that go without saying? Friends didn't have to define the boundaries unless— She broke off her thoughts. Surely Earl wasn't talking about something more than dinners and conversation and exchanging writing tips, was he?

"Anyway, just think about it, Julia." His smile was lopsided, but his quickly blinking eyes told her that he was nervous. She hadn't noticed this tic since the early days of their friendship. What he'd said was more important to him than the casual air he was trying to project.

"I will, Earl," she said softly. Then with a quick motion, she leaned forward, stood on her tiptoes, and kissed him on the cheek. Before he could react, she got into the Jeep, closed the door, and spoke through the window she'd lowered. "I consider you my good friend." She smiled, meeting his eyes, which seemed black in the shadows under the waterfront viaduct where she'd parked. "And I'll let you know if our, uh, friendship gets in the way of dating, okay?"

He nodded. "That's fair." He stepped back as she started the engine. "I'll call you tomorrow."

She headed out of her parking spot to the street,

glancing into the rearview mirror as she drove. He stood watching her go, looking as still and enigmatic as one of the Indian totem poles in a shop window they'd just passed.

She knew that her feelings for Earl were stronger than ever, far more than anything she'd felt for Peter.

She needed to watch it, a warning that had almost become her mantra lately. *I will*, she promised herself.

The house was quiet, the girls asleep when she returned home. After securing the house, Julia went upstairs to bed and was already dozing off a few minutes later. The sound of breaking glass brought her upright so fast that she was on her feet before she was fully awake. A glance at the illuminated clock on the night table told her she'd been asleep for an hour.

The house had gone quiet. Then she heard footsteps in the hall. A moment later Alyssa darted into the bedroom, followed by Samantha, who was several steps behind her sister.

"Mom!" Alyssa cried.

"Shh." Julia motioned them to silence, indicating that they step further into the room and move away from the door.

"Did you hear that sound?" Alyssa went on, whispering. "I think it came from downstairs."

"It sounded like someone broke a window." Samantha's low voice wobbled. "Do you think they're in the house, Mom?"

Both girls looked scared.

"I'm going down to see." Alyssa suddenly looked angry. "It's probably Dad, trying to scare us again."

Julia grabbed her arm, stopping her. "We don't know that."

"It's always Dad," Samantha added.

Both girls' expressions reflected their disappointment in their father, and a belief that he didn't care that he scared the daylights out of them. "Girls," Julia said quietly. "I know it's hard at times to realize your dad loves you, that he does things because he's emotionally disturbed right now, but—"

"Mom," Alyssa retorted, interrupting. "If you don't stop sticking up for Dad's nutty actions, we're going to think you're the one who's emotionally disturbed!"

"Yeah, we aren't babies. We see for ourselves what's going on," Samantha added.

"You both wait here," Julia told them. "I'll see what's going on. Remember, we have an alarm system." She forced herself to remain calm, although her heart was fluttering and a knot of fear was growing in her stomach. Like the exterior doors, only the windows that opened were wired.

Both girls nodded and moved closer together, as if to protect each other, as Julia tiptoed out to the hall. She hesitated at the top of the stairs, straining her ears to listen. The lower floor was absolutely still.

Slowly, she started down to the landing, where she paused, staring ahead along the final steps to the entry, where she could see the door was still latched and bolted. The alarm light glowed red, indicating it was still armed.

Could the noise have been outside? she wondered. The exterior lights were on, casting a faint glow into the dark rooms. From where she stood everything seemed normal.

But she couldn't see much beyond the hallway.

Get going, Julia, she told herself. *Sooner or later you have to check it out.* But still she hesitated, paralyzed by a sense of being watched.

By whom? Someone hiding in the shadows, just waiting for her to come into striking range so they could attack?

Oh, God. She was more of a basket case than she'd thought; Peter's terror tactics were wearing her down. Maybe she should have just called the police from her bedroom. She glanced behind her and saw that the girls had followed her, were anxiously watching from the top of the stairs. Somehow, seeing them was an impetus for action. She continued down the steps to the entry.

Cautiously, she walked through the house, glancing into the living and dining rooms before the family, kitchen and laundry rooms in the back of the house. All appeared exactly as she'd left them.

"Mom! Come quick!"

Alyssa's cry startled her. She was running even before the last word faded into the shadows, turning on lights as she ran toward the sound of her daughters in the living room. Upon reaching them, she stopped in her tracks, her eyes on the huge bay window that had been uncovered when Alyssa had opened the drapes.

"Someone tossed a brick through the window," Alyssa said.

Julia went to the phone and called the police. Peter better have an alibi, she thought. Things were out of control, getting downright scary. It was one thing to frighten her, quite another to terrify his own daughters.

She had no choice. She'd have to press charges.

CHAPTER THIRTEEN

JULIA SAT ALONE IN THE LIVING ROOM AFTER THE PATROL officer left. Both girls were finally asleep. She'd reassured them that she wasn't going to bed yet, that she was wide awake and going to catch up on some bookkeeping. The truth was that she couldn't have gone to sleep if her life had depended on it. She was too keyed up, too apprehensive of leaving the household vulnerable, even though they'd taped cardboard over the broken window.

Irrational feelings, she thought, but she couldn't banish her fears. Surely Peter hadn't flipped out completely. But the officer, a fiftyish man she hadn't seen before, had assured her that Peter would be questioned about his whereabouts, and if he didn't check out, he'd be detained, if not arrested. "We don't put up with this kind of ongoing domestic violence in our community," he'd told Julia at the door. "You and your daughters have endured far more than anyone should have to in this situation." His expression had been stern, like a caring grandfather. "We'll get to the bottom of this one way or another."

She'd thanked him, appreciating his concern.

Once he was gone she'd locked up, seen Alyssa and Samantha to their rooms, and then staked out the living room. When daylight crept in from around the drapes and shades, she went to the kitchen and started the coffeemaker. She needed a caffeine hit. Today was another busy day for her, and she wasn't about to let some crazy nut ruin it. She needed to make her living, and if Peter was behind all the craziness, she'd see to it that he was stopped, even if that meant he had to be committed to a mental hospital.

Julia waited until nine to call Dr. Kornsweig's office and was surprised when Peter's psychiatrist answered the phone. When she identified herself, there was a long pause.

"Are you there, Dr. Kornsweig?"

"I'm here, Julia," he said. "What can I do for you?"

His tone reminded her of that other time she'd called when he wouldn't give her information, when he'd retreated behind patient confidentiality. But he was her only hope now. Even if he wouldn't offer an opinion, he needed to know what Peter was doing. *In case Peter needed to be committed.*

"Nothing for me, Dr. Kornsweig. I only want you to listen and then make your own evaluation."

Another silence went by.

As she waited for his response, Julia could almost see him as he'd looked on her first visit, which had taken place at his request. "Come on in," he'd said crisply, his pale blue eyes noncommittal, the expression on his face probing, unblinking, disconcerting. If she hadn't known better she'd have guessed he was one of the patients. For a moment she'd hesitated, aware that it was after hours, that she was alone with a stranger.

But she'd gone though the door to his office and had sat down in a hard leather chair that was cracked and peeling from age. She'd wondered why their family doctor had recommended Kornsweig, whose bearing was so strange.

"I need your help, Dr. Kornsweig," she said into the phone finally, his continued silence bringing her back to the present and the reason for calling him. "I and my daughters are living a nightmare because of Peter and his accelerating terror tactics." Julia hesitated. "I'm hoping you can influence Peter so that he'll realize how harmful he's being to his girls, maybe use your influence to stop his, uh, destructive activities."

"And what are those, Julia?"

She told him.

A silence went by.

"You must remember, Julia, that Peter is my patient and I can't discuss his case."

"Of course. But we're living in such fear, and the police can't do anything, and—"

"I said Peter is my patient. You're not. I can't comment."

"But you're his doctor. If you can't influence him to stop threatening us, you at least need to know what he's doing."

"I'm sorry, Julia," he snapped. "I can't help you."

"But we're in danger."

"And as I've said, Peter is my patient."

She gulped a breath, trying to stop the quaver in her voice. "I understand that, Dr. Kornsweig. I just want you to consider whether or not Peter needs hospitalization."

"You aren't listening, Julia. I can't give out information about my patient."

"But I'm the mother of his daughters."

"Thank you for your call," he said coldly. The dial tone sounded in her ear.

"You creep!" she hollered into the dead receiver. "How dare you hide behind your professional license." She hung up and spent the next few minutes sobbing. There was no one to help her. After a while she dried her eyes and came to a decision.

She'd help herself. Whatever happened, she'd cope. She just needed to be emotionally prepared for what Peter might do next.

When the front doorbell rang later in the morning, Julia approached the entry with caution, moving through the dining and living rooms from the kitchen so that she wouldn't be seen walking up the hall by the person on the porch. Peeking, she saw that it was a woman, and then realized it was Diana. Quickly she opened the door, greeted her sister, and then closed and locked it right behind her.

"Jeez, Julia, what in hell's going on?" Diana's blue eyes, so like Julia's, were concerned, but direct. "First Alyssa calls me about what happened, that she's afraid for you being home alone, then you creep up on the door like you're hiding in your own house." She sucked in a breath. "You're acting like a person under siege."

"I am under siege." Julia pointed to the living room window. "The glass people are coming later to replace the pane."

"Shit!" Diana took her arm and led her back toward

the kitchen. "I hope you have coffee made, because I'm not leaving until I know what's been going on—and what you're doing about it."

Julia could only nod, then poured the last of the cold coffee into mugs and placed them in the microwave to heat. Gathering her thoughts, aware that her sister was a worrier, she ground fresh coffee beans and started another pot. She figured they'd need it.

They sat facing each other as Julia explained what had been happening, ending with what she'd come up with about Peter's obsession with her and their marriage.

"I can't change Peter," she began. "But I can change my own life. If he doesn't stop these terrifying incidents, and if his own psychiatrist won't talk to me and the police can't arrest someone without proof, then I'll have no option but to move. And hopefully he won't know we're gone until after the fact."

"What about the girls? Are they willing to leave their school? Their friends?"

Julia glanced away. "They may have to." She hesitated. "Our choices are being taken away from us." Her gaze suddenly locked with her sister's. "I believe it could come down to life and death." She gulped coffee, trying to stay calm. "Unless things change here in the very near future."

Diana expelled a long breath. "You think Peter could, uh, kill you?"

There was a silence while Julia gathered her thoughts.

"I don't think the old Peter could do that," she began, her voice wobbling with emotion. "But I don't know about the new Peter, the one who's capable of such inconsideration for his own daughters, who's lost his perspective about what's important." She swallowed more coffee. "If he's not capable of rational thought, and if there's no one who can stop his actions, then I have to protect us."

"Do you really think he's that bad, Julia?"

She nodded. "I don't know how sick he is, but I can't rationalize any longer, and risk a tragedy that alters Alyssa and Samantha forever."

"Like you being dead?"

Abruptly, Julia stood up, and the chair scraped on the hardwood floor. Diana's question was the very thing she didn't want to put into words. "More coffee?" she asked instead.

Diana got to her feet, shaking her head. "I've got to go, but I'm glad to hear that you're open to moving. Both Ted and I think you should."

Julia walked her back to the front door, where Diana faced her again. "Don't take any chances, Julia. And make sure Sam and Alyssa don't either until we know what's going on." Her worry was apparent on her face. "I think Peter is playing his sick games, but just in case he's not, be careful."

"You think it might not be Peter?"

Diana raised her brows, as though considering her next words. "Only that there appears to be a serial killer targeting women in South Seattle, and that same person could be the one shooting at women in our area. You need to be extra cautious, especially since you're a woman who lives alone."

"For God's sake, you aren't suggesting that Peter is a serial killer, are you?"

"Hell no!" Diana looked surprised. "I'm saying we know what we're dealing with if it's Peter, that's all. We don't know anything about how a psycho chooses his victims." She managed a reassuring smile. "So, for now I'm only telling you to be careful. Keep your doors locked, big sister."

With those final words of caution, Diana went out to her car, and Julia headed for her office. Whether she felt like it or not, she needed to work on the computer manual. The deadline was breathing down her neck.

Sitting down at her desk, Julia found it hard to concentrate. Her mind kept going back to what Diana had said about the serial killer. No way could that person be Peter. The possibility was too awful to even consider for a moment.

But the thought wouldn't go away.

She labored over the manual for several hours and was satisfied with her progress. *Maybe I'll really make the deadline,* she thought as she saved her work. A glance at the clock told her it was still a half hour before the girls arrived from school. There was time to check her e-mail messages.

She signed onto AOL, heard the "You've got mail" message and smiled. As she scrolled her mail, she stopped at a handle, My649, one she didn't recognize, although it was also an AOL address. She clicked and opened the message.

Don't delete. It's Earl. His post went on to say that he'd created a secure e-mail address so they could keep future messages confidential. And then he explained how she could create her own private handle that was separate from her regular e-mail, so that no one, on his side or hers, could track their messages. *Let me know that you received this post,* he ended.

Julia reread the post, wondering about his need for such secrecy. And why did she need a separate handle to receive his messages? No one ever read her posts, and she didn't care if anyone read what she sent. It struck her as odd.

She didn't respond. She needed to think about it. Never before in her life had she had to hide her activities. Was it necessary to start now because she had a friend who was a married man? Didn't that imply guilt? She had nothing to hide. Her motives were aboveboard. She couldn't help but wonder about his.

Her inclination was to delete his post even as she saved it and went offline. But his request and how it pertained to her swirled in her mind.

At least it occupied her thoughts, taking away her fears, she reminded herself. She'd respond to his e-mail tomorrow, after she'd slept on it and had a clear head.

He'd have to accept that—or forget her.

CHAPTER FOURTEEN

By midmorning of the next day Julia was still mulling over Earl's e-mail message. What he'd suggested just didn't feel right to her. She couldn't see why he felt a need to hide his friendship with her. It was demeaning. She thought about calling him on the phone but decided against it. He was a busy man at work, and contacting him at home was out of the question. What would she say?

Hello, I'm a writing friend of Earl's and I need to talk to him about our future method of communication?

Finally, she decided not to respond because she had no intention of establishing a secret e-mail address in order to reply. She'd explain her reasons when he called her, and if he didn't understand, she'd have to chalk it up to fate, that despite her feelings for him, her relationship with a married man wasn't meant to be.

She smiled at her pop psychology. And maybe it

wasn't so pop after all. Maybe it was common sense. She went to work on her wreaths, using the dried roses, hydrangeas, and greens from her own garden, feeling resolved about Earl, and not allowing herself to dwell on the Peter situation. Or on the fact that she'd miss Earl if their relationship ended.

The sudden ring of the phone jarred her out of her reverie. She dropped the dried greens in her hand and went to answer it, thinking it was Diana. She'd promised to deliver a winter door wreath to her sister by that afternoon, a birthday present for Ted's mother.

"Hello," she said, pulling off the rubber gloves she used to protect her fingernails.

"Mrs. Phinnortner?"

She recognized the voice this time. "Earl?"

She switched the phone to her other ear so that she could look out over the woods beyond her backyard and shift mental gears.

"Uh-huh. I can't fool you twice with the same trick, eh?"

"If you could, I'd be stupid, not innocent," she said, referring to their earlier phone conversation. Julia didn't add that she'd been thinking about him and that she'd decided she must write him off if he didn't call.

"Uh-oh. I think I blew my cover." His deep baritone laugh sounded in her ear. "I'll have to come up with something else."

"Or you could just be Earl when you call."

A silence went by.

"Yeah, I could be, under normal circumstances." A pause. "Unfortunately, mine aren't."

"What do you mean?"

"Uh, I guess I'd better be up front with you, Julia, because your friendship is important to me." He hesitated. "As you know, my wife is, uh, not well, is, in fact, a little paranoid. Even the most innocent encounters I have with other women are blown out of proportion: secretaries, female lawyers and judges, and lately, women writers. She accuses me of everything from having affairs to plotting her health problems."

"I'm sorry, Earl. I had no idea."

"No one does." Another silence. "And maybe I shouldn't be telling you, either."

"Of course I'll never discuss what you've said with anyone."

"I know that, Julia. It's why I could share my concerns with you in the first place."

She digested his words, wondering how to respond. "Is that why you call me Mrs. Phinnortner when you call, so that no one knows my real name?"

Another silence.

"Maybe, partly." A pause. "I also like to tease you."

"I gathered that."

"I mean it as a compliment. As I said before, your instinct to trust is refreshing. No one I know believes what they hear these days. They question everything."

"That's ambiguous."

"I know. Remind me to explain after we know each other better."

She moved across the kitchen, taking the cordless phone with her. "Explain what, Earl? The need for secrecy now, or in the future, when you're past the problem?"

"Everything."

"So what are you really saying?"

His deep sigh came over the line. "I want us to be friends, so I have to be honest." Another pause. "Because of my wife's mental illness I need to protect myself and any female in my life from repercussions."

Julia didn't know exactly what he meant, but she could identify. If she had a male friend, she had no idea what Peter would do, had no idea if he'd be dangerous to her and the person she dated.

"I understand, Earl," she said finally. "Maybe we should just forget about our friendship, at least for now."

"No way!" His response was instant.

"But—"

"No buts. I refuse to be manipulated, and although I care about my wife and kids, I see no harm in our friendship." A pause. "As long as you're willing, Julia."

A silence went by.

"I also have a volatile situation with Peter, and I don't want to be manipulated either." She stared at her finished wreaths, formulating her words before she went on. "A major difference between us is that I'm divorced and you're married. I'm a free woman who can decide for herself who I want as a friend."

"Does that mean you'll continue our friendship?"

"Yeah, I guess it does, Earl."

"Whew, that's a relief. I figured my e-mail request had offended you."

"I admit it did at first."

He hesitated. "So are you willing to go along with my suggestion, preferably with a man's name, so we can e-mail rather than phone each other?"

She pushed some flowers into place on a wreath as she considered his question. "I could do that now that we've discussed why it's necessary."

"I'm sorry about this, Julia. I hope you can understand that I have no other choice right now."

"I do, believe me." She hesitated. "What's happened to your wife is tragic, and to your storybook romance."

"Yep, that's true." His tone was suddenly distant, as though he didn't want to talk about the past. He changed the subject to discuss the steps in setting up her new e-mail account, and she promised to post a message once it was established.

After they hung up, everything that had seemed so reasonable suddenly felt a little sordid. But it's not, she reassured herself. It was only expedient, because of circumstances. Earl's and hers.

But the feeling didn't go away until she forced it out of her mind by rationalization. Earl was no more responsible for his mentally ill wife than she was for her crazy husband.

"There is a difference," a little voice in her head said, repeating the words she'd told Earl. "I'm divorced and you're married."

She meant to remember that. Earl was only a friend and nothing more.

"Damn," Julia muttered. Who'd be ringing the front doorbell at one in the afternoon? She wasn't expecting company and was, in fact, about ready to leave and deliver her wreaths.

She grabbed her jacket and ran down the steps, wiping excess lotion from her hands onto her Levi's as she headed to the entry hall. A quick glance through the peephole on the door told her it was the mailman. He must have a package that wouldn't fit in her mailbox. Smiling, she opened the door, but his expression wiped the smile from her face as he handed her the mail that he should have left in her box.

"Mrs. Farley, did you know that your mailbox is gone?"

"What?"

"It looks like your box has been stolen," he repeated.

She stepped onto the porch, glancing around him to the cluster of mailboxes down the street. Hers was the only black one, and now there were only white ones in the double line of boxes under the protective shaked roof. Her eyes returned to the uniformed carrier, who was handing her a slip of paper.

"Here's the number to report the theft, Mrs. Farley." He hesitated. "You'll need to get another box up right away and you'll have to fill out a police report, even though the culprit was probably a kid. This type of vandalism is usually done by kids, maybe random, maybe not." He shook his head and then adjusted his hat. "Happens a lot more than people think. Had a situation a while back where a sixteen-year-old boy stole the mailbox of the girl who'd dumped him because she'd returned his letters unopened."

"My daughters don't have boyfriends."

He shrugged. "Could be someone with a crush on one of them. Who knows?" He managed a grin. "All we know at this point is that you need another box so I can leave your mail."

She nodded.

"By the way, what does the A stand for?"

"Pardon me? The A?"

"Yeah, behind you." He gave a nervous laugh. "An A like in Nathaniel Hawthorne's *The Scarlet Letter*."

"For God's sake!" Diana cried from the driveway, drawing Julia's glance over the man's shoulder. She hadn't seen her sister arrive behind the mail truck. "What in hell has happened now? Who spray-painted the front door?"

Julia spun around to see what the mailman and Diana were talking about. For a moment, shock stopped her breath and she couldn't talk. She gulped air, stepping back for a better look at the big red letter A that had been sprayed on her door, just like what might have happened in Puritan New England to an adulteress. But that wasn't the case here.

"I can't believe it. Who would do such a thing?" Julia's voice shook. "It wasn't there this morning when the girls left for school. We would have seen it."

"So it happened between then and now," Diana said. "I wonder if any of the neighbors saw anyone."

Julia shook her head, frustrated, but scared. "The kids are all in school, and almost all of the parents work during the day."

"Shit!" Diana was dressed in a navy business suit, obviously on her way home from work early. "Another reason for you to move, sis. You're isolated here, anything can happen, and no one would know until everyone came home at the end of the day." She wiped stray hairs off her face. "This is not a good situation at all."

Julia was silent, her thoughts going to what was becoming her only alternative—moving. But it wouldn't be an easy decision because the ramifications were immense, life-altering for her and the girls. The acts of violence against them hadn't stopped, were, in fact, accelerating. She had to take the situation seriously, like it or not.

"I know," she said finally. "But for now I need to call the police."

"And I have to get on with my route. You know where to find me if anyone has a question." The mailman gave a salute, then went back to his vehicle.

Diana followed Julia into the house, stood next to her as she called the police, then listened to her account of the mailbox being stolen.

"Jeez, I'm glad I got off early. I figured I'd catch you before you left for my house with the wreath." She gave a wry laugh.

"Thanks, Diana." Julia made coffee as they waited for the officer to arrive. When she heard the patrol car out front, she was relieved. Maybe there was some kind of rational explanation for everything, although she wondered what that could possibly be.

I'm grasping at straws again, she thought as she went to open the door for the officer. But then it seemed that's all she had these days. She could only hope things got better. She could not allow them to get worse.

She recognized Officer Dolby, and her heart sank. He wasn't all that sympathetic to her plight, as though it was somehow her fault. But maybe she was wrong. He might just have a poor bedside manner. As she explained the latest incidents, he just shook his head, asked some questions, and made notes for his report. His expression told her that he was puzzled by the ongoing vandalism.

"You say your daughter's name is Alyssa?" he asked, glancing up from his writing pad.

Julia nodded.

"She break up with a boyfriend lately?"

"I don't think Alyssa has a boyfriend, does she, Julia?" Diana asked, jumping into the interchange.

"No, she doesn't." Julia knew Diana was running interference, that she'd remembered Officer Dolby, too.

He lifted his cap and scratched his head. "Well, you know all of these odd happenings, although destructive and against the law, seem like things a kid with a grudge would do." He hesitated, letting her digest his words. "You realize we talked to your ex-husband about what's been going on here?"

"I assumed that you had, although no one reported back to me," Julia replied. "What was the result?"

"He checked out. He was able to substantiate his whereabouts each time." Officer Dolby gathered up his handheld radio, put his pen and pad into a pocket, and headed for the door, where he faced her again.

"You and your girls be extra cautious until we can figure out what's going on."

Julia swallowed hard, nodding. It was the same old litany.

"And be sure to call us if anything looks suspicious, anything at all, day or night. Okay?"

She managed another nod, then closed the door behind him.

"I think it's Peter," Julia said as they went back to the kitchen.

"So do I." A pause. "For all his poor-me attitude, his mental illness, his downright sociopathic behavior, he sure in the hell knows how to protect his ass." Diana gulped a breath. "I hate that bastard—even though he's the father of my darling nieces that I dearly love."

"I know. Peter always knew how to play the establishment, as he used to call anyone with authority."

For the next few minutes they discussed the situation, finally concluding that they were still uncertain about what was happening. Even when Julia started at the beginning, proceeding from the first threat to her spray-painted door, the whole scenario made no sense. They were still mulling things over when Julia noticed Alyssa in the hall doorway. A glance at the clock told her that school was out for the day. She wondered how long her daughter had been listening.

Alyssa adjusted her short top over her hip-hugger jeans and then stepped into the room. "It *is* Dad," she told them angrily. "And it's time he figured out that he's not still in junior high school. *He needs to grow up.*"

She dropped a kiss on both Julia's and Diana's cheeks, then went to the refrigerator and pulled out a Coke. Soda in hand, she headed upstairs, pleading lots of homework. Then Diana got up, remembering that she needed to get home and prepare her mother-in-law's birthday dinner. With Julia's wreath in hand, she headed for the front door.

"I love you, big sister. Take care, and tomorrow we'll talk about your options." Her gaze was level and determined. "You have to come to some resolution here, right?"

"Right. I'll talk to you tomorrow." As Diana strode outside Julia called after her, "I love you, too, little sister."

Julia went back to the kitchen and had only put the cups into the dishwasher when the phone rang.

"It's Dad," Alyssa said from the doorway. "I just called him, even though I was scared. I told him that we don't appreciate his terror tactics." She sucked in air. "And I hung up on him when he started in on you, Mom."

Julia stared, horrified. "You did what?" She didn't need Peter right now on top of everything else, even if Alyssa had been right on target.

But she went to answer the phone.

CHAPTER FIFTEEN

"Okay, Julia." Peter's high-pitched voice left no doubt about the degree of his anger. "This bullshit's gone on long enough!"

Her own response was instant. "Don't talk to me about bullshit, Peter, not when you're so intent on making my life—and the lives of your daughters—so frightening and miserable." She sputtered. "How dare you!"

She wanted to call him all the names that popped into her head, but somehow she restrained herself. Having her rise to his bait, giving him a platform to vent, was what he wanted. She would gain nothing by confronting him, by throwing all of her suspicions back in his face. He'd just deny everything anyway.

Julia sucked in a long breath. *Stay calm,* she instructed herself. *Sound normal.* "I'm cooking dinner now," she said, lying. "I have to go. We'll have to discuss this later."

"Don't hang up or I'm coming over, police or not!" he shouted in her ear. "We have to talk about this. My daughters are being threatened here and I won't have it!" He broke off, as though formulating his verbal assault. "They're obviously in danger."

She forced herself to breathe deeply, so that her pulse could slow to a normal range. She needed to stay in control of the conversation. A shouting match would only incite him further, motivate him to yet another scare tactic.

"You still there, Julia?"

"I'm here."

"We have to talk about this." A pause. "You believe I'm doing these acts of vandalism, and I'm not!"

"Are you saying that you haven't prowled around the house, peeked in the windows, parked down the street to watch our comings and goings? Is that what you're saying, Peter?"

"I'm not saying I haven't been concerned about my family."

"So you're not denying that you've been stalking us?"

"Son of a bitch! Stop twisting my words, Julia." His sniffle of disapproval came over the wire. "You're crazy if you believe I'd harm Alyssa and Samantha. I'm not the one jeopardizing our girls—you are."

"Get real, Peter, stop projecting—"

"Your paranoia?" he said, interrupting. "You're trying to make me out as the bad guy."

"Are you?"

"Fuck you, Julia. How can you say that? You were married to me, remember? You know who I am."

She sighed. "Unfortunately, I do."

"What does that mean?"

"You want your way to prevail, whatever the cost. You won't accept any change that rocks your boat."

Surprisingly, a silence, rather than an angry retort, went by. "I don't want my family jeopardized, that's all," he said finally. "No one would dare vandalize our house if I lived there. You and the girls would not be in any kind of danger if we were still a family." A pause. "No one would dare."

He went on with his typical ranting, but Julia hardly listened to him; she was somehow relieved by his words. His personal agenda was suddenly clear: scare her and the girls and he would be welcomed back to protect them.

Oh, God, she thought. He was sick. But at least her fears were defused. Like Diana, she was convinced that all of the bizarre incidents had been perpetrated by Peter in order to get back into her good graces.

It hadn't worked. She was on to him.

A few minutes later she was able to hang up. Even though she saw through his crap, it was still a stalemate.

She just hoped she could deflect him, so that he could get on with his life. If he could, then she could, too, and so could their daughters. But for now she went to the garage to look for leftover exterior enamel paint. She needed to paint the front door.

"I just think it would be better to stop seeing each other," she told Earl a couple of nights later after having come to a painful conclusion. "Things are just too uncertain in both of our lives." She smiled, trying to soften her words. "We both have, uh, situations that could be volatile." She hesitated. "And I certainly don't want to put you in harm's way because of mine."

"Harm's way?"

She nodded. "I've told you about Peter, that we're divorced, that he doesn't want to let go, but I haven't told you the whole story."

He raised his brows, waiting, and the candlelight on their table reflected in his eyes, giving them an oblique look that was hard to read.

"Basically, I can't believe the man I lived with for seventeen years is dangerous," she began, "but lately I've begun to wonder." Julia glanced down at her knotted hands. "The incidents"—she broke off with a nervous laugh—"that have been happening at my house are downright scary, to me and my two daughters."

"Explain," he said. "You've told me that your husband doesn't want to let go, but what exactly is he doing?"

She glanced down, considering how much she should say, somehow feeling guilty about the whole sordid mess. Not in her wildest dreams had she ever imagined herself involved in a low-class divorce with a man who was disturbed and obsessed. Slowly, she explained, having decided that Earl needed to know everything, since he was involved in her life. She could not place him in jeopardy, too.

He leaned forward over the table, oblivious to the fact that his white shirt was almost in his pasta dish. "Do you think you and your girls are in danger, Julia?"

Julia lowered her gaze. "I honestly don't know." She hesitated. "But just in case, the worst thing Peter could discover is that I'm seeing another man, even though the man is just a friend." She hesitated. "Until he's gotten beyond his obsession to get his family back, I don't want you in the line of fire because of me."

There was a brief silence.

"I am involved here and I want to help." He paused. "Will you allow me to make that decision, Julia?" Earl asked finally. "I care about what happens to you and your daughters. There has to be a legal recourse, and I'm here to do whatever is necessary for you."

She met his eyes, holding his gaze for long seconds. "Maybe," she said finally, reluctant to say a final no. "It'll depend on what's going on, on what gets resolved between me and Peter."

There was a silence.

"Do you want to end our friendship?"

His question was direct, softly spoken but demanding her honest answer.

"I would hate to end our friendship," she said truthfully. "I just think it may be prudent for now."

"Then we won't end it." His response was immediate. "I hope you'll agree with me that you'll let me help if necessary." Will you?" His dark eyes suddenly held hers. "I look forward to our times together, Julia." He hesitated, but his gaze didn't waver. "I hope you won't end them."

She looked away, considering her problems and his, feeling pulled in two directions—wanting to see him and knowing she shouldn't.

"Don't make a decision now," he suggested. "Will you agree to give yourself time to think this over?"

She hesitated, then slowly nodded. "How long?"

"A few days, a week maybe."

She nodded again, secretly glad for the reprieve. Maybe things would improve on her front, although she doubted it. His sounded pretty static.

"Thanks, Julia." His voice lowered as he explained further, elaborating on problems he'd mentioned in other conversations. "I can't tell you how much I want a divorce, but I can't file until I know my wife can cope without me." He hesitated. "She's an emotional cripple without someone paving her way."

She didn't know how to respond. But, at this point, she couldn't make any promises either. She had her own problems, which might be far worse than his.

"Let's talk next week," she said. "As you suggested, I'll think about everything, mostly my own situation."

"Okay," he said. "But I warn you. My fingers are crossed until then."

"Mine, too."

They finished their meal, chatting about books, autographing, and his latest appearance on a talk show, anything but the subject they were careful to avoid. He walked her to the Cherokee after they left the Italian restaurant, kissed her good-bye, and then headed for the ferry. She spent the drive from Pioneer Square to the East Side wondering what she'd done. Why hadn't she just ended their relationship when she'd had the chance?

But Julia knew why. She'd come to care about Earl, beyond his celebrity status and attractiveness. She could still feel his mouth on hers, and her regret when he'd stepped back to leave her.

Damn, she needed to get a grip. She had enough problems without falling in love with a married man who might never be free.

And then there was Peter, who watched her every move. Not a good situation.

CHAPTER SIXTEEN

Topsy twisted on the chair, unable to meet her therapist's eyes. She felt hesitant to state her fears, the fragments of terrifying thoughts that circled her mind, robbing her of peace during the day and her sleep at night.

If only she could pull them forward, so she could face whatever it was that scared her so much.

Judy, her psychologist, smiled kindly, as patient as ever with her suppressed emotions, her inability to remember. "Tell me what's bothering you now, Topsy." Judy's body language stayed constant: no censure, no judgment, and no recriminations. "What's causing you so much stress?"

Topsy stared at her lap, at the expensive black wool skirt that went so well with her leather boots and jacket. As always, when she stepped out of her house she looked perfect in her designer clothing, the one thing she did right for her husband and family; she was forever the trophy for the people who professed to love her, but who paraded her for their own status.

Dear God, she prayed silently. *Where did that thought come from?* Her magical thinking, as that doctor in the psych ward at Harborview Medical Center had once suggested to her?

If only she could remember some things—*if only*.

"So, what's going on in your life, Topsy?" Judy asked, gently prompting her.

Topsy scoured her mind, desperately trying to remember. *Father in Heaven*, she prayed again. *Help me recall the reason I needed to see Judy today*. She smiled at her therapist, striving to appear upbeat, as though this were just another follow-up appointment to maintain her emotional well-being.

No one could know how badly she was floundering, that fragments of memory would flicker to life only to suddenly vanish again, leaving her unsettled and scared. Then another one would surface in her mind only to disappear with the others, into the foggy place where she stored her fears. She sensed that the last flash of memory had terrified her, and now she couldn't remember that, either.

Somehow she knew that she must retrieve it, that it was the key to unlock everything she'd suppressed. Conversely she sensed that the swirling fog that took her thoughts was protecting her. She didn't understand, even as she pleaded with it to stop.

Crazy, she thought, still smiling at Judy. It was no use. Her issues, whatever they were, had been snatched away beyond her reach, at least for now. *Maybe they'll come back later*, she thought, grasping on to that one hope.

And then I'll begin to get well, be a better wife and mother, she told herself.

But for now, she needed to maintain the status quo. Topsy completed the session, discussing the events in her life, expressing her hope for the future of her marriage and family.

It was all she could do.

The dark place had stolen her mental pictures before she could exorcise them in a therapy session. She began to wonder if they were real, or if she'd just conjured them up out of a need to be recognized as a real person to her husband. She had no idea, and she didn't want to dwell on it.

She only wanted to be a normal wife and mother: keep house, cook, maintain a vegetable garden, cultivate a crop of flowers—and be recognized for those talents by her husband.

Topsy's self-analysis gave her anxiety, and she wondered if she needed an extra Paxil to steady herself, before she had a full-blown attack. But, hearing Judy tell her that she seemed to be making progress, she smiled as she got up to go. She dismissed the fact that Judy seemed troubled, that she may not have bought into Topsy's account of a perfect life.

Topsy wondered what Judy meant when she talked about progress. That Topsy seemed better adjusted, that some of her old demons were not as apparent?

Topsy left Judy's office on a positive note. She'd managed to pull off another session without revealing . . . what? That she felt in imminent danger? That something terrible had happened that she couldn't remember? That it was still happening?

If only she knew.

CHAPTER SEVENTEEN

EARL'S WORDS WEIGHED ON JULIA'S MIND OVER THE NEXT week, and when she didn't hear from him, she was disappointed, but relieved. Their relationship was in the hands of fate: it would happen or it wouldn't.

Although it was not quite the end of October, the local weathermen were predicting snow in the mountains, alerting skiers that the first ski weekend of the season was at hand. Julia immediately thought of Alyssa and Samantha, who were avid skiers, having been going to the nearby mountains ever since Peter had first taken them a decade ago. Peter was an expert skier; Julia was only mediocre. Her family hadn't been into the sport.

"How about a weekend at Crystal Mountain?" she asked them at dinner the next night. "Aunt Diana said Ted's parents are in Hawaii and we could use their cabin."

"Yeah, that'd be cool!" Samantha's expression brightened. "We'd get to ski."

"I'm up for it, that's for sure," Alyssa said.

Julia grinned. "Okay then, we'll plan on it."

A trip to the mountains might give them perspective after all that had happened, she thought. She adjusted her work schedule so they could go.

They drove up on Friday afternoon after school, arriving at the high-peaked cabin around six. The other chalets in the area were alight with activity, the occupants also anticipating their first outing on the ski slopes in the morning.

"Hey, this is great!" Alyssa said as they unpacked the Cherokee and crunched through the undisturbed snow to the front door. She sniffed the air. "It even smells like snow."

"Yeah," Samantha replied. "I can't wait to get on the slopes tomorrow." She glanced at Julia. "I hope you brought something good for supper, Mom. I'm starving."

Julia smiled to herself. She'd done the right thing in coming. It was the break they all needed. She hadn't seen her girls so carefree in months.

"How do chili dogs with grated cheddar and diced onions sound? Of course, with chips, Coke, and hot fudge sundaes for dessert," Julia added. "That is, if there's vanilla ice cream in the freezer as your aunt Diana promised."

Both girls nodded, grinning.

As they went inside and switched on lights, Julia was taken with the coziness of the place: paneled walls, a huge stone fireplace with overstuffed chairs and sofas placed to feel the warmth of a fire, and several bookcases filled with favorite books. It represented the personalities of Ted's parents: comfortable, welcoming, and solid. The same could be said for

Diana's husband, Julia thought, moving on into the kitchen, where she deposited their bags of food onto the counter.

She saw the girls settle into their room, where each one had a bed and nightstand, then she went back downstairs to finish preparing supper. She couldn't help but muse about their need for her being nearby.

Humph, she thought, putting the hot dogs on the stove to boil. She wished there was someone to stand between her and the boogeyman, because she got scared, too.

Over the next two hours they ate, watched television, and then went to their rooms, anticipating an early start in the morning. After she was in bed and knew the girls were asleep, Julia sat up against the pillows and stared out at the falling snow beyond her windows. For the moment she felt secure under the down quilt but sad about her life: being alone, threatened, and uncertain about the future.

Thank you God for Diana and Ted, she prayed silently. *And thank You for giving me the ability to keep on, to not crumble under the pressure, because I'm alone.*

Julia went to sleep with tears on her cheeks, too sleepy to even ponder where they came from.

They spent Saturday on the slopes, riding the lift to the top of the run, then skiing down, only to do it again. At the end of the day, when they were sitting in front of the fireplace, tired but happy, eating the beef stew and rolls that Julia had prepared, everyone agreed that it had been a wonderful day. They retired early, anticipating more skiing in the morning before they left for home in the afternoon. Julia went right to sleep and slept for nine hours straight for the first time in months.

By eight in the morning they had their skis on and were in line for the lift, waiting their turn as the empty seats came down the mountain, circled the platform as people scrambled on, and then started toward the top of the slope again.

"We're next," Alyssa cried, nudging Sam and Julia forward.

Just as the three-seated chair approached, Samantha suddenly lurched forward, stumbling to catch her balance before falling off the side of the platform, missing the moving lift. Horrified, Julia jumped aside, followed by Alyssa, and the chair started up the mountain empty.

"Samantha!" Julia cried, quickly stepping out of her skis. She reached the edge of the deck at the same time as Alyssa, who'd also kicked her skis aside. Some people in line moved to help, while others took advantage of the shortened line. For a few seconds it was pandemonium, everyone talking at once, no one knowing if Samantha had been seriously hurt.

"I'm okay, Mom," Samantha called from the snowbank where she'd fallen six or eight feet below the platform. Her voice sounded faint and shaky, and Julia wasn't sure that she really was unhurt. The snow had obviously broken her fall, but she looked tousled and scared, and there was a cut on her forehead. Several men managed to reach her and help her back to the platform approach, where Julia and Alyssa met them.

"There's a medical aid person back at the lodge," one of the men told Julia. "I think they should have a look at her." He turned to Samantha. "You're gonna be okay, kiddo. You're just a little shaken up."

Julia nodded. "I agree that she has to be checked out."

"Thanks for helping me." Samantha's voice shook as

she talked to her rescuers. "But did you see who pushed me off the deck?"

"Pushed you?" Julia asked, startled. "I didn't see anyone, but then, I was getting ready for our turn on the lift." She glanced at the men. "Did you?"

"I didn't," one of the men said.

"Me either," another agreed. "It seemed like the typical movement of a crowd waiting for the lift."

"But someone did," Samantha insisted. "I even caught a glimpse of the person."

"What did they look like?" Alyssa asked.

"It was only a blur—I don't know if it was a girl or a guy, but whoever it was they wore a red ski jacket and pants."

As one, the men and Julia glanced back to the platform, where skiers were still scrambling for the lift. No one was dressed in red. Julia's gaze went up the line of seats gliding through the air on the way to the top of the mountain. One person wore red but was too far away to identify.

"I'm sure if someone nudged you, sweetheart, it was accidental," the first man said.

Samantha looked about to cry, and Julia thought it best to get her to the medic. She thanked the men for their help, then took Samantha's arm, steadying her as Alyssa took charge of their skis and poles. They headed for the lodge.

"Someone did, Mom," Samantha said, her voice wobbling. "I wouldn't lie about that."

"I know, honey. But I think it was an accident, like the man said." She realized that Samantha was more shaken than she'd first thought.

"But if it was an accident, then why didn't the person stick around and apologize, make sure that Sam was all right?" Alyssa's gaze was as direct as her words.

Julia shot her a glance that said they'd discuss it later, after Samantha saw the medic. But she'd been wondering the same thing. It couldn't have been deliberate, she told herself.

Could it?

Samantha was pronounced unhurt, aside from the superficial cut on her forehead and the shock from the fall itself. But the incident ended their skiing trip early. No one felt like braving the ski lift again.

"Tell you what," Julia said, contriving a cheerful attitude as they loaded the Cherokee for the drive home. "We'll stop on the way home for a nice lunch."

Both girls nodded.

"Can I drive for some of the way?" Alyssa asked.

"I don't think so this time," Julia answered gently, knowing how much Alyssa loved an opportunity to practice her driving. She'd had her permit for a few months and had recently completed her driver's education course.

"Please, Mom." She straightened up after placing her suitcase on the backseat. "Did you forget that I'm taking my driving test next week?"

"We'll get some driving in before that," Julia said, compromising. Although Alyssa was a good driver, Julia didn't need the stress of a student at the wheel today, especially on mountain roads. And a glance at Sam told her that she didn't either.

Alyssa sighed. She, too, had glanced at Sam, saw her sister's subdued state, and didn't press the point. A short time later they were on the road, and within minutes Samantha was asleep on the backseat, her head propped on the jackets that sat on Alyssa's suitcase.

They ended up skipping lunch, opting for dinner out at their favorite restaurant in Issaquah that night. Much better, Julia thought, although she was concerned about Sam, who seemed subdued. She might have to give their family doctor a call later, if Sam didn't perk up. She'd see.

"Someone did push me on purpose," Sam said as they went from the garage into the house. "I wish you guys would believe me."

"We do, honey," Julia said, stopping to hug her.

"I definitely do," Alyssa said. "Or else they wouldn't have snuck off before we could see who it was."

"But why me? What did I ever do to hurt anyone?"

"Of course you did nothing wrong." Julia managed a smile. "We know you were knocked off the platform, we just don't know for sure that it was deliberate."

"I know," Sam insisted. "I'm the one who fell."

Dear God, Julia thought as she stepped into the kitchen. All of the horrible happenings around their house had given her girls the same sense of paranoia that she found in herself lately. Their minds sprang to the worst-case scenario: An accident became a deliberate act of violence against them.

Her thoughts swirled with worry as she went to listen to phone messages. When Earl's voice sounded in the quiet room, she was suddenly uplifted.

"I've been out of town," he said. "Sorry I missed you. I'll call again soon."

Suddenly things didn't seem quite so upsetting. She was already looking forward to his call.

CHAPTER EIGHTEEN

"I'M SO GLAD YOU AGREED TO DINNER," EARL SAID several nights later at the same Italian restaurant in Pioneer Square where they'd dined several times before. His dark eyes seemed black in the subdued lighting; electric wall sconces, lit candles on the tables and the gas flames in the fireplace. "I thought you might turn me down."

Julia pushed back her long blond hair and sipped her wine, considering her reply. They'd just finished a nice meal, and after several glasses of wine, she'd decided to be honest. She had nothing to gain by being coy—by playing some game she didn't completely understand—because she was so attracted to him. Their meetings were not as much about writing techniques these days, although they did discuss the topic in general.

"I almost did, Earl."

A brief silence went by.

"Could you explain your feelings, Julia?" he asked

softly. "You must realize that I'm very attracted to you, that I hope our relationship will continue to, uh, grow."

Her gaze was caught by his, and for a moment she glimpsed what? Insecurity? Fear that she might end their friendship? Or just plain humor because he perceived her to be gullible, his words in the past.

But his directness disconcerted her, and she wondered if she dare explain. Would her words seem self-aggrandizing, as if she'd presumed he was interested in her as a desirable woman he respected, someone with whom he hoped to share a future romantic commitment, and not just a fellow writer friend as he'd always said? Maybe he did only view her as a friend and she was reading into his words and expressions and compliments.

Again, she opted for honesty.

"I enjoy your company very much," she began, and hesitated. "But—" Her voice trailed off into the silence between them.

"But—what?"

She swirled the wine in her glass, contemplating how she could be truthful without offending him. The last thing she wanted to do was seem like a single woman with an agenda—landing another husband.

"I admire you very much, maybe too much, since you're not single. But I'm not a—" She broke off.

"A what?" he prompted.

"A home wrecker." She blurted the term and then lowered her eyes. "I want you to know that I'm not out to catch a man, as women often are who are recently divorced." She met his steady gaze again, unable to read the impact of her words. "I value you as a person before anything else." She spread her hands. "I'm not out to pursue anything other than friendship with you, because you're a married man." She hesitated to sip her wine, wondering if she'd gone too far. "I needed to say that." She managed a smile. "As I said, I value knowing you, but given our circumstances, I felt a need to clarify my position."

He held her gaze for moments longer before being the first to glance away. He sipped his wine, as though he, too, was gathering his thoughts.

"You've been, uh, brutally honest here, Julia, and I need to validate your courage. It's not a common trait these days." His gaze veered upward to meet hers. "Your intuition about my feelings for you is on target." He shook his head slowly. "I could plead ignorance, but I wouldn't do that to you because I respect you too much. There's an odd thing that sometimes happens between a man and woman, a phenomenon called attraction that is beyond their control, whatever their obligations and responsibilities are to others. Some call it vibes, others call it pheromones, and I call it enzymes." He hesitated. "It's what we feel for each other, Julia."

Their eyes locked, and the silence that fell between them was suddenly alive with electricity. The sound of other diners was a low hum against the backdrop of soft Italian music.

Julia groped for a response. He'd just affirmed his feelings for her, the same ones she felt for him. He spoke before she was able to formulate her thoughts into words.

"We have three choices here, as far as I see it." He placed his hand over hers, which was resting on the table, and his gaze was steady.

She leaned forward, waiting.

He blinked rapidly, his tic momentarily beyond his control, but he held her eyes. "We can hurt our loved ones by saying the hell with it and going for our own feelings at their expense, or we can have a European type relationship where men have mistresses, or"—he hesitated—"we can say good-bye forever and never see each other again."

Her heart fluttered wildly, but she pulled her hand from under his, breaking their physical connection. "Tell me what you think, Earl. This is heavy duty for me."

"Have you never had an affair, Julia?"

"No," she said, sounding shaky. "I've never slept with anyone other than Peter." She hesitated, considering whether or not to explain further. "And I could never have a sexual relationship with any man unless I loved him."

"Maybe that's what we're talking about here, Julia. Love."

"Love? Between you and me?"

"Stranger things have happened."

Julia felt at a disadvantage and realized she probably sounded like a Victorian spinster, so out of step with the modern world. And yet, she argued mentally, she wasn't out of step; she just had her own code and knew what she could or could not live with—like stealing another woman's husband, even if that man was desperately unhappy and trapped by his wife's mental illness.

He raised his brows, watching the changing expressions on her face. "You know, Julia, it's not the norm these days to be loyal to a bad marriage. Women, like men, have needs."

"I realize that. But there are important reasons to be loyal, like the example we set for our kids, which takes precedence over our own needs, as you say." She paused. "It's different after a decision like divorce has been made and changes have occurred because of an untenable situation."

"Of course I agree with you." His expression softened. "But there are circumstances where a man, or a woman, has a right to some joy, like having a life beyond an untenable situation where they're trapped by responsibility and obligation."

"Such as?"

"Mine. Maybe yours."

"Those are the two words I'd like struck from my own personal dictionary: responsibility and obligation. I've been shackled to them for all of my adult life," she said, even as she knew that she could never set those words aside. Her two daughters meant more to her than any temporary fix—like an affair, even with a man who might possibly be the love of her life.

If he was that, then didn't fate say that he'd be there for her in the long run—or some such thing? She looked him straight in the eyes. "What are you really saying, Earl?"

"Only that I care deeply for you, Julia. I've never known anyone like you, and I don't want to lose you."

She let another silence go by.

"Exactly what are you suggesting?"

Another silence.

"Only that I'm not free at this time, that I, too, have kids to consider. I'm married to a woman who is emotionally handicapped, unable to take care of herself. If I left the marriage I don't know what would happen to her or to our son and daughter."

She understood that and respected him for his integrity. It was the decision she'd make in that situation. The realization only added to her feelings for him. He was a man who considered his family first, his own happiness second. She identified.

"Do you love her?"

"No, not for a long time, Julia." He took a quick sip of wine. "I hope you won't take this wrong, but I haven't been in love with my wife for quite a few years now, even though I will not abandon her. She's not lovable, is in fact a burden, in that she can't function at the lowest level, like grocery shopping. And our kids are being influenced by her inadequacy." He glanced away, but not before she'd noticed his worry. He wasn't telling her how their kids had been altered, or how they were in their lives right now. "I just hope they aren't permanently damaged by her passive/aggressive behavior," he added, his voice trailing off into his chronic concern, a thing she hadn't seen until tonight.

"So, what do you suggest . . . about us?" she asked gently.

"I don't want to lose you," he said at once. "I want us to continue seeing each other."

She smiled but was direct. "How do you mean that?"

He raised his brows in a question.

"In other words, what does seeing each other mean to you in the long run?" she asked, prompting him.

"I want us to have a relationship," he said. "On whatever level is comfortable to you."

"More than friendship?" she asked.

Something flickered in his eyes. "Friendship between a man and woman always deepens when it's intimate."

"You mean—sexual?"

"If that's where it leads, yes."

"I see." She hesitated and suddenly realized it was getting late, that she needed to get home before the girls began to worry. The realization was a relief; the conversation had become heavy, more so than she was prepared to deal with right now. She placed her glass on the table, knowing she had to respond honestly and hoping she didn't offend him. "I don't know if we're on the same wavelength, Earl." Shaking her head, as if willing him to understand her uncertainty, Julia pulled her napkin from her lap and placed it on the table. Then she grabbed her purse, which she'd placed near her feet, and got ready to push back her chair and stand up.

She managed a smile. "But for now I need to get going. My girls will call out the cavalry if I'm much later. I promised to be home by ten."

"You're a little old for a curfew," he said dryly. "Sure I haven't scared you off?"

Again she shook her head, but she realized that her indecision was showing. "I just need to digest our conversation, and my own feelings."

"Hey, I'm sorry if I came on too strong," he said, grabbing both of her hands, lightly restraining her from getting to her feet. "I understand your hesitancy. It's just that we've got something special . . . and I don't want us to lose it because—"

"I'm too scared or inexperienced?" she asked, finishing his sentence.

"Something like that." His hands held her captive momentarily. "Are you all of the above?"

She stared into his eyes. "Probably. I'm not sure, but I don't want to pursue this right now. I need to think about things."

"I respect that, Julia," he said, abruptly so serious that she dropped her eyes. "Please don't go."

"I think it's best, for now at least," she said, pulling her hands free and standing up. "We both need to think about our feelings, about where we want to go in our lives." She managed a smile, even though she felt like crying. Somewhere in the back of her mind she knew she was hooked on him, married or not. She also knew she needed to fight those feelings; he wasn't a free man, and whatever he'd said thus far didn't seem to indicate a change in his status anytime soon.

He stood, too. And then he walked her to her car and watched her go.

The day after Alyssa passed her driver's test and got her license, she talked Julia into letting her drive the Cherokee to a high school basketball game. Because Julia knew Alyssa was a responsible driver, that the gym was less than a mile away on an infrequently traveled back road, and because she was deep into her work on the computer manual, she finally agreed. She was still working at the keyboard when the phone rang three hours later, about the time she expected Alyssa home.

"Mrs. Farley?" an official male voice asked, then identified himself as an Issaquah police officer.

"Yes." Julia sat forward on the chair, suddenly alarmed.

"Your daughter Alyssa isn't hurt, but she's been in a minor traffic accident."

"Oh my God!" Julia cried, jumping up, oblivious to the fact that her papers all fluttered to the floor around her chair. "What happened?"

"She was run off the road on the way home from her high school basketball game," he said calmly. "The vehicle isn't damaged, but we've called for a tow truck, and an officer is bringing your daughter to your house within the next few minutes." His indrawn breath came over the line. "The towing company will be in touch about your Cherokee."

"Who ran her off the road? What happened?"

"Wasn't your daughter's fault, and the other driver

left the scene, that's all I know. The officer bringing her home will explain the details."

"It was a hit and run?"

"Yeah, as I said, the officer will explain."

A moment later Julia hung up and ran to the front hallway, just as the patrol car pulled into the driveway. She opened the door, waiting to hear what had happened.

Somehow, even though Alyssa wasn't hurt, she knew it wasn't good. It was another unexplained incident.

But maybe it wasn't connected to anything else, Julia told herself. Accidents happened.

CHAPTER NINETEEN

"I CAN'T DESCRIBE THE CAR, MOM," ALYSSA SAID SHAKILY. "I have no idea who was driving because I only saw headlights, not the make, model, and who was at the wheel." She hesitated. "And once I was struggling for control of the car, I didn't have time to pay attention to details." She hesitated. "I just knew I had to keep it on the road and away from the edge, even if the other driver was trying to push my car into the ditch so that I'd have an accident."

"I understand, sweetie, just explain what you can," Julia said gently.

Alyssa shuddered. "I was so scared. I could have been killed." She gulped in a breath as tears seeped from her eyes. "I feel terrible about your Cherokee, Mom. I hope it isn't too damaged."

Julia hugged her again, trying to calm her own fear of what might have happened.

"The important thing is that you're okay, sweetie.

A car can be fixed," she told her frightened daughter.

The young officer, one Julia didn't recognize, watched the exchange in silence and nodded at her evaluation of the situation. Upon arriving several minutes earlier, he'd explained that Alyssa had been run off the road by an unknown vehicle that had left the scene once the Cherokee had gone into the ditch, that there'd been no witnesses, and unless someone came forward the police were unable to investigate further. He handed her the towing company's card showing a number she could call in the morning to find out the status of the Cherokee. It had not been drivable because the front fender had been crumpled against the wheel, flattening the tire.

"It's hard to believe what kids do for kicks these days," he said. "They don't seem to understand that they aren't immortal, that daredevil actions can cause the death of a friend."

"Kids?" Julia's incredulous response soared into the entry hall. "You think the other driver was a teenager?"

"Uh-huh." The officer nodded. "It's a likely answer to what happened. Some teenage boy thought he'd impress a girl by seeming fearless behind the wheel. He probably didn't mean for your daughter to go off the road, so he got scared and fled the scene."

"I don't know anyone who'd do that," Alyssa retorted. "It was someone I don't know, but they intentionally tried to run me off the road."

The officer raised his brows. "Well, it could be someone with a secret crush, we might never know—unless that kid brags at school."

Julia bristled. "Are you suggesting that Alyssa knew the—"

Alyssa interrupted, upset by his analysis. "With all

respect, Officer, I don't believe what you said." She drew in a ragged breath. "I don't know anyone at my school who'd do such a thing, or would even think that trying to kill someone was cool."

Momentarily he looked uncertain, and Julia felt sorry for him. He was young, obviously an inexperienced rookie, and a bit naïve. But before he could defend his position further, there was noise from the second floor, and then Samantha appeared at the top of the stairs, staring down at them.

"What happened?" she cried, running down the steps, her red curls tousled, as though she'd been asleep, her eyes troubled as her gaze darted over the people below her.

"Everything is okay, honey," Julia said. "Alyssa had a little accident, which wasn't her fault."

"What do you mean?" Sam's glance moved from her mother to Alyssa. "Did I hear the officer say that someone ran you off the road?"

Her voice had risen, and Julia saw fear dawn in her eyes. She suddenly knew that Samantha was thinking about her own accident at Crystal Mountain, that she believed someone had pushed her intentionally and was now thinking that Alyssa had become their target.

"This was an accident, Sam," Julia said gently.

Alyssa was silent, and for the first time Julia realized that Alyssa agreed with her sister. She didn't allow herself similar thoughts; she was the adult and had to stay rational. She could not allow her imagination to run away with itself. That would be even more destructive.

After the officer left, she strived to sound cheerful, that these things happen, especially to new drivers, and that they needed to be thankful that no one had been hurt.

"How about some hot chocolate?" she suggested. "I was about to make myself a cup before the police called."

Both girls nodded, and she nudged them along to the kitchen, where she prepared the drink she hoped would soothe all of their nerves. But even as they sat in the peaceful ambiance of their house, her daughters' fears diminishing, her own were becoming stronger.

What if someone had pushed Samantha off the platform at Crystal Mountain? What if that person had then tried to run Alyssa off the road? Why? Who?

Surely Peter wouldn't hurt his own daughters? It went against everything she knew about her former husband.

"Okay, what's going on now, Julia?"

Julia had just gotten into bed and turned out the light when the phone rang on her bedside table. It was almost an hour since the officer had brought Alyssa home.

"How did you know, Diana?"

"Mrs. Bullard told me."

"Mrs. Bullard? My neighbor down the street?"

"That's right," Diana said. "I talked to her last week, explained my worries, and asked her to let me know if anything odd occurred in the neighborhood."

"My God! How could you do such a thing? The woman is the oldest person on the street and just lost her husband last year."

"Precisely my reasoning," Diana replied calmly, as if Julia weren't upset by her words. "She's the only person who's usually home day and night, and who might see what's going on that I need to know about."

"You're kidding."

"Of course I'm not." Diana's sigh came over the line. "I'm only doing what any concerned sister would do—making sure you and my nieces are safe and that I'm kept informed." She hesitated. "You have to know that the situation is dangerous, Sis, and I'm very worried."

Julia sat up straighter in bed, incredulous. "Diana, how could you do—"

"Easy," Diana said, interrupting. "Dire circumstances require dire action." A pause. "Be warned. I'll do anything necessary to protect you and the girls."

A silence went by.

"Thanks, Diana. I love you and appreciate your caring." She shifted position and switched the phone to her other ear. "I'm lucky to have you as my sister."

"Okay," her no-nonsense sister said. "Now fill me in. What happened tonight? I'm assuming all three of you are safe."

"Yeah, we're fine. The girls are both asleep now."

Julia explained what had happened, that the officer had brought Alyssa home, that the police would again check out Peter. "That was beyond my control," Julia said defensively. "It seems our year-long history of domestic disturbances, as the officer described it, automatically means Peter will be questioned."

Another silence.

"He'll love that," Diana said finally. "Be prepared for his reaction."

"I know, and I will be."

"Now tell me about the status of the Cherokee."

Julia told her what she knew, that she'd call in the morning and find out the extent of the damage.

"Let us know, Julia. Either Ted or I are available to drive you down to get your car." A pause. "You may have to rent a car while it's being fixed."

"I know, and my insurance will pay, thank goodness."

"Thank goodness Alyssa wasn't hurt."

"That goes without saying."

"I know."

They hung up after Diana's words of caution. But even though it was dark, peaceful, and quiet, Julia couldn't get to sleep. Her thoughts whirled with the "what ifs" that circled her mind. Her biggest question was what if the person out there wasn't Peter.

Then who? That thought was too scary to consider. But it kept her awake until the wee hours of the morning, and then she only slept fitfully.

She was scared.

Alyssa came down to the kitchen early, much to Julia's relief. She needed to talk to her without Samantha being present. The A that had been spray-painted on the front door had suddenly popped into her head during the night. Had the A stood for Alyssa—because someone had a grudge against her, a grudge Alyssa might not be aware of? In the light of what had happened, they needed to consider that possibility. They sat down at the table, Julia with her coffee, Alyssa with orange juice.

"Sweetheart," Julia began. "We need to think about what happened last night, other than a boy with a secret crush on you."

Alyssa's eyes widened. "What do you mean, Mom?"

"First of all, you've done nothing wrong." A pause. "I just thought we should think about any kid who might have a grudge against you—someone you beat out when you won your position on the student council, a boy who likes you but feels you rejected him . . . anyone you can think of who might be resentful or jealous."

Alyssa swirled the juice in her glass, thinking. Finally she looked up. "I can't think of anyone, Mom. And I've never stolen another girl's boyfriend, or rejected any guy. If someone dislikes me so much that they wanted me hurt it's beyond me." She hesitated. "I may be deluding myself, but I don't think I have an enemy anywhere, especially at school."

Julia nodded. "I'm sure you're right." She reached to pat Alyssa's hand. "So all we can conclude is that the driver of that car chose you at random, simply because you were on the road at the time. It was probably some kid who didn't even know who you were."

"Yeah, you're probably right."

Samantha came into the kitchen at that moment, and the topic was dropped. But later, after the girls had left to catch the school bus, Julia's doubts crept back into her thoughts. The whole thing just didn't make sense.

Just as Samantha's injury at Crystal Mountain made no sense. It was as unreal as a ghost story that had no motive, no base in reality and no probable cause for the story action. But what was happening to her family wasn't of the other world.

It was all too real.

Julia picked up the phone later in the morning, expecting to hear that her Cherokee could be driven home, that the tire had been changed, that the fender had been pounded out until she had free time to have it replaced. Instead Peter's angry words poured into her ears.

"I've had it, Julia. This is the last straw. I'm sick of

this shit of being questioned each time you have a problem in your life."

She caught her breath, instantly angry.

"Are you talking about the fact that your daughter could have been killed, Peter?" Another quick breath. "Because if you're put out by the police checking with you—especially in light of your constant prowling around and threatening me—then fuck you!" She slammed down the receiver and then sank down on a chair, on the verge of hyperventilating.

The phone rang again.

She grabbed it.

"Hey, get real, Julia," he went on as though she hadn't hung up on him. "That's why I'm calling. I'm not the person behind this shit, even the police know that. For your information, they checked out my alibi for last night."

She already knew that; the officer had called her earlier with an update. As far as the police were concerned, the incident was closed.

"Okay, I know that, Peter." She gulped a breath. "I just hope you aren't fooling us."

"Son of a bitch!" he shouted. "My family is in jeopardy because you ended our marriage. This wouldn't have happened if you—"

It was the same litany. She lowered the receiver to its cradle, shutting out his angry words, words she'd heard a thousand times before as he'd thrown things, punched holes in walls and destroyed inanimate objects that were handy when he was out of control.

Thank God his rage hadn't been turned on a person. *At least to my knowledge*, she reminded herself as the phone rang again, and several more times within the next hour as she let the answering machine pick up.

It was decision-making time. She had to do something about changing things, making sure that the girls were safe. And that probably meant moving.

She still resisted that option, hoping it wouldn't really become necessary.

That it wasn't a false hope.

CHAPTER TWENTY

"Yes, it means moving, Julia."

Diana's tone on the phone was emphatic. "The police can't protect you, can't really do anything until after the fact." She sighed. "I don't want to hear something worse has happened, Julia—after it's happened. Last night with Alyssa being run off the road was bad enough, not to mention Samantha's injury at Crystal Mountain."

There was a silence on the lines.

"I'm really at a stalemate, Diana." Julia stood in her kitchen, her hand stilled on the spoon that mixed color into her frosting. "My mind is whirling with options: should I sell, move the girls away from their lifelong friends, take a job somewhere for the most pay a high school graduate can command, and be absent in their lives because I have to commute?"

"Why would you have to commute?"

"Because, unlike you and Ted, I don't have the qualifications for a high-paying job, and the proceeds from the sale of this house would not allow me to live in the greater Seattle area because the prices are beyond my budget—and my ability to purchase another house. In other words, I won't even qualify for a nice little cottage in a safe neighborhood at my present income and projected down payment. I'm completely out of the market for anything comparable to the house and neighborhood we live in now—or even if I wanted to rent a place. The cost, either way, is beyond my means if I leave here."

Another silence.

"But you have a valuable house, Julia."

"With a big mortgage that Peter has to subsidize so long as we live here until both girls are eighteen. If I sell, take the profit and move, he's off the hook. If we stay and wait until both girls are in college, then I only owe him half of the value at the time we were divorced, and I get the benefit of inflation." A pause. "I make more from all of my odd jobs than I could make on a regular nine to five office job, which is why I do all of the things I do. In the final analysis, staying put is the cheapest way to go, and then the girls aren't disrupted from their school and lives." She gave a wry laugh. "Even though their father no longer lives here."

"Why didn't Ted and I know this back then, Julia? Maybe we could have helped you negotiate a better deal. And now we're also mortgaged to the hilt and can't help financially, even though our combined income is good. We're leveraged out for several years into the future, until after inflation overcomes our debt."

"I doubt if you could have helped me make a better

divorce agreement, Diana. At the time my lawyer said it was the best anyone could do for me." A hesitation. "None of us anticipated the terror tactics after the divorce."

Diana's long sigh came over the wires. "Jeez. I don't know what to say except that your safety has to come first." Another pause. "It's a Catch-22. If you leave you'll have to downsize your lifestyle; if you stay you're in jeopardy from Peter."

"I know. If our threat really is Peter."

"What do you mean? Of course it's Peter."

"I know you're probably right, Diana. But lately I've wondered. He's so emphatic that he isn't responsible for these incidents, and although he's mentally disturbed, he's never seemed so uncaring. He's always been protective of his girls."

"What else would he be? His responses to his actions are always skewed."

"Again I know you might be right, and I know he prowls around the house, has threatened me and acted like a crazy lunatic at times." Julia hesitated. "But it's hard to accept that he's so nuts that he'd do harm to his own daughters. That's beyond my understanding of who I was married to for all of those years."

"But he's flipped out, Julia. He's not the person you married, please remember that."

Julia swallowed hard, knowing that if she accepted the fact that Peter was that crazy, she had no option but to move, to change the life she'd established to support her girls, to accept that they'd have to alter their whole lifestyle. Maybe she was in denial, afraid of change, of having to live on the edge of financial disaster, because of giving up what she had. But maybe she had no choice.

"I'll think about this, Diana, and come to a decision—because I must, for the sake of Alyssa, Sam, and me."

"Promise?"

"I promise."

A half hour later Julia had just finished decorating the cake when the phone rang again. She sighed. It had been a long morning, beginning with her daybreak run, which she'd resumed a week earlier on the trail that had spooked her. Since her other neighbors also jogged early, she'd decided it was safe, because there was always another person on the path.

"Hello," she said, grabbing the phone.

"Julia, it's me again."

"What's up, Diana?" Julia could hear, what?—stress? fear?—in her sister's voice. Instantly, her body tensed to full alert. Something was wrong.

"Have you heard the news, Julia?"

"No. I just finished a wedding cake." She gulped a breath, remembering that Diana was the closest of kin to contact at Alyssa's and Samantha's schools. "Are the—"

"They're fine," Diana said, knowing she referred to the girls. "This is about your jogging path."

"The trail behind my house?"

A pause.

"Diana, what are you trying to say?"

"You haven't seen the news?"

"I've been busy. I never watch TV while I'm working." Julia switched the phone to her other ear as she slipped the cake into the refrigerator. "What's happened?"

"There's been another murder on the jogging path."

"What?" She slammed the refrigerator door.

"A woman was found dead, shot in the back, on the trail that you used to jog in the morning."

"I just started jogging again this week," Julia admitted. "But I chose a time when there's lots of activity on the path: people running, walking their dogs, even riding bikes."

"For God's sake. Are you nuts, Julia? Why didn't you mention that before?"

"I guess I knew you'd worry."

There was a long pause.

Julia also knew her sister didn't understand the dynamics of being stalked by an ex-husband, that there was a point where the person being victimized had to make a stand, had to resume their life or risk being controlled by the abuser's manipulations forever. Judy, her therapist, had understood, so long as safety precautions were in place, but then Judy wasn't as emotionally involved as a sister.

"Shit," Diana said finally. Her disapproval seemed to fly over the wires. "Did you run this morning?"

"Uh-huh."

"When?"

"After the girls went to school, probably between eight and eight-thirty, well after it was full daylight."

"The woman was shot before nine."

Julia's breath felt trapped in her throat as she asked the next question. "Has she been identified?"

"Her name hasn't been released yet, until the family has all been notified. But—"

"But what?" Julia braced herself for what would come next.

"The description of this woman sounded like you, Julia, and I—got scared when I heard the news five minutes ago." Her sucked-in breath sounded in Julia's ear. "It's why I called, to make sure you were safe."

Julia nodded, and then realized her sister couldn't see her reaction; she needed to speak it. "I'm so sorry, Sis. I'm fine, just upset that I've caused such stress in your life."

"Thank God you're okay, Julia!" A pause. "And as far as the stress, I guess I'm just making points here." Diana snorted a laugh. "If I'm ever in a bad place, dear sister, you'll have to put up with me."

"You know I would." A pause as Julia's thoughts reverted to the murder.

"Please, Diana, tell me what you know."

A silence went by.

"I hate to scare you, Julia, but you're gonna hear it on the news anyway," Diana began. "The woman was killed less than a mile from you, shot in the back sometime this morning. The reporter said she appeared to be in her thirties, was slender, and had long blond hair—your general description, Julia."

Julia plunked down onto a chair, suddenly chilled to the bone. The dead woman who resembled her was obviously ambushed only minutes after she herself had run that very part of the trail. "Were there any witnesses?"

"None, except the male jogger who found her had heard the gunshot but was too far behind the woman on the path to see anything."

"Oh, God! What next?"

"You moving, Julia." Diana's reply was instant, her concern evident in her tone. "I'm so afraid for you and the girls that I can hardly sleep at night."

"We can't conclude that this woman's death is connected to me, Diana. That's far-fetched—if that's what you're implying."

"I know it could all be coincidental, but in light of all

the weird things that have happened to you in the past year, Julia, we can't just dismiss this as coincidence." Diana hesitated. "I admit that my fear for you was the first thought that hit my brain after hearing that terrible news. For a second, I felt paralyzed, wondering what I'd do if you were the dead woman."

"I'm so sorry, Sis. I hate what's going on, too."

"So, will you promise me again that you'll consider moving?"

Julia stood, forcing her shoulders back, her eyes on the woods that crowded against her backyard fence. Did she really have much of a choice?

"The woman's death could be random." She cleared her throat to remove the hoarseness from her voice. "She, too, could have had a crazy husband or boyfriend. I want to hear the facts before I make a sudden move that will have such a drastic effect on Sam and Alyssa." A pause. "I appreciate you more than I can say, Diana. I don't know what we'd do without you and Ted. But I hope you can understand what's at stake here."

"That's the problem, Julia. I do. It's your life."

After they'd hung up, Julia couldn't get Diana's words out of her head. For all that she wanted to deny it, she realized that Diana could be right. She could have been the dead jogger.

"Jeez! Thank God!"

Julia had answered the phone thinking Diana was calling back with more words of caution.

"Earl?" She hardly recognized his voice.

"Yeah, it's me, sweetheart. I just heard the news, saw a television clip of the dead woman being placed into an emergency vehicle, and was terrified that that crazy husband of yours had flipped out completely."

"Ex-husband."

"I stand corrected—and so relieved that the sawdust has gone out of my legs." A pause. "Good thing I'm sitting down with a desk in front of me."

"You thought it was me, too?"

"Too?"

"Uh-huh, my sister called a short time ago."

"Oh, Julia, joking aside, it was like I'd been hit so hard in the gut that I couldn't breathe." A pause. "Thank the good Lord that you're okay."

For a moment she didn't know what to say. Somehow he'd become an island in a sea of uncertainty, the person who automatically understood her problem with Peter because of his experience as an attorney in high-profile criminal cases, and because he was in his own personal hell with a fearful wife who couldn't cope with life.

The tyranny of the weak, she thought, as she had before. He was cemented to a woman who could never stand alone. And unless he could resolve his marital problems there was no future for her with him—even though it was so obvious that he cared for her.

"I'm flying to San Francisco tomorrow morning, Julia," he said. "I want you to promise that you won't jog on that trail for now."

"I've already promised my sister, and now I promise you, too." She switched the phone to her other ear so that she could continue to box her wedding cake. "How long will you be gone?"

"Two or three days, I'm not sure. I have to be present for depositions in an upcoming case I'm representing."

"Good luck with that," she said, trying to sound upbeat, as though she was not emotionally involved in his life—which she was now—from the wings of his personal stage.

The ensuing silence was so long that Julia wondered if they'd been disconnected. Finally, his voice was in her ear again.

"Be safe until I get back, okay?"

"Okay."

The dial tone sounded in her ear.

Somewhere in the middle of the night Julia heard her bedside phone ring. Still half asleep, she grabbed the receiver, too disoriented to realize that phones never ring in the wee hours unless it's a wrong number—or a disaster.

"Hello?"

"Is this Julia?"

"Yes, it is." She sat up, not recognizing the female voice. "Who is this?"

"Never mind," the throaty voice told her. "I have your man here." A raspy laugh. "Did you know that he's great in bed?"

The woman was still speaking when Julia slammed the receiver back into its cradle. And then, wide awake, she stared into the night beyond her bedroom windows.

What in the hell was Peter doing now?

CHAPTER TWENTY-ONE

It was déjà vu.

Oh God! It was happening again, but on a different level. There was no imminent danger . . . and yet . . . What did she know that her mind rejected, that seemed so forbidden?

Topsy cringed against the car seat, hoping she was wrong. And then she saw the shadowy figure move from the Honda and dart into the woods, the person she'd followed from downtown Seattle out over the Lake Washington Bridge on I-90 to Issaquah.

Her heart almost stopped.

How? Why could this be so?

Hadn't she protected everyone from the horror that her mind wouldn't even allow herself to remember?

It was his fault, because of what he'd done. And hers because she hadn't stopped him, had been in denial . . . but denial of what? Oh God, she couldn't remember. And now this. . . .

He hadn't believed anyone could be on to him, that she would know his secrets, that others around them could pick up on his evil—and be engulfed by it.

Dear God, she prayed silently. *Don't let this be so.* With tears streaming down her face she looked upward, into a night sky devoid of stars.

Help me God. Don't I count?

But maybe I was wrong, Topsy thought. Maybe it was too dark to see clearly.

Let me be wrong, she thought a short time later as she followed the blue Honda back toward the city.

But she wasn't wrong.

Oh Father in Heaven, she pleaded again. *Why have You forsaken me?*

After that she followed mindlessly. She knew that somewhere in the swirling fog of her mind there was an answer.

She couldn't face that yet.

CHAPTER TWENTY-TWO

"SERIAL KILLER STRIKES AGAIN!"

The girls had just left for school, and Julia sat down with her coffee to read the newspaper, unfolding it to the horrifying headline. Another woman had been found dead in South Seattle, apparently brutally murdered, according to the article, which she quickly scanned.

Julia had just been returning to an emotional point where she felt comfortable being on the jogging trail again, and now she was overwhelmed with apprehension once more. As she read she realized that the two cases, although they both dealt with murder, were separate, the M.O. completely different. No one had connected the two, not the police or the media.

She put down the paper, her coffee forgotten on the table. The realization did nothing to help her nervous system, to give her reassurance that the shooting victims on the trail hadn't been targeted because someone thought it was her.

Magical thinking, she reminded herself. Was she exaggerating, reading into incidents, because she'd interjected her own scenario with Peter into the bigger picture of the world?

I need to discuss this with Judy, she told herself. She didn't think she was projecting, but what if she were and didn't know it because she was off kilter about all the scary things that had been happening? Was it possible that, because of several years of extreme stress, she could have lost her perspective, could have become paranoid, even just a little?

She jumped up. *Action cures fear,* she reminded herself. *Get to work. Don't dwell on the unknown that robs you of motivation.*

The suddenness of the front doorbell being rung jarred her. For a second she was paralyzed. Then she moved into the hall, momentarily staring at the door. Taking deep breaths, she told herself that this was her house, a safe neighborhood, and no one hesitated to answer the door—most of which were never locked like hers.

With resolve she stepped forward, flipped the bolt, and swung open the door—to see Mrs. Bullard.

She was of another generation, and not the modern version: short, round, kindly, and inquisitive once there was a neighborhood cause—such as the one Diana had started with her request to be updated about unusual situations in the neighborhood concerning Julia and her girls.

"Mrs. Bullard."

The old woman nodded.

There was an awkward silence.

"Please come in," Julia said, stepping aside.

"My dear," she said, walking into the foyer, "I don't want to disturb your work." She smiled, her face collapsing into a network of lines. "But since my talk with your sister I felt obligated to inform you about someone walking around your house when I knew no one was at home."

"Who? A stranger?"

"Oh, no." She smiled reassuringly. "It was your husband."

"Peter?"

"Uh-huh."

Julia was taken aback. What was the old woman trying to say? she wondered. That her husband was stalking her? Or that she thought it was appropriate that he came back to the house where he'd once lived?

"You know that my husband and I are divorced?"

"Of course I do, dear." The woman hesitated, smiling. "I know that couples have problems and sometimes they can't be worked out." She waved a hand. "It's not for me to say how anyone should solve them." Another pause. "I'm just informing you as your sister requested. "Your husband is often watching you."

"My God, Mrs. Bullard. What do you mean?"

Her neighbor had stepped back onto the porch, where she turned to face Julia. "Well, you know. As he says, he wants his family back." She smiled sweetly, oblivious to the more serious ramifications. "And I can't say that I blame him. Family is more important than anything else."

Julia stared. She couldn't believe that old-fashioned view for one second. The woman had probably never heard the term "domestic abuse."

Julia was direct. "Why haven't you told me this before, Mrs. Bullard?"

The old woman smiled again. "I like you both, dear, and I hate to see you apart. In my day—"

Julia cut her off. "I know, Mrs. Bullard, no couples were divorced back then." With the woman's words still ringing in her head, she added, "They lived together in silent desperation, the woman fearing to displease the man. Right?"

"Uh, yes, dear, we never—"

"Rocked the boat?" Julia said, her annoyance growing. Age or not, the woman had no right to suggest she and Peter should get back together. "Peter is unstable," she began. "And he and I will never be together again, Mrs. Bullard. In my day we women don't have to stay with an abusive husband." She gulped a breath. "We don't have to be trapped by a man who threatens and accuses us, physically or verbally."

Mrs. Bullard stepped back, obviously unprepared for an assault on her own principles. "I'm sure you're right, my dear," she said finally. "But please remind yourself that most men aren't abusive like that."

"I've realized that, Mrs. Bullard. And I hope you're right about most men." Julia sucked in a breath. "Believing that would help me recover from Peter."

And then she saw the old woman walk away from her house. But the one lingering realization was that she was right: Peter *was* watching their lives.

A frightening thought.

Julia drove up to Judy's house the next morning in the Cherokee, which she'd just picked up at the garage, only to discover that her therapist was about to back out of her garage and leave for work. Surprised, Julia parked in front of her house rather than the driveway. A glance at her watch said she was early for their appointment—so Julia could bid on another wallpapering job in return for her therapy sessions. Judy had raved about the last project as being perfect.

"I have an emergency appointment," Judy said, getting out of her car. "I left the house open for you and we can talk about your bid later. Just lock up when you leave." Her smile was brief; she was obviously concerned about a patient.

"No problem, Judy," Julia said, and hesitated. "I need to make an appointment, too. An, uh, professional one at your office."

Judy stopped in midstep, about to slip back behind the wheel of her car. "What's happened?" Her gaze was suddenly direct. "Are you and the girls okay?"

Julia nodded. "I'll fill you in later." She hesitated. "The gist of my current dilemma is whether or not I should move."

"Oh, God! Something bad has happened."

"No, just more of the same." Julia managed a smile. "I'll fill you in later. You need to go, and I need to get to work."

Judy stared a moment longer, then nodded and got into her car. Within seconds she had disappeared down the street. Julia followed a few minutes later, after she'd measured for the job and locked Judy's house.

She'd make that appointment when she got home.

Earl e-mailed her from San Francisco, using the private email address that he'd created for their correspondence.

You okay? Thinking of you. Looking forward to seeing you after I get back.

Me, too, she replied. *It'll be nice to know I have a good friend in greater Seattle.*

Before she went to bed she checked her e-mail, pleased that there was another message from Earl. *What's wrong? Has something happened that I should know?*

The usual, she typed. *Unexplainable happenings: an elderly neighbor who has seen Peter prowling the house, another murder in Seattle and increasing pressure to sell and move.* She dropped a line and then wrote, *Aside from that, everything else is okay.* She included her hope that things went well for him, and then signed off.

A few hours later, unable to sleep, she stared at her computer screen, looking at Earl's latest response to her last e-mail. Aside from anything else, she was impressed. He'd picked up on her distress, the same disturbing thoughts that had robbed her of sleep, the reason she was on her computer at three in the morning.

She decided to explain, because it was easier to type her fears onto the screen than to express them out loud. She hit the Send button, which relayed her message to Earl in California. Somehow she felt better after explaining her fears, and she went back to bed knowing she'd go right to sleep.

She'd hardly gotten under her quilt when the phone rang on the bedside table. She grabbed it on the first ring, at once apprehensive but determined that the girls would not be awakened by the sound.

"Hello?"

"I just got your e-mail," Earl said in her ear, bringing her upright in the bed.

"I only sent it a couple of minutes ago."

"I was online when it came in."

"Don't you sleep?" She smiled into the dark room. "It's the middle of the night."

"I could ask you the same. Why were you still up?"

Julia leaned back against the headboard, her pillow behind her back. "I had some things on my mind, Earl, and couldn't sleep, so I checked my e-mail." She gave a laugh. "You know me, always productive with my time." She paused. "No, you might not know that about me."

" 'Course I do, sweetheart, and a lot more."

A silence went by.

"Like what?" she asked, knowing the question was inane.

"Like you're beautiful, talented, sexy, and a wonderful mother who looks out for her family before anything else in her life."

"Whew! I don't know what to say to such lavish compliments."

"Your thanks will do." She heard the amusement in his tone. "Because it's all true, and much more."

She adjusted the phone away from her hair. "Earl, I'm wondering if you've had too much wine."

He laughed out loud. "Maybe I did, but that was a few hours ago." A pause. "I called because I'm worried about you. Your e-mail sounded like you're having problems."

"Just the usual—Peter."

"Ah, your old nemesis." Another pause. "Is that what's prompting the thoughts to sell your house?"

"Partly."

"Partly?" He repeated. "What else?"

"I'll explain when I see you," she said, evading.

"Explain now, Julia. Or I'll worry away the rest of the night instead of sleeping."

She told him that because the woman who'd been shot on her jogging path resembled her, Diana was worried sick that she'd been the intended target and was encouraging her to sell and move. Also Peter was pressuring her about the danger to his family.

"No shit!"

Another silence while he digested her words.

"And then there was the obscene call last night about this time."

"Explain." All humor was gone from his voice.

She repeated what the woman had said, that she'd hung up before the woman finished her sick spiel.

"Did you call the police?"

"No. I get a little tired of calling the cops, as I'm sure they're getting tired of hearing from me."

"That's what they're there for, Julia. To protect the public, and that means you." A pause. "Promise that you'll call them if this happens again."

She sighed. "I will."

"And I want to hear all the details of this when I get back. Okay?"

"Of course."

They talked a few minutes more about his case and then hung up, but not before he warned her again to be careful. "You're important to me, remember that," he said just before she heard the dial tone.

And those were the words she went to sleep with.

The next morning she drove the girls to school because Alyssa's stack of research books was too big to manage on the school bus. Julia was coming back into the kitchen just as the phone rang. She grabbed the receiver and was surprised to hear Sandi, the bookkeeper at the lumberyard where Peter bought supplies.

"Sandi!" Julia said, pleased to hear the voice that had been so familiar to her when she was still doing the books for Peter's construction company. "Goodness! What a pleasant surprise."

"Hope so after you hear what I have to say."

"Uh-oh. That doesn't sound good." Julia dropped her purse on the kitchen counter. "Go ahead, shoot."

"Guess I'd better, now that I got up my nerve to call."

There was another long pause.

"I don't bite, Sandi."

"I know. Here goes." Her indrawn breath came over the wire. "Peter owes the company a lot of money, he hasn't been paying his bill and—and I wondered if you might talk to him. My boss is getting pretty desperate about this or I wouldn't have called you." She hesitated. "We know you aren't responsible, Julia, but we were hoping you might be able to influence him."

"Oh God." Julia plunked herself down on a counter stool. "I wish I could help, but I'm the wrong person to ask. Peter is too upset with me already to listen to my advice."

"I figured as much, Julia. You were our last hope before we have to turn him over to collections." She sighed. "We hate to do that because you've been such good customers in the past—before you guys split up."

"I'm so sorry, Sandi. I don't know what's wrong with Peter these days. He's—"

"Yeah, I know. He's gone a little crazy. Everyone is talking about it."

"What do you mean?"

"Uh, hey, I shouldn't have said that."

"No, c'mon. I need to know, for my own sake and the sake of my girls."

With a little more prodding Sandi related some of the gossip among the builders, that Peter seemed to have a growing paranoia and odd behavior, that he didn't show up for appointments, that his dress had become slovenly, and worse yet, he was often heard mumbling angrily under his breath. "His cronies are steering clear of him, Julia. Everyone thinks he's lost it."

After they hung up Julia sat staring into space. Had Peter finally gone round the bend completely? God help them if he had.

CHAPTER TWENTY-THREE

"You really need your own kids, Sis," Julia told Diana, who'd come to get the girls for the night. "Isn't it a little early to bake Christmas cookies? It's still a few weeks until Thanksgiving."

"True." Diana grinned. "I'll put them in the freezer until the holidays."

Ted raised his brows fondly from behind his wife. "Hey Julia, you must remember that your little sister is a planner. If one scenario doesn't work, she fits in another one."

Julia grinned. Ted knew his wife, probably better than she knew Diana. Her sister had always been big on traditions, and had dovetailed into Ted's Scandinavian family with their holiday baking and decorations. And once she'd started baking the cookie recipes that Ted's mother had given her, she'd included Alyssa and Samantha for the marathon, which included a sleepover. It had become a holiday tradition for Diana and the girls, and they looked forward to it, in fact wouldn't miss the annual event even if they had to skip a school basketball game.

"Have fun," Julia told them, hugging each girl as they went out the front door with an overnight bag.

"And take care of Bow," Diana replied. "My little Shih Tzu is going to protect you while the girls are at my place."

Julia grinned. The little dog had once been their puppy, until Peter, who hated any animal in his house, had kicked it and an outraged Diana had rescued Bow, denouncing the abuse and adopting Bow on the spot. Julia had no option but to let her, not trusting Peter's temper, knowing his example was not a healthy one for their daughters, and that she couldn't control his outbursts, which could harm the trusting little animal. Both she and the girls had grieved for their loss, but Julia had realized that it was for the best; at that time Peter had just started seeing Dr. Kornsweig.

Alyssa turned before stepping off the porch. "Mom, why don't you come with us?"

"Sweetie, this is your tradition with your aunt." Julia smiled reassuringly. She realized that her oldest daughter was worried about her being alone, a concern that no sixteen-year-old should have as a burden. "Believe me, honey, I have things to do." She shrugged, as though unconcerned. "I'm perfectly fine, and don't forget that we have an alarm system and double locked doors, not to mention that there are many neighbors on our street."

Alyssa came back and kissed her again. "Just checking, Mom. Me and Sam love you and need you to stay safe."

"Of course I understand. And I promise that I'll be safe. I'll call your aunt Diana if anything comes up, okay?"

Julia watched as her girls piled into Ted's Mercedes and waved as they left the driveway and headed down the street. Then she shut and locked the door, bracing herself for the night ahead.

"Whew!" Julia leaned back in her chair, her eyes on the computer screen. She'd just finished the first draft of the manual, and she felt like celebrating. A glance at the clock told her it was going on midnight. Surprised, she saved her work and turned off the computer.

"Hey," she told Bow at her feet. "No wonder you've been so restless. You need to go out to the backyard."

As they moved through the house to the kitchen and the sliding glass door in the breakfast nook, she kept up a running commentary with the little dog, who pranced beside her, wagging his tail at her words.

"You're so good, Bow. You hardly ever bark, you never complain, and you love us all unconditionally." She grinned down at him as she opened the slider so that he could step onto the patio and then the backyard. "You do your business and then I'll let you back inside."

She closed the door and went to the refrigerator for the bottle of Chardonnay that she'd kept until she completed the manual, her way of celebrating a hard job done.

Well, almost done, she reminded herself as she poured the wine into a goblet. She still needed to go over the whole manuscript in one marathon day, so she could concentrate on the details, make sure that the instructions were clear, and that they worked.

But for now, I'm celebrating, she told herself. She'd earned a glass of wine, maybe even two.

As she sipped, enjoying the peace of the quiet house, she decided on a single-serving container of her frozen chicken vegetable soup, complete with her own tomatoes, herbs, zucchini, peas, and beans from her garden.

A very late supper, Julia thought as she defrosted her soup in the microwave. She felt mellow, relishing her time alone, realizing that she would be okay once she really was by herself in a few years when the girls were in college.

Her serenity was interrupted by Bow's sudden barking. As she ran to the draped glass door, she realized that the little dog had backed up to the other side, still barking frantically. She unlocked the slider and flung it open. Bow ran inside, then back to the patio, barking at the nearby rhododendrons and azalea bushes, before darting into the house again.

A mellow Shih Tzu hardly ever barked, unless terribly frightened. That thought hit Julia's brain in a flash.

Someone or something was out there, just beyond the patio.

It was Peter.

The thought came unbidden. Hadn't the girls seen him at night prowling around? Mrs. Bullard?

Her anger was instant.

She stood in the doorway, her eyes on the dark foliage beyond the patio. "Okay, Peter. I know you're out there."

No response.

She stepped down to the patio, even more enraged that he thought he could terrorize her. "Stop acting like a two-year-old—a coward. Show yourself like a man."

There was a movement, and then a dark shape leaped forward.

Instantly filled with terror, Julia's body reacted of its own volition. She jumped back inside the house and slammed the door, locking it instantly behind the drapes.

There was a tug on the outside door handle. The lock held. Then she heard faint scratching on the glass.

Julia stared, her knees folding under her. She sat down hard against the base of the counter, her eyes fastened on the door that was still draped against the night. Bow huddled against her, silent, his face pointed toward the door as well.

But she felt the eyes that probed the exterior glass, trying to find her. She scooted backward, around the end of the counter to the kitchen, where she couldn't be seen from the patio.

Silly, she told herself shakily. No one can see though drapes. Unless it was the devil himself.

Oh, God, please help me, she prayed silently. She knew it wasn't the devil out there, separated from her by a thin sheet of glass, but it was someone evil, someone who'd tried to—to what? Gain access to her house? To kill her?

Peter? The man she'd been married to, had slept with, shared two daughters with?

It was mind boggling. She couldn't even comprehend that Peter could be so crazy.

She lifted her arm, groping with her hand for the phone that was on the counter. When she connected, she lifted the receiver and brought it down to her, where she still cringed on the floor. Quickly, she punched in 911, and when the operator answered, she whispered her address and that someone was trying to get into her house.

As the dispatcher instructed her, she waited on the line until the patrol car pulled into her driveway. "Answer the front door," the woman at the other end of 911 instructed. "It's an officer."

Julia, feeling shell-shocked, did as she was told.

Two uniformed policemen were on the other side of the front door when Julia opened it. Quickly, they secured her property, both inside and out. There was no one in the backyard, and no evidence of anyone trying to get into her house.

Par for the course, she thought, after the officers had taken down her statement about what had happened. But there was no evidence, no proof that what she was reporting was true. They did the usual spiel of caution, that they knew about her marital situation and would check Peter's whereabouts, and then they left, their patrol car moving quietly down the street, so as not to disturb the upscale neighborhood.

She watched them go, thinking dire thoughts about her situation. She needed to move. It was obvious. Something was going on that law enforcement couldn't address without proof. She had no options—unless there was a tragedy—and then she might not be around anyway.

No way, she told herself. She, and her girls, would be long gone before that. They had to be.

Julia knew she'd never sleep, but she got ready for bed nevertheless. She sat down on her quilt, her back propped against the pillows, and she found herself becoming more angry with each passing second.

Impulsively, she grabbed the phone and called Peter.

His voice mail picked up, announcing that he wasn't home, but please leave a message.

"You bastard!" she muttered into the silence of his message machine. "Of course you're not home. You're too busy terrorizing me."

She slammed down the phone. The son of a bitch. She wasn't about to lay down and play dead, allowing him to keep up his threatening presence. Somehow, she meant to stop him, no matter what that might mean to their daughters. She hadn't done anything but divorce a crazy person; she didn't deserve such a stalking presence in her life. Nor did their daughters.

And then, her alarm system armed, the doors locked, she got under the covers—and stared out the windows into the November night. A friend had once told her that insomnia wasn't so bad if you reminded yourself that you're resting, if not sleeping.

I'm resting, she told herself for the next several hours. But her mind would not shut down her fears and the future decisions that must be made. Close to dawn she finally fell asleep and didn't awaken until the phone rang around eight in the morning. She made a grab for it, horrified that she'd slept in, even though it was Saturday and the girls wouldn't be home until evening, after their cookie-baking day with their aunt.

She sat up in bed and cleared her throat before answering. "Yes, Julia here."

"Mrs. Farley?" a male voice asked.

She sat up straighter. "Yes."

"This is Officer Peterson calling from the sheriff's office." A pause. "I'm responding to your call of last night and your request to know if Peter Farley was involved in the disturbance at your house."

"Yes, Peter is my ex-husband."

"He checked out. As far as our department is concerned, this man isn't a suspect."

"What do you mean?"

"Only that our officers tracked him down and he had a legitimate alibi. He was miles away from your house at the time you called 911."

"But that's impossible."

" 'Fraid not, Mrs. Farley." There was a pause, and she

heard the rustle of papers. "He isn't a suspect. Whoever was in your backyard wasn't your former husband."

She thanked him and hung up, puzzled and afraid.

If it wasn't Peter, then who?

The person on the jogging trail?

Don't go there, she told herself. You aren't the target of a serial killer.

Or was she?

CHAPTER TWENTY-FOUR

SHE HAD ONLY STARTED THE COFFEE IN THE MORNING when the phone rang again. This time it was an outraged Peter.

"I don't appreciate this, Julia. You're the one who says we should get on with our lives, and that's what I was trying to do last night."

"So what was that, Peter?" She tried to keep the anger out of her tone.

"I had a date. I was at the woman's place."

Surprise took away an immediate response to his revelation. It was the last thing she'd expected to hear.

"Did you hear what I said, Julia?"

"Of course I did." She hesitated. "So it wasn't you in the backyard last night."

"Hell no! And I'm tired of being accused of things I didn't do!"

"Let's not get carried away, Peter. There are plenty of incidents that you are guilty of, as some of my neighbors have reported." Before he could answer, she went on quickly. "But I'm glad it wasn't you this time, for the sake of your daughters, if nothing else. And I'm happy that you're dating. That's very healthy, for your emotional well-being and self-esteem."

A silence went by.

"Is that advice based on experience?"

Julia's senses went to red alert. For years she'd been attuned to his deceptively calm voice, which really said he was about to explode. *You idiot*, she chastised herself. *Why did you even comment about his date?* He'd interpreted it as an admission that she was dating, too.

"No, it's based on all the self-help books I've read and my therapy sessions." The last thing she wanted to do was undermine his dating women. What she wanted, hoped, and prayed for was that he'd find someone else.

Her words calmed his paranoia about her, and they hung up. Julia's coffee was done and she poured a cup, but her thoughts were on what had happened in the night.

If not Peter, then who?

It was such a disturbing thought that she went to the patio door and closed the drapes. No one could hide in the woods and watch her now.

But it was hard to get started on her work for the day. She felt the presence of someone out there, watching.

Julia sat back in the chair cushion in Judy's cozy office out on Madison Street in Seattle, relieved that all her fears and concerns were out in the open, that she'd aired her big dilemma of whether or not she should move. She'd explained that now that Peter was dating maybe the problem on that front would get better, but then there was her new fear about the mysterious presence in her backyard. Judy, who sat across the coffee table from her, took several seconds to digest what she'd heard.

"So you're saying that Peter is dating now?"

"That's what I understand, from him and the police officer who substantiated that he was visiting a friend at the time of my 911 call."

"Do you think he knows you've been seeing a man too?"

Julia shook her head. "But mine is nothing more than friendship."

"At this point," Judy said, correctly reading Julia's feelings. "I sense that you're really hooked on this guy." Her gaze was suddenly direct, but caring. "Tell me more about this man."

Julia filled her in on some of the details she hadn't mentioned before to Judy: Earl's name, occupation, his best-selling book, and how they'd met.

Judy leaned forward, and Julia could tell that she was trying to keep her professional demeanor but was disturbed by what she was hearing.

"You say that Earl has a bad marriage, is in fact married to an emotional cripple, as he referred to his wife? That he'd like to be divorced but can't until his wife is more stable?"

Julia nodded. "Yeah, he's unhappy about his personal life." She hesitated, then after reminding herself that her revelations to Judy were confidential, went on. "He feels trapped, because he can't abandon his responsibilities to his sick wife and their children, who need him as a stabilizing influence."

"He said that?"

"In so many words, yes. And I sense his frustration

and despair. It comes through in every conversation we have."

Another silence.

Then the timer went off on Judy's desk, indicating that it was the end of the session. For a moment longer she scribbled notes, then put her tablet aside and stood up. Julia followed suit.

"Listen, if I didn't have back-to-back appointments I'd have you stay longer," Judy said, flashing a brief smile. "I feel that we need to talk more about the situation. Can you make another appointment for the near future?"

"I'll call tomorrow after I've checked my calendar." Julia wondered again what had disturbed Judy. She hesitated at the door, her hand on the knob. "Would you agree that I shouldn't make a decision yet about selling, until I see how things go?"

As she spoke, Julia turned to face her therapist. That question had been her main focus for her therapy session today, and she still didn't feel any more resolved about the answer than when she'd arrived. She gave a wry laugh as Judy seemed momentarily hesitant to reply. "Maybe Peter's finally beginning to get over his obsession with his family, and maybe the other incidents were random," she added, her response falling into a momentary silence.

"We'll talk about this at your next session." Judy's professional persona was suddenly restored. She stood in the doorway as Julia left. "In the meantime, stay cautious, Julia," she called after her. "Keep all of the safety measures in place for you and the girls."

And then Julia was in the parking lot headed for her Cherokee. All the way home she couldn't shake the feeling that her therapist had become concerned about something relating to Earl. What? It didn't make sense.

Maybe I'm imagining things again, Julia thought. But she would make that appointment tomorrow. And then she'd be direct with Judy, ask if her perception had been real or imagined.

For now she needed to get home before Alyssa and Sam. She didn't need Judy's caution about safety measures. She meant to keep her girls out of harm's way.

No matter what that meant.

CHAPTER TWENTY-FIVE

TOPSY PULLED HER MERCEDES INTO THE ONLY EMPTY space in the small parking area. She was a little late because of traffic and hoped her therapist hadn't thought she'd forgotten the time again.

Operant conditioning, she thought.

That might be the conclusion her therapist had jumped to, because of all the missed appointments in the past, appointments her husband had paid for and never let her forget about.

But that wasn't the case this time. She needed professional input. She was desperate, even though she hoped her therapist wouldn't pick up on that aspect of her fears.

Keep it together. You can't lose it now.

She went into the empty waiting room, sat down on the edge of a chair, and waited for the slider that separated the inner from the outer office to open and reveal her therapist's face. Topsy knew that a beep sounded in the inner office when a patient came into the waiting room.

She waited less than a minute. The slider remained closed, but the door opened to reveal her therapist, who smiled and beckoned her into the therapy room.

"How are you doing?" she asked Topsy, closing the door.

Topsy hesitated but took the overstuffed chair across the coffee table from where she knew her therapist would sit. "I don't think I'm doing very well." She smiled tremulously, hating the sensation of tremors at the edges of her mouth.

Her counselor sat down, her expression upbeat, as though expecting positive symptoms of emotional growth since their last session.

"So, what's going on, Topsy?"

Topsy was about to respond but was unexpectedly overcome by emotion.

Silently, her therapist handed her a Kleenex, then gave her time to compose herself.

"I thought I loved my husband back then," Topsy said finally, suddenly avoiding facing the answer to the question. "He was so assured, so protective and caring, unlike my own father."

"Your father?"

"Uh-huh." There was a hesitation as Topsy considered. "My dad was thirty-five, my mom thirty-four, when I met my husband, and I was eighteen. My parents always seemed like kids to me.

"You told me that your dad was only seventeen when you were born?"

Topsy nodded. "And my mom was sixteen." A pause. "Their families made them get married because my mother was pregnant with me."

"And the marriage worked?"

Topsy inclined her head. "I think so, as far as I know. At least they're still married."

"Why wouldn't you know?"

"My husband and father never got along in the early years of my marriage, and of course it came down to a choice for me: my parents or my husband." A pause. "Of course I chose my husband, so I have no place to go if I left my marriage, and no way to support myself and our two kids." She hesitated. "I've never worked beyond a couple of months and my parents were angry when I got married—a glamorous career was my mother's dream for herself that was cut short by having me. Then I gave up the very career she'd once wanted."

"So you have no contact with them at all?"

Topsy bit down on her lower lip, willing the trembling away. "My husband forbid it a long time ago, said it wasn't good for me or the kids."

"I see," her therapist said, jotting notes on her tablet. "I hadn't realized you were cut off from your family. You never mentioned it during previous sessions."

Topsy managed a weak smile. "I guess not. There were other, more pertinent issues." She hesitated. "I suspect my parents are still immature in some ways. Their way to cope with serious problems is to eliminate the source." She shrugged, and then her shoulders jerked of their own volition, another of her nervous reactions lately—involuntary movements of her body parts. "Anyway, that's what my younger sister says." Topsy broke off, trying to control her emotions.

"Are you saying that they wouldn't come to your aid if you chose to leave your marriage?"

Topsy nodded, feeling even more desperate. "They'd believe that at my age, I needed to find my own way out, that I'd gotten myself into this situation and it was up to me to get out of it."

Her therapist didn't respond immediately, as though she wondered if she was over her head. "They wouldn't acknowledge that you've been psychologically damaged and needed them to come forward?"

Topsy shook her head. "My sister told me that they consider my husband a psychopath, that I've been under his control for so long that I'm hopelessly crazy now. They washed their hands of me long ago."

There was a momentary silence.

"And your sister? Is she there for you?"

"No, she would be afraid of alienating our parents." Topsy's hands twisted together into a knot on her lap, and she hoped that her therapist hadn't noticed how badly they were shaking. "My sister is taking modeling assignments for her little girl, and my parents help with their expenses, since my sister quit her regular job. Her husband is a salesman and doesn't make much money."

"In other words, your sister is indebted to them."

Topsy glanced away, her gaze drawn to the gas flame in the fireplace. The ambiance of the office had a calming influence, reflecting the kind, but no-nonsense, therapist whose credentials as a Ph.D. were impressive. Topsy couldn't help but wonder how her own life had become such a disaster. Why couldn't she remember what had happened, which was so terrible that her mind blocked the memory? *You have to remember*, she told herself. *Or your children could be the next casualties.*

"Have you made any progress in remembering,

Topsy?" her therapist asked, gently nudging her to the reason she was there.

The tremors moved into Topsy's stomach, vibrating into her chest and throat. She forced them back, holding herself in a rigid posture to do it. "Almost. Sometimes I feel that knowing is just a breath away," she said finally.

Her therapist tilted her head, waiting for her to continue.

"Right now I'm scared for my kids. I've had a sense that they know something."

"Like what?"

"I've told you that I know my husband cheats on me. Maybe that, or God forbid, whatever it is that happened that I can't remember." She paused. "That is, I have had flashes of memory, horrible pictures that are in my mind and gone so fast that I can't make sense of them, or recognize the people."

"So you are closer to knowing what's been bothering you." The woman across from her leaned forward and took Topsy's hand. "Are you up for revealing what you think you saw in those flashbacks?"

Topsy felt the familiar stress sensation settle on her face.

"It might help, Topsy. Once this is out in the open you might even realize that the unknown is far more frightening than what you've been suppressing."

Topsy took deep breaths, leaned back against the cushion, and closed her eyes, willing the images back into her mind. She repeated what she saw, but it made no sense. There wasn't enough to go on: running in a forest she didn't recognize, knowing someone else was there, sensing danger.

She opened her eyes, feeling like she was coming out of her skin, like she needed to get out of there.

She jumped to her feet just as the timer went off. Her therapist got up, too, asked her if she was taking her antianxiety and depression drugs as prescribed. When Topsy nodded, they made another appointment for the following week.

"Please call if anything comes up in the meantime, Topsy. And please understand that what you think is going on might not be as bad as you think, okay?"

Topsy nodded.

"Everything could level out a bit once those drugs have had a chance to really kick in. You haven't been on them long enough yet."

Topsy managed some small talk, then went out to her car. As she maneuvered the rush-hour traffic on Madison, one thought circled her mind. She hadn't expressed her latest fear.

But it might not be valid, she reminded herself. Maybe her mental state was causing her to imagine situations that didn't exist. Maybe her therapist was even right about the thing she was suppressing. Maybe she was schizophrenic, suffering from reality breaks, and the doctors hadn't pinpointed her problem.

All her self-talk did no good. Something horrible was still out there.

Waiting.

CHAPTER TWENTY-SIX

"Do we have to go, Mom?" Samantha asked. She ran her fingers through her unruly red curls, looking even more disgusted. "It'll just be like last time, with Grandma trying to act like Dad hasn't done anything wrong."

"Sam's right. Grandma's blind when it comes to Dad." Alyssa frowned. "Can't we say that we've got the flu?" She paused. "It hasn't been that long since we saw Grandma on her last visit."

Julia sympathized, but she had to be fair. Peter's mother adored the girls and always looked forward to seeing them. It wasn't her fault that her son had flipped out. Peter's mother had always maintained that Peter wasn't dangerous, only histrionic when he wanted his own way. Julia agreed. She, too, had never believed he'd physically harm his daughters, even though he'd turn every trick in his arsenal of manipulations to get his family back. That meant scare tactics, and although that was also abuse, his daughters were on to him. Hopefully, he'd get his act together before any lasting damage was done to their girls.

"I think you girls have to go," Julia said. "Besides, your father seems to be adjusting better now." She managed a smile. "Remember, he's started dating, and that's a good sign."

"But the whole weekend? Please, Mom," Alyssa said. "If we have to go, one night is long enough."

"I couldn't agree more," Sam chimed in.

"Okay, I think a compromise is in order here. How about skipping Friday night and meeting your dad and grandma on Saturday afternoon? I could pick you up on Sunday evening."

"Okay," Alyssa said. "At least we won't have to miss the basketball game tomorrow night."

Samantha sighed, hesitant to agree. "I guess so, Mom." She started for the stairs, then stopped and faced Julia again. "It's not that I don't love Grandma, it's just that Dad is so—so embarrassing at times. I hope he does get better soon."

"So do I, sweetie. Let's keep our fingers crossed."

"And our toes," Alyssa added, and followed her sister upstairs.

Julia smiled as she watched them go, realizing again how lucky she was to have her two daughters. They were good girls who, in the final analysis, wouldn't want to hurt their grandmother's feelings.

And maybe things really were getting better concerning Peter, she told herself as she went back to the kitchen. She hoped so for all of their sakes.

Julia had just returned to the house after dropping the girls off at the game. She wished she'd been able to let Alyssa drive them so she could have stayed home, but that was out of the question for now. She didn't want a phantom driver running her daughters off the road.

Don't whine, she told herself. *You have a whole three hours to make wreaths before picking them up at the school gym.* And then she got busy, watching a small television set on the counter as she worked at the table. When the phone rang she had to put down her dried greens and turn down the volume before answering.

"Yes?" she said, expecting Peter's mother, who still needed to verify the time for tomorrow with the girls.

"It's Earl."

Surprised, Julia sat down on a stool. Earl rarely called in the evening. She braced herself; she'd turned down two invitations for dinner with him since he'd returned from San Francisco, feeling that pursuing a friendship when she was so attracted to him was futile. Was that why he was calling now, breaking his own rules that had never been stated between them but were so blatantly apparent—that he never called from his house or on weekends. A glance at her Caller ID told her that the private number must be his home.

"I'm surprised," she said, stating aloud her mental response. "You never call at this time of the day."

"Yeah, I know, Julia. But I'm a little desperate."

"Desperate?"

"Uh-huh. I'm afraid I'm losing you."

"Earl, that's an odd thing to say."

"Not so odd when you consider my feelings for you." A pause. "And yours for me."

The silence in Julia's ear was long and heavy.

"This is not something I can talk about, Earl," she said finally. "In the first place it's inappropriate, under the circumstances."

"Because I'm married?"

"Yes," she said honestly.

"We need to talk face-to-face."

"I don't know when that's possible."

"How about meeting me tomorrow night?"

"But that's Saturday."

"I know that, but drastic circumstances require drastic action."

There was another silence as Julia's thoughts whirled in her mind. *Oh, God*, she thought. What had she gotten herself into? She knew she was beginning to care deeply for him, but she'd never considered what would happen if he felt that way about her. Did he?

"Julia? Are you there?"

"Yeah."

"Can we meet and discuss this?"

Another pause. "I think that would be a good idea, Earl."

"Tomorrow night?"

"I'm alone tomorrow night, but—"

"Alone for how long?"

"My girls will be staying with their grandmother."

"I'll come to your house."

"But you can't do that. You've always said that—"

"I know what I've said." His tone was slightly— what? Impatient? Or simply upset? "Do you have a garage?"

"Yeah."

"Then I'll call you from the road when I'm close and you can have the door open. I'll drive in and no one will even know I'm there—in case your husband is in the vicinity."

"But—"

"No buts, sweetheart. I'll be there at seven-thirty

sharp. Have the garage open and be ready to close it once I've driven inside."

She started to protest, but he'd said good-bye and hung up. And then she wondered how he knew her address, aside from her being in Issaquah. The conference roster, or even the phone book, she reminded herself. She'd never gone unlisted, even though she'd considered doing so after becoming single.

Oh, God. She suddenly felt panicky. Earl was coming to her house tomorrow night. Somehow her personal space, the place that she governed, was an extension of herself, would be open for scrutiny. Despite her sense of inappropriateness, she was flustered. The man she may have fallen in love with was coming to her home, which reflected who she was, for the first time.

She was truly disconcerted, which overrode her good sense. He was not free, and it was not right that she allow his visit. But Julia knew she would. At this point she had no choice. She was not up to calling his house to cancel.

Earl called as promised, two minutes away from her house. She pressed the door opener, and the panel lifted to access her double garage. A moment later his Mercedes came down the street slowly and turned into her driveway, then her garage. Standing at the door to her house, she pressed the button to close the barrier behind his car. He got out of his car and then came toward her, his dark eyes intense with the reflected fluorescent ceiling lights. Without a word, he took her into his arms and held her against his body, so close that she could smell his aftershave lotion and shampooed hair.

Abruptly, he stepped back, holding her at arm's length. "Jeez, I've never seen you look so beautiful."

Her cheeks warmed at his compliment, the type of which she hadn't heard in years. Julia smiled, uncertain. Although she'd spent a lot of thought on what she'd wear tonight for his first visit to her home, she'd decided to stay casual, dressing in a long-sleeved, high-necked, blue velvet hostess gown, the type her women friends wore for informal get-togethers. Along with light makeup and her hair left long and natural, she felt understated, if looking her best.

They went into the house, and she flipped the bolt lock on the laundry room door to the garage. Her next order of door wreaths was on the kitchen table, ready for delivery tomorrow, and aside from that, the house was sparkling clean. She led him into the family room, where the gas fire in the fireplace was a flickering flame over the fake logs. She'd placed fresh flowers in several vases, had turned on soft music, which drifted out of the built-in sound system, and had a bottle of Chardonnay cooling in an ice bucket on the coffee table. Two glasses and a dish of mixed nuts sat next to it. The room she'd decorated in big overstuffed furniture and family heirlooms and photos was cozy and inviting, the place where her family watched television on their thirty-six-inch screen. Everyone loved this room, the center of family events. Surprisingly, Earl scarcely noticed and didn't comment about how nice everything was in her house.

He pulled her down on the sofa next to him, his action canceled by his obviously agitated state, as though his mind was elsewhere.

Nonsense, Julia told herself. Why would he have come in the first place if he hadn't wanted to?

"Wine?" she asked.

"Sure." The tic that sometimes caused his eyes to blink

seemed more pronounced, adding to her sense that he was stressed about something. Her?

She poured the Chardonnay into two glasses, then handed one to him. "A toast?" she asked, smiling.

"Why not?"

She lifted her glass, trying not to feel that he was playacting for her benefit. "To your first visit to my house."

"Cheers," he said, his eyes narrowed and unwavering.

After sipping, she put her goblet down on the table, uncertain about him being here. He seemed so different. Was that because he was in her house, seeing her in a different light?

A silence stretched between them.

Surprisingly, he scooted nearer on the sofa, his hands taking hold of her upper arms, drawing her closer to him. He kissed her gently on the mouth, and then feathered her face with his lips. Her response was instant. Whatever reservations she had, her body wanted more—of his touch and of his kisses.

Again, he backed away, smiling, reminding her that they needed to talk about their relationship. "You have a nice place here, Julia. Is this where you undertake all of your projects, and your writing?"

Nodding, trying not to feel rebuffed, she grabbed some nuts, chewing each one separately as she considered her answer.

"Uh-huh. The house is conducive to being able to carry out all of my jobs, the combination of which gives me an income to support my family." She gave a laugh. "I think I explained that to you the first time we had dinner together."

He was momentarily silent, and when he stood up,

she was surprised. "How about showing me around your house, Julia?"

She stood too, thinking it was an unusual request, even though some people considered it protocol to be shown around a house they were visiting for the first time.

"Sure, although I suspect you'll find it pretty ordinary."

She led him through the house, from the kitchen, family room, dining and living rooms, to the four upstairs bedrooms, ending with her own.

He hesitated in the middle of the room, glancing around at the blue-hued drapes and bedspread, the antique furniture that had been perfectly restored, the old Fenton glass lamps. "It's lovely, Julia. Just what I'd have expected in your personal bedroom."

"Thank you," she said softly. "Many of the furnishings in this room once belonged to my grandmother. I always feel safe here, because I sense her, and my mother's, presence."

He'd moved into the middle of the room but turned to face her as she spoke. A moment later he was kissing her again, edging her backward toward the bed.

"Wait, Earl," she murmured against his lips. "I'm not ready for this. We were going to talk, remember?"

"Some things don't need to be talked about, my sweet." His kissing deepened, and his hands began caressing her upper arms and back. "We can talk later."

For a moment she struggled, and he suddenly relaxed his hold on her. "What's wrong, Julia? You know you want this as much as I do."

She shook her head, not knowing quite how to respond. She wanted him, too, but she couldn't forget that he was a married man, and where would that leave her after she'd given in to sex with him?

"But not like this, Earl. I care too much to just have this be a . . . a fling."

"You think this is a fling?"

She swallowed hard. "I hope it's not, Earl. But I don't know, and I have to live with myself tomorrow, and next week, if that's what it turned out to be."

He slowly shook his head, but his eyes were suddenly filled with humor. "You are such an innocent, Julia. For all that you were married all those years and have two daughters, anyone would think you were still a virgin."

She didn't know whether to be insulted, if he was ridiculing her in a subtle way. She'd realized long ago that he had a way of seeming so caring about an issue when in fact he was drawing someone out and mentally putting them down. Was he playing with her emotions because he was annoyed that she hadn't gone to bed with him? Was he really angry behind his humor and cynicism?

"Hey," he said. "Let's go down and finish our wine, and have our little talk."

He sounded different somehow, as though he was hiding annoyance under his bravado of indifference.

She suddenly realized he *was* mad, but she nodded, hoping their frank talk about each other's intentions would calm any resentment based on false expectations.

"Oh, shit," he said, sounding even more angry. He glanced at his watch. "I forgot to call home as I'd promised."

She stared, for a moment puzzled. What did that have to do with him being at her house? Shouldn't he have fulfilled such an obligation before he arrived?

"My wife has such a debilitating migraine that she's in bed. I promised my kids that I'd call and check on her."

Julia nodded and indicated her bedside phone. She

felt awkward, wondering about his sudden mood changes. Had allowing him to come to her house given him the message that she would sleep with him? She thought she was being honest, that what she'd told him was what he believed. Maybe she'd been wrong. She certainly was not a woman with dating experience, and she had no clear idea of expectations these days.

While she was considering, he moved to the phone and picked it up. Then he glanced at her before punching in the numbers, his brow raised in a question.

At least she knew what that meant; he wanted to talk to his family in private. She inclined her head, then left the room, again struck by the oddness of the situation. She'd been asked to leave her own bedroom so Earl could call his wife. In fact, his whole demeanor since he arrived had been peculiar.

She waited for him out of hearing range, at the top of the stairs. Several minutes later he joined her and followed her down to the living room, where they sat back down to their wine. He was the first to speak.

"My wife is in a bad way," he began. "My son said she's in terrible pain." He took quick drinks of his wine. "I'll probably have to leave." He expelled a long sigh. "If only she could get beyond those damn headaches."

Julia set down her glass. On the one hand, she understood his concern, on the other, she felt demeaned. The one thing she knew for sure was that she was not up for a repeat performance. Their relationship beyond being fellow writers had to end. It was obvious that his life was dysfunctional, and she had enough concerns of her own without adding his, too.

By the time he emptied his glass and stood up, they hadn't discussed the future of their relationship, and Julia felt he'd avoided the subject.

"I'm sorry I have to leave like this, Julia." He spread his hands. "It seems that my wife's health always disrupts the rare times I'm able to get away from the whole nightmare."

His expression was so worried that she suddenly felt a need to reassure him. Later, in a calmer situation, she could explain her feelings, that there could never be anything between them while he was married. She hated her weakness in allowing him to come over tonight; she'd been wrong.

She led him back through the house to the garage, where he paused, grabbed her upper arms to pull her to him, and gave her a brief kiss on the mouth. Then he stepped back, said he would call next week, and got into his car. When he signaled, she pushed the garage door opener; once it lifted, he gave a salute, backed out, and was soon disappearing down the street.

Julia closed the garage, went back into the house, and poured herself more wine. She needed the uplift, unable to remember a time when she'd felt quite so humiliated. Even Peter had never treated her with such, such what—disrespect?

She was being used. She felt used.

A short time later Julia locked up and set the alarm, then went upstairs to watch television in bed. She felt awful. How could she have allowed Earl into her house so that he could treat her with such disregard?

But maybe he was only insensitive because of his marital troubles, she reminded herself. Maybe he hadn't meant to seem so cold to her feelings. He might be coping with a kind of stress she couldn't imagine, a wife who was far more emotionally ill than Peter.

All of her rationalizations didn't make her feel any better. The house seemed too quiet, and she wished the girls were there, to take her mind off her humiliation. She couldn't stop thinking that Earl had left once he'd realized that she hadn't been up for sex.

Julia sat up straighter in bed, needing to hear a familiar voice that could ground her again. She grabbed the phone. She'd call Diana, listen to the latest events in her sister's life.

Since Diana was the last person she'd called today, she hit the Redial button and waited as the phone rang on the other end of the line.

An answering machine picked up, filling her ear with new age music, mystical-sounding notes that were the background for a low, seductive female voice. The woman spoke in a low tone, saying she was unable to take the call, and then gave a work number.

Jolted, Julia stared at the receiver in her hand. Had she dialed wrong? Was it a crossed wire? She certainly hadn't reached Diana's phone.

Then she remembered. Earl was the last person to call out from her number to his home.

Was the woman his wife?

But his wife didn't have a job.

Julia pressed the Disconnect button, then Redial to listen to the message again, grabbing a pen and pad from the nightstand drawer to jot down the woman's work number.

She tried to convince herself that it was a mistake. Surely Earl hadn't called another woman from *her* bedroom? Her anger was sudden, and it took all her willpower to keep herself from calling his number herself.

Wait, she told herself. *You need to know the facts.* The woman's work number could be called on Monday, and then she'd find out for sure who Earl had called. In the meantime, she tried to sleep.

And couldn't.

CHAPTER TWENTY-SEVEN

Julia didn't hear from Earl all weekend, and by Monday her suppressed anger was more than she'd ever felt in her life. He owed her an apology for Saturday night. He'd insisted upon coming over, then had left abruptly after she'd shown him her house. She didn't like the side of him she'd glimpsed, and although she realized a deeper relationship was out of the question, she still had her own questions about his odd behavior.

And about the woman he'd called from her bedroom.

She waited until ten on Monday morning, then called the number, reaching an office in the Seattle courthouse. It was a receptionist, who told her that they employed many people and she needed to know the woman's name before she could connect Julia with anyone. "I can't attach a number without the name," she told her.

And Julia didn't have a name.

They hung up, but Julia knew one thing for sure. The

person Earl had called was not his wife—as he'd told her.

He'd lied.

As she worked on a wedding cake, she became more and more angry. How dare he call another woman from her bedroom phone. It was kinky—sick.

And she wasn't going to put up with it ever again.

Somehow she got through the day, doing her work by rote. But her thoughts kept swirling in her mind, reminding her about how easily she'd been taken in by a man who obviously had other women in his life besides her, which made her wonder about his *real* relationship with his wife. Had he lied about that, too?

By the time she and the girls sat down to an early supper, she'd made up her mind; she would call Earl at home after Alyssa and Samantha left for a basketball game at school. If his wife answered, she'd simply hang up.

He needed to be confronted, made accountable. What he'd done was an affront to who she was: a decent woman who'd believed what he'd told her. She wasn't playing any game, as he seemed to be doing. In the first place, she didn't know the rules of such a game. She'd been honest with him and had assumed he'd been honest, too.

Stupid, she told herself. *Your daughters are more astute about dating than you are. You're behind the times.*

The girls were picked up by Alyssa's best friend's mother, and after Julia had seen them safely into the car she went back into the house, her focus on calling Earl. It was six-forty-five; he should be home by seven-thirty. She'd wait until then.

She paced the kitchen, checked her drying flowers and greens in the garage, took a shower, put on her nightgown, then sat down on her bed, getting up her courage to call his number, aware that his wife would be there, that she was emotionally unstable. Finally it was time. She picked up the phone.

He answered on the second ring.

"Yello?"

His voice was strong in her ear.

"It's Julia."

There was a long silence.

"Earl?" she said finally.

"Yeah," he replied finally. "I can't talk now."

"I need to talk," she said. "Right now."

Another silence.

"I thought you knew better than to call me at home." His voice had lowered to a whispered hiss. "What in hell is so important that you'd do that? Make it quick then. I only have a minute."

Julia flushed, embarrassed by his reception, but even angrier at his tone. He was treating her as though she were insignificant—*as though she was dirt under his feet*. Even more determined, she gulped a deep breath and went on.

"Do you remember using my bedside phone when you were here?"

"Yeah, to call my wife." A pause. "So?"

She licked her lips, gathering her thoughts. "You didn't call your wife, Earl. You called another woman."

His sucked-in breath came over the wires.

"What the hell are you talking about?"

"I know."

"You fuckin' know what?"

The venomous tone of his response took her aback, and for long seconds her mind boggled for an answer. What had happened to the charismatic man she'd met that day on the writer's panel? Who was this man on the phone? Not the Earl she thought she knew, even as she recognized his voice and knew she'd called the right phone number.

"I know that you called a woman whose answering machine recording is a seductive voice against a background of new age music."

"What in the hell are you talking about?"

She explained the redial process.

"You're scaring the shit out of me. You, of all people that I trusted, are turning into a loose cannon—checking on numbers?" A pause. "If that's the way you're gonna be you could completely bust up my marriage and lose me my children." Another pause. "You and your detective work could cause me terrible problems. I don't like anyone snooping around in my life." A pause. "*I don't allow it.*"

"This wasn't detective work, Earl," she protested, trying to explain. "I was only checking my redial service when I realized you were the last person to call from my phone. The last number called was the one you called."

There was a silence.

"Why would you, a person who is not a part of my personal life, have called that number?"

"Because it was so blatantly on my phone."

Another silence.

"Nothing about this bothers me except that it's detective work—because if you'd do this once, Julia, you'll do it again."

"But Earl, I didn't do anything. I wasn't the person who called that woman from my phone, and I had no thought of spying on you when I hit the Redial button. For God's sake, why would I have done that?" She hesitated. "Stop placing blame on me for your own actions."

"My actions are my own," he said tersely.

"Of course they are." Julia hesitated. "And I want no place in them, Earl. I don't feel good about being a part of your life anymore."

There was a long pause from his end of the phone.

"Hey, I have no explanation for your crazy actions, but I'll have to talk to you later. Please don't call back here." He hung up on her.

He called back a half hour later.

"Hello," she said when the phone rang.

"I can talk a little better now if you can," Earl said in her ear.

"Okay," she said, and wondered why she was giving him such slack when he'd been so rude. But she knew. She'd fallen for him, felt more attracted to him than she'd ever felt for Peter. Her feelings were more than she wanted to admit—to him or anyone else.

"This whole experience just shocks the shit out of me," he said. "First of all, your phone call last night could have been picked up by anyone in my house." A pause. "How could you be that vicious?"

"Vicious?" Her anger was instant. "I didn't do anything to you, Earl. You're twisting this whole ugly situation around so that it's my fault, not yours."

"And you think it is?"

A long silence went by.

"Yes, I do, Earl. You're obviously not truthful, to me, that woman on the phone, or to your wife." She sucked in a breath. "I'm the one who's shocked, because I'm seeing you in a different light, one that isn't very admirable. You aren't who I believed you were, Earl." Another pause. "Please explain why I'm wrong."

A dial tone sounded in her ear.

Slowly, Julia hung up, but she was so angry that she could have thrown the phone through the window—except that she would have had to pay for the window.

She stood up to pace the room. How could he have called her the loose cannon, a vicious person because she'd called him about his call to another woman from her bedroom? Oh, God. He'd transferred his guilt for seeing another women onto her—but she wasn't about to accept that.

He wasn't the man she'd believed him to be—the beleaguered man who was suffering with an emotionally damaged wife. He'd just told her that he would not put up with anyone rocking his boat, *even her*—a woman who'd never thought she was rocking anything with a man who claimed to be so unhappy. Julia felt next to tears.

And his wife might not be the person he'd described as a handicapped person.

Maybe he was lying—again.

Oh, God, she thought. *I'll never see him again. I want no part of this mess.*

What mess? she immediately asked herself. *His life? Or his sick family as he'd projected them to be?*

She'd begun to wonder if that was true.

Earl was not who he seemed.

The phone rang, startling her. Earl?

"Hello?" She grabbed it, prepared to tell him to never contact her again.

Instead a woman's voice sounded in her ear.

"Be careful." A pause. "Please be careful, or you could die."

The dial tone sounded.

Julia stared at the phone. Oh, my God. Was that a

threat? It had sounded more like a warning. From whom?

After a sleepless night, Julia got the girls up for school and managed to keep a lid on her boiling cauldron of emotions. Two women had called her anonymously, one with a middle-of-the-night lewd suggestion, the other with a warning. And she'd called a third woman, the voice on her automatic redial. All three voices had sounded different.

What did that mean? she wondered, but she had no clue, except that two of them were somehow connected to Earl.

Julia halfway expected Earl to call back the next day when he would be at his office. There was no call.

Frustrated because she wanted to tell him off, gain some closure to her feelings for him, and his betrayal of her, she stayed close to the phone. When he didn't call she only felt a sense of sadness, disappointment . . . and ultimately relief.

She would never contact him at home again—or anywhere.

She could never be involved with him in any way—friendship or with any preconceived notion about a fantasy for the future.

There was no future with Earl. Somehow she knew that for certain.

CHAPTER TWENTY-EIGHT

SEVERAL DAYS LATER EARL STILL HADN'T CALLED, AND although Julia was relieved, she also felt let down and angry. What in the world had happened to him? she asked herself for the umpteenth time. He'd changed so drastically in a matter of days.

As Samantha and Alyssa bustled around upstairs dressing for school, Julia thought again about the strange calls from women lately. The more she ruminated, the more she wondered if those calls were connected to Earl, a thought that was even more puzzling when she remembered the man she'd believed him to be. When she opened the newspaper after the girls had left for the day, she discovered one thing that had been bothering him.

"Attorney Questioned in Murder Case" the caption read under a photo of Earl as he left the courthouse.

Julia plunked down on a kitchen chair, her eyes scanning the article. As she finished, she went over it again, slowly, trying to digest the words, unable to credit that it could be true.

The homicide detectives investigating the case had come up with a connection between Carol Norton, the first shooting victim, and Earl, indicating that they were romantically involved. Experts had retrieved e-mails from Earl on Carol Norton's home computer. Although the woman worked as a secretary in the Public Safety Building, Earl was claiming that she was only a cyber friend he'd met on a legal forum but had never met in person.

The ring of the phone interrupted her thought process, jarring her out of a stunned state of disbelief. She grabbed for the receiver, the newspaper still in her hand, her gaze glued to Earl's picture.

"Hello?"

"Julia?"

Her therapist's voice in her ear was a surprise. Judy never called Julia at home, except when the two had discussed the wallpapering jobs, which was unrelated to Julia's therapy. When it came to her patients, Judy was a complete professional; it was her secretary who called to verify appointments.

"Yes, this is Julia."

"I didn't recognize your voice." Judy gave a short laugh. "You sounded different."

"Probably because I just opened the newspaper and saw an article that shocked me."

"About Earl Paulsen?"

"Oh, Judy! I can't believe he's a suspect in this woman's death." Julia drew in a sharp breath. "You know this Carol Norton was the first woman shot on the jogging path near my house."

"It's the trail you use, isn't it?"

"Uh-huh. I'm not jogging right now, especially after the shooter shot at a second woman and a third woman was killed. And that was after my own experience of being spooked out on the trail the evening of the first murder."

"What do you mean?"

Julia explained about tripping on a shoelace that night, then hearing someone in the nearby foliage. "I started running again before this last shooting death, but now I don't dare, especially after all of the other scary happenings around here." She hesitated. "My daughters and sister are too fearful for me to continue, even if I chose a time of day when lots of other folks are on the trail. They thought the third woman looked too much like me, that it was just too weird that I'd just run that part of the trail minutes earlier." A pause. "I didn't admit it to them, but I was uneasy about the whole thing, too. Even though my rational side tells me it was probably a coincidence."

"Jeez, Julia. Why didn't you share any of this with me before?"

"I don't know. I guess I didn't think it was pertinent to my recovery from Peter's craziness, never considered him nutty enough to kill me." She sighed. "Even in light of what's gone on recently, it's hard for me to think he's capable of murder." Another hesitation. "And aside from Peter, I don't think I have another enemy in the world."

A silence went by.

"But you're involved with Earl Paulsen, a man being questioned in Carol Norton's murder."

"I explained that, Judy. He's only a friend at this point. To be blunt, I haven't slept with him."

An expelled breath sounded in Julia's ear. "Thank God for that."

Julia switched position so that she could put down the newspaper. "And as of last Saturday night we aren't seeing each other any longer."

"What happened?"

Julia gave her an abbreviated version of what had happened. "Frankly, I don't know what was really going on. Maybe he was terribly upset about this matter and became nervous about any other woman in his life."

"Then why did he insist on coming over, Julia?"

"I don't know."

Another silence went by.

"Listen, I'd like you to make an appointment and come in. I'll block out two slots in case we need the time."

"Okay. But it'll have to be later in the week, maybe Friday, when I have some time in the early afternoon." She gave a laugh. "I have to deliver a wedding cake by five."

"Say one to three?"

"That'll work."

"In the meantime, Julia, don't see Earl."

"What do you mean?" Julia gave a nervous laugh. "At this point I don't think it's a possibility anyway." A hesitation. "Do you think he's dangerous? The article says that the shootings on the trail aren't connected to the rash of killings attributed to a serial killer in south Seattle."

"Uh, that's what's being reported, but you know I have other clients," she said, evading a direct answer.

"Of course." Julia wondered what that had to do with her question. "Are you implying that you have other information about Earl?"

"I can't explain because of confidentiality issues, but

yes, I do have some concerns that I'd like to discuss with you."

"Connected to Earl?" Julia asked, pressing.

"I can't say."

"Okay, then I'll be there on Friday."

"Good."

They hung up, then Julia remembered that she hadn't mentioned the woman Earl had called from her bedroom.

I'll explain it all on Friday, including my call to him, she told herself as she tried to concentrate on her work. But it was no use.

"Admit it," she said aloud. "You're very upset, and scared. And you don't know what in the hell is really happening." She hesitated. Did Judy?

Throughout the day Julia wondered about Carol Norton, who was already dead before she'd met Earl at the conference, before he'd called the other woman from her bedroom. Was that other woman another of his romantic involvements? Had he left her house to go to her place? If so, why? Because that woman had some hold over him and he was trying to pacify her? Had leaving after he'd only arrived been so important to him that he hadn't minded offending her? Julia had another thought as she worked, remembering the obscene call in the middle of the night. Maybe Earl was turned on by calling a woman from yet another woman's place. Maybe he was kinky. And maybe she'd just been one of many women in his life.

She sighed, suddenly feeling more violated and betrayed than angry. Had she ever really known Earl—*a man who was being questioned in a murder investigation?*

A sudden thought sent flutters into the pit of her

stomach. What if the police found her messages to Earl in his computer?

Don't think about that, she instructed herself. Her e-mails were to a friend, not a lover. Nevertheless, she didn't want her name in the newspaper along with Earl's. Aside from all the horrible ramifications, Peter didn't need more ammunition.

The front doorbell startled her out of her contemplation. A glance at her watch told her it was time for the girls to be home from school, but they wouldn't be ringing the bell. She moved into the front hall, where she glimpsed the person on the porch—Peter.

Her heart sank. It was as though she'd conjured him out of her mind. She wondered if he'd seen her, if she could pretend she wasn't there. But then she saw the girls.

She opened the door.

"Dad picked us up at school," Alyssa announced, and as she passed Julia and headed for the stairs, she raised her brows, as if to say that the situation was beyond her control.

"Grandma had presents for us, and Dad was just giving them to us," Samantha chimed in, looking equally uncertain. "She left on the plane this morning."

"Yeah, I figured since I was in the neighborhood I'd just pick up the girls and bring them home." Peter sounded cheerful for a change, as though he wasn't violating a court order to be there.

Julia nodded. "I'm sure the girls appreciate that."

"They used to when they were little."

He peered around her into the house, but she didn't ask him in. Peter's volatile presence was the last thing she needed today.

"Well, thanks, Peter." She hesitated. "I'm sure the

girls will send thank-you notes to your mother for the, uh, gifts."

"Cashmere sweaters." He grinned. "You might remember my mother's fondness for cashmere."

She nodded again, then stepped back, ready to close the door. "I have to get back to work," she said, grateful that the meeting hadn't turned into an argument.

"Always in a hurry to get rid of me, aren't you?" His tone had gone from friendly to sarcastic.

Shit, she thought. His friendliness had been too good to be true. "No, just busy, and I have to check on something in the oven."

He took a step closer, his expression tight with anger. "You know, Julia, my mother sees no reason why we can't work out our problems, and neither do I." He cleared his throat. "Being divorced is stupid. None of the women I've dated measure up to you."

Julia forced herself to take deep breaths before answering. What was that supposed to mean? That because he hadn't found someone else, she was obligated to go back to the marriage? She wished his mother would stay out of it, even though she could identify with the woman's hope to have Peter in a stable situation. The only problem was that Peter hadn't been stable for a long time now. The divorce was only a symptom of his problems.

"I respect your mother's opinion," Julia began, trying diplomacy. "But it doesn't apply to our circumstances." Then she tried changing the subject. "And tell her the girls will call her soon."

"You're a bitch, you know that?" he retorted angrily. "A fucking bitch who doesn't deserve a good family man like me!"

He'd raised his voice to a shout, and she quickly

closed the door. Alyssa rushed downstairs, looking anxious.

"You okay, Mom?"

"As good as can be expected," Julia said. "It's just the same old thing."

"I'm sorry about him coming. Sam and I had no choice."

"Of course you didn't, sweetheart. This isn't your fault." She managed a smile. "And in time your father will get better."

But as she heard Peter stomp off to his pickup truck, shouting threats and accusations as he went, she felt even more depressed.

She'd chosen the wrong man—twice. At least she hadn't been deeply in love with Earl.

But she had been *a little in love* with him. And maybe he was even worse than Peter.

She hoped not.

CHAPTER TWENTY-NINE

"OH, MY GOD!" JULIA CRIED INTO THE PHONE THE NEXT morning. "I can't believe it."

"Open your newspaper," Diana instructed in her ear. "The article is on the front page."

Propping the receiver between head and shoulder, Julia grabbed the paper and opened it onto the counter in front of her. Scanning the subtitles, her eyes fell on "Another Woman Found Shot," a heading halfway down the page. The woman, Nancy Fredricks, had been a secretary in an office at the courthouse. She, like Carol Norton, had lived on the East Side, and both had jogged the same trail, Julia's running path. The piece also mentioned that Nancy Fredricks was a self-published author of a new age book titled *Your Soul Mate Is Waiting for You*. In another situation Julia's response to the book would have been to laugh if the circumstances hadn't been so tragic.

The final paragraph made the connection to the other

shootings on the trail, but the police were again stressing that the shootings didn't appear connected to the serial killer who'd been operating in another area of Seattle. There was no mention of Earl.

"I don't know what to say," she said shakily.

"This is just another woman who's been ambushed on your trail, Julia," Diana said. "Please, promise you'll never use it again, even if you're with another person, until this lunatic is caught."

"Of course I won't."

"And don't let the girls go there either."

"I'm not the nut here, Diana. Of course I wouldn't let them. Besides, they never use it anyway. They have enough exercise with sports and skiing."

They talked a moment longer and then hung up. But Julia was unsettled. Something kept trying to surface in her mind, but the harder she tried to think what it was, the more it eluded her. She was baking cakes when it suddenly hit her— *The voice on her phone when she'd redialed after Earl left on Saturday night.*

The woman's dreamy voice had left her message against a backdrop of —*new age music.*

It couldn't be, she told herself. Her imagination was leaping out of normal boundaries. Just because Earl had known the first woman shot on the path, the third victim, the one who resembled Julia, had not been connected to him.

Coincidence, she reminded herself. Many health-conscious people came from all over to run the trail, even from downtown Seattle, especially on the weekends. It was a popular destination for serious joggers. It just happened that the two dead women, and the one who'd escaped with her life, were East Side residents with easy access to the trail—like this latest victim.

But all of her mental arguments didn't convince her that there was no connection between the women and her.

Magical thinking again, she thought as she popped the cake pans into the oven and set the timer. *Stop jumping to conclusions.*

Julia suddenly realized there was a way to solve the woman-on-the-phone issue. She could call the work number the woman had left on her answering machine. Julia went to get it.

At the last minute she almost chickened out. *Silly*, she thought. *What would it hurt?* No one at the courthouse would think anything of it.

But what would it prove? Hadn't she called before and been told that without a name or extension number there was no way to connect her with the woman because the number given was the front desk?

Julia had another idea. She pulled out the telephone book and quickly looked up a number for Nancy Fredricks, finding an N. Fredricks with an address in Bellevue, not too far from the upper end of the jogging trail. Before she lost her nerve, Julia punched in the numbers. An answering machine picked up on the third ring.

The same dreamy voice gave the same message Julia had heard before. *It was the person Earl had called from her bedroom.*

She slammed down the receiver, disconnecting.

Shocked, angry, and scared, she still had to make the final connection. The possibility remained that it could be a coincidence. The N. in the phone book might not stand for Nancy.

Bracing herself, she called the work number the

dreamy voice had given. Again, a person at the front desk answered, and Julia asked for Nancy Fredricks.

There was instant silence.

"Are you a relative of Nancy's?"

"Oh, no." Julia managed a normal tone of voice. "A business associate."

Another pause.

"Haven't you read the morning paper?" the receptionist asked.

"Uh, no, I haven't."

"I'm afraid Nancy was involved in a fatal accident."

"Fatal accident?" Julia's voice wobbled. "Are you talking about Nancy Fredricks?"

"I'm sorry, but I am. We have lots of staff here but only one Nancy Fredricks."

"The person I'm talking about is an author."

"Yeah, that was our Nancy." A hesitation. "Hey, would you like to speak to the person who's handling Nancy's desk?"

"Uh, I'll call back. This is upsetting news."

"It is for us, too. She was well liked."

Julia thanked her, hung up, and collapsed onto a chair. She'd identified the dead woman as the person Earl had called from her phone. But the implications were even worse than that.

Earl was somehow connected to two dead women.

And then she had a horrifying thought. Why was the murdered woman's answering machine still on at her home? Wouldn't the police have confiscated it as evidence? Or had they left it on to see who might call? They'd have a tap on it to trace incoming calls.

Julia couldn't stop shaking. She went to the cupboard and grabbed a bottle of whiskey that Peter had left behind. The liquor was old, but it should calm her. She poured herself a shot.

And then drank it all at once.

Later, after the cakes were out of the oven and cooling, Julia felt calm enough to tackle needed revision on the computer manual, which had to be completed in the next week. But her thoughts were still too scattered to concentrate on such precise work. She pushed her chair away from the desk and walked to the window that faced the woods beyond her property. It was a gray day, awaiting the forecasted storm front that was on its way south from Alaska. The woods were still and foreboding, as dark as her thoughts.

Her skin suddenly pricked with apprehension. Anyone could be out there watching. She was a perfect target, framed in the window where she'd earlier lifted the blinds for more light. Her body jumped back of its own volition.

Shit! She'd become a paranoid basket case. What was she thinking? That someone was out there with a gun taking a bead on her?

Get a grip, she told herself. *Don't let this get to you. You don't know the facts. Earl could be an innocent bystander.* There could be a logical explanation for everything, even if she couldn't imagine what it was. She needed to wait before she did anything drastic, like call the police and tell them what she knew. *No,* she corrected herself. *What you think you know.*

And what was that?

She shook away the disturbing thoughts and decided to check her e-mail instead. She would try to figure things out later, after the effects of the whiskey had completely worn off and she had a clear head.

She went down the short list of messages, mostly cake orders, until she came to My649. It was a post from Earl, sent that morning around eight. Surprised, she clicked on it to see two brief lines: *I'll be in touch when I can. Please, let me explain.*

She stared at the screen, then saved the message and went offline. Moments later she shut off her computer and went back to the kitchen. She'd have another jigger of whiskey if the girls weren't due home in less than an hour.

Whatever Earl had to say, she had no intention of resuming their relationship—of being lied to again. Because that's what he'd done, and no words could remove the humiliation from how he'd treated her.

As if to reinforce her resolve, her eyes fell on the newspaper she'd left open on the counter, resting on the second to the last paragraph, which mentioned the legal forum where both murdered women had posted on the internet. Julia stared. That fact hadn't registered with her when she'd first read the article. That was another link to Earl, although he hadn't been mentioned in regard to the connection between Carol Norton and Nancy Fredricks, as he had been in the murder of Carol.

Again Julia wondered if she should call the police about what she knew. Maybe and maybe not. She leaned against the counter, contemplating her options and what they'd mean to her family. How much was real and how much was her imagination working overtime.

I'll discuss it with Judy, she decided finally. Her therapist might not tell her outright, but she'd manipulate her in the right direction. It was time to tell someone.

The doorbell rang an hour later, about the time she expected the girls from school. The person on the porch was Mrs. Bullard, the elderly neighbor Diana had convinced to watch Julia's house.

Julia opened the door, a fixed smile on her face. "Mrs. Bullard?" She raised her brows. "What's up?"

The little woman's mouth curved upward, but her eyes were sharp and alert. "I don't know, dear." She hesitated, pulling her cardigan sweater tighter over her chest, as though she was chilled. "But remember, I promised you and your sister to be on the lookout for strange happenings around your house?"

"Yes, I remember, Mrs. Bullard."

"Well, there was a strange occurrence a couple of hours ago, and I thought about whether or not it pertained to you." Her eyes shifted beyond Julia to the entry hall. "Would you mind if I stepped inside? I didn't put on a coat, and it's pretty cold out here." She gave a weak grin. "My arthritis has been kicking up—the dampness, I'm sure."

"I'm so sorry." Julia stepped aside. "Yes, please come in, Mrs. Bullard."

They moved inside and Julia closed the door. The older woman declined going into the living room and sitting down. "I can't stay, dear. I only wanted to get out of the cold to tell you what I saw."

Julia braced herself but managed a smile. "What was that?"

"Something really weird." She tilted her chin. "You won't think I'm an old woman who's imagining things, will you, dear?"

"Of course not!" Julia's response was instant, convincing her elderly neighbor of her sincerity. "Besides, midseventies isn't that old for a woman these days, Mrs. Bullard."

Mrs. Bullard grinned. "I know, but people your age usually don't credit that."

Julia let the comment pass. "So, what did you see?"

"Uh, yes, what I saw." Her face was suddenly thoughtful, as though she was seeing a mental flashback of what she wanted to relate. "A person in the woods behind your backyard."

Julia was taken aback. "For goodness' sake, how could you see that? You live down the street."

"I was feeding the neighbor's dog two doors down from you. You know, the Swansons are on vacation for a week and I'm feeding Charlie, who's fenced in in their backyard."

Julia shook her head.

"Anyway, while I was back there filling his food and water dishes, I saw a flash of movement in the woods behind your house."

"A person?"

"Uh-huh. I couldn't tell if it was a man or woman because the person was dressed in black and wore a cap." She paused. "I only glimpsed them for a few seconds. But I definitely saw the rifle."

"A rifle?"

"Yep, and it was aimed at your house."

Julia's stomach lurched, but she was able to maintain her cool. "Please explain, Mrs. Bullard."

"That's all I know. One second the person was there, the next they were gone."

"What time did this happen?"

Mrs. Bullard told her.

Julia's air escaped her lungs. She grabbed the edge of the hall table to steady herself. That was the time she'd been working on her computer and had gotten up to look out the window—*when she'd felt someone was hidden in the woods, watching her.*

"I hope you won't think I'm exaggerating."

"'Course not," Julia said with surprising calm. "But I'm sure there's a logical reason for what you saw—maybe a kid with a BB gun, even if they aren't allowed around here."

"I never thought of that." The older woman's expression relaxed. "I was just worried about you."

"Thanks for that, Mrs. Bullard. I can't tell you how much I appreciate your vigilance."

"You're welcome, dear. Even though this was probably a storm in a teacup, I'll continue to be watchful."

"Thank you," Julia said again as she saw the woman back to the porch. "And please let me know about anything else unusual."

Mrs. Bullard beamed. "I will, you can depend on that."

And then Julia watched her as she walked down the street to her own house. But her fingers trembled as she closed and locked the door.

CHAPTER THIRTY

"I NEED TO TALK TO MY THERAPIST," TOPSY TOLD THE SECretary. "Please tell her that it's vitally important."

"Who did you say you were?"

Topsy told her.

"She's just finishing a session with another patient. They aren't quite done yet."

Topsy looked around her bedroom, holding the phone away from her ear for several seconds to listen. Everything seemed quiet.

"I'll stay on the line until she's finished." She drew in a sharp breath. "I know that the sessions begin on the hour and last for fifty minutes. She'll be done any minute now."

"I don't know," the secretary said. "Are you sure I can't take your number and have her call back?"

Panic was a gathering knot in Topsy's stomach. She would have shouted back into the phone had she not been terrified about who could hear her in the house.

Instead, she forced herself to stay calm, her voice hardly above a whisper.

"I'll wait," she said again. "Tell her I've remembered some things, will you write that down?"

"Okay, I've done that, and I'll put you on hold," the secretary said. Soft easy-listening music filled the airwaves.

Topsy glanced around her bedroom. She was alone, but there were others in the house. She suddenly realized how dangerous it was to wait on the phone. If anyone picked up one of the extensions, they could hold Topsy's call to her therapist even if Topsy had heard them pick up the extension and hung up herself. And then they would know she'd called her therapist, and why.

Oh, God! She was trapped.

Yet she waited another minute, hoping for the sound of her therapist's voice. Finally she had no choice. She hung up.

Topsy waited a few seconds, then picked up her phone again. The dial tone sounded in her ear.

Thank goodness. No one else had been on the line, listening.

She'd call back in the morning—if she had a chance.

In the meantime—*Oh God,* she prayed again. *In the meantime.* She hoped it wasn't too late.

But maybe it was.

CHAPTER THIRTY-ONE

JULIA PUSHED BACK THE LEDGER AFTER MAKING HER LAST entry and then stood up. In an hour she needed to shower and get ready for her appointment with Judy, and she didn't mean to miss it. Often in the past she hadn't looked forward to seeing her psychologist, but today she did. In fact, she'd been counting the hours since Mrs. Bullard's visit. She needed to share her concerns, decide on a course of action regarding Earl's phone conversation from her bedroom.

She'd hung around the house, thinking Earl would call because of his e-mail, but he hadn't. If he'd tried when she'd been out, he hadn't left a message.

That figures, she thought, heading to the garage to check on her drying flowers and herbs. She had a sizeable order from a local garden shop for dried herb wreaths, which she intended to highlight with garlic bulbs and small green and red peppers. A glance told her they wouldn't be ready for another couple of days.

That was a relief. She needed to spend her time revising the computer manual in order to meet her deadline. Being paid for that work meant a good chunk of money that would see her through until the first of the year.

As Julia went back into the house, the phone was ringing. She ran to grab the extension in the kitchen.

"Hello," she said, thinking it might be Earl.

"Mrs. Farley?" The female voice was crisp and businesslike.

"Yes, I'm Mrs. Farley."

"Alyssa is your daughter?"

"I have a daughter Alyssa, yes." A ripple of fear ran down her spine. "Who am I speaking to?"

"I'm with the sheriff's department, Mrs. Farley." A pause. "I have some bad news."

"Oh, God! Has something happened to Alyssa?"

"Please," the woman said. "Alyssa is going to be okay. She was hurt on a hiking trail near your house."

"You must have the wrong Alyssa. My daughter is in high school right now."

"I'm afraid not. She and several friends skipped school. She was injured on the trail."

Julia sagged against the counter. "What are you saying? My daughter has never skipped a class."

"Mrs. Farley. Let's stick to the facts, okay? She is on the trail, her leg may be broken, and the aid car is meeting a sheriff's deputy at the trailhead, which I understand is close to your house."

"Yes, it is." Julia's voice shook with fear.

"I'm calling to let you know what's happened, Mrs. Farley. We thought you'd want to be there when she's transported to the hospital."

"I do." She sucked in a breath. "Did this just happen?"

"We got the call only moments before I notified you. One of her friends had a cellular phone."

"I'm on my way." Julia was about to slam down the phone when she heard the woman speak again.

"Good. I'll notify the unit that you're on your way."

Julia slammed the receiver onto its cradle, then ran for her purse and car keys. A minute later she was backing the Cherokee out of the garage to head to the trailhead. Oh, God, let Alyssa be all right.

All the way out of the development and down the road to the trailhead turnoff, questions spun in Julia's head. Why had Alyssa skipped school? Why had she gone to the very trail where women had been shot to death? And what had happened to cause her to break her leg?

Let her be okay, she whispered over and over. *Please, God, don't let anything worse happen to Alyssa.*

Although Julia passed a car driven by a teenage boy going in the opposite direction on the dirt road, there were no other vehicles when she arrived at the trailhead. As she jumped out of the Cherokee, she was suddenly apprehensive. Something was wrong.

Where was the aid car? Had the sheriff's deputy been there and gone? Was Alyssa already on her way to the hospital?

"Mom!" Alyssa's voice sounded behind her. "Are you okay? What happened?"

Julia spun around to see her daughter running out of the woods from the jogging path. Surprised, she was momentarily at a loss for words.

Alyssa's leg wasn't broken.

"What are you doing here?" Julia cried. "The woman on the phone said you'd broken your leg on the trail. I was about to try to find you."

Alyssa came up to her. "My friend Tommy just dropped me off because I got a call at school that you'd been hurt while jogging, Mom. The principal excused us to go." Her face looked pinched from worry. "A woman dispatcher from the sheriff's office said I needed to get up here immediately, before the ambulance took you to the hospital."

"Oh, shit!" Fear took the air from Julia's lungs. It took a moment before she could talk, even as her gaze swept over the empty parking area and the woods, where the underbrush precluded seeing anyone who might be hiding there.

"We've been set up!" Alyssa cried, suddenly coming to Julia's exact conclusion. "The caller was a fraud."

"C'mon." Julia grabbed her arm. "We've got to get out of here." She didn't speak her fears aloud, that the person who'd called them both knew they were there—that they were isolated.

And a target.

Julia yanked open the passenger door, then gave Alyssa a shove as she scrambled onto the seat. After slamming the door, she ran around the Cherokee to the driver side. Once behind the wheel, she started the engine and put the gear into reverse.

As she started to back up, the windshield shattered, spraying glass onto the dashboard and into their laps. Something hit the headrest next to Julia with a soft thud.

She gunned the engine as a second projectile scattered more glass. Julia knew it was a bullet. Someone was trying to shoot them!

Oblivious of bushes scratching the paint job, Julia swung the Cherokee around and floor-boarded the gas pedal to fly back down the road, away from the person who'd taken a bead on them. She scarcely slowed for the main road, making the turn so fast and wide that she almost went into the ditch. Several hundred yards later she turned into her development, speeding along the street toward her house as she pressed the garage opener. Once inside, she closed the barrier behind them. Neither one of them had spoken as they'd fled the shooter.

Julia made Alyssa stay in the laundry room between the garage and kitchen until she went ahead and closed all of the blinds facing the woods. Someone was out there.

Someone who wanted her dead.

But she wouldn't think of that now. There were things to do; she needed to protect herself and her daughters.

Once the house was secure, Julia motioned Alyssa into the house.

"Mom! Someone tried to shoot us!" Alyssa's voice broke with a sob, and then she cried in earnest. "Why is this happening?"

"I don't know, sweetheart, but we're safe now." Julia held her daughter close, feeling the deep shudders that wracked her body. "But we need to be strong right now, honey," she said and led Alyssa to a chair that was not in line with any of the shuttered windows. "I need you to help me, Alyssa. I want you to stay right here while I make a couple of calls, okay?"

Alyssa dropped her head in a nod. "I'll . . . I'll try, Mom." She hesitated. "But I'm so scared. What if the person with the gun tries to break in? What if—"

"Shh," Julia soothed. "Everything will be all right, but I need to make those calls, first to the police."

Alyssa nodded again.

Julia picked up the phone and punched in 911. The

dispatcher answered immediately. Although Julia had steeled herself to sound calm, her voice shook as she told the operator her name, address, and what had happened.

"Mrs. Farley, a patrol car is on its way and will be at your house in about three minutes."

"Thank you," Julia replied shakily.

"I want you to stay on the line until the officer arrives," the dispatcher said.

"But I can't do that!" Julia could hear the anxiety in her voice. "I have another daughter at school and I'm afraid for her. I need to call and make sure she's all right."

"Understood," the calm voice replied. "What's her name, and which school does she attend?"

Julia told her.

"We'll call. Is there anyone who can bring her home?"

"My sister." Julia gave Diana's name and phone number at home and at work.

"Someone is calling your sister right now, Mrs. Farley. Your daughter will be taken care of. Your job is to stay on the line. Don't hang up."

"I won't."

Seconds later the officer, a dark-haired, heavyset man in his midthirties, was at her front door. She glanced out the window, wanting to see his patrol car parked in the driveway before she opened the door. He quickly stepped inside as a second, younger officer, his pistol in hand, moved around the house to disappear into the backyard. A minute later he joined them inside the house. No one had been lurking in Julia's yard.

What about the woods? she thought, even as she realized the forest beyond her fence was not their priority right now. But someone could be out there watching, knowing that they were safely hidden from view, because it would take a small army of policemen to find them.

Both men went out to the garage to inspect the Cherokee as Julia watched. They checked the shattered windshield, then the seat cushions where the bullets had lodged. The first officer made notes of their findings before turning back to Julia.

"We can't do anything more right now, but a crime lab technician has been notified to look over your vehicle."

They went back into the house, where the officers began taking down their statement as to what had happened. The first officer was gentle with Alyssa as he questioned her. Alyssa explained her part, and then Julia explained hers.

The officer's gaze was suddenly direct. "You've had trouble here before, I see. Your husband?"

"My dad would never shoot at us!" Alyssa interrupted. "I know he's been a little nuts lately, but he's not a killer."

The officer smiled at her. "We weren't discussing a killer, Alyssa." He paused. "Only what happened today. Of course we have to look at other reports from this address, but that doesn't mean we're accusing your dad."

Alyssa looked down, and Julia felt sorry for her. It was all too much for Alyssa and Samantha. If today's incident was connected to Peter or not, Peter had to get his act together, for the sake of his daughters.

"I guess that's it," the heavyset officer said and moved back to the front door, the second officer following him. "I see you have an alarm system and good door locks, so I think you'll be okay tonight." He hesitated as he opened the door and stepped onto the front porch. "Is there anyone who could spend the night with you if you and your daughters feel apprehensive about being alone?"

"Yeah," Diana said, overhearing as she came up the steps behind him, followed by Samantha. "I don't know what's going on, but I'm Julia's sister and my husband Ted and I can stay overnight."

The officer nodded, making note of Diana's full name and phone number.

Samantha rushed into Julia's arms. "Mom, what's happened? My principal said Aunt Diana was coming to get me and that I had to go home."

"We'll explain later, honey." Julia managed a smile and spoke softly, hoping to calm her.

"Yeah, come in Sam, and I'll fill you in," Alyssa said, dropping an arm around her sister and guiding her into the house.

The officers lingered for several more minutes, giving Julia the usual instructions to call if she even suspected anything unusual, until another patrol car pulled up in the driveway in front of the closed garage door. Diana looked on, for once not contributing to the conversation.

"The patrolman in your driveway will be here until the forensic technician arrives and finishes their work on your vehicle," the officer explained.

"Forensic technician?" Diana repeated, her eyes widening.

"Uh-huh. The bullets need to be retrieved and examined."

Diana licked her lips, obviously momentarily stunned. As the two original patrolmen left and Julia led her sister back inside the house, she was formulating the words to update Diana without alarming her further. But how could she do that? she asked herself. She only knew the facts, and that's all she could pass on to Diana.

Oh God, how she hated the craziness. If only she knew what was behind it. Please don't let it be Peter, she thought. Her girls might never recover if it was.

As she bolted the door and made sure the shade was securely closed, she was thoughtful. First there had been the ongoing vandalism to their house, then the terror tactics, and ultimately Samantha's ski lift accident and Alyssa being run off the road. Now the shooting. Someone seemed intent on harming all of them.

She faced her sister, knowing she had to explain, that she could no longer dismiss the shootings as being separate from her situation. She wished she didn't have to talk about it, that it would all just go away. But she knew it wasn't about to do that anytime soon.

Just don't let any of us get hurt, she prayed silently. *Especially keep my precious daughters safe.*

Because she was finished if anything happened to either one of them.

CHAPTER THIRTY-TWO

JULIA MADE A POT OF TEA WHILE DIANA TALKED TO TED on the phone, arranging for him to come to her sister's house after he went home to change out of his work clothes. They sat around the table as Julia passed out the cups. Then Julia and Alyssa took turns explaining what had happened, why they had both rushed to the trailhead. Diana and Samantha listened in silence, their expressions reflecting Julia's feelings exactly—terrified.

She hadn't yet allowed herself to dwell on what it really meant. It boggled her mind. She'd mentally searched her background and couldn't come up with anyone who had a grudge against her except Peter—and, lately, Earl. But in her wildest imagining she couldn't picture either man being responsible for such a deadly act. Especially Peter, when it included Alyssa.

Unless his sanity was completely gone.

She'd have to process everything with Judy when—

Oh, my God! she thought, jumping up. She'd forgotten her appointment with her therapist. Quickly she explained, excused herself, and rushed to her office. She didn't want to talk about anything in front of the girls.

She punched in the numbers, then waited while the phone rang in Judy's office.

"Therapist's office," Judy's voice said in her ear.

"It's Julia," she said, surprised that Judy, not her receptionist, had answered.

"Where are you, Julia? It's fifteen minutes past your appointment." Her tone was more concerned than accusatory.

"I can't come," Julia answered. "Something terrible has happened and I can't leave the house. I—that is, Alyssa and I were—" Her voice faltered, and for long seconds she couldn't speak as tears streamed down her face. She hadn't realized how close she was to breaking down until she'd gotten Judy, her sounding board, on the phone.

"For God's sake, what, Julia?"

"Give me a minute," she managed in a shaky whisper, then tried to compose herself.

Judy waited as the silence stretched.

Finally Julia was able to speak, explaining the phone call that had taken her to the trailhead, the similar one that had motivated the principal to excuse Alyssa from school. She gulped a deep breath and related the shooting, their terror as they'd fled the scene for home, and then the police who'd come to the house and were now guarding the garage until the crime scene technician processed her Cherokee.

"Christ almighty!"

"Protect us," Julia added seriously, feeling like they

shouldn't take the name of God in vain under the circumstances.

"Of course." Judy's voice shook.

"Please don't worry, we're going to be okay," Julia said, sensing her therapist's upset.

"I'm very concerned, Julia." Judy hesitated. "I think you might be in real danger."

A silence went by while Julia digested her words.

"Hey, don't be, Judy. My girls and I will be all right even if I have to sell out and relocate." She managed a weak laugh. "And I think I no longer have a choice in that matter."

"Can you come in tomorrow?" Judy asked.

"But that's Saturday."

"I know. But I think we need to talk."

"I can't say right now, Judy. I'll have to let you know after the police have cleared my vehicle as a crime scene."

"Will you call me back when you know?"

"That could be late tonight or tomorrow."

"I know. But you need to stay in touch, Julia. I have concerns that you don't know about that could pertain to you."

Julia shifted positions, suddenly alert. Judy had alluded to this before. What did she mean?

"What are you saying, Judy?"

"Nothing, or everything."

"That's ambiguous, you know that."

"Yeah, I do know. And you know I have confidentiality issues I must adhere to." A pause. "Will you call me when you know a time to meet tomorrow?"

Julia studied the lines on the closed blinds. "I'll call, Judy."

"Good."

And then they hung up, and Julia went back to her family in the kitchen.

"Don't answer the door, Mom," Alyssa cried, jumping up from the kitchen table after the doorbell had sounded. "Someone could shoot you through the front window."

Samantha leaped out of her chair, causing it to slide away from her across the hardwood floor. "Please, Mom, do what Alyssa says." A sob altered her words. "We don't want you to die!"

Julia was taken aback. Her daughters were terrified that she could be shot. After they'd gone through the divorce and their father's unstable response to it, they were even more shattered than she'd believed. And now this, the shooting at the trailhead. She needed to reassure them, no matter how big the toll on her own psyche, because she was as scared as they were.

She put up her hands, contriving a calm persona. "Remember, there's a patrol car with an officer in it out in our driveway. No one could be on our front porch without him knowing it." She hesitated, affecting a reassuring smile. "It's okay, probably the people the police are expecting to check out the Cherokee."

Both girls nodded.

"Your mom is right," Diana said, affecting her own mask of confidence. "No one could be out there if they weren't legitimate and safe."

Both girls nodded, but they got up to walk behind Julia as she headed toward the front hall, her eyes on the window to the porch. She altered her approach to the side of the room, away from her usual path to answer the door. *Just in case.*

From the edge of the shade, Julia peeked outside.

Then she opened the door to a short, middle-aged woman in a navy pants suit, who flashed her badge and identified herself as Pat Bakersfield, the forensic technician. Behind her, the patrolman on duty motioned from the driveway that Julia needed to raise the garage door. She lifted her arm to acknowledge his request.

As the woman started to explain what she'd be doing to process Julia's vehicle, a black sedan drove up to park behind Pat Bakersfield's car. Two men, one about Julia's age and the other around fifty, got out and started up the front walk toward them. Julia's first impulse was to close the door, but Pat Bakersfield put her foot in the threshold, stopping her.

"It's all right," she said. "I know these men. They're homicide detectives."

"Homicide?" Julia's voice quavered.

"Just routine," Pat Bakersfield said, her expression softening with an understanding that probably went with her job. "In light of the women who were shot on that trail, they need to investigate any shooting that might have a possible connection." Her no-nonsense attitude was suddenly replaced by a reassuring smile, and Julia recognized that her professional veneer was only a cover for a caring woman with a job to do.

Then the two men joined the technician on the porch. Both men flipped out their ID. Jim Fitch was the tall, fit man under forty, and Fred Hays was the detective with the expanded waist, flushed face, and thinning hair who was nearing retirement age. In seconds all three law enforcement people were inside Julia's house. A part of her mind couldn't believe it. How could she, the small town girl who'd married at eighteen, be in the midst of a homicide investigation? She suppressed her reservations, remembering her sister and daughters, who were looking on in silence. They were already scared without her adding more fears.

Everyone followed Julia back through the house to the kitchen, where she offered them chairs at the table. The seven people seemed like a crowd, and there weren't enough chairs to go around.

"I don't need one," Pat Bakersfield said after being introduced to Julia's sister and daughters. "My work is with the vehicle in the garage."

Julia nodded and led her through the laundry room to the Cherokee as Pat explained the procedure of extracting the bullets from the seat cushions.

"I won't dig and probe for them or I might scratch the casings and distort the findings by the lab people when they examine them."

"I understand. You hope to match the bullets to the gun chamber."

"Something like that," Pat said. "Which means I'll cut a six-inch square in the upholstery and remove the whole section of cushion and let the experts extricate the bullets."

Julia sighed as a momentary concern hit her. How would she see to her work commitments with her Cherokee out of commission? But paying her bills was the least of her worries right now, she thought. She and her girls were safe, and that's what mattered. She could cope with anything else.

"Please don't worry, Julia." Pat hesitated at the doorway, as though she'd tuned in on her thoughts. "It's going to be okay. I know you're scared and concerned for your family, but at least your insurance should pay for your vehicle damage." She smiled reassuringly. "Be assured that we'll get this thug."

"Thanks, uh, Pat."

"Yeah, that's right. Call me Pat. I don't stand on formality." Her gaze intensified. "And believe me, Julia, I know what you're going through. Many of us women have been there, one way or another, if not so drastic."

And then she stepped into the garage to begin her work, unaware that Julia hesitated in the doorway behind her, wondering what the technician had meant. Obviously, the forensic expert, like so many other women, had suffered through a bad situation. Julia took a deep breath and braced herself to join the homicide detectives in the kitchen.

"Mrs. Farley," Jim Fitch said as she came back into the room. "We just need you to answer a few questions."

She glanced around. "Where are the others?"

His blue eyes were direct. "My partner took them into the living room so that we could talk in private." He hesitated. "I think it best that everything is not discussed in front of your daughters."

She nodded, relieved.

"Hey," he said, "I understand about teenagers. I have a couple of them myself that I'm raising alone."

Her eyes met his. He'd aroused her interest in him as a person, not just a homicide detective. "You're divorced, too?" she asked, taking a chair opposite him at the table.

He shook his head. "My wife died last year."

"Oh." She didn't know what to say, but she wondered if the tragedy was the reason his thick head of hair was prematurely gray. "I'm sorry."

"Yeah, it was hard." His lean face brightened. "But the kids and I are better now. We've gotten into a new routine that works, and we're getting back to some happy times."

A brief silence went by.

"So, tell me what happened today, how you came to be at the trailhead."

She gulped a deep breath and then began, starting with the phone call that Alyssa was hurt and ending with the wild ride home and her call to the police. He took notes as she talked, her shaky voice gaining volume as she spoke.

He glanced up. "You know we'll be examining the bullets for a possible match to other women who have been shot on that trail?"

She nodded.

"I'm aware that you and your daughters have been harassed and that you've experienced quite a few acts of vandalism over the past months. Do you have anything to add to what is already on record?"

She suddenly remembered Mrs. Bullard and related what the elderly neighbor had told her about seeing someone behind her house with a rifle.

"Where does Mrs. Bullard live?"

She told him as he wrote down the information, his expression inscrutable.

"Anything else you can think of?"

"No, not that I can think of at the moment." A pause. "You don't think that the person who murdered those women was the shooter today, do you, Detective Fitch?"

"That would only be a guess at this point," he replied calmly, but Julia had the distinct impression that he did think so. "What about your husband? I know he's been stalking you. Do you think he'd go so far as to shoot you?"

"Oh, God, no!" Her voice had risen. "He's been terribly upset over our divorce, hasn't been able to let go, but I can't see him doing this." She hesitated, trying to gain control over her emotions. "And just lately I've been hoping that he's making progress, since he's begun to date other women."

"I see," he said, and she wondered just what it was that he did see. "Has anyone else been a problem lately?"

She shook her head. Her first thought had been Earl, but she dismissed it—for the moment—until she could talk to him.

They discussed the situation with Peter in depth, and Julia told him everything she remembered, all the times when Peter had tried to manipulate her by fear. She also reiterated her position that Peter would never shoot at his own daughter, however much he wanted his family back.

He shook his head, and although his expression now reflected disapproval, he didn't comment further as he stood up to go. They joined Detective Hays and Diana in the front hall. The girls had gone upstairs.

Julia saw them to the door, where Jim Fitch cautioned her to be careful and told her that a patrol car would be checking the house periodically.

As the men stepped onto the porch, she asked the question that was circling her mind. "Do you think I've become the killer's next target?"

"Don't worry about that yet, Mrs. Farley. We'll be in touch after we have more conclusive evidence. In the meantime, as I said before, you and your girls be on guard for anything suspicious. Fred and I left our cards on the kitchen table, so you have our direct phone numbers. Call either of us day or night."

She nodded, watching as they went out to the driveway, then into the garage, where Pat Bakersfield was still processing the Cherokee. Julia closed the door, then faced Diana. Neither spoke, but Julia suspected that they'd both come to the same conclusion.

The homicide detectives believed that she'd become the killer's next target. Or worse. Her daughters had.

CHAPTER THIRTY-THREE

LATER THAT NIGHT, AFTER DIANA AND TED HAD RETIRED to the guest room and the girls were asleep in their own bedrooms, Julia sat facing her computer screen, trying to formulate an e-mail to Earl. Finally, she left it simple; that she must talk to him, that it was vitally important that he call her. Then she hit the Send key, closed down the computer, and went to bed.

But she couldn't sleep. Too much had happened. There were too many questions. Restless, she put on her robe and went downstairs to the kitchen in the dark, careful to avoid activating the sensors that would set off the alarm system. A cup of tea designed for sleeplessness was what she needed. In the dark she filled a cup with cold tap water, then put it in the microwave. As it heated, she wandered to the window above the sink to glance out at the black woods behind the house, knowing that no one would dare come close after what had happened.

When the forensic investigator had left with the pieces of cushion that contained the bullets, followed by the officer on duty, they'd both reminded her that the house would be patrolled. At the moment, Julia felt relatively safe, especially since Diana and Ted were spending the night and their vehicles were parked in her driveway.

Abruptly, a light flashed in the woods and was gone. A flashlight?

She stared, long after the microwave beeps signaled that her tea water was hot, but there was nothing more. Everything outside was still.

Had she only blinked and imagined a light? Surely no one would be stupid enough to be out there after all the police activity at her house.

She watched the woods for another five minutes, and then decided that she must have been mistaken. She went back to get her cup of water from the microwave, heated it for another thirty seconds, then dropped in the teabag and headed to her bedroom, mindful of not disturbing the sleeping people in her house.

Julia propped the bed pillows against the headboard, then sat against them as she sipped tea, her open blinds allowing some natural light from the starry sky into the dark room. Her thoughts swirled, from all that had been developing in her relationship with Earl, to what had happened today. In many ways, beyond his media persona and his seemingly outgoing personality, he was an enigma. And now any thought of a future relationship with him was gone. She was just grateful that she hadn't fallen too deeply in love with him. His recent behavior, the opposite of anything she'd expected, precluded a further investment of her feelings.

She placed her empty cup on the bedside table and

then scooted under the down quilt, allowing a peaceful lethargy to seep into her limbs.

And then she didn't remember anything else as she slipped into sleep.

Nothing further happened over the weekend, and by Monday morning Julia still hadn't received a return e-mail from Earl. Nor had she had a chance to meet with Judy. There hadn't been anything about her close call with the shooter in the newspapers, or updates about Earl's involvement in the other ongoing murder investigation. She was relieved even as she was conflicted, because she hadn't revealed her own relationship to Earl to the homicide detectives.

Since the shooting, Diana and Ted had been sleeping in Julia's guest room, and her sister had dropped the girls off at school that morning. As Julia completed the finishing touches on a wedding cake, she contemplated calling Earl at his office. She needed to give him a chance to explain, as he'd promised in his e-mail. If Earl's involvement with the dead women was innocent and he'd been cleared, she didn't want to make matters worse by involving him with her.

Still Julia was uncertain, and she felt guilty over not coming clean about knowing Earl and the call he'd made to Nancy Fredricks.

Why should I protect Earl? she asked herself, picking up the phone.

But she knew why. She still remembered the man she'd first met at the writer's conference, the highly respected attorney she'd read about in the newspapers, and despite everything, she couldn't believe that he was really a suspect in a murder case. There had to be a logical explanation. He'd put lots of bad guys in prison;

maybe someone with a grudge against him was setting him up? Maybe his call that night from her bedroom had been legitimate. With resolve, she punched in his office number, and as the phone began to ring at the other end, she took deep breaths, willing her nervousness away.

"Paulsen law office," a woman answered crisply.

"Earl Paulsen please," Julia said.

"May I ask who is calling?"

"Julia Farley."

"And the purpose of your call, Ms. Farley?"

"Personal." The woman sounded like Nurse Ratched guarding the cuckoo nest. Julia decided to be honest. "I'm a writer friend and need to ask him a quick question."

"One moment and I'll see if he's available," she replied, and put Julia on hold.

"What can I do for you, Julia?" Earl's voice was suddenly in her ear, distant but cordial, a tone he probably used when speaking to business acquaintances.

For a moment words escaped her. Her anger was sudden. "I was waiting for you to call me, Earl," she retorted. "Remember? You said in your last e-mail that you'd explain what happened?" A pause. "And I need to know."

"Pardon me?" He lowered his voice, as though he didn't want anyone in his office to overhear. "You need to know what?"

"What's going on? Why the drastic change in you?"

"What in hell are you talking about?"

"Your attitude. Why the police questioned you about Carol Norton, the first woman who was shot." She gulped a breath. "And Nancy Fredricks, the last dead woman. Since you called her from my bedroom I have a right to know what's going on, especially now that someone also tried to shoot me."

"Someone shot at you? For God's sake, when?"

She explained.

A silence went by.

"Son of a bitch! I'm glad you're okay. Do you think that crazy husband of yours has finally flipped out?"

"No, it isn't Peter's style to hurt his own daughter."

"Then what do you believe?"

"I don't know, Earl. I'm trying not to jump to wrong conclusions, which is why I called you for information. But I suspect that the police believe the incident may be connected to the other shootings."

"Jeez." The word whistled over the line. "Did you also tell the police about my supposed call from your house?"

She hesitated. "Not yet. I thought I'd give you a chance to explain first, but I'm thinking that I should now."

"Don't. Not yet. You're right, I need to explain some things to you."

"When?"

"Soon."

"It had better be, Earl, because I feel like I'm withholding information."

"You aren't." His words were clipped with—what? Anger? Or concern? "I told you before I didn't call that woman, nor do I have any connection to the other dead women." A pause. "My secretary just came into my office with papers to sign, so I have to hang up now. We'll talk again."

"I'll wait to hear from you."

For long seconds Julia listened to the dial tone, then slowly replaced the receiver in its cradle. She didn't know what to think. She wanted to believe him, the man she'd been falling in love with before everything suddenly fell apart. He was a respected, best-selling author, and it was impossible to think he had a dark side, a hidden life.

Yet hadn't she witnessed a drastic change in him? As Julia went to change her clothes, questions and doubts rushed back into her thoughts. She just didn't know what to think.

Julia was met at the church by the woman in charge of the wedding reception, who showed her where to set up the cake table. A half hour later she was satisfied with how it looked, having touched up the frosting in several places where it had gotten smudged. She headed back to the rented Ford Explorer, a sport utility vehicle that had been provided by her insurance company. Her Cherokee had been towed to a garage on Saturday morning so that the windshield and seats could be replaced.

She unlocked the door, climbed behind the wheel, and was about to start the engine when she saw a folded sheet of paper anchored under the wiper. She jumped back out and grabbed it, then got back into the Explorer. Expecting a religious flyer, Julia was unprepared for the black, felt pen lettering on the white page.

Careful Bitch! Stop seeing a married man—or die!

The church lot was empty except for the panel truck that had been there when she arrived. It had big emblazoned letters across it that said WEDDINGS MADE SIMPLE, and it was the vehicle driven by the woman who was working in the church basement. And she'd never been out of Julia's sight, had never left the church.

Someone else had left the note on her windshield, *someone who'd followed her there.*

She glanced beyond the parking area to the residential area of Kirkland. Nothing seemed amiss, but she had no idea which of the parked cars along the street belonged to the people in the houses. Goose bumps rippled over her flesh. She had a sudden feeling of being watched as she climbed into the Explorer.

By whom? The person with the rifle?

Grinding the gear into reverse, Julia backed enough away from the curb so that she could go forward over all the empty parking places to the street entrance. Her foot on the gas pedal, she slumped low on the seat so she wouldn't be an easy target, then sped onto the street, heading for the 405 freeway that would connect her to I-90 and the way home. By the time she reached the interstate she was trembling so hard that she had to slow down and take deep breaths. Her eyes continually darted to the rearview mirror. No one followed.

One thought haunted her mind. Who, aside from her family and her therapist, knew she'd been seeing Earl, a married man? No one. So who'd left the note?

Don't be so stupid, she told herself. *Someone is out there watching, someone who tried to kill you, someone so evil that they didn't care if your daughter died, too.*

When she finally reached her development there were no suspicious cars anywhere in sight, so she drove right into the garage and immediately pressed the button to close the door behind her. She got out of the Explorer and went into the house, her eyes and ears fine-tuned to anything out of the ordinary. She knew the house was secure; the alarm system was still on, just as she'd left it.

But she didn't feel safe until she'd walked through the whole house, checking closets and under beds to make sure she was really alone. The phantom out there seemed to materialize in places that seemed secure, and she wasn't taking any chances.

She heated water for tea, seeing that she had an hour before picking the girls up from school. With the steaming cup in hand, Julia headed for her office. There was just enough time to go over her final revisions on the computer manual. She needed another success with the software company in order to get the next assignment.

Before beginning, Julia remembered that she expected several checks in the mail. If they were there, she'd drop them in the bank on the way to get Alyssa and Samantha. She headed for the front hall, checked that no one was on the porch, then opened the door to grab the mail from the box.

Again, as in the church parking lot, Julia felt the prickle of apprehension. She backed into the house and slammed the door. Only then did she look at her mail.

There were several utility bills, a check for the wreaths that had been sold in a consignment store, and another folded sheet of white paper.

Julia stared at it, paralyzed by what it meant. It lay in her hand like a snake about to sink its fangs into her wrist. Her heart swelled in her chest and choked off her breath. She forced herself to take deep breaths, knowing she had to open it. Backing up against the steps, she sat down against the wall. The need to see everything all at once was uppermost on her mind. Slowly, she opened the message.

ADULTERESS! EVIL DESTROYER OF FAMILIES! AS YOU DESTROY SO SHALL YOU BE DESTROYED!

Julia gulped, horrified. She wasn't an adulteress. Until now, she'd never had sex with anyone aside from Peter, although she probably would have if her relationship with Earl hadn't gone sour. And the last thing she'd ever do was try to destroy another person's family.

Oh, my God, she thought suddenly, remembering the spray-painted A on her front door. That incident had happened *after* she'd been seeing Earl.

The A had meant *adulteress* and had been directed at her, not Alyssa.

Shaking, but determined, Julia went to the phone table, yanked open the drawer, and clawed through the contents for Detective Fitch's number. She punched in the numbers on the phone pad with trembling fingers, then left a hysterical-sounding message on his voice mail for him to call, informing him that it was an emergency. Then she called Diana, knowing she would be home from work by now, and asked if she could pick up the girls.

"What's wrong, Julia?" her sister demanded shrilly. "I can hear that something has happened by your tone of voice."

Julia managed to explain that she'd called the detective, that she didn't dare leave. Diana agreed at once and hung up after instructing Julia to pull the blinds, reset the alarm, and stay away from the windows.

Julia did as Diana said, then sat down and waited for the police to arrive. The house seemed to settle around her as if waiting, too. She strained her ears for any odd sound, knowing it could be the phantom out there in the shadows, the one who'd targeted her to die.

Someone had known about her relationship with Earl from that first dinner date. Surely it wasn't Peter, she told herself. He would have accused her of cheating on him, fastened on the other-man scenario as the reason for their divorce. It had never been his way to keep silent. He'd always expressed every complaint and upset he'd ever had.

Or would he have done that now—when he was becoming convinced that she wasn't coming back to the marriage?

Surely Peter's alternative wasn't murder. God help her, she didn't know anymore.

CHAPTER THIRTY-FOUR

"CALL ME, JULIA. IT'S VITALLY IMPORTANT," JUDY'S VOICE sounded in the quiet kitchen.

Julia had been home for fifteen minutes when she'd realized that there may have been calls while she was gone, so she was listening to her messages now. A second message on the voice mail was also from Judy, who asked her to call the moment she returned, that they needed to talk. This time there was an urgent note in her words, as though she was upset about something.

Julia picked up the phone to call Judy when the front doorbell rang. She put down the receiver and headed toward the hall, where she tiptoed to the door and pressed an eye against the peephole. Then she disarmed the alarm system, flipped the lock, and opened the door to Detective Fitch.

"I wasn't far away when I got your message," he explained as he stepped into the house and out of the wind, which was flapping the hem of his raincoat. "What's up?" His gaze probed her face, as though he expected to hear that she'd been the target of another frightening incident.

"Someone left threatening notes, on my car windshield and in my mailbox."

He inclined his head, acknowledging her words. "Can we sit down somewhere?"

She managed a brief smile. "Of course. Would the kitchen table be okay?"

"That'd be perfect."

She led the way to the back of the house, and he took a chair at the table while she poured water and French roast beans into the automatic coffeemaker, anticipating that they could use a caffeine hit. "Where's Detective Hays today?" she asked, making small talk as she worked. "I thought homicide detectives traveled in pairs."

"We usually do." He took a notepad and pen from his pocket, preparing to document her statement concerning the latest threats. "Fred had to take the afternoon off to attend the funeral of a relative."

"Oh, I'm sorry." She glanced up to meet his eyes. "Losing loved ones is traumatic."

"Yeah. I suspect Fred would rather be working."

"I can understand that." The coffee had stopped dripping, and she poured it into two mugs, which she carried to the table. She took the chair across from him, but then stood back up, remembering the notes. Quickly she stepped to the counter where she'd left them and brought both papers back to the table.

Jim Fitch sipped his coffee, but his eyes were on the notes, which had obviously been written with a wide-point black felt pen. He scanned the words, then reached into his jacket pocket and pulled out two plastic baggies.

"You have tweezers?" he asked. "I don't want to smudge any fingerprints on the paper when I put them in the baggies for the folks in forensics. They'll use the Ninhydrin Process to lift any prints."

"Oh, no," she said, upset with her own ignorance. "I've probably already smeared any prints with mine."

"Maybe, maybe not."

Nodding, Julia went to get the tweezers from the downstairs bathroom drawer, handing them to him when she returned. She watched the detective drop the notes into the baggies and zip them closed. Abruptly, he turned a direct gaze on her, as though he'd shifted gear from the physical evidence to the events that produced it.

"Why don't we begin with what happened today," he said. "After that we can go back to the starting point that heralded your reign of terror, and work forward from there."

"Starting point?"

"Yeah, the incidents of harassment, before you felt threatened with the possibility of a life or death situation, when you believed your ex-husband was the sole perpetrator of the scare tactics—and why you've changed your mind."

"You believe there's something else going on here, don't you Detective Fitch? Something beyond Peter's motivation of wanting to come back to his family?"

She knew it was a dumb question under the circumstances, but she had to ask, needed to clarify the focus of her fears—for her sake and the sake of her daughters, who needed to believe that their father was not a serial killer.

"What I do or don't believe has nothing to do with the facts," he said calmly. "And that's what we need to focus on, the actual facts of what has happened."

She nodded, recognizing that he was right, even though her emotional side wanted answers right now, even as she knew that there were none.

"So we'll begin with where you were when you found the first note today, discuss that and then the second note today," he said. "Then I'll need you to go back over the progression of events from the first time that something seemed haywire, however insignificant it seemed on the surface of things." He hesitated. "Sometimes it's the minute perceptions that crack a case. That's why I want to know anything, and everything, you can remember."

Julia glanced at the window above the sink, at the only shade she hadn't closed in her earlier panicked state. The midafternoon light was fading early under a dark cloud cover, which meant another storm front was imminent. Slowly, she began, telling him about finding the paper under the wiper, how she'd fled for the freeway, feeling as though someone was aiming their rifle sights on her.

"Did you notice anyone following you?"

She shook her head.

"Go on. You got home safely, and then what?"

"I calmed down after I realized the house was secure." She explained about checking her mail and finding the second note, how she'd been paralyzed by fear from suddenly realizing the A that had been spray-painted on her front door had meant adulteress and had not been directed at Alyssa by some lovesick boy with a secret crush.

There was a brief silence as Jim Fitch digested her story.

"So you think it meant adulteress?" he asked casually. Too casually? she wondered suddenly as he went on with his questions. "Why would you be accused of being an adulteress?"

Julia couldn't hide her annoyance. What was he implying? That she had a secret life, one that had put both her and her daughters in danger?

"I have no idea," she retorted. "Since I'm not an adulteress, I have nothing in my background that can't see the light of day." She gulped a ragged breath so she could go on. "I'm—"

He put up flat, silencing hands in front of her, stopping her flow of words, as a sudden grin softened his stern expression. "Whoa. I'm only asking questions, not accusing you of having faulty morals." He sobered. "I'm just processing information here."

She held his eyes a moment longer, then abruptly glanced away. "I'm sorry. Just sensitive, I guess."

"How so? Are you dating?"

His question was unexpected, but her gaze didn't waver from his. "If you're asking if I'm having an affair, the answer is no." She hesitated. "Since my divorce my social life has consisted of family and a few dinner dates with a friend."

"A man?"

She nodded. "A professional friend."

His eyes narrowed as he considered her response. "What exactly does that mean?"

"He's a fellow writer that I met at a writer's conference."

Detective Fitch lowered his gaze to the notepad. "He's married?"

"I resent the inference in your tone, Detective."

He looked up, grinning again, as though her moral stance amused him. "I take it that he is, then?"

She sucked in a sharp breath. "Yes, he is, and no, I'm not sleeping with him. He's only a friend who asked my help with his writing. And—" Her voice trailed off.

He raised his brows, waiting for her to continue.

"And he is stuck in a truly bad marriage."

"You think your friendship with him has anything to do with these notes accusing you of being an adulteress?"

"I don't know anymore," she replied honestly.

He flipped the page of his notes over so that he had a clean sheet. "So it's occurred to you that the A that was spray-painted on your front door some time back is connected to these notes today?"

She nodded. "As I explained, it just did shortly before you arrived. Before that I'd almost decided it might have been someone with a grudge against Alyssa."

"It never crossed your mind that it might be Peter, your former husband, who sprayed the A on your door? Maybe because he was jealous that you might have a new relationship?"

She started to shake her head and explain that Peter would have accused her of that immediately, and then stopped, staring at him. "How do you know all of this? The crazy incidents including the vandalism on my front door? I don't remember telling you or Detective Hays about anything other than what pertained to the shooting on the jogging path."

"I do my homework, Julia, and as you know, I was informed about your husband . . . uh, Mrs. Farley."

"Julia is fine."

He nodded and went on. "In this high-tech world of ours, we cops do our background checks by punching the statistics of the victims and perpetrators alike into our computer banks. And bingo, every complaint, infraction, and offence comes up on the people involved."

"So you know all about my husband Peter."

"Uh-huh. He doesn't want to let go, and he's resorted to stalking his family." A pause. "But as you said after the shooting, you don't think he's capable of going so far as trying to kill you. Right?"

Julia nodded, her thoughts spinning, the detective having pinpointed her new perception of what was happening. Her fear had taken on a new intensity; she could no longer blame Peter for everything. She wondered how many incidents had been instigated by someone else. Who? The person who'd shot at her?

Why would someone else stalk her?

"What's your friend's name?" the detective asked.

"My friend?" she repeated. Her mental gears shifted, and then she understood. He was referring to the man she'd mentioned pertaining to dinner dates.

"Yeah, the writer."

"Earl Paulsen," she replied. "I met him earlier in the year when we were on a writing panel together."

His expression didn't change, but Julia sensed the name surprised him. He glanced down as he wrote it on his notepad, but Julia wondered what he was thinking. She would have preferred to avoid mentioning Earl for now, since he'd been connected to one or more of the dead women. Julia still only had his word that it was a mistake, and she was still waiting to hear his version. Being an innocent person in the eye of a murder investigation may have caused his abrupt personality change, or maybe he was the target of the same lunatic who was now focused on her.

Again Detective Fitch surprised her by changing the subject, although she figured he'd get back to it in his own time.

"Why don't you tell me about everything that's happened to you and your daughters?"

"I think you know each time I called the police from having checked your computer database."

"That's true, but it only has your reported incidents. I want to hear about everything, from the very first time you suspected that something didn't seem right, little events that weren't significant enough to call the police."

"I hardly know where to start."

"How about right after you and your husband were divorced."

For a moment Julia thought about those times, when Peter had had to see Dr. Kornsweig daily to keep him under control, when he'd been on antidepression and antianxiety drugs. He'd been crying one minute, angry and accusing the next, but even though he'd scared her at times and she'd known that she could never go back to their marriage, she had never really believed he'd kill her.

"That's denial," Judy had told her, and she'd come to believe that her therapist was right. But now, with all the things that had happened, she was back to square one, thinking that she'd been right about Peter in the first place. He was emotionally disturbed, but he wasn't the person who'd tried to kill her.

"So, when was the first time you were scared?" he prompted.

"I think my fear started that night when I was jogging on the trail." She went on to explain how she'd fallen and then thought she heard someone in the woods.

"Was that after you met Earl Paulsen?"

She shook her head. "It was a few days before the writer's conference, when we were both on the panel together. But—"

"What?"

"It was the same night the first woman was shot."

A silence went by. Julia got up to refill their cups, then sat back down.

"Go on," he said.

She explained everything she could remember, the progression of rocks against her house in the middle of the night to the uprooted plants to the skiing accident and Alyssa being run off the road.

"Uprooted plants?" he repeated, interrupting. "That's so crazy—something a juvenile vandal would do."

She nodded, and then went on to mention the blue Honda that had followed her from Seattle after her luncheon meeting with Earl, and had later been seen parked near the dirt road to the trailhead, and Mrs. Bullard's account of the person she'd seen behind Julia's house.

"Tell me about the blue Honda. I don't think you mentioned that to any of the officers who responded to calls at this address."

"I didn't really think it was significant, because the driver seemed to be a woman."

"Haven't all your anonymous callers been women?"

For long seconds she stared at him. "My God, I didn't make the connection."

Abruptly, his gaze intensified. "How about Earl Paulsen. Have you made any connections between any of these incidents and him?"

"Not until recently."

"Hmm."

"What do you mean, hmm?"

"Nothing, just thinking about all you've said." He put his pen and notepad away, pushed back his cup, and stood up. "I think that's it for now."

Julia walked him to the door, glad their talk was over before the girls arrived from school with Diana. She wondered what he had really meant by the "hmm" but wasn't up to questioning him further. She wanted to avoid discussing Earl until after he'd had his chance to explain. She owed him that much.

"Let me know if you remember anything else," Detective Fitch said. "And for God's sake, be careful."

"I, that is, the girls and I, will be, believe me."

She watched him go and felt a little guilty. Was she withholding evidence by keeping silent about Earl's call from her bedroom, even though she'd revealed knowing him?

And then she realized what his "hmm" might have meant. Nancy Fredricks's answering machine had still been on after her death. If her phone line had been tapped, then Fitch knew she'd called that number.

Don't jump to conclusions, she told herself. But her patience with Earl was waning. He would either clarify things or she'd have no choice but to give the detective the information she was withholding.

And then she closed and locked the door, shutting out the wind-driven rain. The approaching night would be long and black.

CHAPTER THIRTY-FIVE

FIVE MINUTES AFTER DETECTIVE FITCH DROVE AWAY, Diana arrived with Alyssa and Samantha. All three peppered Julia with questions as they walked through the house to the kitchen, where Julia promised to explain what had happened. Diana poured herself leftover coffee as the girls dropped their notebooks and purses on the counter. They all sat down at the table as Julia took the chair she'd sat in minutes earlier.

For long seconds Julia contemplated where to begin and how much she should tell them. The threat of being shot by a phantom killer was very real, and they all had to be alert to the danger. On the other hand, her daughters were only fourteen and sixteen and she didn't want to scare them any more than was necessary. In the end she decided to stick to the facts with her daughters and leave the contemplation of the situation to a private conversation with Diana and Ted.

"C'mon, Mom, what happened?" Alyssa asked anxiously. "Did someone shoot at you again?"

"Yeah, stop keeping us in suspense." Samantha tapped her fingers nervously on the table.

"Just start at the beginning," Diana suggested. "We won't interrupt you."

They were all talking at once. "Shh." Julia waved a hand in the air, stopping their questions. Her sister's advice was exactly what Detective Fitch had said when he'd arrived—start at the beginning. That's what she intended to do.

"I delivered my wedding cake to the church," she began, and then explained finding the note under the wiper as she was leaving.

"What did it say?" Alyssa beat the others to the question.

"Uh, it was just a threat," Julia said, evading. She didn't want to repeat the married man part. "And then I drove home and found a second note in the mailbox."

"What'd that one say?" Samantha's question was delivered with the rapid fire of an automatic weapon. She was obviously upset.

Julia felt terrible. Her daughters were living through a hell that no young teenagers should ever have to think about outside of a scary movie.

"Just more of the same, sweetheart. Vague threats."

Diana sipped her coffee and was silent. Julia realized that her sister had picked up on her hesitancy to scare the girls, even as they had to know what had happened because their lives were also at stake.

"But someone shot at you and Alyssa." Sam said. "Did the notes say they'd do that again?"

Julia reached to grab her youngest daughter's hand. "No, they didn't." She managed a reassuring smile. "And

Detective Fitch said that this nutty person will be caught soon, and in the meantime the police will patrol our street and make sure no one prowls around our house."

Samantha's body seemed to relax at her words, and Julia felt exonerated from the sin of lying. Her daughters wouldn't live in fear, not if she had anything to do with it.

"That's it?" Alyssa asked.

"Uh-huh," Julia said. "Pretty much in a nutshell."

"And the detective said we'd be protected?"

"Yes, he did," Julia told her. "As much as they can, but he wants us to be careful, too."

Alyssa pushed back her chair and stood up. "Believe me, I am, especially since someone shot at us at the trailhead." She picked up her books from the counter, glancing between her mother and aunt. "I have lots of homework, so I'd better get busy."

"Me, too," Samantha said, getting up and grabbing her own books. "We'll be in our rooms if you need us, Mom."

Julia nodded, smiling again. She saw that Diana did the same, and then both girls started toward the stairs and their bedrooms. They'd reached the front hall when the phone rang, and Alyssa answered it before Julia could grab it in the kitchen.

"It's Grandma from Chicago," Alyssa called back. "I'll talk to her upstairs, okay?"

"That's fine," Julia told her, relieved. She wasn't up to talking to Peter's mother right now.

A silence settled over the kitchen once the girls were gone, and Julia knew that she had to give the real version of the notes to her sister. *She knows me too well to accept a soft-pedaling of what's happened,* Julia reminded herself. But conversely, Julia didn't want to deny the seriousness of the situation. She needed to tell someone the truth, because she needed input on how to handle it. The decisions she made now could mean life or death, for herself or her daughters.

"Okay," Diana said as music from upstairs filtered down through the house. "They can't hear. I want to know what those notes really said."

Julia told her.

"My God! This is really serious, Julia. Someone out there thinks you're an adulteress."

"I realize that."

"Do you think it's Peter, who is now assuming there has to be another man?"

Julia shook her head. "No, I don't think this is Peter, although he's done plenty of crazy things, like peeking in the windows, having temper outbursts, and destroying things." She hesitated, feeling the stress building in her. "I think I'd be very foolish to close my mind to the evidence that it might be someone else."

"For God's sake! Who?"

Julia shook her head. "The only man I've been alone with since being divorced was Earl Paulsen for dinner several times to discuss writing." She paused. "And I don't think a respected criminal lawyer and national best-selling writer shoots at people and leaves threatening notes."

"I wouldn't think so." Diana put down her cup. "But he is married, isn't he?"

"Yeah, and apparently to a woman who is emotionally handicapped."

"He told you that?" Diana's gaze was suddenly direct. "Because you do know that married men often use that old cliché when they're putting the hustle on a woman, don't you, Julia?"

"It's nothing like that, Diana."

Diana glanced away. "I hope not."

"In any case, I won't be seeing Earl again."

"Why not, if your friendship is only platonic?"

Julia shrugged. "Because, as you say, he's married, and—"

"And you're attracted to him."

"I didn't say that."

"You didn't have to. Remember? We're sisters, from the same gene pool, with the same upbringing, and I know how you think, just as you know how I think."

An awkward silence went by.

"I guess I don't want to discuss Earl right now, okay?"

Diana shrugged. "As long as you don't think he, or someone connected to him, wrote those notes."

"My God! I would hope not." She wasn't up for speculation about Earl at this point.

"Good."

Another silence.

"Then let's discuss our course of action here," Diana added.

"What do you mean?"

"Get real, Julia. You and my nieces can't remain here unprotected." She paused. "The three of you need to stay with Ted and me, at least for the next few nights, until Detective Fitch gets a fix on what's going on."

"I can't do that," Julia protested. "I have my work, and all of it is connected to this house, like the final revisions on the computer manual I've been writing, my wreath products are hanging in the garage, my cakes that are ready to frost are in the freezer, and all my wallpapering supplies are also in the garage. If I'm not here to work, my income stops."

There was another silence while Diana digested what she'd said. "Oh, God, Julia. I feel like shit because I can't help you out financially so you can move. Although Ted and I have good incomes, we're leveraged to the max. In other words, it takes everything we make to pay our mortgage." She hesitated. "But we're here for you in every other way, even if you and the girls need to move in with us."

Julia smiled, shaking her head. "We'll be okay, sis. This whole awful scenario can't go on forever."

Further conversation was interrupted by the ringing phone. Julia got up to grab the receiver from the bar counter. "Hello."

"Detective Fitch here. I neglected to tell you a couple of things—the patrol of your house is being expanded to at least once an hour, at random times of course, so that anyone watching wouldn't have a fix on the time."

"Thanks, Detective Fitch."

"Jim."

His correction brought a smile even though he couldn't see it. "Thanks, I appreciate that."

"You're welcome." His voice faded and came back, and she knew he was on a cellular phone. "The other reason for the call is that I want to strongly advise you to have someone stay in the house with you at night, and—"

"You sound like my sister," she said, interrupting. "She's right here and just said the same thing."

"Your sister sounds like a smart woman. I agree with her."

"We'll figure something out, Detective, uh, I mean Jim. And thanks for your concern—and for the extra patrol."

"Just doing my job."

"I appreciate that."

"Call if anything comes up, anything at all. You have all my numbers. And I have your sister's phone number."

"I will."

"Uh, one last thing. It looks like we may have a ballistics match. The bullets taken from the Cherokee were probably fired from the same weapon that was used in the other shootings on the trail."

"I see." Now she understood why the patrol had been expanded, his concern that had prompted this call.

Julia thanked him again, and they hung up. Then she turned back to Diana and told her what the detective had said. Her sister looked as shocked as she felt.

A long silence went by.

"You know," Diana began slowly. "I was thinking as you were talking, and I may have come up with a plan, for the short term, anyway."

Julia raised her brows and waited for Diana to clarify.

"Ted and I had skiing plans for this weekend at Crystal Mountain, which we were about to cancel. We'd intended to leave after work on Wednesday evening, and come back late Sunday afternoon. Why can't the girls go with us and you can house-sit, which means all of you are away from here, at least until we get back." A pause. "That way you can still work during the day, especially with that patrol checking your house each hour."

Julia considered her suggestion. "What about tonight and Tuesday night?"

"Ted and I will stay here."

"You know, Diana, it could work. If the girls went with you and Ted, they wouldn't be in danger from the person who is obviously tracking me. But—"

"I know your 'but' and your fears," Diana said, interrupting her sentence. "We don't want to be obvious about what we're doing—so if someone is out there watching, they won't know our plans."

"Sounds like a plot for a suspense novel."

"I'm not being facetious, Julia. I'm dead serious."

Julia nodded, her gaze suddenly direct. "I think your suggestion is the best plan we've got at the moment, Diana. You and Ted take the girls to Crystal Mountain, they'll think it's only a getaway weekend, I'll house-sit and still be able to come here during the day to do my work." She didn't add that the shooter wouldn't hesitate to hurt one of her daughters to get to her, as had already been demonstrated. She wanted to get the girls away, out of harm's way.

"Okay, we'll go with it." Diana pushed back her empty coffee cup. "As long as it's all right that Alyssa and Samantha miss Thursday and Friday from school."

"That'll be okay. They're both good students and can catch up, although they'll miss a Friday night game."

Diana stood up. "Okay, that'll be the plan. We'll revise when we get back from Crystal Mountain on Sunday. You and the girls will stay over until Monday, and then we'll make up another course of action."

"Sounds good."

Julia walked her sister to the front door. "I'll have dinner ready by seven. Is that too late?" she asked.

"Perfect," Diana replied. "Gives Ted a chance to get home, shower, and check his e-mail. We'll make supper fun, like there wasn't an impending danger."

Julia watched Diana go, grateful to have such a supportive person in her life.

Everything is going to be okay, she told herself. By the time her family returned from Crystal Mountain maybe the police would have made progress in identifying the shooter. She hoped so, even as she knew it was probably a false hope.

Stay positive, she reminded herself. She would not give in to a cowardly killer who stalked victims from the shadows. Not ever.

"Mom, you're letting us skip school to ski?" Alyssa sounded incredulous after Julia explained Diana's offer the next morning. "How come?"

"Yeah, it's a first," Samantha chimed in.

Julia busied herself with buttering toast, hoping they wouldn't see any doubt in her eyes. "I just thought it was a nice break, even if you did have to miss school. You'll stay where we stayed, at the chalet Ted's parents own. Aunt Diana thought it would be great if the two of you could go, so long as your grades are good and you can make up class work."

"We can," Alyssa said. "I, for one, want to go."

"Me, too," Samantha agreed.

"Okay, then you're both going." Julia grinned at them. "Wish I could join you, but I have too much work that has to be completed by the end of the week."

"Wish you could, too, Mom," Alyssa said as she picked up her books and followed Samantha to the door, knowing Diana was waiting for her in the driveway to drive them to school.

Julia saw them out to the front porch, where both girls turned back, almost as one, suddenly looking anxious.

"If we go will you be okay alone?" Alyssa asked.

"Of course," she said at once, smiling. "As I explained, I'll be house-sitting at your aunt's house, only working here during the day." She managed a reassuring posture. "And you'll only be an hour or two away, and we have phones, remember?"

Both girls visibly relaxed and then ran to get in their aunt's car. Julia went back into the house, relieved that her girls would be away from the danger that had descended upon them.

What about you? she thought. *Will you be safe?*

She hoped so.

CHAPTER THIRTY-SIX

"Christ almighty! Why in hell wasn't I told about this life and death bullshit? Some psycho shoots at you and Alyssa and then leaves threatening notes and I'm left out here in the dark about what's happening? No way! You're my wife. Those two girls are my daughters! I'm going to demand an accounting from those freaking cops who're always harassing me."

Peter's voice boomed in Julia's ear, and she had to hold the phone away. He was so angry that he was sputtering to get the words out.

"I'm not your wife anymore, Peter," she reminded him calmly. Peter's histrionics were the last thing she needed right now, and she wondered how he'd found out. Then she knew. Alyssa must have confided in her grandmother last night. And then Frances had told Peter, and hence his call.

She sighed. She couldn't fault Alyssa, and she didn't want her girls to be involved in a conspiracy of secrets, what they could or couldn't tell their own grandmother.

It wasn't their fault that a phantom killer had apparently targeted their mother. That was a big enough trip for teenagers to handle without taking their spontaneity away, too.

"Hey," he was saying as her mind went back to the conversation. "You're the mother of my daughters, were my wife then, and therefore you're still my wife when it comes to them. Legally I might not have much to say about what you do, but I have everything to say about what you do that affects Alyssa and Samantha."

Partly right, she thought. And partly convoluted thinking. "I understand your concern, Peter," she said, striving for a proper balance so she wouldn't set him off. He'd seemed better lately, but was he?

"I hope you do, Julia. You turned my whole life upside down with the divorce. I don't want you doing that to the girls because you refuse to live with their father."

She sat down on her bed, having answered her phone while she was packing her overnight bag. "I don't want to argue with you, Peter, but I have to protest. I'm not responsible for your happiness, nor am I responsible for what is happening now, although I'm very concerned."

She didn't want to say 'terrified' and give him a platform for going into his dirge that it had all happened because she'd ended their marriage. She wiped her hair back from her face, feeling totally frustrated. Peter was hopeless, and certainly not a person to go to for help. He turned everything around to further his own cause.

To bulldoze his way back to the family—his safety zone.

It's sad, Julia thought. His compulsive focus was symbolic of some deep underlying feelings he seemed incapable of controlling, so he acted out in frustration, rage, and threats. Again, the thought crossed her mind that he might be playing into the other shootings on her jogging trail, had orchestrated the incident at the trailhead involving her and Alyssa, never intending to kill anyone, just trying to influence her back to the marriage. The thought was chilling.

"That's a convenient argument, Julia." He sucked in a quick breath. "But the truth is that no one would be targeting my family if I were still in the picture, right?"

"Wrong."

His hesitation surprised Julia. Peter was prone to verbal abuse, not silence while he considered his response.

"What's the name of the police officer involved?" he asked finally, his tone indicating that she was a lost cause.

She told him Detective Jim Fitch's name and number.

"Detective?"

"Uh-huh, a homicide detective." She realized it was best that he talk to Jim Fitch rather than continuing their conversation.

"Son of a bitch."

"Pardon me?"

"I'll call him." A pause. "Maybe I'll get more out of him than I've gotten from you, Julia. You're hopeless."

The dial tone sounded in her ear.

Even though she knew it was just more of Peter's verbal abuse, Julia felt the put-down. But at least he hadn't asked what was in the notes, because she would have had to lie. She knew that Detective Fitch wouldn't tell him either, since she was sure that he considered Peter a suspect. Oh, God! When would the nightmare ever end? she wondered.

She stood up and went back to her packing, knowing

she mustn't let his accusations affect her. She hadn't done anything wrong, not during their marriage or after they were divorced. In the beginning she'd believed that they would be together forever. How naïve, she thought. She'd had no way of foretelling a future with his accelerating irrational behavior, which had left her with no other option than to end their marriage. The repressed rage that he'd directed onto her had been turning deadly, and she feared a tragedy if he lost complete control. He was no longer able to cope with business or family.

But her self-talk didn't help. She was going in circles. Surely Peter hadn't been the shooter.

But she was uncertain . . . again.

The girls were packed but not yet home from school. When they arrived, and after they'd changed their clothes, Julia was driving them to Diana's house on Lake Sammamish.

Julia paced the route between kitchen and front door, impatient, feeling jazzed up, as though bracing for the next attack from the phantom who never stepped from the darkness into the light. She was in the entry when the phone rang, startling her.

As she ran back to the kitchen to answer it, an icy finger of fear touched her spine. What's happened now? she wondered, hoping nothing.

But that wasn't the case, she realized, hearing the voice on the other end of the connection. It was Frances, her former mother-in-law. Julia braced herself.

"Julia," the woman began. "I know what happened from Alyssa, and I have to say that I didn't sleep last night. I wanted to talk to you right away, but I respected Alyssa's wishes that I didn't."

"I understand, Frances."

"Do you really?" A sigh came over the wires. "I'm so out of the family loop since you and Peter divorced that I feel I no longer have a say in the lives of my granddaughters." A pause. "But I must have my say this time in order to live with myself in the event the worst happens. In case that shooter hurts you or one of the girls."

Julia was silent for long seconds, suddenly acutely aware of yet another ramification after a family breakup: close relatives got lost in the shuffle. Whatever annoyance her former mother-in-law had been, there'd never been any doubt that she loved her granddaughters.

"I'm so sorry to worry you like this, Frances," Julia began slowly. "But please be assured that everything is being done to protect the girls and me. Believe me; I won't let anything happen to them."

"Or to you, Julia." A pause. "Not to sound like Peter, because I, uh, understand him more than you know, but you'll always be my daughter-in-law. I want you around to bring up my granddaughters."

For a moment Julia didn't know what to say. The compliment was unexpected, but she felt it was sincere. So she kept her response simple.

"Thank you, Frances. I appreciate your words more than I can say."

"Will you keep me informed about what's going on?"

"I promise that I will."

"Thank you."

"And if no one answers the phone here, leave a message and I'll get back to you."

A pause.

"Are you leaving your house, Julia?"

How astute, Julia thought. She must have heard something in her tone, if not her words.

"Only for the weekend, Frances, but my voice mail will be on, and I check messages regularly."

"Are you leaving because of this threat?"

Another silence.

"To be honest, yes."

"My dear God," Frances said. "It is bad. I can't believe you have to leave your own house." A pause. "Julia, Peter just couldn't be responsible for this."

Julia digested her refusal to accept that Peter could be that emotionally ill, realizing Frances was genuinely concerned. Whatever happened in Peter's childhood that had brought him to his present mental problems, Frances didn't share the same affliction. And maybe Peter's mental imbalance hadn't stemmed from childhood conditioning but from a chemical imbalance in his brain, as Dr. Kornsweig, Peter's psychiatrist, had suggested. Peter would take the prescribed pills for a while, then discontinue when he felt better, and then spiral downward again.

"Whoever is responsible, Frances, I have to do whatever it takes to make sure we're safe," Julia said, trying to put a positive spin on an untenable situation. "The girls will be away for four days."

"And you?"

"I won't be here at night."

"But you will during the day?"

"Uh-huh, my work base is in this house, and I have to work to pay our bills."

Another silence.

"I can't tell you how sad I am about all this, Julia. You shouldn't have to work as you do. I-I—" Her words drifted off. "I'm so sorry, that's all."

"Thank you for that, Frances." Julia shifted the phone to the other ear so she could face the hallway door and hear when her daughters arrived. "I'm so glad we had this conversation, even if it is because of the frightening incidents lately. I feel good about knowing you're there for Alyssa and Samantha."

"I am, you have to know I am, Julia." A pause. "And you, too. If the three of you need a safe place, you can fly out here to Chicago and stay with me." She drew in a ragged breath. "And no one need know, not even Peter."

"Thank you, Frances."

Julia could only guess at the significance of her offer, and the fact that she wouldn't tell Peter. Did that mean she didn't trust her son either, that she thought he was behind the reign of terror?

Or was she, like Peter, only trying to deceive her?

Shit, Julia thought. Distrust was another by-product of what was happening. She didn't know whom to believe.

"Where will you stay? How will I know you and the girls are safe?" Frances asked, her tone still sounding uncertain.

"We'll be with Diana and Ted. Both girls are going with them on a skiing weekend."

"Oh, my goodness, Julia. I thought you said you'd all be safely away. Don't tell me you'll be alone at home?"

"I'm house-sitting for someone," she said, evading. "I won't be here in this house."

"So you'll be at your sister's place when they're gone."

"I didn't say that, Frances. No one knows where I'm staying, but the house has a high-tech security system, and the police know where I'll be, and there will be an extra patrol of our house here."

"Good, that makes me feel better."

They hung up a minute later after good-byes and

cautions about safety from Frances. When the dial tone sounded, Julia stared at the phone before slowly resting the receiver in its cradle.

She'd just done what she shouldn't have done—told her mother-in-law about her plans. But Frances had sounded sincere about her concerns. Surely she wouldn't relay the information to Peter. But Julia was suddenly apprehensive.

What if she did?

They were about to leave; the girls packed their skis and suitcases into the Cherokee, which had just been repaired, and they came back into the house to wait for Julia.

"Hey, Mom, we're gonna be late!" Alyssa called to Julia, who had lingered in her office when her fax machine had rung and a page had started to come through the line.

"I'll be right there!" she called back, still waiting as the paper printed a message from someone, hopefully a new customer, she thought. She could use another job now that she'd just submitted the computer manual, hoping it met with approval so that she'd receive her final payment. And how she needed that money.

The fax beeped, and she knew the one page was all she'd receive. She picked it up and couldn't help getting the message, written in big bold letters across the page.

> I'm so worried. I've been unable to reach you. Call me in the morning. It's imperative that we talk. Judy.

Her name was followed by her office and home phone numbers.

Julia stared at the message. What did it mean? Judy must be desperate to send her a fax.

"Mom!" Samantha called. "Aunt Diana and Uncle Ted are waiting for us. They want to get up to their cabin before midnight. Are you ready to go?"

"Coming!" Julia called back. She tucked the fax into her shirt pocket. She'd call Judy back at her home number once the girls were on their way with Diana and Ted.

But she was unsettled. Why would Judy resort to a fax when she could have tried to keep calling on the phone? Come to think of it, there'd been several hang-ups today, but Julia discounted the possibility that it would have been Judy, as she always left a message. Why wouldn't she have this time? Because she was afraid someone else would hear it? It didn't make sense.

I'll find out what's going on once I get the family safely off to the mountains, she told herself. Then she went to join the girls.

At least they'd soon be out of harm's way, and no one would know where they were. Even if she came back into stalking range when she returned to her house in the morning, Julia figured she could take care of herself. She had two homicide detectives to help her.

CHAPTER THIRTY-SEVEN

EVERYONE WAS SO EXCITED ABOUT BEING IN THE MOUNtains for four days that Julia wished she could have gone with them, too. Ted and Diana already had their equipment and supplies loaded in their minivan when Julia drove up the long driveway to the house and parked behind Ted's vehicle. As Ted loaded Samantha's and Alyssa's things into the van, Julia followed Diana into the house so her sister could give her a rundown on the alarm system, door locks, voice mail, and show her the phone numbers of nearby neighbors.

"Just in case you need them," Diana said, pointing out the list that she'd taped next to the phone in the kitchen. "All of us lake residents look out for each other, not just because of burglars, but because weather can sometimes do damage to docks, boats and boathouses."

Julia nodded. Ted and Diana had all three, and late fall in the Northwest sometimes brought bad windstorms or an unexpected snowfall that could sink a boat or collapse a boathouse roof. But she knew her sister was thinking of the shooter.

As Diana went to check on Ted's progress, Julia went upstairs to deposit her overnight bag in the guestroom, flipping on lights as she went. It had been an overcast day, and the light was fading fast as night approached. She wondered if it had been a mistake to stay at her sister's house rather than at home, where she knew every nook and cranny, could identify each creak and groan of the timbers in the middle of the night. Diana's place was bigger, more isolated from neighbors than hers, and the grounds around the house were landscaped with shrubs, bushes, and trees. The whole ambiance at night could be scary.

Fraidy cat, she admonished herself as she stood by the window that overlooked the grassy slope to the lake. The exterior lights were on a sensor and had already come on, illuminating some of the dark places—and Ted's sixteen-foot speedboat, which was tied up to the little dock. Ted and Diana loved bundling up during the holiday season and trolling the lake to see the Christmas lights from the water. *You're safe here*, she reminded herself. *No one knows you'll be here alone.*

Except the homicide detectives, she thought. It was the best move under the circumstances. Unbeknownst to Alyssa and Sam, she'd even made sure that no one had followed them from home. Her vigilance had been subtle; she hadn't wanted to spoil the skiing trip for her daughters.

"Hey, Julia," Diana called from downstairs. "It's getting late. We're ready to go."

"Coming!"

She ran down the steps to the front door, where Diana waited. Behind her sister she could see Ted holding their dog, Bow, and the girls waiting to get into the van. Julia went outside to see them off. After hugs, kisses, admonitions to be safe, and a final good-bye, they piled into the vehicle and managed to buckle up amidst all the gear.

"Be careful, Mom," Alyssa said through the open back window. "I wish you were coming with us."

"Next time," Julia said, contriving a big grin but suddenly feeling close to tears. "Everything will be fine here while you're gone. In fact, I intend to get lots of work done."

"Maybe we should stay with you," Samantha added, sobering. "I hate to leave you alone."

"Nonsense. You're going to have lots of fun, and I'm going to catch up on all of my projects so I can go next time. Okay?"

Both girls nodded.

"Well, we're off then," Diana said from the front passenger seat, but Julia could see that she was also a little concerned. Earlier, she'd tried to convince Julia to go, too, and Julia had again explained the importance of keeping up on her work. Diana had finally settled for the fact that Julia would be safe house-sitting, with the police checking on her when she was home during the day. "We'll call you later, after we get to the chalet," she added.

"Sounds good."

They all blew kisses, Ted waved, and then the van headed down the driveway toward the street. Julia watched it till it was out of sight, then went back inside and closed and locked the door. She went to the kitchen to make a cup of tea, pulling the fax from Judy out of her pocket as she waited for the water to heat. A glance at her watch told her it was going on five, but she'd call the office first in the hope that Judy was still there.

She sat down in an overstuffed chair by the glass

doors to the back deck, punched in her therapist's number, and stared at the wind-rippled surface of the lake as she waited for someone to answer.

It was an anticlimax. The voice mail picked up, and Julia left a message that she would call Judy's house. That call was also answered by an answering machine, but she left her number and where she was staying and that she'd call back later. She put the phone back in its cradle, then took her tea and went upstairs to her room, where she switched on the television set to watch the evening news.

But she was restless. It felt strange to be there, and she missed the routine in her own house. Sighing, she unpacked her long flannel nightgown, went to the connecting bathroom, and filled the tub with water. After a hot soak she would fix something to eat and then call Judy again.

For the moment she quelled thoughts of murder and mayhem. That could wait until after she talked to Judy.

Judy picked up on the first ring. "Thank God you called. I got your earlier messages."

"And I got your fax, Judy. What's happened?"

"Sorry about the fax, but I've been having trouble with my phone line at the office. A technician came to check it out, and you'd never believe what he found."

"What?"

"There was some sort of a device on my line that allowed someone to listen in on my calls."

"My God! That sounds like something in a suspense movie."

"That's what I thought, until I suddenly realized that my phone problems started after one of my patients began to remember things and was calling me, terrified and desperate."

"Remember what things?"

"I can't reveal details, but it involves someone close to my patient, someone who is trying to find out what the patient is saying to me. Someone who may have had my line tapped."

"That's frightening."

"Yeah, especially since this someone didn't know my patient had witnessed something horrific, and only found out by accident."

"So you were afraid to talk to anyone on your phone?"

"The problem is apparently cleared, but I won't take chances, especially since you might have some involvement in this, uh, situation as well."

"Me? Did you say me?"

"Uh-huh, although I'm sure you don't know what's involved here."

Julia stood up from the edge of the bed where she'd been sitting. "That's ambiguous, Judy. You need to tell me what's going on."

A silence went by.

"I'm on the fence here about the patient confidentiality issue, but I'm leaning toward breaching it if I feel someone's in danger."

"Me?"

"I don't know for sure."

"You've got to explain, especially since I've already become a shooter's target, not to mention all the terrifying incidents around my house."

"Can you come to my office tomorrow?"

"Late afternoon?"

"You can't make it in the morning? This is important."

"No. The earliest would be three." Julia didn't add

that her appointment with the software company couldn't be broken or she'd lose future contracts, if not the current one. That could be more important than Judy's fears, which couldn't be that vital or surely she would have called the police.

A sigh came over the wire. "Okay then, I guess it has to be three."

"I'll be there." Julia had been pacing the bedroom as they talked, pausing at the window overlooking the lake, which loomed like the black lagoon at that moment. "Can't you say why you're concerned about me in this scenario?"

"We'll talk tomorrow, okay? In the meantime, be very careful."

They hung up on that note, and Julia doubted if she'd ever get to sleep now, especially being alone and in a strange bed. Diana called to say that they'd arrived at the cabin, and after satisfying herself that Julia was fine, rang off to fix supper. Julia turned up the television, listening for a few minutes about another crisis in the Middle East, then flipped it off. She didn't need more death and violence in her mind before she tried to relax.

What in hell was going on? she wondered. Had Judy heard something from Dr. Kornsweig about Peter that had alarmed her? Surely Peter wouldn't be crazy enough to tap Judy's phone.

Julia turned out the bedside lamp, hoping the darkness would help her feel drowsy. It didn't. She only felt more vulnerable, and the silence intensified the sounds around her. The wind hummed and whined, nipping at the dormers, preening the shrubs and branches in the garden, shuffling the shake shingles on the boathouse roof like a deck of cards. She sat back up, knowing she had to do something.

Julia padded barefoot over the carpet to the master bedroom, where she knew Diana kept a phone on the nightstand. Confident that no one could be in the house because of the alarm system, she didn't turn on a light. Picking up the phone, she punched in Detective Fitch's office number, the one she'd taken the time to memorize, knowing she might need it. When his voice mail answered, she wasn't surprised; the man couldn't be on duty twenty-four hours a day.

The message she left was an abbreviated version of Judy's call, complete with Judy's full name and the fact that she was her therapist. "I don't know what to think of it, but I know it's scared me a little. Therefore, Detective Fitch, I felt I needed to tell you just in case." She laughed, nervously, suddenly feeling a little silly. "Just in case of what I'm not sure." She hung up and wondered if she was overreacting.

No, she told herself. She felt better already. Someone else needed to know what she knew—because someone out there was watching and listening and—waiting?

She went back to bed and dozed off after a while.

Her body jerked, her eyes popped open, and Julia was suddenly wide awake, staring into the darkness. For long seconds she didn't move, her gaze traveling over the room, satisfying herself that she was alone. Only then did she glance at the clock on the bedside table. Not quite midnight. She'd only been asleep for an hour.

What had awakened her? Her own nervous state? The wind, which had grown in intensity while she'd slept? Tree branches scraping the siding like fingers searching for a way inside the house?

Whoa, she told herself. *Tone down the imagination. You woke up, that's all.*

She lay there straining her ears, but the sounds were normal for a stormy night. Finally she had to get up, peek out some windows, and satisfy herself that all was as secure outside as it was inside. She glided across the carpet on the balls of her feet to the lakefront windows, careful to not make a sound.

Standing to the side, she peered into the night, and as her eyes became accustomed to the deeper hues outside, she saw that everything looked normal. But then something caught her eye in the stand of trees between Diana's house and the neighbors.

What? she wondered.

And then she saw it again. A flash of light that was gone so fast she wondered if she really saw it. Julia strained her eyes, catching the next momentary flash, this time farther away.

She suddenly realized what she was seeing. Someone was using a flashlight, turning it on for only a second to get their bearings, and then moving on, only to repeat the process.

She ran to a side window with a better view of the woods between the houses. The final flash was almost obscured by the brush and trees, and she realized that someone had made it all the way to the street.

Her knees wobbled and she went down on them, bracing herself against the windowsill, her eyes on the spot where she'd last seen the light.

A flash of light like the one she'd seen in the woods behind her house, that instant flicker that she'd dismissed as imagination?

Who was it this time? Surely not a neighbor, as the light had traveled away from any of the houses lining the lake. Peter . . . because Frances had told him where she'd probably gone?

Or someone else, who'd been outside, who had made a noise that had awakened her? She didn't know. But she did know that security system or not, she'd probably never get another minute of sleep that night.

Strangely, she eventually did, after she was no longer able to keep her eyes open.

CHAPTER THIRTY-EIGHT

Julia woke up slowly, and for a moment she was disoriented. She sat up, her eyes on the lines of light at the edge of the blinds, and the blankets fell away to drop into her lap. It was morning, and she was in her sister's guestroom, alone in the house.

Shit, she thought, as her mind flashed on the light she'd seen among the trees in the middle of the night. Julia shook her head, clearing the cobwebs, and realized that it was now daylight and she was no longer spooked by thoughts of someone hidden in the dark, watching. In retrospect, it seemed a little histrionic, silly. The light probably had nothing to do with her.

Or did it? Again she was reminded that Frances knew where she and the girls had gone. Had she broken her promise and told Peter?

Don't jump to conclusions, Julia instructed herself. Her mother-in-law cared too much about Peter to have told him. Julia suspected that Frances realized just how disturbed Peter was and didn't want to tempt fate, have him do something even worse than his prior actions.

Swinging her legs from under the covers, Julia stood up and went to the windows, tilting the venetian blinds open so that she could see the grounds surrounding the house. Out front the surface of the lake was capping from the wind, and a light drizzle fell from a low, gray sky. The wooded area where she'd seen the light was shadowy and impenetrable in the stillness of dawn. But it did not seem frightening, as it had hours earlier.

She smiled at her own paranoia. *That's what happens when you're scared to death about things*, she told herself.

After making her bed, Julia went downstairs, stopping in the front hall to disarm the alarm. Then she hurried on to the kitchen to start coffee. Her mind churned with everything she wanted to accomplish in the hours ahead before her appointment with Judy, but she kept stalling on one important fact. She needed to know Earl's version of how he knew the dead women on the jogging trail.

Everything hinged on knowing whether or not she should tell Judy or Detective Fitch about her suspicions.

Which were what? she asked herself, watching the coffee drip. That he'd called one of the murdered women from her bedroom, lying to her about his wife having a headache? Maybe she'd been a client, not another woman he was involved with. Maybe the woman had been fearful of something and he'd called to reassure her. Maybe? Maybe? She poured coffee into a mug and took it upstairs to sip on while she showered and dressed. She needed Earl to level with her before she explained her own questions about his behavior that night to the homicide detectives, and to Judy.

And what were those questions? she wondered again.

She pondered that as she got ready for the day, closed up her sister's house, and drove home. By the time she arrived it still wasn't eight in the morning, and she'd come to a decision.

She was going to Earl's office and insist that he clarify his actions before her late-morning appointment with the software company and her afternoon appointment with Judy. Her immediate work could wait until after that.

Julia stood huddled under her umbrella on the corner of Fifth and Columbia waiting for the light, her eyes on the Columbia Tower, the highest building in downtown Seattle. Earl's office was somewhere on one of its seventy-six floors.

The light changed and she stepped off the curb to head across the street, which sloped down many steep hills to Elliott Bay far below. The wind off Puget Sound swept upward, whining through the corridors between other high-rise buildings, to blast the pedestrians in the crosswalk and pull at the hem of Julia's raincoat. By instinct, she tilted her umbrella before it was turned inside out. Once on the sidewalk again, she ran the final distance to the front entrance and went inside, grateful to be out of the wind and rain. Her dash from where she'd found a parking place on the street two blocks away had left her panting, and she took a moment to catch her breath. Closing her dripping umbrella, she moved to the directory, scanning it for Earl's office. Then she headed for the bank of elevators.

While she was whisked upward through the building, Julia hoped she didn't look too windblown. She'd left her hair long and straight, had taken pains with her makeup, and had worn a new red cashmere sweater with black slacks. She'd wanted to look her best, because—she had to face it—she was still attracted to Earl.

Which was why she'd come. She had to know if there was a logical explanation for his strange actions lately.

Her mind still rejected that it could be otherwise.

Upon reaching his floor she marched toward his suite, afraid she'd lose her nerve if she hesitated. But she almost did anyway when she stepped into his office. She'd known he was successful, had expected that his law firm would be nicely appointed and in good taste, but she was unprepared for the elegance of the high-end antique furniture, deep pile carpeting, valuable paintings and art. But it was the wide, high windows showcasing the city below, the Puget Sound beyond that, and the ragged peaks of the Olympic Mountains in the distance that riveted her attention. The view from so high up was stunning, and for long seconds all she could do was stare. Her next thought was about the cost of occupying such pricey real estate. Earl had to be far richer than she'd imagined.

The woman behind the reception barrier glanced up, pulled off her glasses, and stood to come around the desk. She was tall and elegant, dressed in a black designer suit, white silk blouse and high heel pumps, the protocol penguin outfit, another conformity that Julia hated about working in the corporate world. The only flash of color were her long red fingernails and matching lipstick. It was a surprise to realize the well-preserved receptionist was probably in her mid-fifties.

"May I help you?" she asked, her affect as professionally perfect as her appearance. "Do you have an appointment?"

"Uh, no, I don't." Julia smiled and unbuttoned her raincoat. "I'm a friend of Mr. Paulsen's and hoped I could have a word with him when he's free."

"He didn't know you were coming?" The woman tilted her chin in a question, and there was no return smile of welcome. "He has a very busy schedule today, is in fact in a meeting right now. I would suggest you call him, or"—she picked up a pad and pen from her desk and held it out to Julia—"you could leave him a message to call you."

Julia stepped closer, disregarding the pen and pad, unwilling to be intimidated by Earl's secretary. "Just tell him I'm here. I'll wait until he has a free minute to talk to me."

"I'm sorry Ms., uh, what was your name?"

"Julia Farley."

"I don't think there'll be a free minute," she went on in a haughty tone. "He's already fit his daughter into his schedule and is meeting with her right now, but I'll let him know you're here."

Julia watched as the woman went back to her desk to pick up the receiver and buzz her boss. She heard her say her name and that she waited in the reception area. There was a pause. "No, she insists on speaking to you directly, Mr. Paulsen." The disapproving tone would have intimidated Julia had she not been put out by such unnecessary rudeness. She hadn't done anything wrong, nor did she have anything to hide. She definitely wasn't a bimbo, as the secretary's attitude implied.

A haughty bitch, Julia decided. But, to be fair, Earl's recent newspaper coverage had probably put the woman on edge, she being a buffer between Earl and the press. Maybe she suspected that Julia was really a newspaper reporter, or worse, one of Earl's *other women*. Some of the recent articles on the murders had hinted that he had a stable of women friends. His response had been that all men in his position have many female acquaintances and professional friends. At the time of reading it Julia had smiled at his ambivalent statement, knowing he was trying to protect his reputation. She hadn't believed for a second that he was a womanizer. The press was notorious for sensationalism. But now she was no longer sure about Earl. When it really came down to it, she didn't know him all that well beyond their own dates and his professional persona as a criminal lawyer and successful author.

Suddenly, the door opened to the inner office, and Earl and an overweight young woman stepped into the spacious reception area. The woman, dressed in a business suit that strained the buttons over her breasts, was not attractive: her dark hair had no style, her face was fleshy and marred by acne, and her tense body language denoted suppressed anger. Her dark, penetrating gaze, which had immediately fastened on Julia, was riveting and disapproving.

She could only be Jenny, Earl's daughter.

Julia's eyes shifted to Earl, and their gazes locked. She suppressed a smile, sensing the young woman's eyes were still on her, watchful and stern, an expression reflected on her father's face. Although her mother had been a model, Jenny was not pretty; she'd inherited her father's features but appeared to lack the animation that would give her the illusion of being attractive. Momentarily, Julia felt sorry for the girl.

Earl seemed taken aback to see her, although he was

quick to control that perception behind a brusque manner. "Mrs. Farley, what can I do for you?" he asked, as though she were a client.

"I only needed a few minutes of your time," Julia began, her words stilted by her unwelcoming reception.

"And what does this concern?" His expression was closed. "Something to do with writing, I presume?" He turned to his daughter. "Mrs. Farley is a writer affiliated with the conference I attended several months ago."

She scarcely nodded.

"Uh, yes, it does have to do with writing," Julia answered, taking his lead. He was making sure that she was connected to business, not someone he'd dated, a person to whom he'd confided his unhappy personal life on many occasions.

"You could have written me a letter if you're inviting me to the next conference." He managed a laugh, although his eyelid tic gave away his nervousness. She'd put him on the spot, and he was quietly outraged.

"Yes, I suppose I could have." Julia felt a flash of anger. How dare he treat her with such disregard, like a stranger off the street? Somehow she was able to maintain a normal air. "But since the issue I need to discuss with you needs an immediate answer, and since I was in town anyway, I took a chance that you could spare me a couple of minutes." She was about to go on when he put up a flat silencing hand, an intimidating gesture even though he still smiled.

"I'm sorry you wasted a trip to my office, even if you were already in town. I'm sure my secretary told you I'm scheduled to the max and I don't have a spare minute for a talk, however short it might be."

Julia's face flushed with embarrassment. She nodded, unable to find a polite retort amidst all the angry words that clamored for release behind her pursed lips.

"If you could leave your card, I'll try to call you later today or tomorrow—when my appointments permit."

Without a word, she grabbed a card from her purse, strode to the secretary's desk, and dropped it next to her phone. "Like you say, Mr. Paulsen, when your schedule permits." She flipped back her hair and looked him straight in the eyes. "If you can't manage that, then I'll just carry on with what I have to do without your input."

Something flickered in the blackness of his eyes, and his tic intensified. He inclined his head, then stepped forward and took her arm, leading her back to the entrance. "You'll hear from me," he said in a low tone meant only for her ears.

She nodded and left his office without another glance. The door closed with a soft click behind her, as suppressed as the vibes she'd picked up from Earl.

He was livid.

Once alone in the elevator she forced herself to stop tweezing the fabric of her raincoat between her fingers. He had his nerve being upset with her simply because she'd come to his office. Did he think she'd tell his daughter that her father wanted to date her, a thing she'd never dream of doing? In any case, he'd only kissed her. They hadn't slept together.

Thank God! Julia thought, watching the lighted floor buttons flicker as she descended down through the building.

And then the ramification of her visit hit her. He considered her *the other woman*, and as such she was not allowed to trespass in his life. Affairs were in a separate compartment and not connected to his real life.

The other woman? Or was she just *one* of the other

women? Oh, God. Her thoughts were going crazy because she was so angry. She didn't really know what to think.

But it made sense. She should have realized that earlier, when he hadn't called her as he'd promised. She also understood something else now. He'd changed toward her after she'd refused sex with him. That's when he'd called Nancy Fredricks from her bedroom, and why he'd left so suddenly.

Maybe he'd been having an affair with Nancy, and when she'd turned up murdered, he hadn't wanted their relationship exposed, as his connection to Carol Norton, the first victim of the shootings, had been. If that was true, it certainly didn't mean he was connected to her death. But it would not be a pleasant situation, even if he wasn't guilty of anything more than an illicit affair.

That could explain his reception of her—and that of his curt secretary. His life was probably under a microscope right now.

The elevator suddenly opened and she stepped into the main lobby, hurried to the street doors, and stepped outside. A frigid blast of wind and rain hit her instantly, and she shivered.

As she ran toward where she'd parked, she shook even harder, but not from the cold.

How dare he treat her like a whore! It was time to tell Jim Fitch everything she knew. Let him sort out what it all meant.

And then she drove to her appointment at the software company. She had herself in control by the time she arrived, a smile on her face. Her work was a part of her real world, Earl was not.

CHAPTER THIRTY-NINE

ALTHOUGH BRIEF, JULIA'S APPOINTMENT AT THE SOFTWARE company went well. The manager looked pleased, said he'd be in touch soon, and that they looked forward to working with her again. "We like people who meet their deadlines," he said. She left knowing she'd have more work with them.

Arriving home earlier than she'd expected, Julia realized there was time to get some work done before her appointment with Judy. It was a relief to look forward to wreaths and cakes, anything to take her mind off the visit to Earl's office. Once in the house she turned off the alarm, so glad she had the system in place. It gave her an immense sense of security. In fact she wished she hadn't agreed to house-sit. Her own place felt safer.

Sighing, Julia checked her phone messages, annoyed as the first one played out into the quiet kitchen.

"It's your husband," Peter said. "I want to know where my family has gone." He went on to say he needed to be informed when his daughters skipped school and left town.

Julia sat down to listen to the rest of them: a couple of orders for wedding cakes, a possible wallpapering job, and several more calls from Peter, each one sounding more irate.

Going around the counter, she put the teakettle on to boil, then took a mug and teabag from the cupboard. As she busied herself she thought about the content of Peter's messages. He obviously kept close track of all of them, knew that the house had been empty overnight. She also realized that Frances had kept her promise to not tell him where they'd gone. Julia felt reassured and knew that the woman wanted the best for her granddaughters.

The person with the flashlight in the woods last night hadn't been Peter.

The thought came unbidden, sending a shudder of fear through her. Then who? A neighbor looking for their dog? No, she told herself. They wouldn't have kept turning off their flashlight, as though they didn't want to be seen. But that still didn't mean the incident was connected to her.

Pouring the water over the teabag, she stood over the cup as it steeped, trying to make sense of all that had happened over the past months. There was no real pattern, aside from the fact that the incidents were ongoing and accelerating. Peter was the logical suspect, but she knew that he wasn't responsible for everything.

She took her tea back to the phone and called Detective Fitch, realizing he hadn't returned her call concerning Judy. *I'll just leave another one*, she told herself. She felt better when she reported her fears, even if they turned out to be silly.

"Detective Fitch," she said after the beep sounded to record her message. "I need to talk to you about another issue, my friendship with Earl Paulsen. This isn't an emergency, but I'd appreciate a call back when you can."

Julia had just hung up when someone knocked on the front door. Startled, she jumped, and her tea splashed from her cup to the counter. She put it down and crept to the front hall, careful to stay hidden from the person on the porch who was ringing the bell nonstop.

Peeking from the side window, she saw Peter's pickup truck parked in the driveway. She shrank back into the alcove under the stairs. No way in hell was she answering the door. If he kept his finger on the doorbell much longer, she intended to call 911.

Abruptly, the ringing stopped.

Hidden from his view, she watched him return to his truck, back out of the driveway, and head down the street. Her sigh of relief rushed out of her mouth in a long swoosh. Then she went back to the kitchen to return her calls, hoping to take cake orders and set a time for bidding on the wallpaper job. With a pen and pad ready, she sat down in front of the phone. It rang under her hand as she was about to lift the receiver.

"Hello?" she said in her best businesslike manner.

"Julia? Earl here."

Julia switched the phone to her other ear, suddenly apprehensive. She could hear that his rage was barely suppressed under a veneer of cordiality.

"Yes, it's Julia," she said, and waited.

She heard him suck in a breath, as though he was holding himself on a tight rein.

"I'd like to know the meaning of your brazen act this morning?"

"Brazen?" Her own anger surfaced, but she managed to maintain a calm tone. "I don't consider going to your office as being a *brazen act*."

"Oh no? Then what do you call it when you behave like a whore?"

His term took her words, and he went on before she could gather her thoughts to answer.

"You placed me in a compromising position in front of my daughter and my secretary." His voice rose with each word. "What in the hell did you think you were accomplishing—proving that you're a loose cannon bitch?"

"How dare you speak to me like this!"

"I dare because of what you did."

"Inform me. What did I do that was so bad?"

"You came to my office."

"So?" She gulped a breath. "How does that make me a whore? Why can't a friend drop in at your office, hoping you have a minute to discuss an important issue? For God's sake, Earl. We aren't having an affair, and I'm not asking you for anything." Another pause. "Why are you overreacting like this?"

A silence went by.

"You compromised me, Julia. I couldn't even call you back from my own phone. I've had to use a public street phone."

"Do you realize how crazy this sounds, Earl?"

"Crazy? Crazy?" His voice rose up the scale to sounding manic. "Is it crazy that you came to my office—a woman I've been seeing? How was I supposed to act in front of my daughter? Welcoming? Did you want to be introduced to her? Did you think being there would force me into making a decision about you?"

"My God, Earl," Julia retorted. "What are you talking about? You have no decision to make about me. *We were only friends.*"

"Were?"

"That's right. Our *friendship* is a thing of the past now."

He didn't acknowledge her but went on in the same accusatory manner. "What was so fuckin' important that you couldn't have e-mailed or called me?"

"You haven't responded to either one, Earl." Her voice shook with anger. "I wanted to give you the courtesy of explaining, as you'd promised to do, before I talked to the homicide detective or my therapist."

"For Christ's sake, surely you're not talking to them about me?"

"Not yet."

"What in hell does that mean?"

"Like I said, I was giving you the opportunity to clarify why you'd called one of the murder victims from my bedroom." She stood to brace her trembling body against the counter. "That was the only reason I came to your office. Since you hadn't contacted me, it was the only choice I had to let you know what I was doing."

Another silence.

"And what was that?" His tone had gone manic. "Going behind my back to cause trouble?"

Who was she talking to? she wondered. He had no resemblance to the Earl she'd met at the conference. Or the man she'd shared pleasant dinners with, discussing their mutual passion to write.

Had he flipped out? Or was she only seeing a side to

him that he usually kept hidden but didn't now because he was so stressed that he couldn't control himself?

Because he was under investigation?

"I'm not your enemy, Earl. On the contrary, I was being considerate of you."

"Like hell you were being considerate. Would a considerate person tattle to the police about things that didn't concern them?" He sucked in several quick breaths. "You're obviously trying to hurt me on both a professional and personal level. I won't have that Julia, not even from you."

"That's paranoid! Are you threatening me?"

"Just telling you the way it is. My family comes first, and I won't allow them to suffer because of a jealous bitch."

"What?" Was he talking about the same family he'd complained about—the wife he wanted to divorce?

"You heard me."

"Yes, I heard you, Earl. But you won't be hearing from me again." She gulped a ragged breath, devastated by his verbal assault. "You have to do what you have to do, and so do I. From here on out I'll express my concerns to the homicide detective or Judy."

"For Christ's sake, who's Judy?"

"Judy Gaston, my shrink."

A long silence went by.

"Out on Madison?"

"That's right. You know her?"

"I don't want you saying anything about me to a shrink. You got that, Julia?"

"My God! What's wrong with you, Earl? What's happened to change you so drastically?"

"Uppity whores, that's what. Whores who suddenly believe they've got me by the balls."

"This is so crazy. I'm hanging up."

"Not before I have your word that you leave me out of your discussions with detectives and shrinks."

"No promises." She sighed. "I think you've lost it, Earl. You're talking irrationally."

"I'm warning you. If you—"

"If I what? Tell the truth?"

"Fuck you, then! If you gossip about me, I'll see you in court for slander."

"Is that another threat?"

"It's a promise."

There was another silence.

"You obviously have a dark side, Earl, one I hadn't seen before. Just leave me alone or I'll tell the detective about that, too."

She slammed down the phone, and then stood staring at it, shaking from the emotional intensity of his unexpected attack. All of a sudden she felt better.

And fuck you, Earl Paulsen. You can't control me. You can't even control yourself.

Julia went to take a long, hot bath before she got ready for her appointment with Judy. She intended to tell her everything she knew about Earl. She needed to get it off her chest.

And then she stopped in her tracks. What had she done by forewarning him? The answer was instant.

CHAPTER FORTY

THE PHONE HAD RUNG FIVE OR SIX TIMES BEFORE SHE GOT out of the house and headed for the ferry. Oh, God, Topsy had just known it was him and hadn't answered. He always seemed to tune in on what she was about to do, especially if he felt threatened in some way, as he had been since overhearing her telephone conversation with her therapist.

She'd hung up quickly, not knowing how long he'd been listening. He'd questioned her, seemed satisfied with her answers, and then dropped the subject. But something about how he'd looked at her made her wonder. Was he suspicious?

Within the hour she drove the Mercedes off the ferry into Seattle traffic, and was immediately impatient with hitting every red light on the way up the steep hills from Elliott Bay. When her cell phone rang she turned it off, knowing it was him.

Once she was on Madison Avenue it was a straight

shot over the crest of the hill toward Lake Washington. Her therapist's office was located just a mile short of the lake, in a funky area that was home to vegetarian restaurants, high-end consignment shops, and a nationally recognized AIDS hospice.

As she drove, Topsy concentrated on taking deep breaths, hoping to slow her speeding heartbeat and stop the invisible moths fluttering in her chest. Her doctor, had she called him, would have said she was having an anxiety attack. But she couldn't call him now because he always reported to her husband, the respected man who paid her medical bills. She'd never had anywhere to turn—until her current therapist.

He didn't know what she'd told her counselor about him.

He'd never even guessed that Topsy knew. Did he now? The thought was frightening. Until recently he'd dismissed her counselor as a harmless therapist who simply gave positive reinforcement to her female patients, not solid psychiatric help. He'd often commented that the woman didn't even have a doctor's degree in her field, was lucky to have a practice at all. He had no idea just how good she was. But again Topsy wondered if his opinion had changed.

Topsy was so terrified around him now, since she'd begun to remember, that she could hardly meet his eyes, those brown eyes that had once seemed so warm and caring, whose very glance had melted her heart. She'd loved him so much back then, had believed in him, and had been so shocked when his dark side had begun to surface.

No, she instructed herself. *Don't think of that now. Stay focused or you'll lose it again. You're coming back now, but you might not next time.*

Go forward, she chanted mentally. *It'll be okay. The others can get well, too. It's not too late, regardless of what they've done. They can recover.*

They must recover.

She made the turn off Madison and headed for the parking places next to the small medical building. The entrance to the lot was blocked by a police car, and a small group of people had gathered on the sidewalk. She put on the brakes and lowered her window.

"You can't park here," the officer said.

"I have an appointment," she replied, her eyes darting over the unexpected scene.

"With who?"

She told him.

"Can I have your name?" he asked, pulling out a pad and pen. "I'll also need your home phone and address and some identification."

She dug in her purse for her driver's license and a personal card, then handed them over to him. "I need to know what's going on, Officer. I have an appointment that I'll be charged for if I don't show up."

He nodded. "I understand, but your therapist was just transported to the hospital. I'm sure you won't be charged, Mrs. uh—" He glanced at her card and repeated her name. "Your therapist will understand."

"What happened?" There was a knot of fear tightening in her stomach. "Did she have an accident? What?"

"I can't say," he said, handing back her driver's license. "But someone will be in touch with the details."

"Why can't you say?"

"Because someone shot her!" a man cried from the crowd on the sidewalk. "We heard that she's in critical condition."

Topsy glanced at the man, who was close enough to have heard her conversation with the officer. "Who shot her?" She addressed her question to the officer.

"We don't know, lady, but like I said, someone will be in touch."

"But you must tell me if she'll be alright." Topsy's stomach lurched with the thought that her therapist could die.

"She's alive, that's all I know."

Another car had driven up behind her, and Topsy was forced to move on. But her heartbeats fluttered even faster. She felt light-headed, as though she could float away at any second.

Deep breaths, she told herself. *Don't succumb to the madness.*

But how could she not?

As she drove back to the ferry, sudden tremors wracking her body, she wished there was somewhere else to go, a place where she could hide. *There are no options but to go back home*, she reminded herself. She had obligations, responsibilities to the people she loved. Their lives depended on her being strong now.

But could she be? She didn't know.

All she knew was that she had a thirty-five-minute ferry ride to prepare herself. And then she must be ready to face him.

The devil.

CHAPTER FORTY-ONE

JULIA DELAYED HER BATH SO THAT SHE COULD RETURN calls, which she'd been about to do before she talked to Earl. No way would she allow him to affect her work as well as her emotional state. After taking two cake orders and making an appointment to look at the wallpaper job, she finally went upstairs for her bath. It had been a good day on the work front. She figured her stress level would improve as well once she'd talked to Judy.

She filled the bathtub with water, dumping in a half bottle of bubble bath. She needed downtime before she met Judy and unloaded all of her concerns. Once in the tub she lay back, allowing the warmth to seep into her body. As the water cooled she added more from the hot tap. Finally, as her skin began to look shriveled, she stepped out, grabbed a towel, and dried herself.

She felt better, more relaxed and ready to face what she had to do. Quickly, after a glance at her bedside clock, she pulled slacks and a sweater from her closet, socks and underwear from a bureau drawer, and got dressed. Then she applied makeup and coiled her hair into a knot at the back of her head. Finally she went downstairs, pulled a jacket from the hall closet, and went back to the kitchen, where she'd left her purse. The blinking light on her answering machine caught her attention.

She pressed the Message Play button.

"Hey, Julia, I got your messages, made note of the light you saw last night at your sister's house, and I'm interested in hearing about Paulsen. You said this wasn't an emergency, so I'll give you another call later. In the meantime, the patrol has been alerted about that light and is keeping a close eye on things. Call if anything comes up, and definitely call 911 if you have a problem. I'll be notified immediately."

Detective Fitch said good-bye, and she had no other messages. For a moment she was thoughtful. He must have called while the water was running and she hadn't heard him.

Actually, it's a good thing, Julia thought. Although she intended to tell the detective what she knew, she wanted to run everything past Judy, wanted substantiation that she wasn't just overreacting—as Earl had accused her of doing.

Grabbing her purse, she went out to the garage and got into the Cherokee. After locking the car doors, she hit the door opener and backed out, her eyes darting everywhere. Nothing moved on the quiet street.

Then why did she have that feeling that hidden eyes were focused on her?

Nerves, she told herself. And paranoia. Everything seemed ominous these days, even a light in the woods that had probably meant nothing at all.

But all of her self-talk didn't help. Her neck prickled

as she drove along her street and out of her development. She didn't relax until she was on I-90 headed for the bridge to Seattle.

Once on the other side of Lake Washington Julia took the first exit that led over to Madison, then headed east toward Judy's office. Coming down over the hill into Judy's area, the traffic slowed to a crawl, and as she inched along, wondering if there'd been an accident up ahead, she began to worry about meeting her appointment on time. At this rate she'd be late.

When she finally reached her turn, she was waved on by a police officer in the street, not allowed to exit Madison. A glance toward Judy's two-story building momentarily took her breath.

"Oh my God!"

Police cars were parked along the curb, with blinking bubble lights that swept the side street beside Judy's office. A small crowd of people was being restrained behind a barrier of uniformed policemen, and a yellow tape that said Crime Scene had been looped all the way around Judy's property.

Quelling a growing sense of panic, Julia followed the traffic along Madison for another block, and then zipped into a parking place. Quickly she jumped out of the Cherokee, locked it, fed the meter, and crossed the street. In seconds she was back at Judy's place, again confronting the policeman, who wouldn't let her cross over the yellow tape.

"But I have an appointment here. What's going on?"

"Sorry, lady, we can't let you through."

"Why not?" Julia felt like there was no bottom in her stomach. "What's happened?"

"Can't tell you, miss. There's been a shooting, that's all I can say."

"Someone has been shot?"

"Uh-huh."

"Who?"

"Dunno." His blue eyes narrowed in his round face. "And I wouldn't be at liberty to tell you if I did."

"But I have an appointment—"

He held up a hand, interrupting her. "I'd advise you to call the office then, find out from them what's going on. Okay?"

She nodded and turned to go. It was no use to argue. Something terrible had happened to someone.

She just hoped it had nothing to do with Judy.

Julia pressed her cell phone to her ear, listening to it ring in Judy's office. The answering service picked up, and a recorded message stated that all appointments had been canceled, that someone would be in touch with the patients in the next day or so. She hung up, even more disturbed.

As she headed back toward the bridge, Julia decided to check in with Detective Fitch when she got home, before she left for Diana's house. She didn't know what had happened at Judy's office but figured he could find out, if he didn't already know. She prayed Judy was okay. She wouldn't allow herself to think otherwise, even as Judy's recently voiced words of concern surfaced in her mind.

Driving into her development, Julia was again reminded how secluded it was, that her street was completely deserted as she drove into the garage. The silence was instant when she turned off the engine, and for a moment she sat there, suddenly apprehensive.

Don't be silly, she told herself. No one was in her house or the alarm would have sounded, and at the very least, Mrs. Bullard, her elderly neighbor, would have called the police. *Stop being such a fraidy cat. You're in your house, you're safe.*

But the ominous quiet was oppressive as she hurried into the laundry room from the garage and turned off the alarm. She needed to hurry. Daylight was already starting to wane, and she wanted to be inside Diana's house before dark.

She glanced at her answering machine, saw that there were no messages, and went on upstairs to get her cosmetic bag. Coming back down to the front hall again, she veered to the door, unlocked it, and grabbed her mail from the box before resetting the bolt. Then she headed to the kitchen, glancing at the mail as she went.

Just bills, she thought, except for one plain envelope that was addressed to her. Probably a cake order, she decided as she opened it and pulled out the single sheet of lined paper, her eyes fastening on the words.

Protect yourself or you'll be next to die!

She dropped it faster than if it had been laced with anthrax.

Her knees buckled, and she sagged against the counter, her operant conditioning to fear these days. The stillness around her intensified, roaring in her ears, and for a moment Julia thought she would faint. She forced deep breaths, and the gray space that edged her mind began to recede.

Someone had left the note while she was gone. *Who?*

She grabbed the phone and punched in Mrs. Bullard's number, hoping her voice had enough volume to be heard. Her elderly neighbor was probably the only person who'd be home right now. She might have seen who had come up on her porch.

The old lady answered on the third ring. "Yello," she said faintly.

"Mrs. Bullard?"

"Yes?"

Julia identified herself and then explained that someone had left something on her porch and she wondered if Mrs. Bullard might have seen who it was.

"Oh no, dear," she replied. "I've been in bed all day with one of my dizzy spells and had the shades drawn."

"I'm sorry you aren't well," Julia managed in a normal tone, not wanting to alarm the old lady.

"Nothing serious, is it, dear?"

"Oh no," Julia replied at once. "Probably just a customer or a friend." She shifted the phone to her other ear so she could see out through the window above the sink. The day was darkening fast now. "I'm sure they'll call soon, after they remember they forgot to sign it." A pause. "I hope you're feeling better by tomorrow."

"Me, too. Let me tell you, Julia, it's no fun getting old."

Before Mrs. Bullard could get started on her health issues, Julia was able to get off the line. And then she went to the cupboard where she kept baggies and dropped the note and its envelope into one, remembering what Detective Fitch had told her about fingerprints. She just hoped she hadn't already messed up the evidence . . . again.

She put the baggie in her purse, careful not to crush it. Then she left another message for Jim Fitch, explaining what had happened and that she was leaving for Diana's house.

Quickly, she grabbed her things, reset the alarm, and headed to the Cherokee. After backing out to the street, she waited to make sure the door was completely closed before starting away from her house.

Again, she felt like a moving target. But now several of her neighbors had come home from work and she didn't feel quite so vulnerable.

But her bravado collapsed once she made it to the freeway. She kept her eyes glued to the rearview mirror, making sure that no one followed. She wondered about Judy, about what was going on. One thing was obvious. Whatever it was, it was coming to a fast climax.

The thought almost took her breath as it knotted in her stomach.

I'll call Detective Fitch again when I get to Diana's, she thought. She had to. Something was imminent. She could feel it in every nerve and cell in her body.

CHAPTER FORTY-TWO

JULIA TURNED FROM THE STREET ONTO DIANA'S DRIVEWAY, suddenly wishing she'd arrived a few minutes earlier, before night had overtaken the day. But that hadn't been possible. Too much had happened.

Oh, God! She was so worried about Judy. *Whoa*, she told herself. *Don't jump to conclusions.* No one had said it was Judy who'd been shot.

But Julia couldn't help but remember Judy's insistence on seeing her, that something was wrong. And her own resistance to an appointment until she had accomplished her own obligations.

The bottom dropped from her stomach.

Maybe she'd been wrong, been in denial.

She'd never credited, for even a second, that Judy's concerns might have been life threatening.

She drove into the half-moon driveway in front of the house and then veered into the space beside the two-car garage. She turned off the engine, but she hesitated before leaving the Cherokee, her gaze darting over the grounds and the wooded areas that separated Diana and Ted from their neighbors. Everything seemed serene.

Julia got out of her vehicle, locked it, and ran to the back door. Quickly, she inserted Diana's key and turned it, then went inside, stepping from a small back hall to the kitchen. The alarm beeped until she punched in the code and turned it off. That meant everything was secure.

No one was in the house.

But it felt cold, empty and foreboding, and she resisted an impulse to turn and leave. Again, Julia wished she'd stayed in her own house, but it was too late to change her mind now. Her family would worry if she did, and they would probably come home early.

After turning on lights as she went through the house, Julia ended up in Ted's den, where the answering machine was blinking a red light for messages. Julia pushed the button, and Diana's voice suddenly filled the room.

"Hey Julia, we're all wishing you were here. We've had a wonderful time on the slopes today and we're about to broil steaks."

Julia smiled, feeling good about the safety of her girls.

"Mom!" Alyssa said next. "Uncle Ted let me ski from the highest slope." A giggle came over the line. "Course Uncle Ted went down with me. It was scary at first, but now I love it. I can't wait until you can see me do it."

"And Auntie Diana and I went up the lift, too," Samantha piped up. "But we came back down and skied on the shorter slopes. But I'll be with Alyssa by the end of the season." Julia smiled as she listened, envisioning her younger daughter's serious expression.

Diana came back on the line, still enthused about the great time they were all having, and she instructed Julia that she didn't need to call back since they'd all be in bed after supper. "Unless there's a problem," she'd added.

There were no other messages, and Julia went to the kitchen, thinking about finding something to eat. As she looked through the refrigerator and freezer, she sipped on a glass of Chardonnay, from a bottle that Ted had already opened. Finally she decided to steam fresh vegetables from the drawer that was filled with them: carrots, broccoli, spinach, mushrooms, cauliflower, onions and garlic. There was shredded parmesan cheese to sprinkle over the finished result.

As the food cooked, Julia went upstairs and got into her nightgown. She expected that a return call from Detective Fitch was imminent, but there were none by the time she'd returned to the kitchen, so she left him another message before dishing up her vegetables. Plate in hand, she started back to the stairs, pausing to turn out lights and set the alarm in the front hall. Although the second floor was not alarmed, she made a mental note to remember to turn off the system if she came downstairs during the night for a cup of tea. Then she continued to her room, where she planned to eat while watching television.

Happy that her family was having a great outing, Julia hoped that she'd be able to sleep soundly for a change, without night terrors and fear of what would happen next.

But she didn't.

Instead she tossed and turned, got up once and turned off the alarm system so she could go to the kitchen and make Sleepy Time tea. Then she rearmed the system on her way back upstairs, climbed into bed, and stared into the darkness as she sipped her tea, praying it would calm her nerves so she could sleep. Intermittent dozing was all she managed, only to be jolted awake again, straining her ears for strange sounds. Her mind would not let go of her fears. The message in the letter was too raw, she still didn't know what had happened to Judy, and Detective Fitch hadn't called her back.

Finally dawn began to brighten the night, and Julia got up and put on her robe. It was a relief to head downstairs and start the coffee. She was in the kitchen when the doorbell rang.

She spun around, facing the doorway that led to the entry hall. Who could be out there at this early hour? It was barely daybreak. The paperboy? A neighbor? *The stalker?*

For long seconds she didn't know what to do. Why had she turned on the lights as she'd made her way downstairs? Stupid! Stupid! And she'd also turned off the alarm.

Finally she tiptoed from the kitchen into the dining room and on to the living room, where she hesitated under the archway to the hall. As the bell rang again, this time more urgently, Julia crept forward to the side of the door. Before her courage failed her, she peeked outside from the edge of the blind. Her quick glance told her all she needed to know. Unlocking the door, she opened it to frame a tired-looking Jim Fitch. He immediately stepped into the house.

"Got any coffee?" he asked and managed a grin.

"It's dripping now." She peered at him. "Are you okay? You seem beat."

"Just tired. Haven't slept all night."

"How come?"

"I was on a stakeout."

"Where?"

"Here." His grin widened. "I was at my son's basketball game last night, and by the time I got my messages, it was too late to call you back."

Julia was puzzled. "What does that mean?"

He hesitated. "Only that I'd gotten the information about the shooting in your therapist's office, that you'd left a message and I was concerned. Because I felt it was too late to call after the game, I simply staked out the house. I wanted to make sure you were okay until we could talk and figure out what's going on." He gave another weak grin. "When I saw your light go on a few minutes ago I knew you were up, and that's why I rang the bell."

"And scared the daylights out of me."

"Sorry. I'll be more tactful after I've had that coffee."

She grinned back, relieved he was there. Leading him back to the kitchen, she indicated that he could sit at the kitchen bar or at the nook table. He chose the bar stool as she poured the coffee, and after pulling another stool around the counter, she sat down facing him.

"This is quite the house," he said, glancing around. "Your sister and brother-in-law must do well in their careers."

"Uh-huh, they have good jobs and no kids—yet," she replied, realizing he was making small talk. But her thoughts were on Judy, and she tried to be patient. She knew he'd tell her what he could when he was ready.

There was a silence as they both sipped coffee.

"Jeez, I needed that jolt of caffeine." He sighed, and she could hear the fatigue in his voice. "Minutes can seem like hours on a stakeout."

"Couldn't you have gone for coffee? There's an all-night convenience store right down the hill."

He shook his head. "A stakeout is to protect people and property from a real threat. That threat, or person, is looking for that kind of window of opportunity."

"In other words, if someone is watching, they'll use that unguarded time to act."

He took another drink, but his eyes were noncommittal. "Something like that."

"Thanks, Detective Fitch, uh, Jim. I appreciate your concern."

"You're welcome, and I'll have a refill." He lifted his cup.

Julia grabbed the carafe and filled both mugs. Then she sat back down and waited for him to begin.

She could see him gathering his thoughts, as though he didn't want to shock or scare her with his first statement. She braced herself.

"We've had an extra patrol checking out both your house and this one since yesterday," he began. "Everything seems fine. That is, nothing unusual happened in either place."

She nodded.

There was a silence. Abruptly, his gaze was direct.

"Your therapist, Judy Gaston, was shot yesterday afternoon as she arrived for her afternoon appointments."

Julia sucked in a sharp breath. "She didn't, uh, she didn't—"

"She's alive," he said, interrupting. "In critical condition." A pause. "She's still unconscious, and we haven't been able to talk to her yet."

Julia splashed coffee as she put down her mug. "But she will live, won't she?"

"She's in the trauma unit at Harborview, and the doctors are hopeful. We'll have to wait and see."

"And pray."

"That, too."

Julia stood up abruptly, fighting tears. "I'll be right back. I have something to give you." She went upstairs to the guestroom, retrieved her handbag, then ran back down to the kitchen. For a moment she stood next to her chair, her mind in a quandary, wondering what the note and everything that was happening to her and the girls had to do with Judy's situation. Maybe Jim Fitch would have some insights into what it all meant.

She reached into the top of her purse, grabbed the baggie, then handed it to him.

"This is the letter I found in my mailbox," she said.

He took it and then glanced up, meeting her eyes. "A baggie?"

"Uh-huh. I remembered what you said about compromising fingerprints."

"The forensic guys did lift a couple of prints from those notes," he said. "Trouble is no match was found in any of our computer banks."

She raised her brows, waiting for him to explain further.

"That only means the prints aren't on file anywhere. But if we get a live suspect we'll fingerprint them and then compare their prints with those on the notes. A match means physical evidence, which can mean a conviction."

She digested his explanation as he opened the baggie and pulled out the envelope by its corner edge, so that he didn't ruin the evidence. Unfolding the page, he quickly scanned the one line that cautioned Julia to protect herself.

He stared at it, and a silence went by while he digested the message. Finally, he placed the paper back in its envelope, then looked up. "The tone is different from the others, like the writer is concerned for your safety. It's not necessarily a threat."

"Yeah, I thought that, too. It's like two different people wrote the notes."

His gaze was suddenly direct. "So what can you tell me about Earl Paulsen, Julia? What is it that you haven't told me?"

"Why would you assume that?" she asked, trying not to be offended.

"Because I'm a homicide detective and my antenna is up." He hesitated. "Besides, you told me there were some things you needed to discuss in one of your phone messages, remember?"

She glanced down, unable to hold his eyes. "There may be a couple of things I haven't revealed."

"Such as?"

"My relationship with Earl Paulsen."

He lowered his gaze. "Explain?"

She hesitated.

"C'mon, Julia. You need to clarify."

She nodded, then launched into a rundown of meeting Earl at the writer's conference panel and their subsequent dinner dates to discuss writing techniques concerning plot.

"So this was not a romantic relationship?"

"No, not exactly. Earl always said that he was totally committed to his family, although he'd told me how unhappy he was with his marital relationship. He claimed to want a divorce but felt his wife was so mentally ill that she wouldn't be able to cope without him. He said she was an emotional cripple, too handicapped to manage on her own."

"I see." Fitch only nodded, but he'd pulled out a pad and pen to take down notes as she talked.

"I didn't have a sexual affair with him, Detective."

He glanced up from his notepad. "I didn't say that you had, Julia." His gaze intensified. "But he came to your house?"

She lowered her eyes. "Once. And that marked the place in our relationship where he showed another side of himself, a mean-spirited side. I now believe that having a sexual affair was his only intention from the beginning."

"How so? Explain."

She did to the best of her remembrance, how he'd insisted on coming over that night so they could talk about their feelings for each other, how he'd driven into her garage so no one would see his car, and finally how agitated, abrupt, and on edge he'd been. When she'd rejected his advances for sex, needing to first talk as they'd planned, he'd suddenly used her bedroom phone to call home after he'd asked her to leave the room.

"He was in your bedroom?"

"I was showing him the house." She glanced away. "He'd expressed an interest in seeing it, but I realized later that it was only a ploy to get to the bedroom. I was such a dope for a woman who'd been married for years and had two half-grown daughters."

"I think you were only being honest and trying to be fair." A pause. "I'm picking up on something else here. You have a bigger concern about his visit, don't you?"

She nodded.

"Who did he call?"

"He said his wife."

"And was it?"

She shook her head, then explained using the redial to call Diana but being connected to another woman's answering machine instead. Julia gulped a breath and went on to relate how she'd realized the woman wasn't Earl's wife and how she'd eventually discovered the woman's identity. "It was Nancy Fredricks. I recorded her recording on a tape, and I still have it. And I know the phone company can verify the call from their records if need be."

He nodded, staring at her, his expression unreadable. "You're telling me that Earl Paulsen called Nancy Fredricks from your house only days before she was murdered?"

"Yeah, and I'm sorry I waited to come forward with the information." Julia spread her hands, as though in supplication. "I was wrong to do that, however well-intentioned my reasons may have been."

"Because you couldn't believe that a man of Earl's stature could be involved in murder?"

"No, because he's a criminal lawyer and I thought she may have been a client. Of course I confronted him right away about calling another woman from my bedroom, long before I'd learned the woman's name. He'd promised to explain, and then he didn't, and that's why I went to his office yesterday morning for his explanation."

"It was after that visit that you called me, right?"

"And I left another message after he called me when I got home."

Jim Fitch drank more coffee. "Care to tell me about what happened?"

Julia nodded and gave him the rundown on what had transpired yesterday, from Earl's suppressed anger when she'd gone to his office, to his vicious phone call, when he'd threatened her, and how shocked she'd been when he'd turned on her. She left nothing out, even though it wasn't a pleasant experience to repeat his vulgar accusations.

"He sounded totally negative about women in general, as if they were the root of all his problems," she said.

"So Earl knew Judy Gaston was your therapist, that you were going to discuss him with both her and me."

"That's right." She hesitated, suddenly overwhelmed with the whole sordid mess. "I hope to God Judy is okay. She's so special, so understanding of what women are up against when faced with a wrong choice."

"I hope she makes it, too. We don't want her to be our next shooting homicide."

She stared. "You think Judy being shot is connected to the others, don't you?"

"It's my suspicion at this point, even though it looks like the gun used on Judy was a smaller-caliber weapon. As I told you before, the bullets from your Cherokee are a ballistic match to those that killed the other women."

"A smaller gun was used on Judy?"

"Uh-huh. A pistol rather than a rifle. We're hoping it's not a Saturday Night Special."

"A what?"

"It's a term for a street gun, one that is virtually untraceable."

Julia drained her mug, her thoughts in chaos. She felt awful. It was as though someone out there was tarring her with an evilness that was permeating every part of her life. Who? Why? She'd never intentionally harmed anyone, was only trying to live a decent life with her daughters.

As though Jim Fitch sensed her feelings, he suddenly reached out to pat her hand. "Don't worry, Julia. You haven't done anything wrong. Single women fall for these smooth-talking guys every day. At least you've realized that Earl Paulsen is a cheating husband who lies."

"But do you think he's involved in these murders?"

"Dunno. We're still checking things out, and he has a little explaining to do."

He pushed back his cup and stood up, closing the conversation. After he'd retrieved her baggie with the note, she walked back to the front door with him and opened it. Then he faced her again.

"When does the family get back?"

"Late tomorrow night."

"Tell me the routine again? You'll go to your house to work today, and then come back here for the night?"

"Yeah, that's the plan."

He inclined his head. "So promise me a couple of things."

She waited.

"No contact with Earl for now, or with Peter. And let me know right away if you think of any more information that could be pertinent, okay?"

"Absolutely." She managed a smile. "And will you keep me posted about Judy?"

"The minute I hear anything." A pause. "And we'll have someone watching both this house and your house round the clock. But be careful. Close the blinds before turning on any lights, things like that."

"You mean so I'm not a target?" Her stomach was swimming again.

"Look, just remember that there's a cold-blooded shooter out there. This person has no remorse and no empathy and will kill again given the chance."

"I won't forget," she said, and then watched him head down the lane to wherever he'd parked his car.

Within the hour Julia drove home, but she didn't see the stakeout patrol that Jim Fitch had promised, not at her house, nor at her sister's. The officer was hidden somewhere, she told herself. But where? She saw no vehicles anywhere. She decided that the officer on duty was purposefully staying out of sight. She just hoped the eyes she felt following her progress were his.

And not the killer who was intent on harming her.

CHAPTER FORTY-THREE

Topsy jerked upright on the bed, panting, trying to catch her breath. For a moment she was disoriented, unable to clear her mind of the terrible scene she had witnessed in the woods over a year ago—the living nightmare that had finally resurfaced in her mind a few days ago.

She forced herself to slow her intake of air, to bury the horror one last time. But it gave her no peace. She didn't dare close her eyes. It waited until she slept, until she was vulnerable to relive its evil—the murder of an innocent woman barely out of her teens.

For a long time her mind had protected her with amnesia, only allowing brief flashes of memory that made no sense. But lately, with her therapist's help, it had gradually emerged, circling puzzle pieces that had suddenly connected into a terrifying video on her mental screen. She could no longer pretend that her life was normal. Now that she knew the truth, there was only one way back to innocence, to the place where she could never be hurt again.

Like the place where her therapist had gone.

Her breathing had slowed, and she got up to pace the room. A glance at her watch reminded her of why she was there, in a rented hotel room. She'd checked in under an assumed name, flashed a credit card, and then paid cash.

It was a necessary precaution.

When she turned up missing, he'd check hotels until he found her, then trump up a charge to have her committed to a mental hospital. He suspected she knew. Topsy could tell by how he'd been watching her, trying to control her movements. And now the one person who'd helped her was gone. There was no longer anywhere to go for help.

The realization sent new tremors through her body.

It was almost time.

Pausing at the window, she stared out at the distant islands in Puget Sound, misty and mysterious through the soft rain. Brigadoon. That was how she'd always felt about Seattle, an enchanting city that sometimes hid in the fog that swept inland from the bay. She had once believed that a mystical place could change things, even bad things.

But it couldn't. Nothing could.

She turned back into the elegantly appointed room, her gaze sweeping over the highly polished antiques, the Oriental rug, and the brocade draperies and bedspread. Her lips twisted into a smile. She had chosen the best hotel in town, one last selfish indulgence to showcase the destruction of a sadistic madman.

Sitting back down on the bed, she propped herself against the decorative pillows, smoothed her dress over her legs, and made sure the note she had written was still on the night table next to the wine she had ordered from room service. What she was about to do could still rescue precious lives.

Oh, God. She had to believe that it would. Somehow, she had to save them from the evilness.

Her denial in the past, her pretense that nothing was wrong, had been cowardly. She acknowledged that now. She had not allowed herself to face the truth—or to admit that she was equally responsible for his killings *because of her silence.*

If only she'd been stronger, hadn't blocked what she'd seen, been able to go to the police with proof. But she had been too traumatized, and now it was too late.

Back then, on that terrible night, she had outsmarted herself, following him because she suspected he was seeing another woman . . . again. What she had discovered instead had flat-lined her brain for over a year.

Even now she could not remember how she had gotten through those days, a mindless robot, terrified of him and not understanding why. And now, after recalling the horror of his secret life, she knew he'd kill them all to protect himself.

She glanced at the door to check the lock. The housekeeping maid would open it in the morning.

Bile rose up in her throat, and she swallowed hard. *Don't be afraid*, she commanded herself. *You can do this. You must do this.*

It's all you have left.

Her hand shook as she reached for the wineglass, which she'd laced with her antidepression prescription. About to put it to her lips, she hesitated, remembering. How could she have known way back, when she'd fallen in love with the perfect man, that it would end in disaster? Murder was something she had only read about in the newspapers. A killer was not supposed to be someone you trusted—*someone you loved.* All she had ever wanted was to be a wife and mother.

And she had failed at both.

You're doing it again, she thought. *Making excuses—trying to justify your own inaction.*

She shook her head and slowly raised the glass out in front of her. Tears seeped from her eyes.

"To you, you sick bastard." Her whispered toast soared into the quiet room. "You've destroyed us all. Now it's your turn."

And then she drained the glass as words from her childhood sprang to her lips.

"The Lord is my Shepherd . . ."

CHAPTER FORTY-FOUR

JULIA SPENT AN UNEVENTFUL DAY INSIDE HER OWN HOUSE working on her various projects. Jim Fitch called several times during the afternoon, the last time around four.

"It's time for you to pack it in and head over to Diana's," he told her. "You want to be inside the house before dark."

She'd been working on a children's story for one of her regular magazines, and the time had gotten away from her. A glance out the office window told her he was right about it being time to leave. The night was moving in fast over a gray, rainy day.

"You're right. I'll leave within ten minutes," she told him. "Thanks for reminding me."

They hung up, she saved her work, and turned off the computer. As she headed for the kitchen, where she'd left her purse and overnight bag, she couldn't help but wish she didn't have to go. Her own house had been deemed unsafe, but she didn't feel any more secure at her sister's place.

It was not the location that was necessarily dangerous, she realized as she armed the security system and stepped into the garage. It was the person out there who'd targeted her to die, a killer who could find her anywhere.

The thought was chilling, and not conducive to being alone tonight. She climbed into her Cherokee, pressed the door opener, then backed into the driveway. All the way out of the development she was aware that someone out there could be observing her every move.

But maybe not, Julia reminded herself. Hadn't she seen the security patrol several times that day? And she knew they were staked out somewhere nearby. She wouldn't allow herself to dwell on what it all meant, or else she couldn't keep going.

But she was vigilant as she drove away. She had no intention of becoming the next victim of a cowardly sniper, whoever the person was—Peter, Earl, or a random stalker. Her bet was on Detectives Fitch and Hays to catch the killer.

Her mind boggled to think it could possibly be Peter, unless he'd shot the other women to make it look like a serial killer had also killed his ex-wife.

Impossible, she told herself. She'd lived with Peter all those years, shared two daughters. He'd flipped out, but how could he be a killer?

And Earl? Julia realized she really didn't know the man, only his professional persona—the mask over his real self, a superficial personality that hid the real Earl. The man she'd been falling in love with was not the same man she'd come to know. Although they wore the same face, they were two different people.

As she approached her sister's turnoff, she couldn't speculate on a possible random stalker who'd singled her out to die. It was just too unbelievable. If someone had targeted her, there had to be a reason. If only she could discover what that was.

Just before she turned into the driveway, she noticed the car parked across the street, the person at the wheel hidden behind a newspaper. She grinned. She'd have to tell Detective Fitch that his stakeout was a little obvious.

But as Julia drove up the lane, under the overhanging tree branches that dripped from a day of rain, she was glad the man was there to protect her. It was a dark, spooky evening that promised to be an even blacker night. She was relieved to see that all of the automatic exterior lights were already on, and once she'd parked and unlocked the back door, she was grateful to step into the safety of the house. Quickly, Julia turned off the security system so that she could continue into the kitchen.

But once within the house, Julia had a sense of how quiet it was, how shadowy and big and . . . empty. Her apprehension crept up on her. *Be an adult*, she chided herself. *Your imagination is working overtime . . . again.*

She couldn't allow herself to consider why she was so scared. If she did, she would never be able to undress and get into bed. Sleep meant vulnerability.

The ringing phone distracted her, and she picked up the receiver.

"Hello."

"Hey Julia, it's me, Diana. Just checking in to make sure everything is okay."

"It is," Julia replied. "I'm about to fix something to eat and go to bed and watch TV."

"Good. We've had another great day on the slopes." Her laugh came over the wires. "Those girls of yours are fearless, great skiers. I think they may be Olympic material."

Julia laughed, too. "And I think you're a typically fond aunt." A pause. "But thanks, Diana. I appreciate your and Ted's place in our lives."

Another brief silence.

"Julia, are you sure everything is okay?"

"Positive."

"Okay then. We'll see you Sunday night. It might be late, because we intend to ski until dusk."

"I figured. I'll be here waiting for you."

They hung up, but Julia felt disconcerted. While they were having a great time away, and she was happy that they were, something evil was lurking on the periphery of her life. It was unreal. She'd told her sister that everything was okay, even while she knew it wasn't. But she was glad that they were safe, at least for the time being.

Julia busied herself by watering Diana's houseplants, then she rechecked the door locks and made sure that all of the exterior lights were on. She chose a low-calorie TV pasta dinner and placed it in the microwave to cook. When it was ready, she rearmed the security system and took her food upstairs to the guest bedroom, just as she'd done the night before. Once she'd changed into her nightgown and gotten into bed, Julia ate her dinner as she watched *Hollywood Squares*.

I lead a boring life, she told herself wryly, then realized the craziness of the thought given the fact that someone was plotting her death. She'd momentarily forgotten that.

A few minutes later she settled down in bed, still watching television. She didn't know she'd dozed off until she awakened with a start, sitting up in bed. The news at eleven was just beginning on channel four. She couldn't believe that she'd been asleep for three hours.

And then the current news caught her attention.

An unidentified woman had been found unconscious in a prestigious downtown hotel room. She had no identification, but was well groomed and dressed in expensive clothing. Authorities were checking out a suicide note, and the woman had been transported to Harborview Hospital in critical condition.

"We've heard, although it's not substantiated at this point," the newscaster said, "that the woman is married to a prominent person, and her note may connect him to the serial murders in the south end of Seattle. We'll keep you updated on this breaking story."

There was a replay of the hotel scene as the woman was placed in an ambulance. For a moment it swept over the investigators in the background, and Julia thought she recognized Jim Fitch.

Could have been him, she thought. There weren't that many homicide detectives in Seattle.

But who was the woman? And who was her prominent husband?

Not Earl, she told herself and switched out the lamp. But Julia was amazed that her mind had instantly clicked on him even as she'd dismissed the thought the next second. She settled under the down quilt and pondered her reaction to the news. If the reporter had said the connection was to the shooting victims and not the serial murders, she might have considered that the prominent husband was Earl. But the brutal murders of prostitutes in a seedy section of south Seattle seemed unthinkable.

Julia needed sleep. Her thoughts were all over the map and out of control. Earl had fooled her, but he couldn't have fooled her that much.

She hit the TV remote control, and the screen across the room went blank. She plumped the pillows and then slipped deeper under the covers, determined to go back to sleep. She just hoped that her dozing earlier hadn't taken the edge off her fatigue and now she'd toss and turn for the next few hours. If she did, she'd be doomed to another night of insomnia while she dwelled on her fears.

The first discordant sound was obscured by her own movement as she tried to get comfortable. She went still, listening.

Had she really heard something?

Silence pressed down around her, so intense that it made a low humming sound in her ear.

Then she heard something again.

What?

She strained to hear, her heartbeat accelerating in her chest. She tried to stay calm, reminding herself that Diana's house was not her own, that she wasn't familiar with the odd sounds that might be unique to the beams and timbers of the structure around her.

The next disturbance was louder, like something had scraped the siding. A branch? A loose gutter?

But there was no wind even though the rain had been steady all day. So what had made the sound?

She had no option but to get up and look, feeling brave because she knew the alarm system was armed. It would go off if anything, or anyone, tried to get inside the building.

Still, she felt uneasy and decided not to turn on the bedside lamp. Careful not to make noise, Julia slipped out from under the covers and tiptoed to the doorway, hugging her long flannel nightgown against her body.

Hesitating, her eyes scanning the darkness of the hall, Julia oriented herself to the furniture, the black shapes in the lighter hues of charcoal gray space. The long window at the end of the corridor allowed a faint reflection of light to penetrate the shadows. Slowly, she glided forward, headed toward the window and the staircase beneath it.

Before starting down the steps, Julia glanced outside into the night. Her eyes caught on the top of two obstructions that lay against the house to rest on the sill.

Then she noticed that the window was ajar.

Her breath caught in her chest, stopping her heart. She sucked in a breath, starting it again.

It was a ladder. Had someone climbed it? She knew the upstairs was not alarmed.

Was someone in the house?

CHAPTER FORTY-FIVE

JULIA CRINGED BACK INTO THE SHADOWS, EVERY ONE OF her five senses on high alert. Silence pressed down on her. Everything was still; there wasn't a ripple in the air around her. It was as though nothing had changed in the house since she'd come upstairs to bed.

But something wasn't right. She couldn't remember the window being ajar, or seeing the ladder. Surely Ted and Diana would have seen it even if she'd missed it. The seriousness of why she was even there would have led them to check and double-check all of the windows and doors.

Maybe Ted had been cleaning gutters and forgotten to put the ladder away in their rush to leave for Crystal Mountain. Julia pressed into the side of a tall bookcase in the hall, its shadow giving her temporary cover while her mind swirled with all manner of fears. Her reasoning about Ted cleaning gutters didn't fit. Ted was the most organized man she knew. He always put everything away, motivating Diana's complaint that he was a perfectionist, which at times was annoying to her sister.

Damn that she hadn't grabbed her cell phone from the bedside table; the very reason it was there was for an emergency call if the house phones were disconnected—a safety feature Diana had insisted upon in the event of a problem.

Julia waited, considering her options. It only took seconds for her to realize that she only had one. She had to get down to the alarm pad by the front door and push the emergency button. There was another pad in the master bedroom, but to go there would cut her off completely from an escape route—just in case there was someone in the house. She would explain to the police later if she was wrong.

Staying put, Julia remained absolutely still, and as her eyes adjusted to the darkness, she scanned the hallway and staircase down to the landing, beyond which she couldn't see. Minutes passed, and everything stayed quiet. She began to wonder if she was really losing it, jumping to conclusions because of completely normal props, like Ted's ladder, which he might have forgotten to put away.

Finally, she got up her courage to step out of the shadows, to approach the stairs. Anyone who'd gone beyond the downstairs entry would have set off the motion sensor in one of the rooms, and thus the alarm. From the landing she could see if anyone was down there. If there was even a suggestion that something was wrong, she'd have time to run back to the guestroom, lock the door, and call 911 from her cell phone—and hope the officer on stakeout could get there in time.

Julia started down the steps to the landing, where she

hesitated, her eyes scanning the entryway below her. At the door the alarm pad glowed red, telling her that it was still armed. Nothing moved, and although she couldn't distinguish the dark places, it appeared that no one was there.

Goose bumps suddenly pimpled her body, and a sense of danger loomed over her, like a giant fist about to grab her from the darkness and squeeze the life from her. Her legs moved of their own volition, slowly taking her toward the alarm pad as she tried to control her panic. Even as she worried about exposing her presence, tried to dismiss the idea of an intruder, Julia *knew* she was in jeopardy. She had the same sense of hidden eyes trained on her as she'd had many times lately.

The heebie-jeebies, she thought. She was just on edge these days, expecting the worst, because on a primal level she was scared to death.

But what if she was right? What if someone had entered the house?

Who? The person in the woods behind the flashlight last night?

Reaching the bottom of the steps, she leaped toward the glowing alarm pad by the front door, her hand outstretched, knowing she'd never feel safe until she pushed the emergency button.

Her finger was only inches away when she was stopped short, her body yanked back against the hard body that had materialized out of the darkness.

"Help!" she screamed, and twisted and squirmed in an attempt to free herself. It was useless. The grip around her chest tightened instantly, taking her breath. And then a hand pressed against her mouth, silencing her.

The person behind her was bigger and stronger, but

puffing from the exertion of constraining her. She tried to brace herself for what she knew would come next; an attempt to kill her.

Somehow she had to get free.

As hard as she struggled, Julia couldn't break the hold on her, and she found herself being dragged backward to the stairs. The sound of his panting telegraphed that her assailant was a man, and he was pulling her back up the steps to the second floor.

Why? It was crazy. Why not just kill her where she was?

And then she knew when they reached the top of the stairs under the window with the ladder propped against it.

He shoved her against the wall face forward so that she still couldn't see his face, held her there with a knee and one hand while he raised the window over the ladder with the other. And then he shoved her toward it.

He meant to push her out.

Then he would climb down the ladder after her, to see if she was injured, dead, or unconscious. In any case, he would finish her off.

Her mind boggled momentarily. Who hated her that much? Who would go to such lengths to kill her? She still couldn't believe it was Peter, and Earl would have to be crazy to attempt such a thing. It had to be the random shooter, someone who'd fixated on her.

As her assailant tried to push her through the open window, she struggled, kicking his legs, biting the hand that pressed against her nose and mouth. He hit her on the side of the head so hard that bright dots danced in front of her vision. She was on the verge of passing out.

She went limp. Her mind said to free herself, but her body wouldn't respond to her mental commands.

His grip relaxed. He thought she was unconscious. It was her only chance.

Coming alive, she took him by surprise. Before he could react, she kneed him in the crotch.

"You bitch!" he growled hoarsely. She didn't recognize the voice.

A second later she was free, flying down the steps two at a time, her pale nightgown splayed out behind her, to the bottom and the front door. She heard him clambering down the staircase behind her. But he was too late to stop her escape. Twisting the locks, she yanked the door open and fled into the night, the alarm siren following behind her.

She ran down the curve of the driveway toward the street, only to be cut off by her pursuer, who'd taken a shortcut across the grass to head her off. Julia had no option but to veer off toward the lake, wishing she had her car keys in her hand so that she could have gotten into her locked Cherokee.

Then she remembered the spare key she had stuck under the front bumper because Alyssa had left hers locked inside the Cherokee twice. Although Alyssa didn't drive that often alone, she'd been absentminded about the keys. But there was no time to get the spare key now. If she slowed her pace, he'd be on top of her.

As Julia neared the lake, her gaze darted from left to right, trying to see a route that would take her back to the main road, where she surmised the police stakeout was parked. There was no path away from the house that wouldn't lead right back to the person behind her. The lakeside was her only hope to escape being murdered.

Where was the officer? she wondered. Hadn't he heard the siren that was still screeching in the night?

Running zigzag, she braced herself for a bullet, remembering the women who'd been shot on her own jogging trail. Why hadn't she been shot already? she wondered. She'd been a perfect target since leaving the house. Why had he changed his MO for her? Because he wasn't the shooter of the women on the trail? Then who was he?

Dear God, no! Please don't let it be Peter.

Julia pushed herself to run faster, her breath burning in her chest from the exertion. She fought panic, not knowing what would happen when she reached the lake, a dead end unless she jumped into the icy water.

The dock loomed in front of her. Ted's rowboat, the very boat she'd thought was stupid to keep outdoors during the winter, was only a short distance away. The boat became her instant hope of escape. If only she could get on board and cast away from its mooring before she was caught.

Behind her the mysterious assailant closed the gap, and she ran even harder to hurtle herself onto the dock. When Julia reached the boat she jumped down between the benches without hesitation, the boards under her feet wobbling from the sudden movement. With shaking hands, Julia concentrated on unhooking the mooring line, her breath caught in her throat and her heart fibrillating in her chest. Fumbling frantically, she finally managed to separate the boat from the dock. Then she grabbed the oars to row herself into the lake and out of reach.

But her assailant was right above her, poised to leap on top of her, a man in a ski mask with a knife in his hand.

Before her mind could even process the situation,

her arm lifted the oar and swung it with all of her might against his head. The blow knocked him into the lake.

For long seconds she sat frozen in the rowboat. What had she done? Killed him?

Then as reason reasserted itself, Julia leaped out of the boat, knowing he could surface and climb onto the dock before she had a chance to get away. Running back to her Cherokee, she groped under the front fender for the key.

Damn it! Where was the freaking key? Then her fingers made contact and she yanked it free, tossed the magnetic holder aside, and unlocked the driver's side of the Cherokee. Jumping onto the seat behind the wheel, she slammed and locked the door, then started the engine.

As she was starting down the driveway, the man was suddenly in front of her, his wet clothes plastered to his body. By reflex, she slammed on the brakes, unwilling to run over him.

Seconds later she knew she'd made a mistake. He'd counted on her normal reaction to not hit him. And then he lifted something and swung it against the windshield, shattering it. As he hoisted it to hit the Cherokee again she saw that it was a garden shovel. He was determined to stop her, to finish what he'd come to do—kill her.

He was mistaken about her unwillingness to hit him. She was in a life-or-death situation.

Julia floor-boarded the gas pedal, and the headlights connected with him like a wild animal trapped in sudden illumination. In the second before the bumper connected with him, the man, whose ski mask had been ripped from his face by their confrontation on the dock, leaped onto the hood, his bloodied face pressed against the splintered windshield.

Her breath caught in her chest as their eyes met, hers shocked but questioning, his glinting with evil determination.

She couldn't believe it. But it was *him*.

CHAPTER FORTY-SIX

"No! Oh, no!" she screamed, shaking so hard that her teeth rattled against each other like castanets. "Get off, Earl! I don't want to hurt you!"

"You bitch!" he shouted back, his features distorted with such rage that she scarcely recognized him. "You wouldn't have had to die if you hadn't turned into a whore!"

She pressed the accelerator to the floor as his bloodied hand reached through the shattered windshield, groping for her. She twisted away from him, but he'd grabbed the wheel, trying to yank it from her grasp.

"I have no choice!" His voice was high pitched and sounded crazy. "You have to die, like all the others!"

"Why?" she shouted above the whistle of wind through the broken windshield. She squinted, feeling the shards of glass against her face like tiny needle pricks on her skin. "What others? Who are you, Earl? I thought I knew you."

His maniacal laugh rang in her ears as he grunted out the words. "I'm the angel of death, and I've come for you."

The Cherokee careened against the shrubs lining the driveway while Julia fought to control the wheel. As she was nearing the street, a police car suddenly turned into the lane, blocking her exit.

She slammed on the brakes, and Earl bounced against the windshield to rebound off the hood, the abrupt stop tearing his hold from the wheel and his grip from the wipers. Before the officers could get out of their car, he'd already staggered to his feet to run back up the driveway toward the lake, the only escape available to him. They ran after him with drawn guns while several other cars pulled up, blue and red bubble lights flashing.

Julia couldn't move. Reaction had set in and she shook harder than ever, leaning against the steering wheel for support. Oh God, it had been Earl from the beginning. Her reasoning faltered. It didn't make sense to her. Where had Peter's stalking stopped and Earl's intent to kill her begun? She'd believed he'd valued her as a person before he'd desired her as a woman. How could she have been so mistaken?

What was wrong with him? How could the highly respected Earl Paulsen be a psychopathic killer?

The driver's door opened, and Jim Fitch was suddenly there, prying her fingers off the wheel, pulling her against him, letting her know that she was safe.

"It's okay, Julia. We'll get Paulsen. He can't get away."

She lifted her head and their eyes met. Behind him, Fred Hays was issuing orders to the local uniformed officers who'd responded to the call. "You knew it was Earl?" she asked him through chattering teeth.

Jim Fitch nodded. "He's been a suspect for a while now." He hesitated, observing her state. "C'mon Julia, I'll explain later, after you feel up to it."

She felt like a rag doll baby, and she allowed him to help her out of the Cherokee. Once on the ground she realized that her legs would have folded had he not been holding her up. She was vaguely aware that her windshield was completely destroyed, the hood pressed into the engine and one front headlight out. The damage was all because of Earl and the shovel he'd wielded in an attempt to stop her from getting away.

A new wave of weakness washed over her, and Julia's knees buckled again. Jim Fitch caught her before she fell, and he pulled her erect to brace her against him.

"Sorry," she said shakily. "My limbs don't seem to respond to my mental commands."

"It's okay," he said, and she knew he was contriving an upbeat tone for her benefit. *He's a nice man*, she thought as he helped her to the backseat of his own car, where she sank back against the cushion, her eyes closing momentarily. He pulled a car blanket from the trunk and wrapped her in it, then closed the door.

"Call for an ambulance," she heard him tell someone, and her eyes popped open.

"For who?" she asked.

Fitch smiled encouragement. "You."

She straightened on the seat and unwound the window. "No way. I don't need medical help."

"You're in shock, Julia."

"I'll get over it." She moved to get out of his car, show him she was okay. There was no doctor who could fix her disillusionment, her realization of how completely she'd been fooled by the charming façade of a deadly killer. Only time could do that. "I refuse to go to the hospital. Cancel that order."

He stared at her, considering, the officer still hovering behind him. "Okay," he said finally. "You don't have to go, for now."

"What does that mean?"

His eyes were suddenly distant, as though he'd retreated into his professional persona. "I'll hold the call for an ambulance if I see that you're okay in a few minutes." A pause. "I'm on the line here. If you're not all right by then I'm up for a reprimand by my department chief for not calling and sending you in for a checkup at once."

"I'll be okay. In any case, I'll tell them that I refused your order, as I'm not physically hurt in any way."

"Agreed," he said crisply, but she saw a flicker of admiration in his eyes. "You've got five minutes to get yourself together, or you go to the hospital."

Despite her state, Julia suppressed a grin as she leaned back on the seat. That was the same approach she used with Alyssa and Sam when she delivered an ultimatum about a behavior problem. She felt her own tactic in progress with Detective Fitch and knew he wasn't kidding. She made a huge effort to steady her emotions—and her balance.

"He dove off the end of the dock," one of the policemen who'd come back from the lake told Detective Hays. "And he didn't come up. There are at least six or seven officers watching that he doesn't take refuge against a dock piling or under the boathouse or in the foliage along the shoreline. His injuries might have precluded him from surfacing, may in fact have caused him to pass out when he hit the icy water." The reporting officer paused. "We've called for the search unit to drag the lake in the morning."

Julia's senses reeled again. Death by drowning? How could Earl be dead? But then, how could he be a serial killer? Remembering Jim Fitch's five-minute concession, she willed herself to stay focused, to not give in to tears. And to her own guilty feelings for having hit Earl with the oar. Misplaced emotions, she realized, and knew what had happened to him wasn't her fault. She'd acted in self-defense.

"Hey, you okay?" Jim said, poking his face into the open car window, having realized that she'd overheard.

"Not really." She met his eyes and hoped he couldn't hear the wobble in her voice. "I can't accept that a man like Earl would shoot women on a jogging path, especially if he was involved with them in extramarital relationships."

A silence went by as Jim Fitch considered her remark. "Julia, Earl Paulsen was not a suspect in the East Side sniper shootings."

His explanation robbed her of a response. She stared at him. "But I thought—"

"That he was your shooter?"

She nodded.

"We now have another suspect in that case."

"But someone shot at me. He just tried to kill me."

He hesitated again. "I know you're confused, and I promise to update you when you're up for it, as I said before."

"Then what has Earl done, if he's not your suspect?" Shaky or not, she had to know.

"Remember I told you that the serial killing of

women in south Seattle is not related to these East Side shootings?"

She was stunned by his implication. "Are you saying that Earl might be that killer? Then who is the shooter who shot at Alyssa and me?"

"I believe I told you before that they're two different cases," he replied, evading.

"Then why was Earl after me? I was his friend."

A silence went by.

"A man like Earl has no friends, only people in his life that he can use."

"Please explain why I became his prey. Was it because of that call he made to Nancy Fredricks, or because I confronted him? Did it have anything to do with Judy being shot?" She gulped a ragged breath, remembering that she'd told Earl about Judy. She couldn't think about that now.

"All in due time, after we've gotten the facts together," Detective Fitch repeated.

"Facts like whether or not Earl drowned?" she asked. "Or why he intended to kill me when I was already the target of another killer? Nothing makes any sense."

"But it will," Jim repeated, all at once the professional homicide detective. "Once we put the evidence together, I'll be able to clarify everything." His expression softened. "It's possible that this whole thing could be wrapped up by the time your family gets back. Everyone in the department, including forensics, will be working overtime on both cases."

Her family. Thank God they'd been spared the terror this time. She thought about calling them and decided to wait, if that was okay with the police. Several officers were already stretching yellow tape to block the driveway from the street, and the dock and boathouse from the yard. The tape repeated two words over and over: *Crime Scene.* She wondered if she'd be allowed to even go back inside the house.

"What is that evidence?" she asked Detective Fitch, going back to the beginning of his argument.

"I'm not at liberty to say right now. By tomorrow sometime I may be able to."

"It's not fair to keep me in the dark."

He nodded. "I know. But necessary at this point."

They were at an impasse, and she felt too spent to keep insisting. In the final analysis she knew he wouldn't explain before the evidence was solid, not willing to risk contaminating the case by letting something slip.

He slid onto the seat next to her. "Do you feel up to explaining what happened?" he asked kindly.

She licked her lips, considering. Julia knew he'd wait until morning, but she needed to talk about it now, having realized that sharing her fears might give her some closure. And then she explained everything she remembered, from the ladder to the shovel Earl had used to smash in the windshield, to the knife he'd had in his hand when he'd tried to leap into the boat. Even talking about it started the deep shivering tremors inside of her, and she broke off.

He reached to cover her hands, which were knotted together on her lap. "Thanks, Julia," he said. "You don't need to say more now. I've got the picture."

He smiled reassuringly, then got out of the car to speak to several of the officers. Because her window was still unwound, she heard snatches of what he told them. "The guy had a knife, so make sure the divers know about it when they dive for the body. It could be crucial to pinning him to the murders."

He came back to the car and climbed behind the wheel. "I'm taking you back to your house, Julia," he told her. "The crime lab guys want to go over the window where he entered and the stairs and entry hall for fingerprints."

"Not the whole house?"

"Probably not necessary. The motion sensors would have set off the alarm if he'd been downstairs." He hesitated. "The upstairs is a different matter. Since it isn't alarmed, he could have wandered around a little more, although we doubt he did."

He didn't elaborate, but she knew what he meant. If Earl had been inside for any length of time, she would have been dead—in her bed.

Julia tried not to lose it again, or even consider Earl's motive in trying to push her out the window, that her body may have ended up in the south end of Seattle.

"Do I have to call Diana and Ted, let them know what's happening to their house?" she asked instead.

He shook his head. "Not unless you want to. Our guys won't hurt anything, and since this is a major crime investigation, the search will take place regardless of whether or not they're here."

She nodded, her eyes lowering to her hands knotted in her lap.

"You okay with going home?" he asked gently. "If not, we could take you to the hospital for the night, as a precautionary step."

She shook her head. "I'll be fine at home. Besides, I want to be there in case Diana calls."

"Understood. And of course we can put a man right in your house if that would make you feel safer."

She met his eyes. "I thought you said Earl has probably drowned."

Jim Fitch glanced away as his partner came back to the car and slipped next to him on the front seat. Detective Hays smiled kindly and didn't interrupt as he handed Julia her handbag. "I said he's presumed dead, but we can't substantiate that yet," Fitch said.

She leaned forward. "You think he's still alive?"

"No, I don't. It's unlikely under the circumstances."

Moments later she was being driven toward home, the blanket still wrapped around her flannel nightgown. Ten minutes later, they turned into her driveway and stopped, and she suddenly remembered that her garage door opener was still in the Cherokee.

"I've got the opener," Detective Fitch said, holding it up as he pressed the button. Then he handed it to Julia. "I figured you'd need it."

All three of them went inside, and she turned off her alarm. Julia welcomed being in the familiar surroundings of her much smaller house.

The men checked out the rooms, made sure all of the exterior lights were on, and then got ready to leave.

"You sure you don't need an officer in the house?" Detective Fitch asked.

She shook her head. "My house is safe so long as you have someone outside." She managed a laugh. "I have the alarm system, but then my sister has one, too."

He got the implication of her words. "Someone will be close by at all times," Detective Fitch said. "No one will sneak past our patrol again."

"And we'll continue to guard your house until Earl Paulsen is confirmed dead," Fred Hays added.

Then they left, and Julia was alone in her place, which suddenly seemed cold and silent. But not dangerous, she reminded herself and turned up the thermostat. The danger was past.

Then why did she feel so scared? Because there was still a phantom shooter out there?

CHAPTER FORTY-SEVEN

EVEN THOUGH THE DETECTIVES HAD GONE THROUGH THE entire house and pronounced it safe, Julia couldn't even change her nightgown until she'd done her own walk-through, checking the closets, looking under the beds and all of the known hiding places. Finally, she felt secure enough to head for her bedroom and get ready for bed.

She also felt terribly sad.

Don't think about Earl, Julia instructed herself, knowing she was incapable of processing what had happened. It was too soon. She needed to block her thoughts, focus on sleep and on her hope that she would feel stronger in the morning.

But once in bed she couldn't relax, even though a glance at the clock told her that daylight was still a few hours away. And she needed sleep to face the realities that would surface tomorrow.

Going back downstairs, Julia turned off the alarm by

the front door and then hurried to the kitchen, where she put the teakettle on to heat and dropped a Sleepy Time Extra tea bag into a big mug. She wished she had a sleeping pill, anything to make the whole terrible experience vanish, at least for a few hours. That thought reminded her that she still had some whiskey in the house from the Peter days.

Abruptly, she changed her mind about the tea and turned off the burner under the kettle. A gentle nudge to doze off would never work tonight; she needed a big-time tranquilizer.

She went to the cupboard and pulled down the half-filled bottle. The contents were old, but she remembered reading that liquor only got better with age. Whatever, she thought, and poured some into a glass, then added ice water from the spigot on the refrigerator door.

Julia gulped several swallows, coughed, and then hoped for a quick lowering of her senses, if not her blood pressure. She hadn't told the medics at her sister's house that, although she wasn't injured, her veins were singing, a strange sensation she'd never felt before. She realized her blood pressure had probably gone through the roof. She needed to bring it back to the basement, where it had always resided.

She swallowed more of the drink, topped off her glass, turned out the light, and headed back to the front hallway, where she reset the alarm. She would not allow herself to think about the vulnerability of her second floor, which, like Diana's, hadn't been wired into the security system, a common practice for many homeowners who wanted to save money. Faulty thinking, she thought wryly.

But the danger was in the past, she reminded herself, and again she forced her confused thoughts away from Earl, the East Side shooter, and what both cases meant.

One thing was for sure, Julia told herself as she reached the second floor: She needed major counseling before she ever entered into another serious relationship. Her marriage to Peter had turned into a disaster, but her relationship with Earl had been a hundred times worse—because he was so much sicker than Peter—and she hadn't even seen the similarities.

As before, she realized that she'd been attracted to the same type of man twice, even though their outward personas and ways of life were so different. In effect, they were both sociopathic, the difference being the degree of the personality disorder.

But how do you know that? she asked herself. She had no answers. She was not the expert. Peter was predictable; Earl was an enigma, as far as his reactions to any given situation. She was not a professional who could make the determination of who would or wouldn't kill to reach his sick goal.

It was all so horrible that she couldn't think about it now. Her mind needed a reprieve.

Your picker of men, as Judy might have told her, has malfunctioned because of your bad experience with your husband. And then Julia's thoughts went from Judy's subtle advice to Judy.

Oh God! she thought. *Please don't let Judy die.* Instantly, she had to force her thoughts away from Earl again, that he might have had something to do with Judy being shot.

She placed her drink on the nightstand and climbed into bed. Grabbing the remote television control, she punched the Forward button to surf the channels for a mental diversion. Finally she gave up. There was nothing on that could take her mind off what had happened. She was not able to divert her thoughts from her fears, and from her sense of loss. She pressed the Off button and dropped the remote control onto the bed beside her in case she wanted to try again.

Her window blinds were open, and she sat up in bed, her eyes on the woods beyond her backyard, the black treetops etched against the lighter hues of the sky. She sipped her whiskey and wondered how anyone could ever prefer to drink the stuff over wine, even beer. As far as she was concerned, it was rotgut.

But it was making her drowsy.

And nostalgic, sad about everything: Earl, his family, the women who'd died, and herself. Tears ran down her cheeks—and then she drifted off, wondering if her world could ever right itself.

Her awakening was sudden, and she sat straight upright in bed, her covers falling around her. All of her instincts were on full alert as her mind came fully awake and her body went to its conditioned state of emergency. Her heart was beating so fast that she couldn't have gotten a word out of her mouth if her life depended on it.

And maybe it did.

Someone stood at the foot of her bed in the darkness.

As Julia's eyes focused, her chest compressed on her heart. She could hardly breathe.

The shape of a woman stepped closer, and the gun in her hand was leveled on Julia. She knew her death was moments away.

"Wait! Who are you?" she cried into the silent room. Even as she spoke, Julia's fleeting thoughts were on how the woman had gotten past the police patrol and the alarm system, why she was even there.

Was she having a nightmare?

Then the woman spoke, and she knew everything was all too real. "I know who you are, Julia Farley—a destroyer—and that's all we need to acknowledge here."

"What?"

"You heard me." The voice was low and threatening, and as the woman stepped even closer, Julia had a sense of having met her before, although she couldn't distinguish facial features in the dark. "You wanted to destroy my family, like all the others tried to do." Her words quavered between them. "And you're going to pay just as they did."

"Who are you?" Julia started to get out of bed. "I haven't destroyed anyone, ever!"

The woman fired, and the bullet shot past Julia's head into the wall behind her. Her whole body jerked backward, the inadvertent reaction bringing her hand down on the remote TV tuner that still rested on the bed.

Instantly, the screen came to life, the sound blaring into the bedroom.

Startled, the woman whirled around, the gun waving in her hand. "Bitch!" she cried, turning back toward Julia.

But Julia was already out of the bed and running for the doorway. In seconds, she was in the hall on her way to the stairs, her eyes darting ahead in the dark house, knowing she had to get to the alarm pad by the front door and press the emergency button.

As she ran she felt a cold draft on her bare legs and realized that an upstairs window must be open somewhere. And then she knew how the woman had gotten inside.

It was déjà vu, a rerun of what had happened earlier at Diana's house. The intruder had bypassed the alarm system by entering though an upstairs window. Alyssa always kept her window open an inch or two in winter, claiming her room got too stuffy. And Alyssa's windows were above the garage roof, which had climbing wisteria vines that grew up trellises on both sides of the car bays.

Oh my God, Julia thought. She'd been too upset to even think about Alyssa's window, let alone check it out. But the person with the gun must have spotted the open slider and used the trellis as a ladder to access the roof. Entering the house after that had been easy—and it hadn't set off the alarm. The woman wasn't dumb, Julia thought as she flew down the steps. She'd realized the upstairs wasn't alarmed, probably because she was also the person who'd been watching the house for weeks now.

"You fuckin' bitch!" the woman's voice was shrill and hysterical behind her. "You piece of shit adulteress! You're going to die for what you did to my dad and mother—to my family."

A little warning bell went off in Julia's mind, and she suddenly knew the identity of the woman—the shooter. But how could it be so?

There was no time to contemplate. She had to get out of there and get outside, where she could find help. She knew the woman with the gun had every intention of killing her.

Her foot had barely hit the hall floor when the light came on, illuminating the stairwell, entry hall, and herself. There was nowhere to hide, and she was still a couple of feet from the front door and the alarm pad.

Julia turned to face the woman coming down the stairs who had a gun pointed directly at her.

It was Jenny, Earl's daughter.

She moved slowly now, sure of her target, her eyes never wavering from Julia's face, her finger on the trigger, ready to press it. With each of Jenny's downward steps, Julia took one backward, until her back was against the front door but still several feet from the alarm pad.

"I detest the likes of you." Jenny's words hissed out of her mouth like a deadly snake about to strike.

Julia knew that she'd never make it to the panic button and that she only had seconds to do something. With one hand hidden behind her, she groped for the bolt lock on the door. When her fingers fastened on it, she forced them to move slowly, to gradually turn the lever and unlock the door so that it wouldn't click and give away what she'd done.

At the bottom of the stairs Jenny waved the gun, indicating that Julia should step away from the door. "Turn off the alarm," she demanded.

Julia nodded. "But first I need to know why you've fixated on me."

"I don't need to tell you shit." The young woman's harsh talk didn't fit her image. She was overweight, had bad skin and stringy hair. It was hard to believe she was Earl's daughter. One eyelid twitched, the very tic Julia had seen in Jenny's dad. Her gaze darted nervously, and her overall bearing was of an emotionally disturbed young woman.

A deadly young woman.

"Then I won't punch in the code." Julia slowly edged toward the alarm pad, her one hope on the panic button, and then to flee through her unlocked front door so that the alarm siren blared behind her. Déjà vu.

"Stop, bitch. If you won't unarm it I'll simply shoot you now and leave the way I came in."

"You're going to shoot me anyway!" Julia hesitated, her mind spinning. She saw the determination in Jenny's eyes and wondered why she hadn't fired yet. Then she realized why. If Jenny had stalked the neighborhood all these weeks, then she'd noticed the recent addition to the area: a police stakeout. Jenny wanted to kill her and then slip away unnoticed, through the woods behind the development.

"You were lucky coming in that window, Jenny," Julia said, stalling. "There's a policeman out there, and I can't imagine why he didn't see you."

"You know me?"

"I saw you in your father's office, remember?"

"I remember everything, bitch. That you tried to seduce my father, that you didn't care that he was a happily married man, that he had a family. You, and the other women who were out to trap him, destroyed my mother, who was the only woman my dad ever loved." Her lips twisted on the words. "All you cared about was yourself—and trapping a rich and successful man."

"That's not true, Jenny. I wasn't out to trap anyone."

"Yes you were. You wanted my dad!"

"I rejected your dad, Jenny. I'd only wanted a friend, not a problem."

Julia saw the girl wavering and pressed on, suppressing feelings of sorrow for her, a child only a few years older than Alyssa. "I believed your dad, Jenny, and he deceived me." She took a step closer to the pad, feeling the girl's anguish and emotional upset. "I would never have anything more than a friendship with any man who was still married, happily or unhappily, even though he told me your mom was mentally ill, that their marriage was over."

Julia sucked in a breath, hoping her words wouldn't send Jenny over the edge. Quickly she went on, "I admired and respected your father, but we were not romantically—or sexually—involved."

"You were! You're lying. You aren't any different from the others who destroyed my mom."

"They were wrong if they were involved with your father, Jenny," Julia said, for the moment forgetting about the gun in her sympathy for the girl. "But they were deceived by your dad just as your mom was. He—"

"Shut up!" Jenny shouted, and Julia realized she'd said the wrong thing to the disturbed young woman. "You should have died a long time ago, on the trail that day." She stepped closer, aiming the gun at Julia's chest. "I wanted your daughters to suffer, like my brother and I have suffered. Those two don't know what it's like to be an outcast in your own family, to be called names and to not have friends."

"You were the one who tried to kill me?" Julia's question was a long sigh across the space between them.

Jenny's laugh rose up the scale to a hysterical pitch. "And pushed that dumb red-haired kid off the ski platform, and ran the ditsy blond off the road, and all the other fucking stuff that scared the shit out of you." Her expression tightened with resolve. "I'm just sorry I didn't get you out of the way before it was too late."

"Too late?"

"Yeah, bitch. Before it was too late for my mom."

Julia saw that reasoning with Jenny was hopeless. She was completely unhinged by her environment, conditioning, and probably many other elements Julia could not even guess. But one thing was certain. Jenny meant to murder her, blaming her for the destruction

Earl had done to his family by his extramarital affairs and only God knew what else. She couldn't even begin to comprehend the extent of what had happened. All she knew was that Earl's evilness had caused a terrible loss to everyone, not to mention the lives of the women who'd imagined themselves to be in love with him.

"Did you shoot Carol Norton and Nancy Fredricks?" Julia asked, playing for time, seeing that Jenny was about to end their conversation permanently.

"Yeah. Both of them thought they were going to step into my mother's shoes."

"What about the second woman?"

"She was a mistake."

And then Jenny edged closer, forcing Julia away from the door, taking her place near Julia's escape route. "You won't punch in the code to disarm the system?"

Julia shook her head, her eyes holding Jenny's gaze. "You'll have to shoot me, and then the police guarding my place will catch you, and how will that help your family?"

Jenny was silent.

"Give me the gun, Jenny," Julia said. "Believe me, I'll help you."

"Get back!"

Jenny, her back to the front door, lowered the gun on Julia, who now stood in the hallway to the kitchen, only a short distance from the area that was alarmed with motion sensors. She was poised to run for it when she noticed a movement at the front door behind Jenny.

The doorknob was turning.

There were only seconds to spare. Julia dived toward the archway to the kitchen. The alarm siren went off instantly, just as the front door burst open. Jenny was caught off guard.

In seconds Detectives Fitch and Hays, followed by two uniformed police officers, were in the entry. A moment later the gun had been knocked from Jenny's hand and she was subdued. Julia repeated the code, and one of the officers disarmed the alarm system.

Jenny broke into hysterical sobs as she was arrested and led from the house. Julia felt weak all over and sat down on the hardwood floor. She'd had enough. It felt as if the whole world had gone crazy. She lowered her head into her arms, unaware that she'd begun to cry, that tears were streaming down her cheeks.

"C'mon, Julia," Jim Fitch said gently. "It's over. It's really over now."

Julia nodded, but she couldn't stop crying.

CHAPTER FORTY-EIGHT

"STOP!" ONE OF THE OFFICERS ON THE PORCH CRIED.

"She's running for the woods!" another one hollered.

Julia jumped to her feet, her exhaustion forgotten for the moment as she followed Detective Fitch outside. Somehow Jenny had broken free as she was being handcuffed and was headed for the trail. She disappeared into the trees, but seconds later the two policemen had recaptured her and led her back to the street. One of the officers was carrying a rifle.

"She went for the rifle she'd hidden," the first officer told Fitch.

Fitch nodded. "We'll take it in as evidence, see if it's the weapon used in the other shootings." He turned to Jenny. "You go with the officers. We're going to see that you get some help, okay?"

Jenny struggled against the hands that held her, glaring first at the detective, then at Julia.

"My mom is dead. No one helped her, so she had to kill herself."

"She didn't die, Jenny." Detective Fitch spoke softly. "She's been asking for you."

"You lie. You just want me to confess to the shootings."

"I wouldn't lie to you about your mother. I know you love her."

Fitch's words suddenly got through to her. Instantly, her whole persona changed from crazy rage to a mentally ill young woman who sagged against the men and sobbed like a lost child. The officers led her to the police cruiser, and seconds later they were headed down the street, on their way to the station. Julia watched them go, heartsick for the girl. What had gone so terribly wrong in Earl's family?

But she knew. It was Earl who'd wrought the damage, a twisted psychopath who had no empathy with his fellow humans, not even those closest to him. His wife and children had been controlled, manipulated, and then destroyed by him. But he'd worn his mask so well that he'd fooled everyone, including her and all the other women who'd been seduced by his winning ways. It was only when the mask had come down that the real Earl had emerged in all his ugliness, as she'd seen earlier that night. Every woman in his life—wife, daughter, mistress, and street prostitute—was the other woman to him, and all were throwaways in the face of his twisted needs. Earl was a monster.

"C'mon." Detective Fitch took Julia's arm and led her back inside. Fred Hays locked the front door, and then they all went into her kitchen, where she started coffee. When it was ready, they sat down at the table. Julia had so many questions she didn't know where to start.

"Before we discuss what happened tonight, I want you to know that Earl Paulsen is dead from drowning."

Julia glanced down, giving herself time to digest the news. Even though she'd anticipated it, the reality of Earl being dead was an emotional adjustment. He was a man she'd begun to love. But he wasn't the man he'd portrayed himself to be, she reminded herself. She'd been attracted to his façade, the person he'd been play-acting to win her affection—and God only knew what else he'd wanted.

She looked up and swallowed hard. "Go on."

"Did you ever meet Earl's wife, Kaye?"

"No, I've never even seen her." Julia hesitated. "But as I said before, Earl referred to her as an emotional cripple, that he wanted a divorce but couldn't for the sake of his children until his wife was better."

The detectives exchanged glances.

"Go on," Detective Fitch prompted.

"I don't think I know much more than I've already said." She expelled a long breath. "Guess I only knew what he wanted me to know."

"That was his M.O.," Detective Hays said.

A silence went by.

"Kaye was a successful model and only eighteen when they first met, a woman whose professional name was Topsy," Detective Fitch went on. "She was the woman he decided would showcase him the best, so he married her."

"A trophy wife?" she asked.

"Something like that," Fitch replied. "But like all sociopaths he had to control her, manipulate her into his own comfort zone even if that meant destroying her mind. Unfortunately, Kaye had already been groomed for modeling by a stage mother type who was only sixteen years older than her daughter, and who lived vicariously through Kaye. The end result was a disconnected child who wanted to please adults. I suspect Earl may have been a father figure to Topsy because he was so much older. He molded her into a submissive wife, and shortly after their marriage she was estranged from her parents, no doubt orchestrated by Earl."

Detective Hays shook his head. "It's typical of a psychopath like Paulsen to isolate his wife so that he has total control. She was prey to Paulsen, but in a different way than the women he's suspected of having killed."

Julia put down her cup, her heartbeat accelerating to a chest-clenching rate. "I realize now that Jenny was the East Side shooter," she managed to say. "But surely you aren't saying that Earl was the serial killer who operated in south Seattle."

Again the detectives exchanged glances. "That's what the evidence suggests," Jim Fitch said. "We can't say much more until our case is solid, but there are a few facts we can share."

"I'd like to hear whatever you're at liberty to say."

"You sure?" Fitch asked.

She nodded, not knowing if she was or not.

"An unidentified woman checked into an upscale hotel and then tried to commit suicide yesterday. She left a long letter stating who she was and why she was killing herself."

"I heard about that on the eleven o'clock news last night," Julia replied. "Before my own terror began."

"Okay, so you know that the woman wanted to remain anonymous."

"Uh-huh." Julia stared at the detective, bracing herself for what he'd say next.

"Because she knew if she didn't her husband, who was prominent, highly respected, and successful, would discredit her again. Everyone believed him that she was unstable."

"You mean—?"

"Yeah," Fitch said, interrupting. "Kaye Paulsen was finally identified as the woman in the suicide attempt. She'd suffered a mental breakdown over a year ago, had completely blocked the traumatic incident that caused her loss of memory, and she was seeing Judy Gaston, a psychologist out on Madison Street."

"My Judy?"

"That's right. Seems Kaye had recently begun to experience horrific mental flashes and was on the verge of complete mental recall. She was scheduled to share those flashbacks with Judy just before her therapist was shot. According to Kaye's note, Earl had overheard a conversation between Kaye and Judy and realized that his wife knew he was a serial killer."

Julia expelled a shaky breath. "And then I mentioned to Earl that I had an appointment with Judy and was going to share my concerns about him."

"Afraid so," Fitch said. "Earl knew the therapist would put two and two together, since she knew everything about both you and Kaye and your connections to him. Hence, he had to shut Judy up."

"And you," Detective Hays added softly.

"So Earl shot Judy." Julia couldn't comment on Earl's intentions for her, not yet. His deceit was still too raw.

Jim Fitch nodded. "That's what we believe, and it's substantiated by Kaye's suicide note. Kaye covered everything from Earl's murderous activities, to his affairs, and ultimately Jenny's break from reality and misdirected desire for revenge. Kaye knew Jenny was stalking Earl's other women but not that Jenny was shooting them."

"It was Jenny's homicidal actions that drew attention to Earl in the first place, that he'd been romantically involved with the shooting victims," Hays said. "And that in turn threatened to expose his even darker side."

"How ironic," Julia said.

"Jenny blamed all of her family dysfunction on those women," Detective Hays went on. "We've learned that Jenny has always been a troubled child without friends or a close relationship with her parents due to Earl's coldness and Kaye's mental illness. At some point she took matters into her own hands and started eliminating the other women in her dad's life, believing that would change the family dynamics."

"Of course Jenny didn't know that her dad's problems weren't fixable," Fitch said. "Had no idea that when his maniacal rage overcame him, he killed prostitutes—the women who would first play out his twisted games." His gaze was suddenly direct. "He was probably behind the woman who called you in the middle of the night with the obscene suggestion. That kind of thing turned him on, gave him a sense of power and control."

"I was so fooled," Julia said, remembering other things, like him e-mailing coded assignations from his wife's house, calling one woman from another woman's bedroom. It had all turned him on, and he hadn't cared about any of them beyond his perverted needs. "How did Earl become such a monster?" Her question was a whisper.

"We can only guess at this point." Hays shrugged. "Probably a number of things: a disconnected childhood, hatred of his mother, abuse, neglect, and maybe even a genetic predisposition for violence."

"What Fred means is that we're trying to investigate his background, but he obviously went to great lengths to erase his past before he went to college," Jim Fitch said. "We do know that he grew up poor in Pittsburgh, that his mother prostituted herself to support them, and that he never knew the identity of his father. His mother was found dead on the street the summer before he left for college."

"How did he afford college?" she asked.

Fitch shrugged. "Don't know that yet either. All we know is that he was a really bright kid, if a loner."

"Yeah, his charming personality was only a mask," Hays said. "The rage beneath it was the real Earl he hid from the world. Only his victims saw him exposed, just before he killed them."

Julia glanced away. She'd seen that man tonight, because he'd meant to kill her. It was sobering.

"Poor Kaye and Jenny," she said finally. "They never had a chance."

"According to Kaye's note, that's what she thought she was doing by committing suicide—exposing Earl and saving Jenny," Fitch explained. "She either knew what Jenny was doing or she'd blocked the realization, unable to believe that it was already too late."

Detective Hays took up the story from his partner. "Kaye's note said Earl would have to kill her to keep her quiet, and she was confident he'd get away with it, given her mental history. She believed he'd already killed her therapist and knew she had to act at once, so she checked into the hotel under an assumed name, knowing he'd be looking for her once he realized she was missing. If he found her before the note was discovered, her death would have been in vain. Her letter outlined everything she knew or suspected about Earl, and included her fear that Jenny had been sucked into his homicidal world. Then she took an overdose of an antidepressant drug. But lucky for her, she took too many pills. Her stomach couldn't handle the huge dose, and she threw up enough of them to save her life. A maid found her and called 911."

Julia chewed on her lip. "I feel a little responsible for Judy's death because of my role in all of this. Judy even tried to warn me, but patient confidentiality kept her from explaining on the phone. I knew she was concerned and I should have gone in to see her sooner."

"Judy didn't die, Julia," Detective Fitch said. "My dispatcher says that both she and Kaye will recover."

"Thank God!" Julia's relief was instant.

After a brief pause, the detectives explained more of Kaye's note that detailed Earl's killing spree, one murder she had secretly witnessed. The cost of Kaye's criminal secrecy was her sanity. But, because she was concerned for her daughter, Jenny, she had tried to make things right, and she'd warned Julia by calling and leaving a note in her mailbox. It was Jenny who'd made the threats, by phone and by leaving other messages, like the spray-painted A on the front door. Jenny had watched Peter's prowling and taken over from there, thinking Peter would be blamed, as he often had been. But Kaye had not been able to change her very sick family, who'd been controlled, manipulated, and ultimately destroyed by one man . . . Earl.

As she and her girls might have been, Julia thought. Thank God she'd escaped Kaye's fate.

She walked the detectives to the front door, where they paused for her reassurance that she was okay. Then she watched as they climbed into their unmarked car and started down the street. The morning air was still, awaiting the first light, which was already shading the black horizon with a sliver of silver. Gently, Julia closed the door and locked it.

The tremors within her had subsided. She and her family were safe. She headed upstairs to rest, her thoughts on Alyssa and Samantha, who were coming home tonight. Thank goodness she would be here to welcome them.

She was lucky.

For days Julia was apprehensive when she was alone. For weeks she relived the nightmare when she slept and woke up in the middle of the night with her heart pounding. Judy, who'd been released from the hospital, still counseled Kaye and Julia from home via phone conversations. The three women had something in common: Earl.

Julia thought it best that she not meet Kaye, a decision Judy endorsed. "It's enough that you both go on with your own lives in your own directions," Judy said.

Kaye was recovering from her ordeal, and she and her son were thriving, although they had many emotional issues to work out to stay mentally healthy. Jenny had been evaluated, deemed completely delusional and psychotic, and had been committed to a private mental hospital where she would probably stay for many years, escaping prosecution for the shootings of which she'd been proven guilty. The rifle she'd used along the hiking trail had been traced to a former client of Earl's, a weapon Earl had been holding in his little arsenal in his home basement. The pistol that he'd used to shoot Judy had also come from that same stash. The knife that had been recovered off Diana's dock linked him to the serial murders of the prostitutes. Julia hoped Earl's son had a chance to grow up normal. But she wondered.

Mostly she was grateful that the whole horrible time was over, that she was alive, that Samantha and Alyssa were safe and thriving. The frightening events had receded from their life, for which she was eternally grateful.

Even Peter was moving forward with his life. Julia suspected that he'd had a reality check when he'd been a suspect in a murder investigation. His bizarre behavior had suddenly ended as far as she was concerned, and she'd realized he wasn't a psychopath like Earl, even though he had his own problems. She suspected he hadn't really changed, only shifted focus to the new woman in his life. She wished them luck and hoped for the best.

Over the following months Jim Fitch dropped by occasionally, checking on their progress. "Just making sure," he said each time. She appreciated his concern. He was the type of man she would be interested in dating sometime in the future.

But not yet.

Although her life was moving forward, she had no intention of jumping into the dating scene too soon. But finding someone special was definitely a goal for her future—when she was ready. She hoped that would happen before the girls were in college and she was alone. Whatever.

"Everything in its own time," as Judy always said. "You won't pick the wrong man a third time."

And Diana had added, "Next time will be it." Thinking about her sister's prediction made Julia smile. Somehow she believed her. It was something to look forward to.

All in all, life was good for all of them now.

Visit
❖ **Pocket Books** ❖
online at

---

www.SimonSays.com

Keep up on the latest new releases from your favorite authors, as well as author appearances, news, chats, special offers and more.

2381-01